GLOVES OF EONS

GLOVES OF EONS

THE KALLATTIAN SAGA

VOLUME THREE

ANDREW D MEREDITH

GAMES AFOOT, LLC

Books by Andrew D Meredith

NEEDLE AND LEAF SERIES

THRICE

FOUR-SCORED

FIFE AND DRUM (*UPCOMING*)

SWEAR BY THE SIXTH (*UPCOMING*)

THE KALLATTIAN SAGA

DEATHLESS BEAST

BONE SHROUD

GLOVES OF EONS

DREAD KNIGHT

SIDEWAYS TALES

QUAINT CREATURES: MAGICAL & MUNDANE

To Wendy, my Little Rose.

You smiled and stole my heart on your first day in my arms. Our quests together, both today and tomorrow, promise to be just as full of joy as that first one.

FORWARD

The writing of *Gloves of Eons* was a lesson in furthered ideas. I had long beforehand written the first two books of the series, and they had gone through many iterations through my growth as a writer. That growth spawned the ideas that would be carried forward into the book you read now, *Gloves of Eons*. It was my intention to see it act as a stepping off point into the rest of the series, as well as fulfill the consequences of actions taken in *Deathless Beast* and *Bone Shroud*.

With all of these goals sitting firmly on my shoulders, I began writing this book back in 2021, right as I was in the midst of publishing *Thrice* and the *Kallattian Saga*. Many of the themes started in those early books carry through into this one, including one I had not realized I was doing until I could look back in hindsight – the passing on of legacy.

Mentioned in the previous books was the conflict the previous generation faced: The Protectorate Wars. Their actions during and after the wars had their own consequences, culminating in the events of the *Kallattian Saga*, just as our intrepid heroes now must make decisions and suffer their own consequences. What will the new generation decides to do with their lives? Who will flee in fear, and who will run to their fears and face them head on? Who will act as though they have no choice? And who will take responsibility?

Thank you for taking the time to read *Gloves of Eons* and I hope that your path leads you to where you too can inherit the legacy of past actions and future promises.

—*Andrew D Meredith*

MORIN
MORRAINE

BRONUE
JINRE
CENDIN

MAHN
FULHAR

MAHNDÜR

ALNIR

DONIG

PRECIPICE
ORACLE

OREEN
BASTION

ZEBUDE

BRAHZ

BORONI

GRISDEN

ESCHENFÜR

HAVEN

ABINGEN

VAREA

LIMAE

ABDALON

NIKGREST

BIRIN

DÜRAN

RESDAM

REDOT

GRYPH'S
NEST

JERTGON'S
HOLD

LIBERTE

OUIQUIMON

ŒRON

SAL-DU-MARS

ADWALL

CASTENARD

VITTS

AUNTE

ORMACH

BOSCOLON

SIDIERATA

EDI
CITY

Gasota Tribe

NOR-VIO

IRONA

TASHAR

EDI

Oracle Marches

AMMAR

TRONSHU

KANDAR SEA

ZIRYSIR

SEA'LAER

QUSLOR

ZILYNTOL

TRYANTON

YRKNO

KRYSON

PRAE

VALNYAM

AVENDAR OCEAN

WESTERN GANTHIC

EASTERN GANTHIC

SUMMARY OF EVENTS THUS FAR

After Black Sentinels Hanen and Rallia Clouw travel north with Searn VeTurres and his apprentice Ophedia del Ishé to protect a detail of sight-bound monks, an ex-colleague of theirs, Ghoré Dziony, attacks them. Blessed by a dark god with the ability to control vermin, while cursed with a visage matching his minions, he is defeated by Black Sentinels and Paladins of the Hammer only when a dark figure bearing a cloak made of bone assists them, the dark power in his own cloak stripping Ghoré of power and flesh. Sentinels then successfully deliver their charges to the city of Mahn Fulhar and take up the responsibility of establishing a new office in the Blackiron Hall near the castle. The city does not take kindly to them due to the Black Sentinels' history of extortion.

Jined Brazstein, now champion of his god, Grissone, takes on a second vow and under that new burden re-learns who to navigate a life as a Paladin in the city of Mahn Fulhar. The religious organizations hold a grand council and the mysterious Watchers of the Dead make an appearance, revealing that a dark figure has murdered many high ranking individuals to some unknown end. The investigation Jined Brazstein undertakes reveals the Moteans, the heretical sect that seeks to destroy the Order of the Hammer.

Katiam Borreau, now with the sprouted Rotha in her possession, works with the botanist Asenath Chloïs to unlock its secrets. The Matriarch Superioris of the Paladames of the Rose journey to the oracle with her church, and her husband goes after her, fearing it a trap. When the oracle reveals the future, and is then destroyed by a dark tool of the Moteans, his fear is made real. This deals a mortal blow to the Matriarch and her church, leaving all in disarray, and in the aftermath, Katiam finds herself in a land far off any map—the Dreamscape, or Veld. Jined and the twins, Loïc and Cävian, journey to a lighthouse where they find and defeat the Motean leader, who turns back to the faith when their god reveals himself. But he is killed by the boneshroud wearing figure.

The monk, Seriah Yaledít bears witness to the death of her order's leader by the man in the boneshroud, and in her mourning visits the dying in hospitals where she is asked by a mysterious figure to give a message to her goddess. In doing so, it is revealed she spoke as messenger for a dark god, and the message she gives her goddess ushers in a new era.

To stop the Moteans from completely destroying the Order of the Hammer, the Paladins march against an allied heretic/Sentinel force. The boneshroud worn by Searn VeTurres commands the shades of the dead and he fights against Jined with a regenerative invincibility, and dominion over the minds of his followers granted him by the gauntlet of black metal he wears. Jined only gains advantage as he submits to taking on a third vow to his god. His beams of light fight back on even footing against the cloak that makes Searn invisible to the gods. He is only defeated when Hanen Clouw notices the shades' weakness to flame, and the Clouws, with Ophedia del Ishé, rush to help. With their ingenuity and the light pouring off Jined, Searn is defeated. After revealing that Ophedia is his daughter, Searn drives a long pin through his own eye and he dies.

With Searn dead, Hanen is given a journal and a piece of bone revealing his old mentor to still lives on within the bone, and he is guided to take the Shroud for himself.

Katiam travels through the Veld, the realm of Dream, returning to the world to find the Rotha seed has awakened, and is now a thinking, moving plant child.

Jined, infused with the power of his god after taking on a third vow, struggles with the silence that he will face while hs god leaves off to other responsibilities.

PART 1

BLACKIRON

THE STONE

ABECINIAN
CATHEDRAL

ROSE CONVENT

DULAR
TAILORS

GROTTO
MARKET

CITY OF MAHN FULHAR

NORTH HILL

GUILDHALL

CANAL

GROTTO

QUAYSIDE

NASUN

MORIN

MORRAIN

MAHN
FULHAR

MAHNDÜR

ALNIR

PRECIPICE
ORACLE

GREEN
BASTION

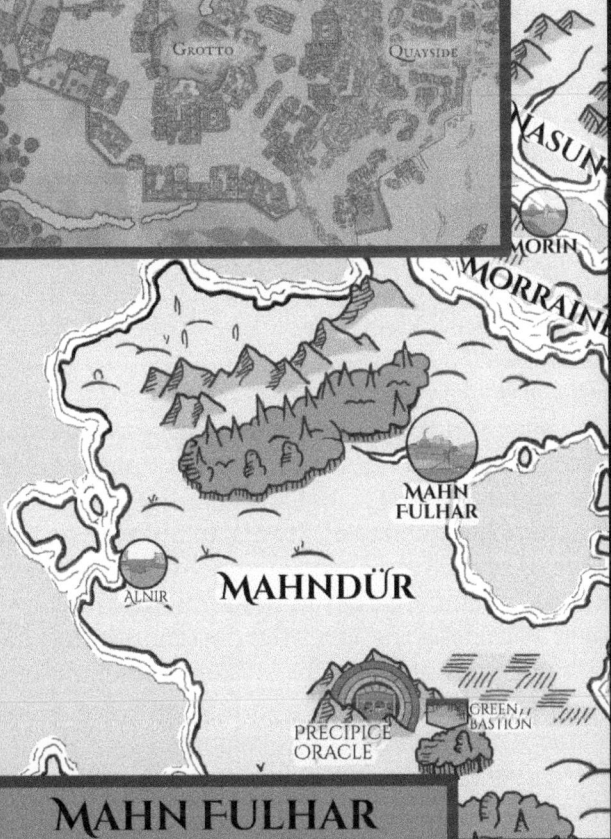

MAHN FULHAR
CAPITAL OF
MAHNDÜR

PROLOGUE

He looked across the small camp from his tent to the fire. The wind off the lake shore was as cold as the glacial water that fell from the long waterfall. Nodding satisfactorily, he turned back to the cot set up for him by Adjutant Haal. He sat down and opened his satchel, pulling the small velvet sack free. Turning it over, the black leather-bound book fell into his hand.

He touched the new leather, admiring the work the binder from Hraldor had done. He opened it and took up the bone quill that sat inside the leather cover. He touched the tip to the back of his wrist, and pressed until blood beaded—quickly siphoning into the quill. He touched it to the page.

Has he broken yet?

The page suddenly blossomed with words written over one another, different hands, and even a couple in older languages, barely legible.

He chuckled to himself. It was an unforeseen side-effect of the binding of several shadebooks together. The shades had fallen to bickering, bound together in the same soul prison with others as learned as themselves. Over the past month they had begun to form into a natural hierarchy, albeit a reluctant one. As they had no means of recourse to attack one another, it soon turned into a parliament of deceit and political guile.

He watched the words argue over one another, trying to vie for interaction with someone still living. Finally a single stroke of red covered the page and then faded.

What have you for us? a single hand wrote.

Have you broken our friend? he wrote.

He had been waiting for this moment, when one would finally begin to barter and deal with him, rather than merely screaming in rage for having bound them together. He had made the first move when he pointed out that the one silent voice continued to listen to them, and they didn't know that the soul was even among their number—Jakis Gladen, the Motean turned back to the faith, and murdered by Shade.

The page remained unblemished for some time.

He remains silent, one line bloomed. *Though we know he is here. His faith reeks.*

Be sure he doesn't let it soil your own power, he wrote in reply.

You bound fifteen of us in here. To what end, I do not yet understand. And you kept the likes of Cup to yourself.

I do not have the shade of Cup, he wrote.

Then why does he speak to us?

He looked over at his left hand, to see it writing of its own volition, the words fading almost before he could read them.

The quill in his left hand, which he had picked up without being aware of it, appeared possessed by some unseen power. He took out a separate piece of paper and his left hand began to scribble quickly.

We need not write back and forth, the left hand wrote.

"What?"

The quill Searn pierced through my eye. He never put me in a book. Perhaps you should shove me into your arm.

"Why would I do that?"

So we can speak more clearly, the left hand wrote.

"No. No one has done that."

Of course they have and you'll eventually do it. If you're willing to take a toe knuckle to prepare your own shade, the knowledge that you could put me into your arm and have access to me at any time will be too great a temptation. You are as much a scholar as I was in life.

"Aeger. What did you tell the shades bound in the book?"

I introduced myself, and let them know that we're going to work together to take what belongs to all of us. Searn was his own unwitting pawn, and his betrayal of the cause shows his true colors. Imagine what you and I could do, better scholars than he, if we could unlock and wear the Dreadplate.

I

BEGIN

Spake Existence "Begin!" unto the void, and with that word, All began. First brothers Aben and Wyv and again with the word the sisters Crysania and Sakharn were born. With power bestowed these four then spoke the word "Begin," and all four worlds were created.

—BOOK OF SAGES, ABECINIAN HOLY BOOK

The sun rose over the Lupinfang Sea announcing the beginning of spring. While on most days the edge of light that carved its way out of the sparkling sea began with little fanfare, on the Vernal Equinox bells across the city began to chime and peal. For most, the beginning of the year was a celebration of life renewed. To Hanen Clouw it sounded like a funeral dirge, one he had been anticipating for the past five weeks, when his mentor and leader, Searn VeTurres, had betrayed all the Black Sentinels and sentenced their organization to death.

Blackiron Guildhall was quiet, with only his sister and him there now. Most Black Sentinels left the city soon after that humiliating night, when their wills had been overpowered and they had been made puppets.

A black creature sat in the middle of the room, which Hanen observed in the early dawn's light. Sitting with its haunches on the ground, its head rose no more than two feet high. Thumbnail-sized scales covered its sleek frame and its long tail. This was Whisper,

Hanen's ynfald, watching the door. Even before it opened, Whisper's tail struck the flagstone with a rattle, several times.

Rallia Clouw quietly entered, covered in a light sheen of perspiration. Her blonde hair was slicked back on her head and pulled into two shoulder-length braids behind her, ending in two silver caps, the sides of her skull shaven clean. She stood four inches shorter and as many years younger than her brother.

Hanen stood with a groan and ran his fingers through his black hair. He grabbed a leather thong and tied it up loosely on the back of his head and pulled on the black clothes he had worn the day before. He scoffed at the worn, slightly pungent garments, and then smiled, remembering that his new outfit was awaiting him at the tailor. He adjusted the large gold medallion stashed in his boot, making sure it sat comfortably.

"You're definitely losing weight," Rallia said to him as she sat in a cushioned chair, a chunk of bread in her hand. "You need to eat more."

Hanen tore off a piece of bread from the larger loaf that sat on his table, and shoved it into his mouth.

"Begin," Rallia said with a smile.

"Hrm?" Hanen replied. "Oh. Yes. Begin."

It was the first word spoken at the creation of the world of Kallattai, and the greeting people gave on the first day of the year.

"What do you want to do today?" Rallia asked.

"Probably the same things we've been doing," Hanen replied. "Think about the failure of the caravan. Try to make a dent in the list of the contracts the king keeps adding to. Make a trip to the Grotto to pick up my new outfit."

"We should do that before the crowds get too dense. The word is that the Grotto is where the main Beginning Day Celebration takes place."

"Wonderful," Hanen said under his breath. He looked up at his sister. "We should have left when we had the chance. Sticking our necks out didn't help anything."

"We stopped him."

"Yes. Then the Paladins left. We received no reward for it. Just an empty office, and a debt to the crown that Searn forced us all into."

"We're still getting paid," Rallia said.

"But we have no choice. We're no better than the castle guard guild, the Voktorra."

As though on cue, there came a swift rap on the door, and a man walked in.

He wore a dark gray uniform with blue trim that looked black in the dim room, though the gold thread clasps still gleamed in the dawn's light from the door. He wore a thick black beard that covered his collared throat, and he was armed with the short poled, crescent hawk-billed poleax most Voktorra carried, hanging from a hook on his belt. He took the wide domed metal helm from his head and tucked it under his arm, and then held out a letter with his other hand.

"Hanen and Rallia Clouw, of the Black Sentinels," he said stiffly.

"The daily addition to our assignments, Abenard?" Hanen said.

"That's Captain Navien," the man corrected. He handed the letter to Rallia, who had risen as he entered. He then held his forearm and hand up in front of his chest, in a salute befitting a soldier, and turned to leave.

Rallia broke the seal and pulled out two pieces of paper. She unfolded one and began to read, while handing the other to Hanen.

"The king is summoning me with a personal assignment. I'm due to appear this afternoon."

"That's odd," Hanen replied. "The rest of them have been assignments through Abenard."

"I'm hungry," Rallia said, changing the subject. "Let's go see what the city is up to."

In response, Whisper shot toward the door, pausing for a moment to look back and make sure the two of them were following.

The Clouws and their ynfald walked the southern circumference of the inner wall and came to the south courtyard of the Stone— the common name for the royal castle complex. Dozens of gray-clad Voktorra practiced their drills in the graveled courtyard. Captain Navien stood under a tree and watched them pass, signaling two of his guards to follow them. It was the usual drill: Except when they slept, they now spent every moment no further than fifty feet from one of Abenard's guards. After the Prima Pater of the Paladins informed the king of Searn VeTurres' treachery, all his crimes formed a cloud of suspicion around Hanen and Rallia.

They left the castle and walked out onto the castle green. To their right stood the bustling cathedral complex of the Church of Aben. Monks in gray shuffled about, and priests from all corners of the world seemed to have come to pay their respects. To the left stood the abandoned complex of Crysania. The doors had been boarded up, and no one approached it. Within three days of the events that had changed their lives, the Paladins had closed up and left, offering to take any of the servants with them on their travels.

Whisper sniffed at every tree, roaming at times ahead of them and other times lagging behind, only to race past them again, silent as a black dart across the green, chasing warbling four-winged dwovs that hovered over a few early-spring flowers, sampling their nectar. The little birds zipped away from Whisper like white streaks in the air, leaving behind clouds of powder that made the ynfald sneeze. If caught escapading in the night, the tiny birds, glowing in the dark, would leave sprays of glowing mist that stained clothes horribly. Once, Whisper had returned late at night looking like a pale specter, covered in the glowing dust, likely having scattered a flock of the four-winged creatures during a nighttime patrol.

They moved through the gate and into the next city green, surrounded by the homes of the rich and powerful. Hanen glanced toward two homes in particular. They belonged to the first two merchants who had canceled their plans to travel with the caravan.

"Why the sigh?" Rallia asked.

"Did I sigh?" Hanen replied.

Rallia nodded. "Thinking about the caravan?"

Hanen didn't respond, he just hunched his shoulders forward. They walked out the gate, leaving the upper quarter, and looked over the city. A few boys nearby kicked balls of leather between one another. If a boy didn't catch the ball in time, it threatened to roll down the steep street all the way to the sea. This was the main thoroughfare of the city, built into a canyon with bridges overhead, shops lining the streets and with houses carved above the shops into the canyon walls.

"Surprisingly quiet today," Rallia said.

Then she bit her tongue, for the clamor that arose as they came around the corner and within earshot of the Grotto.

The wall of the canyon opened up to the right, revealing a large area, half underground, half exposed to the sky. People there were dressed in their brightest clothes, with their arms bare to the frigid, early spring air. Peddlers hawked easy-to-eat and overpriced food to one and all, while the barest trickle of water, leftover from a once-robust stream, fell into the pool along the back wall. Hanen pressed through the crowd toward his destination. The crowd became denser, and while he could see the Dülar tailors, the people around him no longer let him pass. All craned their necks to try to see the pool.

Drum taps and a horn cut down what silence remained.

A door opened up in the cliffside at the same level as the outlet of water, boasting a ledge Hanen had never noticed before. Two men stepped out wearing light grays and blues. One looked no older than Rallia and the other was elderly, with a long white beard that almost reached his belt. They both walked the ledge, and when they reached the water they stepped through the stream and then stood with their backs to the wall as a third figure emerged from the door. He wore deep blues and grays, with flashes of gold on his hands and across the breast of his uniform.

"The king!" someone nearby hissed in excitement.

King Velab Erdthal II had a short black beard and long black hair that lay over his shoulders. He carried no scepter, nor any symbols of office, nor did he wear a long cloak. He came and stood next to the stream of water, across from the other two men.

"Death and Dream have taken the warmth from us!" the old man proclaimed.

"While the Gift-Giver has given us nothing but snow," the young man replied, "and the Lord of the Forest has not yet come of age!"

Hanen realized the speech was a variation on many Beginning Day speeches, and referred to the last months of the year.

"O, King Velab Erdthal II, King of Mahndür and Nasun, Ruler of the Fulharian Guilds!" the old man said, looking over at Erdthal. "What shall we say to you that you would bestow spring upon us?"

"Have your reservoirs of kindness not been filled all winter?" the young man asked.

"Aye!" the king announced. "I have water aplenty to give you."

"Will our crops grow with this water?" the old man asked.

"Only by the will of the gods" the king said. "I shall offer my services to them and to my people as I am able."

There was a long silence. Then the king raised his hands out to the people.

"Begin!"

The people held both hands out, their palms up, and as one shouted, "BEGIN!"

The hole in the rock face, from which the trickle flowed, grew wider, and water began to pour from it in a sudden torrent. The people began to cheer. The clamoring grew into a chant, "Begin! Begin! BEGIN!"

The old man suddenly threw himself off the ledge and down into the freezing water below with a cry of glee. The young man next to him followed suit. Soon people down below began throwing themselves in with abandon.

Hanen watched as the king turned and left, unnoticed by anyone but him. Rallia stood with a smile plastered across her face, watching the people in the ice-cold water. Hanen pulled on her elbow.

"Come on. We can make it through now."

It was another hundred yards to the side of the grotto, where a line of pretty shops edged the market. Windows stood wide open, paned with the clean, clear glass produced by the city. There was no mannequin on the street this time, as the crowds were too dense, but there stood in the window a mannequin with a rich green brocade and a blue brocade ribbon hanging from its neck. A young girl stood in the window looking like she was sprucing up the display, but she wasn't fooling anyone as she watched the crowd, craning her neck to see the Grotto Pool with fully-dressed people splashing about in the frigid water.

Hanen took a single step up to the recessed door and pushed into the shop. To his left sat the ancient master tailor Abgenas Dülar. He wore a simple white shirt as he stitched a piece of brocade. He did not look up. A middle-aged woman stood at the counter. Her long blond hair was ribboned in blue and fell over her left shoulder to her hips. She smiled at Hanen and Rallia.

"Begin," she said. "Alodda saw you coming, Goodsir Clouw. She will be out shortly."

"Thank you," Hanen replied.

The shop had few decorations. There was one wooden display with embroidered ribbon lying out on it. The only mannequin was the one in the window with a dress on.

"Why so few dresses on display in a tailor's shop?" Rallia muttered to Hanen.

Whisper had gone over to the window and sat next to the young girl, Runah. She dropped to pet him while they both watched the crowd outside.

"No point in making surplus Spring Fashion now," the old man said in reply from across the room. "We've already completed many orders, which have been picked up. Tomorrow we'll get another rush of young people looking to update their wardrobes. But not on a holiday like today."

"When last I was in here there were several mannequins displaying your fine craftsmanship," Hanen replied.

"Those garments were not for sale," the old man said. "They were orders we were working on. Too many tailors hide their work. If a blacksmith can work on his metal for the whole world to see, we might as well, too. Not that we're ever in need of work."

A blonde girl perhaps a year older than Rallia came out of the back. She wore a pale blue apron over an even lighter blue dress. A sash made of un-dyed material was richly embroidered with a darker natural twist. Over her shoulders she wore a cape not much darker than her apron, held on by a string of pearls. Her hair was loose and blonde, and framed her round cheeks and chin. Her blue embroidered ribbon hung from her shoulders.

"Begin," Alodda said cheerfully as her eyes met Hanen's.

"Begin, Alodda," he said, smiling back.

"Did you watch the ceremony?" she asked.

"I did."

"Rallia, is it?" Alodda asked, turning away to look at Rallia.

"Yes ma'am," Rallia said.

She laughed a bubbly laugh, "I'm no ma'am," she said.

"Is it ready?" Hanen asked.

"No need to cut to the chase," she said, looking back to Hanen. "And of course it is. I promised it would be done today."

She indicated to a doorway hung with a curtain. "Follow me and I'll show you."

"I'm going to see if I can find some food," Rallia said, walking to the door.

Hanen followed Alodda through the curtain. In the outer hall stood two curtained dressing rooms. Outside of one stood a mannequin dressed in a black outfit. The black tunic-coat was long and thin, to match Hanen's frame. The sleeves were a part of a blousy shirt, dyed black. Over the shoulders hung a short mantle, stretched with pillowing and the tall neck of the mantle had black sable lining the inside. It reminded Hanen of the fur that lined the outfit Alodda had worn all winter. As he got closer, he saw that the pillowed squares on the mantle were hand stitched with a deeper black embroidery. A soft smell of flowers and sawdust lingered in the air around the outfit.

"I had run out of fur from the winter, so I stitched in the fur from my own winter collar," Alodda said, "if only to remind you who made the outfit while you're away on your travels."

"I won't forget," Hanen said, smiling.

"Well, step into the dressing room and strip down to your under gown. I'll hand you parts of the outfit to wear."

Hanen did as he was told, and moved into the spacious room beyond the heavy curtain. He soon stood in his black stockings and boots. She handed through each piece, which he pulled on, admiring the work in the mirror that hung from the wall.

"I embroidered the straps with the Abgenas' Knot," she said through the curtain as he fastened the tunic-coat.

"It's well done," he said as he pulled the mantle over his shoulder. Alodda's aroma surrounded him from the fur on his throat. It wasn't a dense fur, but it would keep him warm. He turned once in the mirror, and then stepped out to show off the outfit. Alodda wasn't there.

"Come out into the main room," she called.

Hanen took a deep breath and stepped out, where Rallia was offering a sweet bun to the old man. Alodda stood in the center of the room, with her mother and sister beside her, each already holding sweet buns in their hands. The smile on Alodda's face was broad, and full of pride for the work she had completed. She nodded, a replication of the same nod her mother gave.

"Well done, my daughter," her mother said.

Hanen stood feeling awkward as the women sized him up.

"What do you think, Hanen?" Alodda asked hesitantly.

"Your embroidery work is unmatched."

Alodda blushed.

"While it fits my frame, it doesn't feel stiff. It feels right."

Hanen held out a medallion of qavylli gold and dropped it into Alodda's open palm as she stretched it out. "In payment for the suit," he said.

She looked at it in astonishment. Her mother glanced over Alodda's shoulder. "Is that a qavylli gild-pound?"

Hanen nodded.

"This is too much. I am sure we can't find a banker who will easily break it up for us," the mother said.

"Then keep it," Hanen replied, smiling.

"I can't take this," Alodda said, her face blushing. "It must be worth at least twice what the uniform is worth."

"Then consider the rest a gift."

"We'll make your sister an outfit too, then," Alodda's mother, Eimeé, said.

"If you'd like," Hanen said. "But please don't feel you need to. I have been trying to find a place to spend it for some time."

"Let me take your measurements," Eimeé said, ushering Rallia over to a mirror.

"Will you and your sister be in town for a while?" Alodda asked.

"Yes. Our caravan was canceled."

"I'm sorry to hear that," she said. They both went to stand behind the mannequin in the window so they could look out at the crowd. "You have not been for want of work, though?"

"No. We're fine, I suppose," Hanen replied. "The king has been giving us a long list of contracts to keep filled. Mostly guard work for his extended family."

"Good, good," she said absentmindedly.

"We can make you something completely different," Alodda's mother was saying to Rallia as they approached. "I think something you can move in. We've got a fairly clear schedule after the spring orders die down. Perhaps we can have it done in a month?"

"I'd like that," Rallia said.

"I should be going," Hanen said to Alodda.

"Don't hesitate to visit," Alodda said. "Please." The last word sounded more like a demand than a request.

Hanen nodded and walked to the door, where Alodda's little sister, Runah, held his own clothes up to him in a bundle. Hanen took the clothes and called to Whisper, who had spent the entire time relishing the attention of Runah. Then they left the shop. The door shut behind them, almost closing on Whisper's tail.

"Alodda's nice," Rallia said.

"Yes."

"You should visit her more often, like she suggested."

"That's my business."

"No need to be testy with me," Rallia said. "I'm just observing she'd be a nice companion."

"Leave it off, Rallia."

"Why?" Rallia said, stopping. "You've been distant these last few weeks. I know Searn's betrayal was hard, but that's no reason to take it out on me."

"Searn's betrayal was a pretty good example of the curse our father bestowed on us."

"What curse? He had bad luck. That's all."

"I've had word from Father that says otherwise."

Rallia's mouth dropped open. "Father's alive? Where?"

"We can talk about it when you return from whatever assignment the king is sending you on. But let's not speak of Alodda. I'm not subjecting her to the family curse of lucklessness. Their family is successful enough. She doesn't need us dragging her down."

"That's nonsense," Rallia said, shaking her head. "But if that's the way you want it, fine. I'm marching on ahead to see the king."

Rallia walked into the crowd and quickly disappeared from sight.

By the time Hanen returned to Blackiron, Rallia had packed up and left. Hanen walked around the office to make sure no one was around and then went and pulled out the lock box hidden under his bed. He took out the wrapped object and opened it, revealing the bone-colored mail. The two books wrapped inside of it fell into his hand, after which he made his way over to the unused cupboard. As Whisper slunk under the bed, Hanen lit a candle and closed the door of the cupboard behind him, finally alone.

2

DARKNESS

The world it flew beneath them,

Her hand now clenched in his,

They came to maw of black night,

Beckoning he come in.

The Judge now weighing sin.

—*THE TRAVELER*, EPIC POEM BY

JUREN LIEFSEN OF BORTALI

Have you been reading? The words across the flat pin of bone bloomed like blood soaking through a bandage, and quickly faded.

"Yes," Hanen said. He had quickly found that Searn's shade was more or less hard of hearing. Hanen had to whisper directly onto the bone with his lips nearly brushing it.

Very good. Keep doing so. There is much to learn.

"What do you hope for me to learn?"

The secret of immortality. I have made a living shade, and I would that you knew how.

"But you died."

My body died. But a part of me still lives. You and I could break the bonds of death.

"Necromancy."

No. Not necromancy as your twice great-grandfather would have done it. Besides, that truth was a lie.

"What do you mean?"

What I mean is that we could truly cheat death. Imagine if I could return and make another shade.

"Then if your new body died you'd once again be able to rise."

Yes. Keep reading. Learn more than I did. I am heir to the Warlord. You could be heir to all of it.

"All of what?"

Dream. Walking. Dreadcraft. Even Deceit.

A chill ran over Hanen's shoulders. He touched the door to the little closet and pushed it open a nudge. When people came into Blackiron, it forced a small breeze to enter the closet. Hanen peered out to see figures walking around the barracks in the half-light. They didn't wear the cloaks of Black Sentinels, but held the short polearms of the Voktorra. They approached his bed and the empty chest sitting there. Hanen closed the door.

"Voktorra have come. They found the chest I keep the boneshroud in."

Then they must know you have it. If they find that out and tell the king...

"That can't happen."

No, it cannot. Take them for a chase.

"Where?"

There is a door to the left of the altar in the cathedral of Aben. Go there.

"Altar of Aben?" Hanen said to himself.

He peeked again. They had gone. He came out and walked over to his bed, and then pulled his Black Sentinel cloak over the boneshroud he wore. He looked under the bed. The ynfald underneath whimpered.

"What did they want?" he asked himself.

He walked to the door and peeked out. Five Voktorra stood guard outside, their backs to the door as they chatted.

He moved to the back wall where the canvas office Searn had set up still stood. He pulled back the curtain to reveal an old exit and hall that led him away from the castle.

"Whisper?" he said. "Are you coming?"

The ynfald's nose peeked out and then disappeared again, rattling in response.

Hanen shook his head and entered the darkness.

With the boneshroud over his shoulders, hidden by the black of his Sentinel cloak, Hanen found he could make out things in the dark by some unknown means, not well enough to read the journals—that required candlelight—but enough to see where he was going. He took the turns as he remembered them, and came to an old moldering door. He pushed it open with a heavy creak and entered the abandoned cellar. He could hear the scratching sound of scribes at work on the floor above, and finally came to his destination—a ladder that led up to a grate against the inside of the wall of the castle.

He climbed up and pushed the grate open. With no one around, it was easy to climb up and out of the cellar, where he found himself fifty feet from the final gate of the castle complex. He walked briskly and turned the corner just as several Voktorra saw him through the inner courtyard gate. One of them took off running toward Blackiron to alert the men that waited there.

Hanen began running across the green. Instead of heading toward the Abecinian cathedral, he turned left and sprinted toward the abandoned Crysalas convent, where the main gates were nailed shut with wooden beams. When he'd climbed to the top of the gates, he looked back to see the five guards running toward him. Hanen dropped ten feet to the cobblestone floor and ran as hard as he could, trying to find a way in. The stables were unlocked, and he was soon within the dark corridors of the complex. Passing the throne room, where Searn had stood against the Paladins of the Hammer, he took turns until he reached his goal—the storage closet at the back of the gallery.

He heard the clamor of the Voktorra, weapons drawn, far off behind him but nearing quickly. Opening the door to the storage closet, he gathered and dropped enough debris on the floor to keep anyone from entering easily. Then, having laid these obstacles down, he continued to the back door and on into the tunnel that would take him under the capital green to the Abecinian complex.

When he was partway through the tunnel, he saw light coming through a crack under the door at the very end, which let out into the gardens. As he came out into the light he heard someone raking. He spun and saw a monk with his back to him working leaves into a pile. He turned quickly to the nearest door and pulled it open with its heavy iron ring. He had walked into the now-derelict paladinial bastion. When he closed the door behind him, the silence was disorienting. Hanen stopped several times to listen to sounds that bounced off the walls only to realize it was his own breath or the swish of the two cloaks that hung from his frame. It took a few minutes for him to find his bearings, but he finally made his way into the stables. He remembered when he had slunk into the stall, and that cold dread had overwhelmed him as Searn, wearing the mantle now upon his shoulders, spoke. It was odd to now feel nothing. No shade had ever wafted out of the bone rings, as they had when Searn wore it. Instead he felt nothing.

The door leading out of the stables was unlocked. After opening the door and peeking out to check for guards, he proceeded toward the cathedral's front door. As he approached, he glanced to the green and caught a glimpse of a few Voktorra searching for him. He made it to the door and ducked into the torch-warmed cathedral, which was surprisingly empty. Hurrying to the front of the church, he passed the black bench dedicated to Wyv-Thüm. The entrance to the catacombs was cut into the wall beyond the bench. This doorway led down into the blackness of the grave. Darkness enshrouded him, and he felt himself disappear.

There was a light up ahead, dimly lighting a large room lined with open recesses boasting piles of the desiccated bones of long-dead priests, monks, and guildmen. Someone approached from the far end of the room, wearing a black robe that flowed to the ground. Hanen, who had not been seen, pushed himself up against a wall and watched as the figure passed by, stopping to observe an ossuary before moving on. The man in question was not from a priesthood Hanen recognized. He felt he should follow, and began to ghost behind the priest in black.

The man stood not much taller than Hanen, and glided with an otherworldly grace that inspired fear rather than peace. The figure came to a stop at an archway with even deeper blackness within. He took something out of his pocket and lit a torch on each side with a flame of almost greenish hue at the center. Neither torch burned bright, but they shed enough light to see by. Then the figure, looking once more over his shoulder, disappeared into the archway. Hanen waited for a moment before he heard a door along the hallway grind closed against the stone threshold, the two flames on the torches guttering out. Then he walked to the archway and peered down the hall. He could just make out another door further along, the boneshroud enabling him to see things in the dark.

He took out a flint, steel, and lit oil-soaked tinder, then set the two sconces aflame. The greenish fire came back to life, and Hanen was aware of dense currents of air moving up the passage from a distant opening. He quickly walked the fifty paces to the door he knew would be there, a door that had begun closing again after opening at the command of the flames. He took a deep breath and stepped within, where the air around him pressed down upon his shoulders, making his body feel twice its weight. The two cloaks hung heavily on his frame, and as he peered around he found himself in a vestibule rather like the manor houses in Edi. There were rich black rugs, lit by bright torches. A door opened up across from Hanen, and he pressed himself against the black banner that hung from one of the walls.

A figure dressed in a black robe entered, took hold of a small silver bowl on a table, and turned to leave. His gaze went over Hanen as if he weren't there, though Hanen knew he must be visible to him. The figure then left the room. Hanen slowed his breath to keep his heart from pounding and approached the door, putting his ear to it. Once he no longer heard footsteps he entered the next dark hallway. This hallway was not lit by torches, but by windows out into the world beyond. The glass in the windows was thick and outside there stood a vista he did not expect to see.

A large cavern stood outside, stretching for miles. The ceiling of the cave was far too high to be directly under Mahn Fulhar, for Hanen had not come more than three hundred feet into the catacombs below, with only a handful of steps in descent. There were ephemeral forms standing in a long line that ran to and fro along the floor of the cavern, all shuffling toward a large doorway, over which the massive stone-carved form of the wyloth-winged and three-eyed Wyv-Thüm, Judge in Noccitan, looked down.

"Noccitan?" Hanen whispered hoarsely. It came out as both statement and curse.

He walked down the hall that encircled this entrance to the underworld, glancing down on the lost souls continuing their death march toward their judgment.

A figure in black came walking in the opposite way, carrying several tomes, and walked through a large set of doors. Hanen glanced in as he passed, and saw a library that stretched off so far into the distance he couldn't see the end of it. The figure was handing the books to a person sitting at the front desk.

"Here are yesterday's recorded deaths," the former said to the latter.

"A good day," the other said.

"Yes. Perhaps one in twenty were given judgment to proceed to Lomïn."

"A very good day indeed."

Neither paid Hanen any attention, and he continued to walk the hall. He passed a door just as it opened, and saw within it a procession of black-robed figures preparing to exit. None looked up at him, and Hanen quickly rushed on ahead as they filed out into the hall and began to proceed along behind him. They moved with a stately but intentional march-step, pushing Hanen further and further into the underworld. None of the doorways were deep enough for him to press into so they could pass, and all were locked. He ran on ahead, feeling certain he was now asleep back in bed, dreaming this nightmare.

A double door stood before him. Hanen pushed through and into a large amphitheater. Instead of a stage at its center, a window opened toward a doorway, through which Hanen could see an ephemeral form entering to stand under a dim light. The figure threw himself onto the ground at the feet of someone Hanen could not see. Near to the window a scribe sat at a desk and wrote down what was spoken. Hanen approached him, but the scribe did not look up. This was a dream or a vision; that would explain why no one could see him. The scribe had his ear to a horn that came out of the wall. After standing nearby for a moment, trying to make out exactly what was being said and failing, Hanen finally went and sat at a nearby desk, unsure of what to do next.

Just as he sat, however, the door opened, and a throng of black-clad monks began to fill the seats of the amphitheater. When someone approached Hanen's desk, Hanen threw himself away to avoid being sat on, then turned to find a place where he could stand. He went to look behind a black curtain in a far corner and found himself in a room with a single monk sitting on a chair by himself. There was a heavily studded door, locked by countless locks and bolts, allowing nothing to pass through. The man was tall and thin but sat on his throne, gazing at the world beyond the door through a small porthole-shaped window. Hanen came and stood next to him, peering at the view.

What Hanen saw took his breath away. The porthole looked

GLOVES OF EONS

over the shoulders of two massive figures, their shoulders rising
and falling with deep breaths. The figure to the left had soft,
curved shoulders that glowed a purple hue. The shoulder of the
other was cloaked in blackness. A shade lay in prostrate
genuflection nearly sixty feet below Hanen.

"State now your claim," the figure on the right said. The voice
was ancient, and full of unmatched wisdom. "That you may be
judged."

The spirit giving its account muttered something Hanen could
not make out.

"Nevertheless," the Judge said, "you will give an account."

"I walked the path," the witness spoke up. He hesitated, and
finally said, "But I never sought it."

"What you say is true. Your life does not show you worthy of
journeying on to Lomïn."

The shade threw itself to the ground once more and began
begging.

"And yet," the Judge said, "there was a moment, when you were
twelve, where you offered your cloak to an ailing woman. She
blessed you with words of wisdom, advising you then to continue
in service to the helpless, and you did for a time, until greed
became your sin. That act of kindness might have been enough,
had you stayed the course it set you upon. You are sentenced to
two hundred years in silence to consider your actions in life."

The spirit stood, opened his mouth to speak, but nothing came
out. Hanging its head, it turned and floated away.

The massive figure to the right turned his head, and suddenly
Hanen could see the Judge's profile. Upon his brow he wore a
crown made of bone with a single tip that rose above his forehead.
The figure continued to turn, in order to look over his shoulder
through Hanen's porthole with a single black eye in the center of
his forehead. The eye looked directly at Hanen, who suddenly
wanted to throw himself to the ground and bow, as the spirit
before the throne had done. But something protected him from the
baleful stare.

"So that is how it is done," the giant said calmly, with no malice
in his words, merely interest in his eye. Hanen felt a hand reach
into his mind; like someone running their hands along the spines
of books, Hanen felt Wyv-Thüm, Judge in Noccitan, riffle through
every one of his memories, browsing for something. The
boneshroud had done nothing to protect him. He was naked

before the god of Death.

"You are incorrect," Wyv said. "About many things, of course, but mostly about your not being protected."

Hanen tried to open his mouth to speak, but could not.

"You are protected. You should be seen by my followers, by most eyes that see only spirits. Yet you are invisible, seen only by my third eye. Even then, only barely. You should be struck dead, for no mortal has looked upon a god as they truly are, and yet you do. You are protected from my telling you what to think. No person who comes to these halls may leave, save for permission from myself. And yet, I expect you shall walk from these hallowed halls untouched—but not unchanged."

"Why do you not strike him down for such insolence?" the voice of the purple-hued Queen asked.

"I may not see the future as our sister does, but I see what has happened, and I can infer that it is in our best interests to allow this one to go."

"But who is it?"

"I shall not tell you, for your healing is not complete."

The rich female voice growled, more to herself than in anger.

"You have been here too long," Wyv said to Hanen. "Next time we meet, you shall stand before the throne and not behind it. Come in the arms of Nifara or bearing the skull of a fallen god, for I will grant permission for your appearance no other way."

Hanen took a deep shuddering breath as Wyv turned away and another soul entered to be judged. The first breath was followed by a quick succession of breaths that turned to a blind panic. He turned and ran toward the door, pushing through the curtain, unnoticed by the monks beyond as they clamored and argued with one another over Wyv's words to Hanen, which they had heard from the amphitheater. One of them had lowered their hood to reveal a featureless face of grey. Another waved their arms animatedly to reveal grey hands, whose fingers barely had individuality. Hanen did not stop running until he came to the entry vestibule and passed back into the catacombs, where he crouched down behind a sepulcher and tried to catch his breath in the much thinner air, sobs wracking his body.

Soon the sobs turned to deep, painful breaths. He stood, his composure slowly returning to him, and finally went out of the catacombs. He saw five figures standing near the door, all wearing the gray and blue of the Voktorra.

"So they did follow me here," Hanen muttered. He had looked into the eye of a god. He now feared nothing. Then he remembered what Wyv had said about those that entered the black monastery. He took out his tinder again and lit a candle, which he held up while stepping back into the darkness of the catacombs. He moved the candle about to make sure they saw it. As they crept forward to investigate, Hanen matched their stride yet kept in front of them. They followed the light, which seemed to float in the air by itself, his cloak enshrouding him in darkness.

They were hesitant, but he led them on. He neared the portal to Noccitan and lit one of the green flame torches. The Voktorra startled. One of them threatened to flee while the others pressured him to stay. Hanen reached out with his candle and lit the second one, and the doorway opened. Then he pinched the flame of his candle and pressed himself up against the wall.

One of them stepped forward, examining the black portal, and stepped through, followed by each one in turn. The door next to Hanen slid closed, and there was no sound from the other side.

He stepped out of the shadows, returned to the cathedral, and made easy passage back to Blackiron. He calmly removed his cloak and the boneshroud, and sighed in relief as he shut the chest that held both. Whisper came out from under the bed.

"Am I asleep? Dreaming? Or did I just cheat death?"

Whisper sat staring at him, cocking his head, considering.

A knock came at the door of Blackiron. Captain Navien entered.

"Did my guard detail find you?" he said, walking toward him. "The king has summoned you."

"I did not see any guards," Hanen lied. "I've been here all day."

"You're to join me to see the king, then. Once you're in the service of the king, you are at his beck and call."

"And once you're in the service of a god, tricked into it or not, it never ends," Hanen muttered to himself as he reached back into the chest, pulled out his Black Sentinel cloak, and pulled it around his shoulders.

3

PURPOSELESS

I was twelve when Zephyr first showed me the Heptagrammaton, although it was another year before I was allowed to see its pages. It was within that text that he'd buried the secret of the boneshroud. He had never spoken of it, but allowed me to find it on my own. I think he thought he was clever, leaving it as the only portion of the book that made any sense without explanation. But I understood much of what was written there— more than Scepter did, and he had been formally educated as a prince in Mahndür.

—JOURNAL OF SEARN VETURRES, ENTRY FIVE

"What does the king want?" Hanen asked as they walked through the main gates into the castle proper.

"That's none of my business, nor yours until the king reveals it to you," Captain Navien said.

They walked along blue-carpeted halls. The last time he had been summoned before the king was when he had joined Searn. Since then all messages from the king had been through Navien. At that time, they were led to the Blue Room. It had been easy to reach, and easier to leave from. This time the Voktorra led Hanen through several back hallways, with turns enough to confuse an ynfald following a strong scent, before coming to an open door which looked into a spacious and cold room with south-facing windows. The fire in the hearth at the far end of the room was doing little to combat the chill. Near the hearth, the king sat on a cushioned throne.

"I leave you here," Captain Navien said. "But I'll be watching."

Hanen nodded and stepped toward the king without anxiety. Being addressed directly by a god had removed any fear he had of anyone, it seemed. As he approached the chair, he saw the king wore plush furs over his shoulders, though his feet and calves were bare. He had a stack of books on a side table, and a small journal in his hands. He glanced toward Hanen as he approached and waved a hand beckoning him to come closer.

When Hanen was near enough, the king held up a hand for him to stop.

King Erdthal was the same age as Hanen, with long black hair that fell around his face, his matching beard kept trimmed short. He wore a white shirt and short leather pants dyed blue.

"I find the contrasting warmth and cold stimulating as I read," the king said. He turned the page and marked his place, putting it down on his lap, looking out the window. He took a deep breath and nodded to himself, then looked up at Hanen.

"You are not fulfilling your end of the bargain your predecessor made."

Hanen looked the king in the eyes and said nothing.

"Searn VeTurres promised me that you were going to put a caravan together, and you'd be making money that would come directly to me. Yet, since he mysteriously disappeared, you and your organization have failed to fulfill my requests. You're in breach of contract."

"I understand your concern," Hanen replied.

"You do? Because spring is upon us, and you've not sent a single caravan south."

"The merchants who agreed to travel with us have backed out."

"Then what have you done to procure more merchants?"

"Given that most Black Sentinels have left the city, my sister and I have done what we can to fulfill your requests ourselves. It has left us little time to find new clients. The caravan was not to leave for another two weeks, regardless."

"Then you had best see that you find a caravan and begin collecting gold."

He patted the book mindlessly and said, "Have you heard from your missing mentor?"

"I don't understand," Hanen said. "Searn VeTurres is dead. This was reported to you—the Paladins of the Hammer reported that to you."

"That doesn't mean I believe it."

"I was there when he killed himself. He shoved a pin through his eye."

"A pin? That might gouge an eye out. But it wouldn't kill him."

"It was a sail needle six inches long. It killed him. I helped move the body."

"Then you know what he had on his shoulders when he died?"

"His Black Sentinel cloak," Hanen lied.

The king frowned and looked back at the book on his lap. "Do you know what this book is?"

"It looks to be a journal."

"It is the journal of my uncle, Bakkdin. I believe I mentioned him when last we met."

"A mentor to Searn," Hanen said.

"Yes. My uncle left before I was born, and this journal confirms that he became a Paladin of the Hammer. That would lead me to believe that Searn VeTurres was a Paladin himself."

"This is true," Hanen said. "I learned that the night before he betrayed us."

"Thank you, Clouw. That confirms something I needed to understand. I may need to pay my guest a visit tonight."

The king went silent for a time, awkwardly pondering something. "Did you meet the new Prima Pater of the Paladins?"

Hanen nodded.

"Did you know that a new Prima Pater is only established after the previous Prima Pater dies?"

Hanen shook his head.

"Interesting, then, that a new Prima Pater was announced when the previous Prima Pater was still alive, isn't it?"

The night of the incident, the new Prima Pater came to Hanen and Rallia, questioning them about the boneshroud and the gauntlet, which had both gone missing from Searn's body after they moved it to the bastion. He also asked both the Clouws to remain silent about Dorian Mür being alive. Rallia had made Hanen vow to say nothing, out of respect for her if not the Paladins.

"I hadn't heard that," Hanen lied.

"You don't know much, do you?"

"Only as much as I need to know."

"Very well. I have nothing more to say to you. I expect you to keep quiet about what we've discussed this day, including the fact that the old Prima Pater still lives."

"Yes. And I ask you to reduce your demands on the Black Sentinel office until we can launch the caravan again."

"No. I'll be canceling your contract. You've given me what I need, and now I need to continue my search to find out who took that cloak from the body of Searn. I should be able to gather more information from the old man now. You and your sister will move out of Blackiron by the end of the day. You're free to go."

Hanen's shoulders fell.

"Actually," the king said, standing up. His feet slapped the cold stone ground as he walked up to Hanen, who had not realized how much shorter he stood. "I do have an assignment for you. A singular one that would make all my other demands null and void."

He held up the journal. It had a sketch of the boneshroud within.

"Does this look like the cloak Searn wore that night?"

"I'm not sure. Maybe," Hanen said. He could feel a cold sweat breaking out across his head.

"I'm not even sure what it is called. It might be called a bone cloak, or something. I want you to find it and bring it to me. If Searn VeTurres began creating this cloak when he was still apprenticed to my uncle, then the cloak belongs to me. Are we understood?"

Hanen nodded, tilted his head, and walked toward the door. Navien entered and crossed the room at a gesture from the king. Erdthal spoke, just loud enough for Hanen to hear. "Please summon the old Paladin to my private dining room after you see a meal prepared for the two of us."

Hanen walked quickly back to Blackiron, locked the door behind him, and sat down on his bed. Whisper came out from his place and put his head under Hanen's hand to be petted.

"We've been kicked out," Hanen said, "and we have no way to reach Rallia."

Hanen paused in his scratching; Whisper looked up imploringly.

"If we're going to pretend we're seeking the shroud, we need to be out where the Voktorra can see us."

He took a deep breath and began to pack. He soon had everything out of the chest under his bed and into his travel pack after checking all of Rallia's hidey holes and ensuring she had taken all her things. He put heavy rocks in the chest, locked it, and pushed it back under the bed for the Voktorra to find, hoping they would drag the heavy thing back to their barracks, only to open it and discover nothing. He placed the folded-up boneshroud at the bottom of his pack and laid everything else on top of it. His charts and notes had long ago been packed into a long leather tube, which he threw over his shoulder once his travel pack was securely on his back.

"Come on, Whisper," Hanen said, walking to the door. He stopped and considered checking the room for anything he might have missed, but decided against it and left just as the sun was setting. Hanen hoped to find an inn with a decent room for tonight before searching for permanent arrangements. Despite his hopes, he found himself walking for hours without success. As dawn was breaking he decided to seek a room at the Ship Tack Inn where they had first stayed in town. On his way there, the smell of baking bread took him to a small baker's window, where he bought a loaf of sweet bread, set his pack down against a wall, and began to eat as the sun rose.

He heard the long-gaited tap of a staff approaching and he knew who it was before they came to stand over him. The aroma of exotic spices followed.

"*Leq'aw y dis,*" Ymbrys Veronia said. "May I join you?"

Hanen nodded. The qavyl sat down, crossing his dog-like legs, and laid his long leather-topped staff across his lap.

His face was the shape of a heart, but his head, while short, extended back. His eyes were round, with large eyelids that fell to a squint in the brightening light. He had only two slits for a nose, from under which two tendrils drooped. Two boney protuberances rose from the top of his head, marking his age, and were covered with the same soft leathery skin as his body. His ears stuck out sideways from his head, and fell toward his shoulders. Attired in many thin layers of silks of closely matched shades, he wore under them a blousey tunic, and his hands were left bare, revealing four fingers on each with thumbs posable to the left and to the right. His long flat tail curled around him, seemingly with a mind of its own.

Whisper quickly got up and curled up next to the qavyl.

"I am glad to see you still have this worthy companion," Ymbrys said.

Hanen just nodded.

"You are packed to leave town, it seems. The caravan is ready then?"

"The caravan was canceled and the king just kicked us out of our offices."

"I'm sorry to hear that."

"Are you sorry?" Hanen turned, snapping.

"I was only passing by and saw you," Ymbrys said. "That's barely a good reason to become angry with me."

"Then why do you seem to always find me at my lowest?"

Ymbrys placed a hand on Hanen's shoulder.

"Young man," Ymbrys said. "I swear to you, I was not seeking you out."

Hanen rolled his eyes, hoping the qavyl couldn't see it.

"I was looking out for your sister, however."

"Why?"

"It is early morning. She is often out walking at this time, and I had intended to pass on a message for the two of you."

"And what is that?"

"I will be leaving town. I have business to conduct in Haven in Limae. Perhaps I shall see you both there."

"Why would we go to Limae?" Hanen asked.

"To perhaps tie up loose ends with your organization?"

"What business are you seeking out there?"

"You'll recall my saying that I have been seeking out your family's bloodline for some time. Now that I've found your family there are other questions that remain unanswered. Do you remember my mentioning the Alvarian branch? When I traversed north with you and your companions?"

"I think so, yes."

"There were two lines to the Alvarian branch, which may be significant for reasons I can't tell you at the moment. You and I will meet again, I have no doubt. Until then, I have much to learn."

"You always seem to speak in riddles."

"I'd prefer not to share anything that I've not confirmed." The qavyl rose. "I look forward to seeing you and your sister again. May your journey find you traveling in the right direction."

Hanen watched the qavyl walk away then went to the Ship Tack Inn, where he made arrangements for a room and set about unpacking.

He spent the next week formulating his plan, spending time near the upper city while waiting for Rallia to return. At the end of the week, she did. Hanen was traveling back down the city to the inn when he saw his sister walking the opposite way.

"Rallia," Hanen said.

She looked up and smiled.

"Hello, brother," Rallia replied.

"We've been kicked out of Blackiron. I've moved our things to the Ship Tack."

Rallia's smile dropped. "That was sudden."

"It seems our favor with the king has run out, yet we're not out from under his thumb yet, either."

"He won't like what I have to tell him, then. My mission was a failure."

"What did he send you off to do?"

"He wanted me to find Dorian Mür. I was in Zebüdé."

"Why would he send you off to do that? I suspect he's got the old Prima Pater at the castle here."

"Excuse me?" Rallia stopped again, staring at Hanen incredulously. "Was I just sent on another false mission?"

"I guess so," Hanen said. "I think the Prima Pater is his house prisoner. He's been questioning him, and wants me to start hunting for the cloak that Searn was wearing."

Rallia was shaking her head. "No. We're not doing that. We need to get out of this business. I just want out."

"At least you didn't get your face beaten this time," Hanen said, forcing a smile.

"Not yet," Rallia said, scowling.

"I've been thinking about it," Hanen said. "I think we can at least get away from Mahn Fulhar; then we can decide what to do."

"Leave Mahn Fulhar? Impossible."

"Why not? You just said you wanted out."

"We can't let Dorian Mür remain a prisoner of the king. The king has no business holding him hostage. The Prima Pater is the highest authority on Kallattai, save perhaps the Emperor of the Hrelgren Empire."

"He's not the Prima Pater anymore," Hanen said.

"That doesn't change the fact that he was the Prima Pater. That should stand for something."

"You're not suggesting we try to help the Prima Pater escape from the castle?"

"It's the right thing to do."

They came to the inn. Hanen took a plate of meats and cheeses from the barmaid, Rallia took up two tankards of ale, and they made their way to their room.

"You're serious?" Hanen asked.

"Of course I am. Ophedia might help us," Rallia said.

"She left town after Searn died."

"I know," Rallia said. "But I ran into her in Zebüdé. She's working there as a bodyguard, gambling her money away. She told me never to hesitate to call for her help."

"Fine. You can send a message for to her to meet up with us."

"I can't believe I got sent on a fool's errand again. Why does no one want me around?" Rallia asked.

"Because you're observant and you're capable."

"Then why do they want you around?"

"Because they take me for a fool. I guess everyone thinks I'll believe anything."

Rallia threw herself onto her bed and sighed.

"Tell me about Father. You said you found him? You promised you'd tell me more later."

"Not much to say," Hanen said. "He's alive. I'm not sure where he is."

"You said he mentioned something about being cursed? That doesn't sound like him at all."

"Nonetheless he's alive, but no better than before. Nothing ever goes well for him. Luckless. And since these things keep happening to us, it must be our curse to bear too."

"I refuse to believe that," Rallia said. "After this is all over, I'm going to find him."

4

CHALICE

I saw the children play upon the woodpile.

I looked upon the books of history.

And in both I saw the same.

We make much of our lives, and draw conclusions when we cannot see the whole.

All is foolishness.

— ABEDOIR OF OIQUIMON

Hanen sat with his back to the wall outside the Ship Tack Inn. The wall across the street, overlooking the drop to the Lupinfang Sea, blocked some of the wind blowing off the water. Tradesman moved goods up and down the street from The Hill to the richer folk in the Grotto and the canyon leading up the city. The briny scent in the air was pleasant in the cold, early spring air, and the fish smelled fresh, which was better than the stench of his hometown of Garrou. Rallia sat next to him, and Hanen saw the blank look in her eyes. He knew she was thinking of that night in the Rose convent as she shuddered, and tried to shake the thought away.

The Voktorra guardsman assigned to them stood leaning against a wall down the street, the curve of the road exposing him to the uncomfortably cold and shearing wind. Rallia glanced down the street at the guard, shook her head in derision, and returned to the inn. Hanen and Whisper quickly followed her.

Rallia took a table near the back, and held two fingers up for the barmaid as Hanen moved to join her.

"When do you think Ophedia will arrive?" Hanen asked.

"Soon, I should hope," Rallia replied. "If we don't present findings to the king soon, we'll have to leave town."

The clack of wooden-soled boots marked the long strides of an approaching person. Hanen looked up and turned. Ophedia del Ishé held four beers in her gloved hands. She wore a fur-lined vest with many pockets, and a heavy woolen blouse over baggy trousers that were tucked into her knee-high boots. There was an almost imperceptibly auburn highlight to the black hair that flowed over her shoulder, and her long nose crinkled as she smiled at them. A young boy followed in her wake, carrying her cloak and bag.

She set all four tankards down on the table.

"The barmaid could have carried those over," Rallia said.

"I didn't carry yours over," she said with a smirk. She threw herself into the booth next to Rallia. She put an obviously protective arm around her tankards, then waved at the boy. "You can take those to the room belonging to these two."

The boy nodded and waddled off. The barmaid approached with Rallia and Hanen's tankards, and eyed Ophedia's beers. Ophedia held up a finger, then proceeded to drop one of the tankards back in one fluid gulp. She handed it to the girl.

"Make enough of an entrance?" Hanen muttered.

"I always make an entrance," she said. "It's good to see you too, Hanen."

"Hello Ophedia," Rallia said.

"Where's Whisper?" she asked. She gasped at something under the table, and smiled as Whisper stuck his head out, demanding to be petted. "What's the big news?"

"No platitudes?" Hanen asked.

"I've never heard you talk about the weather. Why should I?" she asked.

"We're glad you're here," Rallia said. "We need your help."

"Why me?" she asked.

"Because we trust you. And you're in the same boat as us."

"What is that supposed to mean?" she asked.

"Hanen and I were practically announced as Searn's acolytes.

And you, well..."

"I'm his daughter."

"Yeah."

"So why do you need me?"

"Because we need to do something that will vindicate all three of us."

"And what's that?"

"Dorian Mür," Hanen said. "The old Prima Pater?"

"What about him?"

"The king has him either imprisoned, or under house arrest at the Stone."

Ophedia lowered her head and stared at Hanen from under furrowed brows. She spun her head and looked at Rallia, lifting another tankard to her mouth and taking a long pull.

"You want me to help you jailbreak an old man who can barely walk out of a heavily guarded castle, making us capital criminals in Mahndür, in order to make everything right with the Paladins? Because my father, whom I never knew as such, was their mortal enemy and wanted to destroy them?"

Rallia nodded.

"All right," she said, upending the second tankard.

"That easy?"

"Why not?" she smiled. "I'm bored. Life was so much more exciting with you two and Searn. I'm also in debt here, so any excuse to flee the country and never return seems like a good idea."

"What kind of money do you owe?" Hanen asked.

"Not really your business, but I also may have maimed the goon of one of the men I'm indebted to."

"Speaking of goons," Rallia said.

Ophedia's smile dropped as she shot a glance at the door.

A Voktorra pushed through the door and held it open for another, Captain Abenard Navien, who pulled his brimmed helmet off his head as he entered, and placed it under his arm. Smoothing his hair down, he looked around and glared at the three of them as soon as his eyes fell on them. The other guard stayed by the door as Navien approached.

"It seems you've returned to town," Navien said, standing over Ophedia.

"I was passing through."

"As a former apprentice of Searn VeTurres, may I ask where

you've come from?"

"Zebüdé. You probably won't find Searn there, however. He is dead, after all."

"Everyone seems to be under that impression," Navien said, sizing up the room. "However, given that the Paladins never produced a body for me to see, I do not have good reason to believe it."

He took a deep breath and continued speaking more to Ophedia than the other two.

"You may consider yourself a guest of mine while you're here. My men will make sure you don't get into any trouble. Of course, given you've come directly to the inn the Clouws are staying at, I'd ask you not to make any false moves, or you'll no longer be my guest, but a guest of the Stone."

"Is there any other reason you've approached us, Abenard?" Hanen asked.

"That's Captain Navien," he corrected. "I came when I heard our friend Ophedia del Ishé had arrived, just as I received word from my commander that special guests will be arriving today. You'll hear it from other Voktorra on the street corners, I'm sure, but I wanted to make sure you knew directly from me, and attended at my invitation, and not out of some moral obligation."

"Attend what?" Rallia asked.

"All denizens of Mahn Fulhar are to appear along the main thoroughfare to welcome the arrival of the Praetors of the Church of the Common Chalice."

"The guilds may not appreciate those orders," Hanen said.

"This order does not come from the king, but from the High Priest Klent Rigal himself."

"I consider myself a Grissoni," Rallia said.

"The only church recognized in Mahndür and our neighboring countries is that of the Church of Aben, under the authority of the High Priest of Aben, Klent Rigal. If the king of Mahndür can submit to his authority, then you can too. The procession starts soon."

He walked away, glanced back over his shoulder with a frown, then disappeared out the door.

"What's the plan then?" Ophedia said, starting in on her third tankard. She wasn't slowing.

"First we need to scout out the Stone," Hanen said.

"Which will be difficult if Abenard is going to be watching all three of us," Rallia interjected.

"Secondly," Hanen continued, "we need you to distract Abanard for a day or two."

"Lead him on a chase or something?" Ophedia asked.

Hanen nodded.

"The third thing will be breaking Dorian out," Rallia said.

Hanen gave her a faint smile.

"How do you plan to find the old man in the castle? It's massive," Ophedia objected.

"I spent a few early mornings on the walls encircling the castle," Rallia said. "The guest quarters are on the opposite side of Blackiron. Hanen thinks the old Prima Pater may be held there."

"Or he's in the dungeon," Hanen replied. "Under the keen eye of the Voktorra."

"Or in one of the private rooms with the rest of the royalty," Rallia said.

"Yes. But I doubt that," Hanen said. "When I was leaving my audience with the king, I overheard some conversation which suggested he's being kept somewhere within easy reach of Captain Navien, who is rarely away from the front gates. This indicates either the dungeon or the guest housing."

"Except when he's tramping around the city watching you two," Ophedia said.

She placed the third empty tankard down carefully and reached for her fourth. Rallia put a hand on it.

"That's probably enough for now," she said.

Ophedia yanked her tankard away while shoving an elbow at Rallia, who scoffed and stood from the table.

"Stop this," Hanen said.

"I'll drink what I want," Ophedia said. "It's not your business to parent me."

She picked up the fourth tankard and left.

"She's going to make herself sick," Hanen said, once she was out of earshot.

"I hope she's not going to be much trouble for us."

"We'll see," Hanen replied. "If she can distract Navien long enough for us to get into the Stone, we'll be fine."

"Are you anxious about the plan?" Rallia asked as they left together.

"No, not yet. It's once we get out of the Stone with Dorian Mür that I'll have a few dwovs in my innards."

Thousands of people were milling about the Grotto when they arrived, with not a few young boys looking for trouble in the crowd. Alodda and her sister, Runah, were trying to rescue a mannequin that had somehow left the shop and found its way across the cobblestone street.

"Let us help," Hanen said, taking the mannequin from her arms. Rallia and Ophedia shouldered clear a space for him to move.

He carried the mannequin into the shop, which was empty except for the Dülar family.

"Thank you, Hanen," Alodda said. "Where are all these people coming from? They just showed up a few minutes ago in droves."

"The Voktorra are going through town announcing the arrival of honored guests of the High Priest," Rallia said. "Everyone is to situate themselves for a parade of sorts."

"Rallia," Alodda's mother said, approaching. "We finished the outfit. Perhaps while you're here you could try it on?"

"I'm happy to," Rallia said.

"Who is coming to visit the High Priest?" Alodda asked.

She stood next to Hanen, their shoulders brushing.

"Praetors from Œron," Hanen said.

Alodda gasped.

"What's wrong?" he asked, glancing down at her.

"My mother, Eimeé," Alodda said. "She was born in Œron, and her mother was a member of the Crysalas church. Her parents were taken by the Chalicians after their vault was seized, and she only escaped because another member brought her to Mahndür when she was a little child. If the Church of Œron is making peace with the High Priest...."

"I thought the High Priest held them under his own authority."

"The Church of the Common Chalice doesn't make deals that don't benefit itself," Alodda said, her countenance darker than Hanen had ever seen. "This won't be good."

Rallia reappeared from the back. Her blouse was dyed gray, with a lighter gray embroidery worked through it.

"How does it feel?" Alodda's mother asked.

"The sleeves will take some breaking in, I like what you did."

The older woman nodded.

"What made you decide to embroider with gray?" Rallia asked.

"Alodda's suggestion," she said. "It matches your eyes."

Hanen nodded. "You look good. Is that oilcloth on the arms?"

"Yes," Alodda said. "For traveling in the elements. It will keep its color longer than the rest of the outfit."

She walked up to Rallia and touched her arms. "There is woolen padding within. When you remove the sleeves in the summer, pull out the wool. You can use it for kindling. Then, find a seamstress and have her replace the wool before autumn. It will last longer that way, and won't get lumpy."

"What of your friend over there?" Alodda asked, pointing to Ophedia, who stood by the window watching the crowd. The four beers had left her as unsteady as a ship in windy waters.

"What about Ophedia?" Hanen asked.

"Is she a Sentinel, too?"

"When she feels like it," Rallia said smiling. "Mostly she's a nuisance we can only rely on when we need help."

"What kind of help?" Alodda asked, cocking an eyebrow..

A horn blasted. Her father rose, with the help of his younger daughter, to stand in the window. People outside parted as a lone rider on a sleipnir marched through.

"Make way and show respect!" Captain Navien called as he came into view atop a gray steed. He stopped several strides before the shop, looking over the heads of the surrounding people. "By order of His Royal Majesty, Velab Erdthal II, King of Mahndür and Nasun, Grandmaster of the Fulharian Guilds, all must show respect and honor to the guests of the Church of Aben, and hear the way in which you shall conduct your lives this year."

He looked up into the shops and directly at Hanen.

"Their proclamation is law, for their authority is granted directly over all humanity by Aben, High King in Lomïn. Disregard this, and you forfeit your souls."

He kept his eyes on the Clouws as he proceeded down the loop of the Grotto and made the announcement at a new point in his route.

"What is that supposed to mean?" the old tailor Dülar asked.

Suddenly the people at the edge of the Grotto dropped to their knees, followed by more and more people in the crowd. A rider in a red-sashed gray robe came forward. "Kneel! In respect!" He ordered with so much authority, Hanen almost dropped to a knee without thinking.

"Hanen?" Alodda said. He turned to see she had knelt, as had Rallia.

"What are you doing?" Hanen asked his sister.

"I should ask the same. It will not harm you to bow when the church says bow."

Hanen reluctantly came down on one knee. The herald moved on as a group of riders came into view.

Hanen had never seen the Praetors of the Church of the Common Chalice, but he knew at first sight that they were similar to the Paladins. They each wore cylindrical helms, wide at the top, symbolizing a cup. They each had full and well-trimmed beards. Where the Paladins of the Hammer had their jawlines obscured by gorgets, the breastplates of these Praetors were form-fitted, and covered by gray tabards so light as to be almost white, with a blue chalice embroidered on the front. They each held in their stirrups a long spear, the tip like a barbed arrow with decorative fletching at the other end. Hanging across their chests on silver chains was a book bound in red leather, and chained to their their belts a bejeweled chalice.

The central Praetor sat a head taller than the others on a special saddle, and he wore a regal blue sash across his chest.

"I, Provost Zehan Otem, second to the Praetor Praeposit Anhouil Chétain, bring word. It is hereby decreed, by the High Ecumenical Priest of Aben, Klent Rigal, seconded and established in doctrinal agreement by Benefactor Missioner Abithu Omrab, highest on the Path of Aben, that all kings under Aben's authority shall recognize He Who Reigns in Lomïn as High King, whose authority shall be given by the executors of his church, the Praetors of the Chalice. For it is by the revealing of his will, through the mysteries of our faith, that his authority is established.

"Therefore, let it be known that the Praetors have been given the authority to rule over your lives, guiding you to the salvation you cannot know without our permission. You shall live in safety, under our supervision. This has been acknowledged by King of Mahndür, and by High Ecumen Rigal. Thus you have no recourse.

"As first command, recognize or else find thyself cast from the church and from communion with all others—follow the statutes set before you."

Praetors with no helmet or armor, but wearing the blue chalice across their tabards, marched forward and pushed through the crowds, holding hammers and pieces of parchment. They came to each door or to the posts at the vendors' tents and swiftly nailed the parchment to the wood. Then, they reached to their belts and held up wide rimmed chalices, and held them out for all nearby.

"It is an honor for you to see they who bear the chalice, upon their chests and in their hands. Your duty is to fill their vessels with silver and with gold. If you fail to do so, know that a mark shall go upon your record. Give only trifles, and you insult your hosts upon this earth."

Hesitantly at first, a few put coins into the chalices waved before them. Then coins came out in a flood.

"Second, know that as newly adopted members under the Common Cup, this city of Mahn Fulhar now enters a time of observance—a time that shall see you purified through holy worship, and through strict denial. Therefore, none shall walk the streets once sun has set. None shall leave by gate without express permission of the Church or one of their officers. Any act to the contrary shall be seen as sedition."

"Where are the Paladins?" an unseen woman called out.

"The Paladins of the Hammer have been cast from these lands, for their sins come down upon their heads as a rain of fire. Their heresy has condemned their order to a slow and painful death. As it is written: Should one fall to heresy, then let his sins be known, or else his be yours."

He stopped speaking for a minute and let that sink in.

"Lastly, let your eyes turn to the study of the *Book of the True Path*, by which you shall learn of Aben's will for your life."

The men with the chalices had returned to pour out the gold and silver into the chest on the side of the speaker's sleipnir. He looked down and frowned.

"Each shall appear before the Abecinian Cathedral before the week's end, make a donation to the church, and in return receive the *Book of the True Path*. But for your lack of faith and paltry giving to the chalices held to you, know that a silver conta shall be your contribution."

"Follow the path," he intoned in conclusion.

The other Chalicians around him replied in loud chant, "Follow or despair!"

The parade moved along and the crowd stood there in shocked silence.

"They've instilled a curfew?" Rallia said.

"And a locked gate," the old Abgenas Dülar said. He opened the door, pulled free the parchment nailed there, and frowned at the mark on the paint. After reading it, he scoffed and handed it to his wife. "It's written in Œronzi."

She glanced over it, shaking her head.

"It provides complete authority to the Church of the Common Chalice, and dictates that priests over other Abecinian orders are granted certain levels of authority in the Church but not over the Praetors. Effectively, it states that the Œronzi have authority over citizens of other countries."

"What does that mean, Mother?" Alodda asked.

"It means I need to go and see some friends. Abgenas, you'll need to go and pay the Church for the book. Bring it home. Don't bother reading it. It's only written in Œronzi, in their 'holy tongue.'"

"This is going to make our plans much more difficult," Ophedia said.

"What plans?" Alodda asked.

Rallia gave Hanen a look and a nod.

"Prima Pater Dorian Mür," Hanen said.

Abgenas Dülar turned to look at them. Alodda's mother stopped to stare at Hanen.

"I have reason to believe that the king has him under house arrest at the Stone."

"He will not last long there," Alodda's mother said. "The Praetors will either use him as a pawn or execute him."

"That's why we need to get him safely to a country beyond the authority of the Chalicians."

"Tell me what I must do to help you," Abgenas said. "I served under the Prima Pater in the Protectorate Wars. I will not have the leader of the church I recognize, and protector of my wife's faith, murdered to further the wicked goals of the Œronzi church."

"The curfew is going to make that hard," Rallia said.

"If you can see the Prima Pater safely away from the Stone," Alodda's mother said, "then I can find a way to see you safely out of the city."

5

SAINTS

Be unto them a scale to judge against.

Be a paragon. Be flawless in your steps.

I call you to higher than you be,

For you must remember that you are mortal such as they,

But I am perfect, such as they should strive toward.

— *STAFF OF WISDOM*, SPOKEN BY NIFARA

IN THE 9TH CENTURY

The line of monks shuffled down through the switchbacks, their staffs tapping against the waist-high walls that kept travelers from plummeting down the steep hillside. Seriah Yaledít recalled that they still had half a mile or so, after they came out on the valley floor, before they reached the north gates of Birin. Although the smell of the city was usually the first thing she noticed, with muddy spring runoff coursing through the city as people moved about for the first time since winter first forced them to buckle down those many long months ago.

This time though, the first thing she sensed did not come from her nose or ears, nor from her eyes bound by the cloth she had long ago tied around her head when she first took her vows. The first thing she sensed was the growing dread of the presence of Nifara, who had vowed to protect the city from harm.

Seriah had, after all, been the harbinger of a new age, bearing a message from the dark god Achanerüt, who had appeared to her with Coldness as his attendant, and asked her to deliver a message to her own goddess, Nifara, a message that had caused Nifara to cry out in fear and flee from her. Achanerüt had regretted how she had shunned him, talking of how things might have been different if she hadn't done so—for everyone. Seriah had not known who had given her those words, at least not at the time. That was Achanerüt's deceit. Now she traveled with her guilt, knowing that she was the one who'd caused her goddess to sob.

Koragh Neyarn, known to everyone else as Cräg Narn, was an immortal saint of Nifara, one of only nine in history. He had made a world-changing decision for their goddess, and was in return granted immortality in service to her. The elderly man had ensured Seriah made the journey back with them to Birin. They had tramped through the long winter, through dangerous passes that had taken one of their number, a young assistant who had not yet taken his vows. Kerei Lant led the five remaining monks out of the original ten, having been chosen as the acting Archimandrite until a vote could be held in Birin. She did not know she walked with a saint, and she also did not know she walked with a betrayer—Seriah.

They continued across the valley floor as the sound and fragrance of the city washed over them, the scent of people dusting their homes of a winter's buildup, the sound of market stalls being opened, the feel of pleasant crowds of people in sunny squares. She was home—in a place she could never call home again.

"You'll be joining me," the old gentle voice of Koragh Neyarn said. "I have to speak with the other saints, and you'll be giving your testimony."

"So that you can decide what to do with me?"

"Don't be silly, young lady."

They walked in silence for some time, their staffs clacking on the flagstones, the three rings hanging from the single standing ring jingling with a jin, jin, jin.

"We're not going to do something to you. I'm aware that you were an unwitting messenger. But the consequences of your actions still need to be weighed, so we can decide what actions we need to take."

"There are nine saints?" Seriah asked quietly.

"Yes. But only six of us are likely to be at the Templum. Unless

Eregar is gone off on mission while we were away."

"Do the Archimandrites know of your presence?"

"We do not reveal ourselves to them, but a few of them have put the pieces together from time to time."

"Why did you travel north with us?"

"It was decided one of us should go. We thought that the meeting of the orders would be important, and it was, but not as important as what occurred in that hospital."

Seriah sighed once more.

They came to the entrance of the Templum and walked in. The sound of the large city square outside dulled to a murmur. Ahead Seriah heard a few sets of sandaled feet upon the bronze welcome plate—thousands of tiny bells underneath that jingled incessantly as people stepped on it. She and Koragh Neyarn stepped upon it when their turn came.

"Greetings in the name of our most holy virgin goddess, Nifara!" a voice said. Seriah thought she could make out the same ancient tone of voice she had come to recognize at quiet times with Neyarn around the campfire.

"Greetings, Belligar," Kerei Lant said.

"Ah, young Councilor Lant. Returned already? But where is Archimandrite Moran?"

Kerei sighed. "He has gone from us, as has Gregor Hans. If you'll allow us to enter, we are weary."

"Of course, of course."

He tapped his staff on the ground and the doors opened. Seriah was about to enter with the rest when Koragh took hold of her arm. "Please wait, Sister." Then the doors closed.

"Belligar," Koragh said.

"Brother Neyarn," Belligar Mand said. His voice sounded as though he was smiling.

"We need to hold meeting tonight."

"Very well. Who is this with you?"

"A harbinger of a new age."

"I am interested to know more. We shall meet in my study, then," Belligar said calmly.

"You may retire to your chambers," Koragh said to Seriah. "You will return here tonight, after dinner has concluded. Do you understand?"

"Yes, holy Nefer," Seriah said.

Seriah turned and walked inside as the door opened for her,

making her way through the outer chamber as the whispers of the faithful filled the place with a constant drone. Entering the corridor that led to her living space, she counted her steps and the doors she passed until she came to her own and touched the marker next to it, which bore her symbol meaning "Greeter." She had always wondered why she had been given this symbol and what it meant, but now she knew. She had greeted a new age; she had spoken to three gods and twice stood face-to-face with a man who had sought and failed to kill the Pantheon.

She took comfort in her small room, although her bed was cold to the touch, the sheets unused since she had left many months ago. On the side table were three items which she knew by touch, one being a single scale from her childhood pet ynfald, Olvier, and another being a braid of her own hair, cut when she took the cloth. The third was a small knife, the blade of which she had blunted long ago, although she still kept it. She'd held this knife in her hands the day she'd resolved to murder the men who had killed her parents. She tucked it into her sash, hidden from view. It was against the rules of her order, but it made her feel safe. Searn, at least, could not threaten her anymore, but she was a witness to the murder of Pell Maran and the battle that had ended with Searn's death. But a nudge at her heart told her that if two gods had spoken to her, and their enemy had tried to take her life, then she was in constant danger. A knife, even blunted, was better than nothing.

The bell tolled for dinner, and she took up the braid and ynfald scale on a whim and put them into her satchel. Then she left her room and followed the procession of other monks toward the dining hall. She said little during the meal, as food was passed around, not feeling social. Her appetite was lacking as well, so she took some breads and put them into her satchel for later. As dinner concluded, she walked to the monastery's front door and stepped off the brass bell plate, next to Belligar Mand's station.

"Good evening, Sister," Mand said.

"Greetings, holy saint."

"Tsk. Keep your voice down. I don't need the attention."

"I'm sorry."

"It is well. Please go on in," he said. "I will be in shortly."

She felt along the wall and found a small door. She entered and could tell it was a small room. There were perhaps two others already sitting in chairs there.

"Who enters?" a male voice said.

"Seriah Yaledít."

"Yes," the voice said. "Koragh said you'd be along. I am Nefer Reddo."

"Reddo Dotti? The founder of Redot?" she asked. "My homeland."

"You are informed, then. Have a seat. I'm interested in knowing why such a young girl has been asked to join us in this meeting."

"I shall remain quiet until Koragh asks me to speak."

"Ha!" a deep female voice bellowed. "I've never heard of anyone being frightened of Koragh."

Seriah recognized the voice. It was Zelline, the librarian, and that meant she was actually Zellina Dosk, one of history's greatest lawyers. Seriah took a seat as her knees began to buckle.

"You're overwhelming the girl," a soft voice from further off said. The woman who spoke sounded demure, and no older than Seriah—like sweet Rystan Amiré, whom Searn had killed alongside Pell Maran.

Someone pressed a bottle of tea into her hand. "Now, young dear," the demure voice said, "it's overwhelming for anyone. I know I'm still a bit overwhelmed by the idea, and I've had a couple hundred years to get used to it."

"Then you must be Luphini Gollin?"

"Yes. Now drink your tea."

Koragh Neyarn entered, the sound of his familiar step welcome to her ears. Another entered behind him and took a seat next to the entrance.

"Belligar never actually leaves his post. He's greeted every single guest since the day the first brick was laid," Luphini of the sweet voice said, having taken a seat next to her.

"Nefer Yaledít is here?" Koragh asked.

"Yes, Brother," Luphini said.

"What is this all about, Koragh?" Reddo asked.

"We shall get to it. First, you're all aware of the death of Pell Maran?"

A couple of them murmured consent.

"I asked not to be told the full story," Belligar said from the door. "I wanted to hear it from you."

"Very well." Koragh proceeded to detail the attack that took the life of Gregor Hans and poisoned the Archimandrite Pell Maran, beginning with the meeting of the Paladins and Paladames and their journey to Mahn Fulhar, up to the sudden murder of Pell Maran. "This is where young Seriah's tale begins."

The room fell silent.

"I..." Seriah began. The woman next to her squeezed her arm encouragingly. "I was there when Pell Maran was killed by that dark figure."

"You heard it?"

"Yes, but I saw it as well. Let me explain. I was going to join the Archimandrite, to attend to him. When I got to the door I heard voices—Archimandrite Maran's voice, and a dark voice that filled me with dread. The dark one took Pell Maran's life, and, at that moment, I could see. Because Nifara arrived to take their lives, I could see her holy aura through my blinder and through the wall. Yet I could also see the shadow of the dark figure, untouched and unseen, by the goddess."

"Unseen?" the lawyer Saint Zellina Dosk asked.

"Yes," Koragh replied. "It seems the murderer, Searn VeTurres, had made a garment known as a boneshroud. It has since gone missing, but from what I've gathered, it was created and empowered by the blood of innocent people. It casts a shadowed cloud the gods cannot see into, and the shades of those it is made from can be sent to attack others."

"You are witness to this event, then, Nefer Yaledít. Is there any more to your story?" Saint Dotti asked.

"Yes," Koragh said. "She has more."

"Let us hear the rest from her without any interruption, then," Saint Dotti said.

"I felt drawn to those that were dying," Seriah said, "so I journeyed to the infirmary, to sit with a dying woman whose orphanage I helped take on. It was there I surmised who Saint Neyarn was. We both sat with the woman as she died, and Nifara came to take her away. I could not see her this time, but Koragh spoke with her and assuaged my fears for the souls of Nefers Maran and Amiré."

She paused.

"Then what?" Koragh goaded.

"Give her a moment," Luphini said.

"I spoke with the goddess, and delivered a message to her that I was instructed to give many days prior, by a figure I should have known was evil."

"What do you mean?" Saint Luphini encouraged her.

"The night after the Solstice Council, I was alone on a street and a coldness came over me. A figure sat beside me at the judgment tree, self-described as ugly. He dispelled the coldness by telling it to leave and then we spoke. He bade me to deliver a message to Nifara when I saw her, even if it was at my death. When I was before Nifara with Saint Neyarn, I felt compelled to speak the words."

"And what were those words?" Saint Dotti asked, although his voice sounded as though he knew what they would be.

"Saint Neyarn asked Nifara for permission for me to speak, and I heard her voice telling me to speak quickly. So I said the words, 'He said he wished you had not shunned him. And that things might have been different for everyone if you hadn't.'"

The room took a collective gasp, then, after a time, they all gave a long sigh.

"Nifara fled," Koragh said, "sobbing like a little girl."

Luphini, sitting next to Seriah, gave a sob herself.

"And so the end begins," Saint Dotti said. "I pray the scales are balanced well enough."

"What begins?" Seriah asked. She felt frantic as she said it. "I don't understand what has happened, and Koragh has been vague."

"Yes. I'm sure he has," Belligar said. "This is probably best explained by Zellina."

The woman across from Seriah grunted. "Very well. I will explain.

"Achanerüt appeared before the gods, first to Kashir, who is now called Kos-Yran. It was he who ushered Achanerüt to Lomïn, before the other ten. Achanerüt introduced himself, but he only hinted at his origin, and it took some doing to unveil that he had been created from the imagination of Sakharn, the wife of Wyv-Thüm. Achanerüt turned to each god and asked them to accept him into their number. He turned to Nifara first and begged her to acknowledge him, but she turned her face from him and dared not look at him from that day on."

"There was no anger in our world before that time," Koragh spoke up. "It is said the Deceiver seethed, and tersely asked each god, not caring what they said, but instead dwelling upon Nifara's shunning."

"And my words somehow fulfill some prophecy?" Seriah asked.

"Yes," Zellina answered. "When the Deceiver left, Crysania

spoke with Nifara, her daughter, and told her that when she heard the words of Achanerüt again, one era would come to an end and another would begin. Eras have come and gone since then, but this is the only one with a sure sign—one that would come from Nifara."

"What era has begun?" Seriah asked.

"An era that the gods have striven toward. The White Pantheon seeks a balance between good and evil, in which the Tenth will have to make a decision that will shake the foundations of the earth once more."

"And the Tenth is Nifara? She was born after Kos-Yran," Seriah said.

"Yes. Also, a tenth saint of Nifara has not yet come to make their decision," Belligar offered from the door.

"I think that will give us plenty to speak of," Saint Dotti said.

"I may go then?" Seriah asked, standing.

"Yes," Luphini said.

Seriah walked out of the room and leaned against the wall, hoping no one would see her eavesdropping.

"What should we do?" the lawyer Zellina asked.

"Do?" Saint Dotti replied. "Nothing. We pray. Koragh, visit the sick and dying as you always have done, and see if you are able to speak with our goddess when she comes. I shall see about speaking with the Chronicler in the Noccitan Monastery, though a message to Mahn Fulhar for that will be difficult."

"What of the girl?" Koragh asked.

"What do you mean?" the doorman, Belligar, asked.

"How will we keep her from speaking out, and telling others of this?"

"We can assign one of the acolytes to watch her," Saint Dotti said. "Perhaps she has a part to play in this still."

Seriah had heard enough. She quietly reached down, pulled off her sandals, and crept toward the front gate. It was evening, and the night was cold. She had friends in Temblin, and perhaps the war perpetually brewing there might hide her from these saints.

6

INTERLUDE

He traced the words in ink as they bloomed. It didn't matter what was said by the shade within. The final page of the book was filled with scrawling madness. He nodded to himself, and took up the razor, drawing it gently against the first page.

The parchment broke free, and he placed it down on the desk. Touching the quill to the bead of blood on his wrist, he touched that single page.

Have you done it? The words bloomed.

"I have," he spoke. "You are confined to a single page now. I'll bind you with the others when the time comes."

And my shadebook?

"Filled with mad scrawling. And ready for the fire."

And you are sure it will have no risk to me?

"It did not harm the shade of Nocturn."

The words hesitated for a time.

Very well. Bind me to the others.

A knock came to the door. He placed the parchment piece under a book.

"Come in."

The door opened and two Paladins walked in.

"Pater Zoumerik," the almoner, Stevan Filip, said with a salute. "It is nearly time."

"Have you both said your prayers, preparing your hearts and minds for our call to contrition?"

"Grissone guides me down paths of penitence," the other man said. He wore a brown burlap robe rather than the normal woolen habit. The chaffing could already be seen around his throat and wrists.

"Very good, Brother Marric. I anticipate you'll speak your mind to all who would hear, and not only to men."

Dane blanched at those words.

"Yes, Pater Minoris."

"Brother Marric. Do not forget that our mission is to bring all to true repentance. That sickness continues to run rampant is a sign that there is still unconfessed guilt."

"We must seek it out."

"No. I agree with your late Prima Pater and his successor, if only on that point. Like sin, a weed is easily pulled when it is visible, but you don't always get the root underneath. Let's not waste our time tearing weeds out but leaving the roots. Lowering yourself in humility to preach to those you consider beneath you will deepen your journey of contrition."

Dane bowed his head.

"We shall wait in the courtyard," Brother Filip said.

"I will be along shortly."

They both turned and left.

Zoumerik took out the parchment page once more.

They are further along the path, it would seem.

"Stevan is nearing harvest and Dane Marric will run into the arms of our brotherhood soon. His zeal need only be aimed in the right direction."

You do not fear he shall expose us?

"Oh, I mean to use him to expose us. He'll be a wildfire that shall spark a Motean rise to power. By his hand I'll be made equal to the foolish High Priest in Mahn Fulhar."

Even in life, I saw that spark of ambition in you. It isn't a spark anymore, is it, Dusk?

"Spark? No. It is a blazing sun."

PART 2

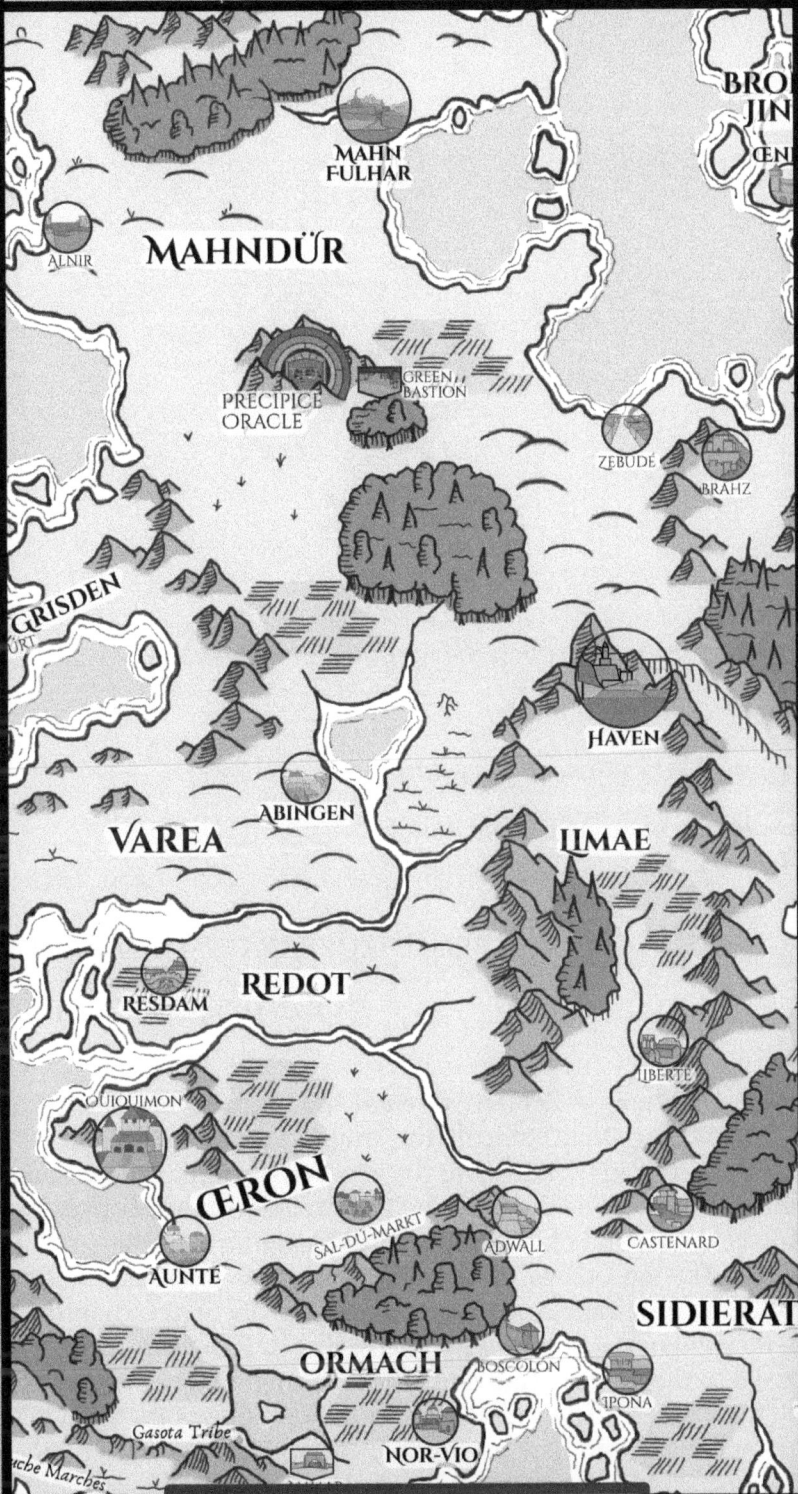

MAHNDÜR

BRO
JIN

CEN

MAHN
FULHAR

ALNIR

PRECIPICE
ORACLE

GREEN
BASTION

ZEBUDÉ

BRAHZ

GRISDEN

ÜRT

HAVEN

VAREA

ABINGEN

LIMAE

REDOT

RESDAM

LIBERTÉ

OUIQUIMON

ŒRON

CASTENARD

SAL-DÜ-MARKT

ADWALL

AUNTÉ

SIDIERAT

ORMACH

BOSCOLON

IPONA

Gasota Tribe

uche Marches

NOR-VIO

NORTHWESTERN
GANTHIC

7

ZEBÜDÉ

Every flower, a verse upon the tongue of the world.

Every petal fallen, a prayer.

Every seed, a promise to the future.

Every leaf, a testament of past bared.

—FROM *PROVERBS OF THE GARDEN,*

CRYSALAS SACRED TEXT

The buildings of Zebüdé were tall and narrow, made of the stark gray stone cut from the ground they sat upon. The walls looked menacing to the two new arrivals, the buildings looming over them as they entered the streets with hoods over their faces, the wind off the Lupinfang screaming over the rooftops. The few others walking the streets also wore their hoods up, and hurried past them without notice. As daylight began to dim, they entered a deserted plaza edged with filthy snowdrift. Exposed to the violent wind here, they cowered in a corner to catch their breath. The whistling coming from one of the women's cloaks subsided, and they proceeded, navigating the rest of their way through the city to the small side door of a warehouse. One of the figures knocked; the other rocked back and forth, trying to stay warm.

Even over the wind they could hear the lowing sound of cattle within.

The door opened, revealing a round-faced woman with her long blonde hair braided up on the top of her head. She had a heavy scarf tied around her neck.

"Greetings, dear ladies," the woman said. "I'm afraid all the cream is gone for the day."

"We're not here for cream."

"I am not expecting any other visitors."

"What about Sisters of the Crysalas seeking emergency asylum?"

"I'm afraid I do not know what you speak of," the woman replied.

"It is very cold out here," one of them said as she dropped the hood, revealing a face almost as round as the woman's at the door, framed by short black hair. "If you would please allow the niece of our late Matriarch Superioris to warm herself by a fire, we would both be eternally grateful."

"Oh dear! Of course. Come in, I recognize you. Yes!"

She stepped back so they could enter. The wooden floor hid from view the dairy aurochs kept on the lower level, though it did not mask the smell of the creatures, nor block the warmth of their bodies.

"Sister Borreau, is it?" their hostess asked as she walked them across the room to a side door.

"Yes, Katiam Borreau. My companion is Astrid Glass."

In response the other dropped back her hood to reveal blonde hair cropped close to her skull. She reached into her satchel and pulled out a steel ringlet of metal-crafted leaves, and placed it on her head.

"Sister Borreau's companion and guard," Astrid said.

"We've a fire in my home," the woman said. "You can warm your hands while we make arrangements in the vault for your stay."

"Thank you," Katiam said, smiling. "That would be nice. I'm sorry that we did not know the secret passwords for the city. We've only just arrived."

"In the midst of this storm, too," their hostess said, clicking her tongue. "We'll have you warm soon enough."

The hostess nodded to herself and pushed through a door to the blazing warmth of a hearth. Katiam sighed and took a seat. Astrid walked the room, as she often did, examining their surroundings.

"Please make yourself comfortable. I'd offer you food, but I haven't any. There is a communal feast in the vault tonight, though."

Astrid was sniffing at the cauldron boiling away on the hearth.

"Laundry, I'm afraid," the hostess said.

Astrid turned back, nodding to herself.

"If you'll excuse me, I'll see about a room in the vault."

"May we know your name?" Katiam asked. "Perhaps where you recognize me from?"

"Yadvi Sahne. I visited the Rose Convent in Mahn Fulhar during the Solstice ceremony," she said and left the room.

"Make yourself comfortable," Katiam said to Astrid, who was checking the bolts on the window.

"You know I can't sit still until I've gone through my routine," Astrid said.

Katiam scooted her stool closer to the warmth of the fire and pulled the bundle from her cloak. A leaf stuck out of the cloth, and she clicked her tongue as she began to unwrap the contents. The leaves and vines within were tightly bound together and the flower had receded protectively back into a bud. In the heat of the hearth the first leaf began to unfurl, and then the next, until all five came free. The lowest leaf was now the smallest, withering as it diminished, and a new leaf bud was toying free near the stalk below the flower bud, which began to quiver and open up.

"Good," Katiam said. "Get some heat, Little Rose. Be warm."

She touched the petals softly.

The two little thorns on the stalk began to sigh rapidly, then slowed to a whispering breath.

"Veeewahmmm," the thorns whistled.

"Yes," Katiam murmured. "Be warm."

"It is uncanny to me," Astrid said over Katiam's shoulder. "After two weeks, it still astonishes me when a plant tries to say words. How is this possible?"

"Crysania had a purpose for the Rotha. That it can speak is astonishing, but I guess I'm not surprised."

The vines and leaves had relaxed into a lounging posture in the heat.

"We're not to be here long," Katiam said, "so I'll need to bundle you up again, but at least you're warm now."

"If they keep aurochs," Astrid said, "I imagine we can get some good warm manure for it to settle in. My mother kept several herbs alive over winter that way."

"That's a good idea. We can ask them to provide that for us if we must leave soon, but let's find out if there is any word from the others. We can determine if it's worth catching up with them, or if we should wait until closer to spring."

"This is a stark and ugly city to settle in for the winter," Astrid muttered.

"But safer than the road and mountains in mid-winter."

The door opened, and Katiam, her back turned to the door, gently pulled the wrap around the Rotha and turned to smile at their hostess.

"If you'd both like to join me," Yadvi said, "the vault is ready."

"How protected is this vault from the prying eyes of the city?" Astrid asked.

"Our city cares little about the vault. There is enough change to keep people distracted, with sailors coming and going. And, across a vast distance, we bear strong ties to the Shieldmaidens of Bronue Jinre, stronger ties than Mahn Fulhar has."

"Yet it appears that you are still cautious."

"It is our responsibility to be cautious, no matter what. With deep winter comes the long-term mooring of ships in the harbor, bringing many sailors who sometimes get restless. Some go looking for trouble, although we've never experienced an actual threat to our vault. It's not unheard of in more western ports, so we've chosen to err on the side of caution ourselves."

She took them down a flight of stone stairs onto the milking floor. Several women attended the large aurochs in their stalls, feeding, cleaning, and caring for the animals. They passed through the door on the other end and took another flight of stairs down into the cool earth.

"I've noticed that while the tops of buildings are high, the upper stories do not look lived in," Katiam said.

"Ours is a city that carved itself deeply rather than rising. The entire city is carved from the hard marble it sits upon," Yadvi said. "It was one of the Crysalas Vaults that discovered it, in fact. A few hundred years ago Zebüdé was nothing but a ramshackle port built on mud flats, but the makers of the vault dug deep in order to remain hidden from the town, and discovered flat and untouched marble bedrock. They secretly carved their way down into it, and sold the excess off. Women associated with the vault convinced their husbands to dig theirs, and soon nearly every other son became a stonemason. In a few generations, the city became a place of tall, thin marble houses of stone, with deep, cold cellars. Money and prestige followed, and while our desolate location and climate make winters difficult, Zebüdé prospers."

She pushed her way into the vault's interior, revealing a small number of women sitting at various tables. An elderly woman rose from her seat and came to greet them.

"You must be Sister Borreau," the woman said, holding out her arms. "I am Sister Superioris Geldin."

"Thank you for your hospitality," Katiam said, leaning in to return the embrace.

"And Sister Glass," Geldin said, as she offered a warm embrace to Katiam's quiet companion. "I heard you are now the sole occupant of our beloved Oracle."

"Now my duty sees me following those that journeyed before us."

"The rumor was that you were lost," Geldin said to Katiam.

"I was," Katiam said. "But now we seek those who journeyed homeward."

"Come with me and we can speak privately."

"I left my armor in a pack at an inn at the edge of town," Astrid said.

"We can have it retrieved," the Sister Superioris said.

"We're in no hurry. We can get it when we leave town."

"You expect to leave soon?"

"That is something we must also speak with you about."

"Very well. Come, take refreshments, and we can speak."

The Sister Superioris had hearth-warmed blankets placed over their laps as they sat in her office. The books lining the shelves in that room would have caused envy in the most well-read members of the Crysalas. Geldin herself prepared a tray of flavored biscuits that met Katiam's diet of the Aspect of St. Klare, and placed it on a small table between the two of them.

"We have rooms for the two of you to repose in after we share our meal together," she said as she took her seat. "But first I wish to learn what brought you here, away from the Oracle."

"As you said, Sister Superioris—" Katiam started.

"Please," Geldin interrupted, "while you are my guests, you may call me Avine."

Katiam smiled. "Very well, Avine. As you mentioned, I was thought lost. Indeed, I was gone for several days. The World Rose whisked me away on a journey that brought me to the root of the Dweol."

The older lady raised her hand to her mouth.

"The root is dying. Others were brought to the root, like me, and they confirmed the Dweol is truly dying all over the world. I was returned to Kallattai by Maeda Mür herself."

"Then Maeda Mür lives?"

"No. She was in Lomïn, in our goddess's garden."

"And yet you have returned."

"My purpose is not completed."

"What is that purpose?"

"We cannot say," Astrid said, "but we can ask you to trust us nonetheless. It is within my sacred duty to act as guardian of the World Rose on this secret mission."

"Then you mean to restore the Dweol," Avine said, "and you have been instructed by someone how to do so."

"That is very insightful," Astrid said. Katiam saw her brow arch in suspicion.

"You can tell by my collection of books that I am a scholar. I became a member of the Crysalas after my brother's wife, Fedelmina Barba, was changed for the better by it."

"We met your sister and traveled with her for a time in Bortali."

"So your company told me when you last passed through here," Avine said. "I've received letters from her with news since then. But we'll get to that."

She rose and walked over to one of the shelves.

"I have made an effort to procure several important books pertaining to our Order. As a young woman, I was skeptical of the gods and their interactions with us. My research took me far and wide, from Hrelgren archives to the vast libraries of the qavylli."

She took a book bound in a blush-pink cloth and brought it over to them.

"This is a book I wrote that summarizes my career so far, in which I examine and come to several hypotheses about the nature of the World Rose. I've sent one of my copies with the company that went before you, the company fleeing with the Paladins from Mahn Fulhar. I think perhaps this copy ought to go with you."

"And what shall we find in it?" Katiam said, receiving it from Avine gracefully.

"It does not tell the story of our order, exclusively. We are only one petal of the entire Rose, I believe. Our history, and the history of those who came before us, is part of a larger purpose. The actions of which have a meaning behind them that we will only understand later."

"I will cherish this gift," Katiam said.

"Have you ever watched a rosebush grow?" Avine asked. "As the plant matures, it surpasses what has already grown, and evidences of future growth are there. Surely injuries may change it, and it may grow to the left instead or to the right, but it still grows. All things continue. A flower dies so that it may bear fruit. Dead rose blooms are removed so that more will come. So too, I believe the Future Tapestry is merely the observation of the lowering tendrils of time, observed as it is passing and guessed at for the future. The goddess, in her infinite wisdom, reads it better than any. Even without the Worldrose, I believe that the flowering of the future can still be read in the things that occur."

She looked Katiam squarely in the eyes. "That is what the book you hold contains. My theories on the reading of the past to predict what is coming. All that comes to pass was intended, and will come to be."

"You mean to say," Astrid said, "that there is no hope save for what will be? That nothing will prevent either glory or destruction from happening if such things are willed?"

"That is not what I am saying," she said, turning to Astrid. "I am saying all things work to the will of He that is greater than the gods. The will of the Existence is in all of it. We simply watch and observe it as it unfolds."

"If it is to be, no matter the journey, what hope do we have?" Astrid replied.

"There is always hope," Avine said, offering a comforting smile. "An injury to a stem may cause it to grow in ways unexpected, but not in purposelessness. Thus, do we not have the duty to ensure that injuries to the bloom do not happen? Yet, if they do, then we coax forth a thorn to mark the occasion. The rose smells sweet, and blooms even in the desert, but it is no rose if it hasn't thorns. For this reason it is the queen of all flowers. For even in its indignity it is beautiful."

"Well said," Katiam replied. "Now, what of the company that

came before us?"

Avine's smile faded. "Speaking of thorns forming where there are wounds...."

Both women looked at each other, then back to Avine.

"The sisters from the Oracle came bearing news of what happened at the Dweol. A Paladin came not long after that, riding hard with news of their own order being ousted from the country. Then, only two weeks ago, Prima Pater Guess arrived."

"Nichal Guess is Prima Pater now?" Astrid asked.

"Acting Prima Pater, as I understand it. He offered to take any who would journey with him east to Pariantür. He and his second-hand man, a champion of Grissone, say they persevered against some dark figure bent on destroying their order, but lost against the political might of the Church of Aben, and the King of Mahndür. The holdings of Pariantür have been seized."

"Then Mahndür is no longer a friend of the Hammer," Katiam said.

"Likely not to the Rose, either," Astrid offered. "The arguments the High Priest gave in defense of the Chalicians spoke volumes at the Solstice Ceremony."

"Prima Pater Guess said as much," the Sister Superioris said.

"You'll remain here? To continue the work?"

"Of course," Avine said. "What else would I do? There are other vaults worse off than ours."

"When did the Paladins leave, and how many went with them?"

"They left two weeks ago," she replied. "Any who came from the Oracle joined them."

"And how did they travel?"

"Against our advice, they insisted on taking the coastal road to Brahz."

"How bad is that road?"

"Oddly enough, they have had two weeks of calm weather. Only yesterday did the winds return. I suspect their god protected them,"

"Grissone's Champion, was he a big man?"

"A head taller than most of the other Paladins, and broad. A Boronii man."

"Two beads upon white cordons across his chest?" Astrid asked.

"Three. On black cordons."

"Then Grissone did deliver them," Katiam said. "But it is not a path you'd advise us to take."

"Not if you plan to live through winter."

"What of the southern passes?"

"There is no safe pass," Avine said. "Not until the spring thaws. By then, I suppose we could find a guide to take you to Brahz, if that is your intent."

"Very well," Katiam said. "May we stay here with you until spring? I'm sure there is much we could learn from your library."

"You are more than welcome, of course. We'll make good use of both of you. Is there anything you require for your rooms?"

"I'd like to retrieve our packs," Astrid said, "if we're to stay that long."

"And I will need some rose water daily," Katiam added, "and some sacks of dirt mixed with some of your auroch manure in my room."

"An odd request," Avine said. "I don't doubt you have your reasons."

Katiam smiled. "Thank you, Sister Superioris. Your hospitality is most welcome."

8

VOLDÉ

Service without care is meaningless.

It is a gnat in your drinking water and a husk in your bread.

— CRYSALAS PROVERB

Women came and left the vault on a daily basis. It was not as extensive as some of the larger vaults the Matriarch had visited on her journey west, but it was well supplied, and the five or so permanent sisters in residence were never overtaxed. Although Katiam's expertise lay in caring for the elderly, she was more than capable of treating wounds, bruises, and infections. She often knew better than to pry into the personal affairs of those seeking help. They would speak when they felt comfortable—and the sisters who had escaped such lives themselves knew the best way to draw the truth out.

One evening, Astrid distractedly looked over Katiam's shoulder toward the entrance of the vault as they picked at the last bites on their plates. Katiam turned to see what had drawn her attention. A few new women had arrived for the evening meal. Most quickly rushed to embrace or clasp arms with old friends. But one woman in particular had drawn Astrid's gaze. She was thin, with angular cheekbones, and bore the long, straight auburn hair of an Ikhalan. She appeared twice Katiam's age, but Katiam felt she had merely seen much in her life. She couldn't have been more than thirty.

The woman kept to herself, with an arm across her middle, holding her other elbow. At first glance, Katiam thought her shy, but she observed the room and all its people with piercing eyes that probably understood much more than she let on. When she did finally move through the room, she reminded Katiam of a kicked ynfald, or a wild tosker, taking swipes at the table for bites of food as she passed. To any city guardsman, she'd have been eyed with suspicion and watched for signs of thievery. But Katiam knew she was probably just hungry, scared, and likely only dangerous when threatened.

Katiam wished Avine was nearby so she could ask about the woman. Meanwhile, Astrid walked across the room to the food-laden table and took up a handful of nuts, leaning up against the wall by her.

"Have you had these?" Astrid offered out her hand.

"No," the woman replied, shying away half a step. "I don't care for them."

"Oh?"

"They remind me too much of home."

"And where is that?"

The woman took several dense trenchers from the table, stuffed the bread into a short-strapped satchel, and left the vault without another word.

"What did I say?" Astrid muttered to herself.

Avine approached from across the room.

"I see you've met Voldé."

"Is that her name?" Astrid asked.

"No. It's what we call her, an Üterk word for a female vül."

"I can see how she got the nickname. What is her story?"

"No one is really sure. As far as we can tell, she came to Zebüdé on a ship from the east. Possibly as a crew member, or of a less savory role. No one knows her real name, so we all just refer to her as Voldé."

"She has a name, though," Astrid said.

"Not one she's told any of us. I'm not even sure who began calling her Voldé."

Voldé appeared at nearly every meal, at random times. As soon as Astrid spotted her she would try to make her way over, only to find that Voldé had grabbed her food and left. Other times, Voldé arrived when Astrid was already seated with others and unable to free herself from a conversation.

One evening Voldé made her appearance too late. The food had already been cleared and was already in the process of being secreted across the city to a poorkitchen. Voldé looked on edge and visibly disappointed. Katiam watched from afar as an unarmored Astrid appeared next to her. Voldé practically jumped five feet in fear toward the wall, flashing her teeth menacingly. Astrid calmly lifted a kerchief-wrapped bundle to the woman, which Voldé considered for a moment then took the package and left.

Astrid turned and scanned the room. As her eyes met Katiam's, she smiled.

The following evening, Astrid sat across from Katiam at the dining table. She reached out to take up her napkin and gasped.

"What is it?" Katiam asked.

Astrid held up a white kerchief.

"I wrapped the food I gave Voldé in this."

"So she must have returned it."

"It had a berry tart in it, yet there is not a spot of red on it. She cleaned it better than the washers the vault employs."

"Perhaps that is her trade," Katiam replied.

"Maybe," Astrid agreed.

Sightings of Voldé became fewer and farther between after this. Katiam suspected the woman had merely become better at avoiding them at mealtimes. Nearly every day trinkets were left behind for Astrid, from bent coins to pieces of ribbon. It reminded Katiam of a story of a girl near Pariantür who had trained a small black gryph to bring her gifts in exchange for food and a safe windowsill to sleep on. The girl began receiving gold coins stolen by the bird from a counting house that had not treated it kindly.

She dismissed the thought that Voldé might be a pickpocket, preferring to think of her as an opportunistic washerwoman.

One evening, Astrid was bandaging a burned arm when Voldé entered the vault. She only came in a few steps and leaned against the wall, her eyes falling on Astrid before glancing away. Katiam approached her friend and offered to take over for her. Astrid smiled in thanks and crossed the room to a small table where she took up a parcel and brought it to Voldé. They did not look at each other, but exchanged words, after which Astrid held out the parcel. After a moment of cautious consideration, Voldé took it and left without another word.

Astrid crossed back to Katiam, a broad smile across her face.

"What did you give her?"

"A small box to collect her keepsakes."

"Did she tell you where she gets them?"

"She finds them in the gutter, or trades for them. I think she's a rag-and-bone woman."

"A sorry existence," Katiam said.

"She is doing what she must," Astrid said. "I got her to brag a bit. She told me that last week she found a half-gold and with it bought a cart. I suspect she is hoping to trade up and become a tinker."

"That can be just as hard a job," Katiam replied.

"But it offers the freedom I suspect she craves."

The next evening Voldé sat across from Astrid at the meal. Astrid looked up in surprise, the food in her hand almost dropping onto the plate in front of her. The woman was in a good mood and filled up her trencher of bread with any food she could reach.

"You are in good spirits," Astrid finally said, filling a tankard with cut-mead from a bottle and passing it to the woman.

"Today was a good day," Voldé replied.

"In what way?"

"The sun was out," Voldé replied. "I followed the carriage of a rich woman, and as I suspected, she tossed from her window a used silken handkerchief. I used it in a trade later."

"Oh?"

"I've the wood I need to repair the wheel of my broken cart."

"Congratulations!" Astrid said. "You are almost there."

"Now I need only find the tools for tinker repairs."

"My family are glaziers," Astrid said, "far off at Pariantür. I know how important a set of tools can be."

"Not many artisans are willing to part with them," Voldé said. "Especially not to a woman."

"What would you give someone who had a set of tools to trade?"

"The favor of the Riverfolk would ever bless their path."

"There are not many that can make that claim. Even a local Üterk tribe would not have the audacity to bandy a blessing such as that."

Voldé blushed, rose, and took up the trencher of food before exiting the vault.

"What scared her off?" Katiam asked.

"She is not a local Üterk. She's a true-blooded Riverfolk of the Yutrak River."

"What do you mean?"

"I've suspected she was related to the people of the wood, but she bears a slight Ikhalan accent. My father traded with a few Riverfolk that had come to live on Lago Crysan. If she was only a local Üterk, she'd have dug herself deeper into her bluff. But if she is Riverfolk of the original Yterk people, close cousins to the Üterk from the Yutrak River in Ikhala, then her promised blessing is legitimate."

"You mean to find those tools, don't you?" Katiam asked.

"I do."

"Why bargain? Why not give it with no debt?"

"She would not take it. 'Nothing is free unless found,' her people say."

Katiam lit the fire in the small room she and Astrid had been provided with. The Rotha lay on her bed, the dirt brushed free by Katiam and awaiting the heat of the small hearth to make the pot of soil next to it warm. The Rotha moved lethargically, uncomfortably, its four vines feeling around, and tiny barbs along the underside of its leaves plucking at the blankets. Katiam had examined the barbs with a magnifying glass, finding them to be more like small soft hooks with which to grasp things. Although the Rotha had taken hold of her plenty of times, it never hurt her.

The door opened and Astrid walked in.

"It was easier than I thought," Astrid said, putting a canvas roll down on her bed.

"What is that?" Katiam continued to stoke the fire.

"The tools. The vault has an old, dilapidated leather shop that no one is using. Avine told me I could take what I needed from it. I managed to find the right tools and rolled them together. When Voldé arrives tonight, I'll present them to her."

Astrid was barely able to eat that evening, nearly jumping to her feet every time the door opened and another person entered. Voldé arrived late to the meal. Katiam placed a hand on Astrid's arm to calm her, and suggested she wait while Voldé settled into the meal. After ten long minutes, Astrid could stand it no longer and circled the room as Voldé rose and moved toward the table, where satchels of nuts had been prepared for those leaving.

"I have something for you," Astrid said.

The woman turned and considered her.

"I've gotten all I needed," Voldé responded.

Astrid held out the roll.

"What is this?"

"You said you needed tools. I found some."

"I don't need help," Voldé countered.

"Then you can give me what you feel they are worth."

"What do you want for them?" Voldé asked.

"You mentioned a Riverfolk Blessing, but I've something else in mind."

"What?"

"Your name."

The woman cringed and took a step back.

Astrid smiled. "If that is asking too much, then perhaps you can offer me something else."

"I will tell you where I am from, but I will not give you power over me by telling you my name."

"That is an acceptable payment," Astrid said, smiling. "Where are you from?"

"Nevenhal."

"Ikhalan, then?"

"My father is said to have been. I'm Riverfolk."

"Why so far from the Yutrak?"

"I had little choice. You know the Yutrak?"

"I had the honor of taking a Riverfolk barge up the river as an escort to a sister being sent to a vault in St. Nevenhal."

"I pity them and the squalor they live in now."

"I thought much the same when I visited. I would not call it squalor so much as impermanence."

"Mud and wood. Filth and lack of care."

"What do you think of this town?"

"Zebüdé? It is a stark town of angles, stone, and suspicion."

"Is there a place where you do find beauty?"

Voldé eyed Astrid, then looked away.

"I mean no offense," said Astrid. "I'm merely making small talk."

"The only time I have known beauty is in the solitude of my mind. It was there I dreamed of a pasture."

Katiam let out a little gasp.

Voldé shot a glance her way.

"You are new to town," the woman replied, turning back to Astrid.

"I'm only here for the winter," Astrid replied, "yes."

"Zebüdé is a city of people running or hiding from their past.

You'd do wise to remember that."

"I'm not sure I understand the warning," Astrid said. "What you describe is exactly the purpose the vaults serve in every city."

"Your friend is staring at me. She ought not to."

Katiam looked away, blushing furiously. She heard Voldé begin walking toward the door.

"Please wait," Astrid said.

The woman did not stop.

"Voldé!" Astrid called.

The room went silent. Voldé stopped and turned slowly, her face red with fury and darkening to the blackest stare Katiam had ever seen. Astrid froze in place. Then the other woman turned and left.

After several long and awkward minutes, Astrid turned around, her eyes going from Katiam to Avine. "What did I say?"

"I have made a grave error," Avine said.

"In what way?"

"I told you that woman was known as Voldé, but I forgot to mention that none of us has ever called her such to her face. But then, none of us has ever been able to break through and enter a conversation with her before."

"Then I've just insulted her," Astrid said, sitting down on a nearby bench and burying her head in her hands. She did not sob. Katiam doubted she had any more tears left in her after her brother died the year before, but she sighed deeply. Katiam placed a hand on Astrid's shoulder. Her friend looked up, her eyes red and hot. She gave a forced smile.

"Thank you for being here with me, Katiam, but I need to be alone now,"

Katiam returned to the room she and Astrid shared and moved through the nightly ritual she had settled into, refreshing the Rotha's dirt with new mossy loam and a little manure. As Katiam placed the Rotha into the loose soil, it moved like a child in a tub of water, tossing brown debris around playfully.

Astrid entered, changing out of her armor and into a brown robe and cloak.

"What are you doing?" Katiam asked.

"I'm going out to look for Voldé."

"What is the weather like?"

"It doesn't matter," Astrid said. "I've offended her and I have to make amends, or else she may never return to the safety of the vault.

"And if you don't find her?"

"Then I shall continue to search."

As Astrid walked to the door, Katiam leapt up and placed a hand on the doorknob.

"Why are you doing this?" Katiam asked.

"Why are you stopping me?"

"I'm not," Katiam said, taking her hand from the knob. "But I want to hear you say why."

"I've questioned the purpose of the vaults on the road from Precipice to here. If they were never the first purpose of the Crysalas Church, then why continue with them?"

Katiam opened her mouth to speak, but Astrid continued.

"Being here in this vault reminded me that they have become places of protection and community. It is no bad thing that has been established. It is not against the Life Mother's will. They exist because they must. They still fulfill a purpose, just as the Aspects of Purity do. Some aspects exist to better oneself. Others exist for the sake of Purity. Most are there to be an example and to provide Purity for others. My true purpose is the safety of the Rotha. But that does not mean we are to abandon the Aspects we have picked up along the way. These vaults are an Aspect of our church, and shall continue to be. I'll not allow my mistakes to drive that woman away from the only place of safety she may know. I shall make amends, and if she will not have it, then I will have done all that I can."

Katiam threw her arms around her friend. "Be careful, Astrid. I'll see to it that the Sisters are praying for your success."

Astrid gave a weak smile, followed by a deep breath, and left the room.

Katiam returned to the little pot of dirt and the Rotha sitting there, contented and still.

"Let us pray Astrid remains safe," she muttered.

"Praastriiiihd," the Rotha whistled.

"Yes," Katiam said, smiling. "Pray for Astrid."

Technically the Rotha never slept, although, after a time, it became bored and fell still. Katiam tried to bide time leafing through her copy of Esenath Chloïs's *Book of Flowers*. Then she took out a needle and thread and occupied herself with mending a tear in her travel cloak. After several hours she left the room. It was late in the evening and the only other person in the vault was an old lady asleep before the hearth. Katiam fed the fire quietly and sat down in another chair across the hearth from the sleeping woman. In what seemed like mere moments she woke with a start as the door to the vault burst open and two snow-covered women fell through. One supporting the other, and they stumbled across the room together, dropping in a heap before the fire.

The old woman leapt up from her chair and began building up the fire for them.

"Astrid?" Katiam cried out, dropping to the ground next to them. One of the snow-encrusted figures rose from the ground.

"You found her?" Katiam said, and began taking the wraps and gloves off the fallen form. "She was sleeping on the street in a snowstorm?"

The standing woman took her wrap from her head and face. It was not Astrid. It was the Riverfolk woman.

Katiam removed the scarf from the other woman's face, revealing the still and blue-lipped Astrid.

"Strike the bell," Katiam ordered. The old woman rose and walked across the room to ring the alarm.

"I want the fire blazing. If it gets too hot, we'll move to block the heat, but this room needs to be warm and we need to thaw her out without moving her. How long has she been like this?"

"She fell at the entrance to my alley," Voldé said. "In the storm, the inns would not take us in, or could not hear me as I beat upon their doors. It took us an hour or two to get here."

"That is far too long," Katiam said.

"What kind of fool is she, walking the streets in this blizzard?"

"The kind of fool who sought to make amends with you and ensure you weren't doing something equally as stupid."

"But why?"

"Because none of us should be alone, and none should pass along with their name unknown."

"I have a name," the woman said, "but no one deserves to know it."

"This vault," Katiam said, "has given you food and warmth while asking nothing in return. Doesn't it deserve to know your name?"

"No one has ever asked."

"Because when someone does, you flec. When my friend uses the only name she knows for you, you turn your back on her without seeking to understand why anyone would call you such?"

"The name Voldé is what my husband called me when he sought to drag me down. I fled from him and came here."

"Did Astrid mistreat you?"

"Her name is Astrid?"

"You didn't know?" Katiam asked.

"I never asked..." she replied, blushing.

Women rushed into the room, gathering blankets as Katiam instructed them. Soon the room was warm enough for them to strip the wet clothes from both and cover them with blankets. Warmth returned to Astrid's fingers, and the darkening skin returned to its normal luster.

When morning came, the kitchen brought out hot gruel for those who had stayed up with the women before the fire.

Katiam sat in a chair nearby and had nearly dozed off when Astrid croaked from the ground.

"Food," she said. "Tea."

Katiam dropped down to her friend, a laughing sob escaping her.

"Astrid!" she cried.

"Where am I?" Astrid asked.

"The vault. She brought you back here!"

"Who did?"

"I did," Voldé said from near the hearth.

Astrid's eyes widened. "You?"

"You fell at the entrance of my alley."

"I had lost hope that I would find you. I stumbled to that alley to find a place out of the snow."

"And in doing so, you found me. I brought you here, in out of the cold."

"My fingers and feet hurt," Astrid said.

"We'll have to watch them carefully, to ensure you don't lose any of them to frostbite," Katiam said.

"May I have a moment with her?" the Riverfolk woman asked Katiam.

Katiam nodded, rose, and crossed the room to make a bowl of porridge for Astrid.

When she returned, Voldé was gone and Astrid had a smile on her face.

"Let's get you sitting up," Katiam said.

She helped Astrid to a sitting position and, with the aid of others nearby, moved her to the wall near the hearth, out of its blazing light. Astrid took the bowl from Katiam, the smile never leaving her face.

"That's one of the few genuine smiles I've seen on your face in a long time," Katiam said. "What is it for?"

"She told me her name," Astrid said.

"Oh?"

"Volanya."

9

COASTAL ROAD

The gray rocks rose alongside

The path that cut through stone.

A danger stalked and promised

To grind him down to bone.

No hope upon soul shone.

—*THE TRAVELER*

Sister Superioris Avine Geldin personally walked Katiam to the city gates. The rain fell heavily upon them in the spring storm coming in off the Lupinfang. Despite the cold dampness that covered the gray marble town, everyone moved about in a buzz.

"I'm sorry to see you go," Avine said. "Your company has been a pleasure these past five weeks. I certainly do not desire your discomfort. The early spring is going to bring misery along the coastal road."

"We must continue our journey," Katiam said. "While I would love to have stayed longer and learned more, our road has only just begun."

"I understand," Avine said.

A group of sailors were being urged out of an inn by the captain of their vessel, all walking in a single meandering line toward the docks. A few women leaned suggestively out of the windows above waving with false smiles at the sailors passing by.

"Port towns are all the same," the Sister Superioris sighed.

"I was..."

"You were wondering what we've done to help, and you know as well as I that we can only do what we are asked. Three of those women I know personally. Two of them come to the vault to have their injuries and sicknesses tended to. The third comes to confess her sins. I think one day I'll convince her to stay, if she doesn't die young."

"You say that so flippantly," Katiam said.

"It is the only way I know to cope with the sadness that gnaws at me. Of the thirty or so bawdy inns, it is that one woman that gives me the most hope, and the most sadness."

"That is the most hope you have, for merely one of these women to join our cause?"

"Perhaps that one soul will make all the difference. Until then the vaults will remain, and we will take in the children they bear and continue to hope. The Dweol is gone for now, but our mission still remains."

They turned a corner to see the gate far off ahead. A single figure leaned on the wall, watching their approach.

Avine slowed her pace and said, softly, "I have not wished to speak of this until you were leaving..."

"Speak of what?" Katiam asked.

"When the company of sisters came through, there was one among your number, Esenath Chloïs, and she was outspoken about the loss of something of great importance—a seed pod that had miraculously bloomed. When you asked for a pot of soil on the day you arrived, you confirmed to me that perhaps this seed pod was not truly lost."

Katiam pulled to a stop and looked at Avine.

"At this time, it is an important secret to keep," she replied.

"Then it is what the goddess charged you with safekeeping."

Katiam nodded.

Avine did not look surprised. "My suspicions are confirmed, then."

She pulled out a small box. "I have not had time to bind this, but these are copied notes I have made on the subject. Disparate lines from ancient texts pointing to a lost people who once followed our goddess Crysania. I think these notes will help you on your journey."

"Thank you," Katiam said, taking the ribbon-bound box and putting it under her cloak.

"I believe I understand the importance of your mission," Avine continued gently, "and that agents of the Deceiver, both inadvertent and intentional, will try to stop it. Esenath called the seed pod a Rotha. What name did you learn when you were taken to the Dweol?"

"There was a female T'Akah there, and she called it an Iwarat. Crysania called it..."

"A Warotha," Avine interrupted.

"Yes," Katiam said.

"And you go east."

"We were commanded to find one another out, those of us summoned to the Dweol after its disaster. So I'll do that."

"In the box you'll find I changed some of the language. I never refer to it as a Warotha, but as the Sacred Child; just in case the notes should fall into the wrong hands, I do not wish for the Rotha to be known. You will understand what I mean by what is inferred. If you say the T'Akai call it an Iwarat, then that will also confirm the tale you'll find of a Dweol bloom, in some unknown land, which is worshiped by any who seek it. There must be something lost in the translation, but in the ancient texts, this bloom is called Diwarith, which is similar in sound and meaning to Iwarat."

"I will be on the lookout for any signs of that name."

"Crysania guide and protect you," Avine said. She pulled Katiam into a gentle embrace as they neared the gate. Astrid was speaking with a cloaked woman, who placed something in her hand and left just as Katiam and Avine approached. Astrid stepped, then vanished into a nearby courtyard and emerged guiding a pack-sleipnir.

"Once you arrive at the coastal road," Avine said, "stop at every inn you pass and they will give news of the road ahead, as portions of the road are often washed away in the rains of spring. We shall pray the road is safe, as there are few options but to stop and wait if it is lost."

"Thank you for your hospitality," Astrid said.

"And your companionship," Avine replied.

Astrid turned to walk out the gate. Katiam followed close behind and they began their long trek toward a range of mountains obscured by the misty rain that swirled around them.

"Who was the cloaked woman who spoke to you?" Katiam asked.

"Volanya. She gave me a token of the Riverfolk."

"Oh?"

"She thought it might come in handy as we journey east, although she wanted me never to show it to an Üterk. Only the people of the Yutrak River. What did Avine say to you?"

"She shared some knowledge of the Rotha with me."

"Oh? She knew, then?"

"Yes. More than we realize."

The weather didn't relent during the three days it took to reach the foothills, above which they could sense the looming mountains, even if they could not see them. The first inn they came to was as damp and quiet as the weather outside. The barkeep provided little conversation, and gave no indication that the road ahead had any difficulty. Katiam got a fire going in their room as Astrid cared for the pack-sleipnir, and later appeared with a bucket of fresh soil for the Rotha, which contentedly whistled a tuneless, breathy song, like a bird not yet strong enough to warble.

The following morning heralded a fresh wind that had cleared the air of the enshrouding mist, and the clouds that kissed the higher reaches of the black shale mountains blew away. The foot traffic of the past several days had cleared a trail between the bits of shale that lay scattered in the road as it climbed to the cliffs, drawing nearer at times to the edge that overlooked a long drop down to the sea and the razor sharp boulders peeking up out of the surf.

Astrid took the lead, guiding the pack-sleipnir, and Katiam could see her hesitance when the track led closer to the edge. Perhaps this was her friend's first hint of fear. Katiam recalled the precipitous leap from St. Rämmon to the secret path and the dead look Astrid had given Katiam. But now, in the light of day, her concern was visible.

Their progress was slow and cold, and the dark of night descended too soon. They passed a series of small shelters, most of which had been ruined by the weight of snow, ice, or shale. When they came to one that was fairly intact, Astrid doubled back to tear away some of the broken remnants of a ruined hut for firewood.

The Rotha was lethargic in the cold, preferring to remain in its bundle while Katiam slept fitfully. When the gray morning dawned, Astrid didn't appear to have slept at all, having tended the fire all night. She warmed the legs of the sleipnir as Katiam rose and folded their blankets. The Rotha almost appeared to watch the two of them, despite having no eyes, taking in the air of the little shelter with sniffs and whistles. When they were ready, they continued along the path as it led away from the cliff and into a meandering scree field. The shale had diminished, giving way to the granite boulders that had long ago tumbled down the high slopes.

"How far would you say we came yesterday?" Katiam asked.

"Not as far as I would have liked," Astrid replied. "Although we might have made it seven miles," she added.

"How far is it to the border?"

"The innkeeper thought it was three days' journey to the border of Boroni, but he also said we wouldn't see a station for at least five. Even then, we might not see a guard."

"This must be a good road for smugglers, then," Katiam replied.

They found another set of shacks before night fell and made themselves comfortable, only to be awakened just before dawn by a howling gale from the mountains above. It sheered the wetness off the rocks and cleared the sky to a brilliant blue as the sun rose, which, at first, was welcome. The wind remained relentless, and the path neared the sea again. If it weren't for the large rocks lining the sea side of the road, they would have considered stopping and finding shelter until the windstorm died away.

That night, ensconced in yet another shelter, Katiam bolted awake. The wind outside the shelter had stopped abruptly, and for the first time in several days, she could hear herself think. Three sounds returned to her in the eerie calm, first, the slow and steady snores of Astrid, then the rolling crash of the waves from the sea, and finally a small whistle from the Rotha, wrapped tightly in its blanket and kept between the two women for warmth. She rose, pulled her blanket around herself, and stepped out into the cold air exposed to the clear, starry night sky.

A single star fell, streaking across the constellation of the Grazing Beast and through the Keep. Katiam raised her hand and traced a line through the two of them to a bright blue star, Elzar. Memories flooded back, of nights spent with her stargazer father as he taught her of the constellations and their purposes for divining the seasons. She smiled as she traced out the bright speckles of the Sleipnir Herd stars, grazing their way through the Healing Vine and its long path through the heavens.

A tear rolled down her face. Neither she nor her brother had learned all of what their father knew before they journeyed to Pariantür. She hoped he had found someone to teach his profound knowledge to. The thought of his knowledge being lost blanketed her in a wave of sadness.

Turning back to the shelter, she thought of the Rotha in her care, and wondered what she might learn if she pulled back the veil on its little mystery, and if she would be able teach it anything as it grew. The thought brought a smile to her face.

When Astrid woke up Katiam had a small fire going, and together they sang a hymn while they readied breakfast, boiling water that had pooled in a nearby rock. The whistle of the Rotha grew louder, and they opened the blanket and settled the Rotha in the nearly-empty pool of water.

"Does it think?" Astrid asked as she finished packing their blankets into a roll and strapping it to the pack of the sleipnir.

"The Rotha?" Katiam asked.

Astrid nodded. "Like you or me?"

"Perhaps not exactly like us," Katiam said. "But it appears to think, in some way."

"It doesn't seem to do much, though, other than whistle and lap up water."

"Neither does an infant," Katiam said.

"I suppose that's right," Astrid said. "It has only been a few short months since its awakening."

"It's grown a lot since then," Katiam said. "I can almost hear my mother now, speaking to me after my brother was born, as I complained that he didn't play with me."

"What did she say?"

"He is doing what he was meant to do. Suckle and grow, as a calf or a sapling."

"I hadn't realized you were the oldest," Astrid said. "Killian was several years older than me, and we had no younger siblings ourselves."

"There were four of us," Katiam said. "Our younger sisters were born several years later."

"Your brother didn't stay and become a Paladin, though."

"No. He failed to take the vows."

"He returned to your parents then?"

"He could not face the shame," Katiam said. "He never left the Protectorate of the Hammer. He was killed by a T'Akian raid.

Several years later my parents wrote and asked after him."

"Did you ever tell them?"

"I didn't feel it was my place, although at my request Auntie increased the stipend paid to them. Some of it came from my own stipend, but I've never dipped into it."

"I've never needed to dip into my own stipend, either. When we reach Pariantür, we can talk to the bursar about giving us what we need to continue on our journey."

Around midday, as the sun warmed their backs, Astrid pulled up suddenly.

"What's wrong?" Katiam asked, coming to stand next to her.

"There is something moving in the boulder field ahead," Astrid whispered.

"A person?"

"No, a creature of some sort."

Katiam saw nothing as she scanned the rocks where Astrid looked.

"I don't see anything."

"It's hard to spot. It's the same color as the rocks."

Katiam scanned the rocks for a while, but saw nothing to alarm her.

"It appears to have gone up the slopes," Astrid said. "We'll move forward cautiously. But keep your eyes open."

"What do you think it was?" Katiam asked.

"I don't think it was an urswine, if that's what you're worried about. It is early spring, but those are brown or black. Not gray."

"I wasn't thinking of an urswine," Katiam said, though she shuddered at the thought of the lumbering, big-nosed, violent creatures. "But I am now."

They entered a small path leading through the gaps in the boulder field. Astrid handed the reins of the sleipnir to Katiam and indicated she continue on; then she took out her mace and pulled herself onto the boulders to scan the field above them.

"Do you see anything?" Katiam said.

"Shhh," Astrid hissed. "No. Don't draw attention."

Katiam wanted to flee and force the sleipnir faster down the road, but then realized bolting might cause even more trouble.

The pack beast suddenly pulled up short. Katiam stepped out in front of it and tried to urge it forward, but it would not budge.

"Come on!" she hissed at the six-legged creature.

"Katiam," Astrid said calmly from above. "Don't. Move."

She let go of the reins and her arms went protectively around the bundle strapped to her chest. Turning her head slowly, she looked down the path ahead.

At first she saw only rocks and boulders. Then one of the boulders moved forward, snuffling through the small rocks, shoving them out of the way as it moved down the trail. She became aware that she was looking at the backside of the creature, whose summit almost came as high as her chest. It lifted its head to sniff at the air, and paused for a moment before turning its head around to consider what was behind it.

The head was massive, with two huge shovel-like tusks jutting out from its jaw. It had only just enough space on the trail to turn around on the narrow path and consider the sleipnir and women behind it.

It was a Tusk-Jaw, or Ipoter to some. It was larger than the smaller knee-high ones found on the plains near Pariantür. It considered Katiam with its beady black eyes, its two slotted nostrils steaming in the cold air. The sleipnir stamped its hoof to encourage the creature to move along. The tusk-jaw suddenly lunged forward, offering a counter threat, then fell back and grunted, swinging its tusks menacingly.

"Katiam," Astrid said calmly. "Take my hand."

Katiam glanced up at her friend, standing on the boulders above her.

"Can they climb?" Katiam asked.

"No, but it doesn't mean it can't come after us. Give me your hand."

The sleipnir began to back up, wresting itself free of Katiam's hand, leaving her exposed.

"Give me your hand," Astrid said firmly.

Katiam turned to the tusk-jaw, which took a tentative step forward.

She reached up and felt Astrid grab her wrist.

Suddenly the creature charged, its tusks clattering against the rocks.

Katiam tried to scramble up the rock but fell against it, the Rotha whistling in surprise. She tried to roll up onto the boulder, but felt a hammering pain hit her in the heel as something struck and ground her foot against the rock. She winced and looked down as the tusk-jaw, which had hit her, continued crashing down the trail toward the sleipnir, which reared up and began to kick down on the head of its enemy, and the armored, fleshy plates along its back. The two beasts fought, for the sole purpose of forcing the other to back away.

The tusk-jaw suddenly thrust its head up once, then twice, hitting the ribcage of the sleipnir in the same spot. The second thrust broke flesh, and the tusk went deep into its body. The sleipnir went rigid and fell over with a scream, after which the tusk-jaw snuffed at the body in the startling calm of victory, rummaging through its pack and tearing away hunks of treated leather to get to the dried mushrooms found there.

Katiam and Astrid watched as the creature destroyed their supplies; Katiam touched her left foot, now pulsing with pain. The bundle against her chest moved slightly, and she opened it up and examined the Rotha.

"Oh no," she whispered.

Astrid knelt down next to her. "What's wrong?"

"One of her vines was crushed when I rolled over her."

"It could be worse," Astrid said.

"But what must it think?" Katiam said.

Astrid took hold of her arm and helped her up. Katiam winced as she put her foot down.

"You're hurt?"

"Yes. It hit me with its tusk."

"Once it goes, we'll try to get down and collect what we can from the packs."

The creature was soon snuffling along the trail, having completely forgotten the two women who had interrupted its morning. Astrid climbed down and rummaged through the packs. She handed up a satchel with Katiam's medical supplies, and Katiam began wrapping her foot.

"We are within a day of the checkpoint," Astrid said.

"Two, if I can't walk as fast," Katiam answered.

"All right, two. We'll stash important things nearby, and instruct whoever we meet there to find them. Otherwise, we'll take only what we need for the next two days, as well as anything irreplaceable, in case things go wrong."

The tusk-jaw had not found most of the dry goods. All of the heavy cooking vessels and even their armor had been spared, and she lugged them up over the boulders to a crevice, where she hid them under a covering of waxed canvas before returning to Katiam.

"How is the Rotha faring?" Astrid asked.

"It appears to be all right. The other vines are touching the break like a small child examining a sore."

Astrid took the bundle from Katiam and helped her slide down. Katiam winced again as her feet touched the ground.

"Bad?" Astrid asked.

"It could be worse," Katiam said. "It's not broken, but the bone might be bruised."

"Then let's see how far we can get today."

As night fell they saw no sign of the tusk-jaw or anyone else, and, during their journey the next morning, they were pleasantly surprised to arrive at a view of a verdant valley and see the outpost they had been looking for.

"We made it," Katiam said. A sob escaped her.

"We did," Astrid said.

Katiam turned and saw a smile emerge on the her friend's face for the first time in far too long.

IO

SACRED SPACES

Calm thee now thy hammer.

Lay aside thy forging, and let us together till this land.

If thou needs a garden for thy flowers, I shall see it done.

My flowers will not grow in a lumber yard.

Nor our friendship grow in a desert.

By strength of our backs, a burden taken upon shoulder.

Hammer and Rose ever stand now as one

—CRYSALAS-PARIANTI POEM, UNKNOWN AUTHOR

Katiam was thankful when their carriage and escort arrived to guide them into the hill country leading to the city of Brahz, which would have been a difficult climb even with two good legs. In the city itself, they wended their way on sloping streets, up a system of inner-city switchbacks. Most streets were lined with terraced walls and looked out over the falling-away green hills, a landscape dotted with shepherd shelters and white fleeces of capricörs. Brazhstone Keep crowned the city, a collection of buildings surrounding an ancient central tower, which was nearly swallowed up by rooftops and the side of the mountain it clung to.

The red tapestries hanging in the receiving hall of the Keep portrayed a mountain and two capricörs rampant, indicating they were either ascending, or fighting one another. A servant or two stepped through, touching up the room as they went. All of the servants they had seen wore the red of the Brazh Jarldom, but they each wore a small hanging badge upon the right shoulder, with various household insignia from their native town or village.

The door on the other end of the room opened and a tall, elegant woman stepped in. Her long black hair had been plaited with gold ribbon and nearly touched the back of her calves. Loose red robes hung on her thin frame, not quite hiding the signs of a child growing in her. A moment later, a man rushed through the door behind her. He was only an inch taller than her, if only for the heeled boots she wore, and they looked the pair—slender but powerfully built Boronii nobles.

"Greetings," the woman said in a low, rich voice. "I am Lady Ketiva Vaur-Brazstein. This is my husband, Baron Arthoss Brazstein, son of Jarl Brazstein."

"We thank you for your hospitality," Astrid said. "I hope it was not an inconvenience to request an escort to your home."

"Certainly not an inconvenience," Lady Ketiva said. "But we should like to know the story of you women. You are obviously traveling somewhere, with large packs left in the care of our stables. What are your names?"

"Perhaps you'll recall the two of us, having traveled here with your company last autumn. I am Astrid Glass, a Paladame of the Crysalas Honoris. My companion here is Katiam Borreau, niece and physician to our late Matriarch Superioris. Given the hospitality your household showed us on our journey through this city, we thought that perhaps you might have offered that hospitality once more to our friends who preceded us."

"Those who preceded you?" Lord Arthoss asked hesitantly.

"We were delayed in the middle of winter, and there were those of our order, and of the Order of the Hammer, that went on ahead of us, retracing our steps through Boroni, Bortali, and toward the Fortress-Monastery of Pariantür."

"We understand you came from the coastal road," Lady Ketiva said. "It was too treacherous for the entourage you speak of last autumn, and yet you braved that road during the spring rains and survived. How did you fare?"

"We were more foolish than brave," Astrid said. "Our pack-sleipnir was killed by a tusk-jaw."

"The story becomes all the more interesting," Ketiva said, raising an eyebrow.

"We understand that the new Prima Pater, Nichal Guess, as well as several members of the Paladins of the Hammer, joined up with our sisters in Zebüdé and took that coastal road. We were several weeks behind them, and the window for travel along that road closed just as we arrived in Zebüdé."

"Anyone in the Northern Scapes might know the name of a Prima Pater, and use his name to access important places. I hadn't expected it might be two women, and although I admit that your face is somewhat familiar, I also admit that my mind was on other matters last autumn, and I did not pay much attention to our companions from Donig."

"You require more proof from us, then?" Astrid said, her tone shifting.

"Our country is at war with Bortali," Arthoss said.

Ketiva held a hand up for him to be silent.

"My husband prefers to jump to the heart of the matter. Two women, with accents no northern country can claim, come to the gates and declare that they traveled from Mahndür on one of the most difficult roads in our country, then they insist on immediately speaking with Jarl Brazstein."

"That is true," Katiam said.

"You carry some bundle inside your own robe," Ketiva said, indicating toward Katiam, "despite our servants offering to take your burdens from you. I should imagine it is something very important to show our Jarl. No doubt some less-than-subtle attempt to shift the power of balance in favor of Bortali, or perhaps another Jarl."

"If you believe we have come to do some harm to the name of Brazstein, you are sorely mistaken," Astrid said.

"I think I've heard enough," Lady Ketiva said. "You mentioned going to find your own people. Perhaps it is best you do so."

The doors behind them opened and four guards entered.

Katiam turned from the guards to look at the two nobles standing before the hearth.

"We ate with you at the feast of Jarls," Katiam blurted out. "I sat at the Tosch table. When your house was announced, I watched the face of Jined Brazstein blush red at the mention of his own house name, and we were both there when we watched his god, Grissone, bless him with miracles as he took on a second vow."

"Hold," Ketiva said.

The guards froze.

"While I was not present in Mahn Fulhar," Katiam continued, "we both understand that he has perhaps now taken on a third vow, and bears signs of that upon his breastplate to that effect. We only wish to seek out both he and the Prima Pater, so we can join them on their return to Pariantür."

"And that bundle upon your breast?"

"As precious to me as the life which grows within you now."

Ketiva reflexively touched her own belly.

"It is not for me to show you that which I carry," Katiam added. "But it will not leave my person. If your Jarl will not see us, and if you will see us out and onto the street, then so be it. But if you have word of our people and where they went, then please tell us."

The woman waved a hand, and the guards relaxed. Astrid did likewise.

"Wait here," Lady Ketiva said. "There is someone in our city you ought to speak to."

She turned and left the room with her husband in tow.

"A rather cold introduction," Astrid said.

"No doubt cooler once I called out her past," Katiam said, "and in front of the man who was forced to take her as his wife after the incident."

"I'm not sure I follow," Astrid said.

"As I understand it, involvement with that woman is what drove Jined to become a Paladin."

"We all join for different reasons."

"He killed her betrothed and went east to avoid execution."

"Then why was his younger brother forced to marry her?"

"Apparently, she carried Jined's child, unbeknownst to anyone at the time."

"Well, that'll do it."

A servant entered, bringing a bowl of nuts and meats and a loaf of bread. Katiam picked a handful of nuts for herself and gave the rest, including the meat, to Astrid. Astrid offered Katiam some of the softer portions of the loaf of bread. It had become a habit of theirs, though never acknowledged. A leafy vine of the Rotha had escaped its swaddle, and searched blindly around. Katiam offered the leaf a few seeds, which it took back into the wrap at her chest.

Arthoss Brazstein entered the hall, a robed man behind him, his face obscured by a hood. The host turned back to the other man, and they exchanged a few words before Arthoss left.

"Greetings by the Hammer and the Rose," the man said, lowering his hood. Katiam did not recognize him, and Astrid didn't seem to, either.

"In Faith and Purity," Astrid replied, stepping forward.

"I am Pater Minoris Didus Koel," the man said. "I understand you seek word of the Paladins who journey east?"

"We have been traveling east," Astrid said, "taking some time to winter in Zebüdé during the snows, and now we find ourselves here, in search of members of our sisterhood gone before us and the Paladins who fled with them."

"Then you were not in Mahn Fulhar during that fateful night?" Koel asked.

"None of our number were," Astrid said. "Not after the pilgrimage to Precipice and the Oracle. I was Paladame guard to the Matriarch Superioris, and this was her physician."

"Then you were members of the Entourage?"

"We were."

"I'll need to know something that proves this. Who is Prima Pater?" Didus asked.

"Nichal Guess is the Acting Prima Pater," Astrid said. "His status was given to him by Dorian Mür himself. The Sister Superioris in Zebüdé is Geldin."

Didus nodded. "Very well. Follow me."

He turned and walked to the door. Astrid took a tentative step forward.

"Come along," Didus said.

"You'll not offer us something to quash our own doubts?"

"Jined Brazstein spoke with your companion, Katiam Borreau, at the Dweol before he closed it off."

Astrid looked at Katiam, who nodded with a smile.

"Where are you taking us?" Katiam asked.

"Please trust me, and put your hoods up."

They left the castle and meandered through town, avoiding the main thoroughfares, and eventually came to a street built along the side of the mountain. Katiam took one tentative look over the wall and saw nothing but plains a quarter mile below. She quickly retreated and returned to the middle of the paved walkway, where they soon came to a shop selling ropes, flanked by a ruined old chapel that stood more as centerpiece than as functional chapel, while the other buildings grew up around it.

Didus approached a small door between the shops then turned to speak to them. "This street, anchored by that old chapel, is the original town of Brahz, founded on the wealth of two copper mines and a tin deposit. The chapel is one of the few non-Parianti chapels dedicated to Grissone. It wasn't well-tended to when we arrived this winter, but it has served us well."

He opened the door and signaled for them to follow. They stepped onto a staircase that twisted and turned between the buildings, after which they came into a vestibule with a new wooden door. Katiam could still smell the fresh woodwork. As Didus pressed his hands on it, the door swung in on well-oiled hinges to reveal a sunken rotunda room with steps down to its center, where a large stone vessel of oil sat. A bronze candle rose from the oil, the wick shedding light on a figure kneeling before it with his back to them, draped in a golden-yellow blanket.

Didus touched his finger to his lips and stepped onto the top stair, crossing his hands in front of him as he waited. The figure below was muttering to himself. At the end of his prayer he stood, ignited a lighting stick with the flame from the centerpiece, and lit a candle that had been waxed to the edge of the basin. Turning, Katiam saw a face she recognized all too well, from his broken nose and heavy brow, to standing taller than all three of them from a step below.

"Hello Katiam," he said in a low, commanding voice.

"Hello Jined Brazstein. A Primus now too, I see."

He looked down at the black cordon pinned across his robe, with three vow beads hanging from them.

"A gift from my god, when I took up a third vow."

"If you're still here," Astrid asked, "where are the others?"

"It is good to see you too, Astrid," Jined said with a weak smile. "Let's get some food together, and I'll tell you all that has happened since last we spoke."

"Fine," Astrid said. "Is it just the two of you here?"

"The end of the book before the beginning?" Jined replied. "Very well. In short, both Rose and Hammer are spread across the Northern Scapes. Didus and I are here, and last I heard Nichal and a few others are still in Donig. Others have gone ahead to Waglÿsaor."

"Astrid," Katiam said, "let him tell us what he knows. Nichal shared only a little with the vault in Zebüdé. I'd like to know everything that would cause the mighty warrior Nichal and his guards to leave behind their holdings."

"We hope we can salvage these lands from war," Jined said, "and make it back in time to Pariantür to ensure that the entire order does not collapse on itself."

Astrid was eating the cold chicken off her plate, a bit more amiable now there was food in her stomach. Jined picked at his cheese and dried fruit, and refilled Astrid's cup with more ale.

Didus appeared from the kitchen with a plate of bread and butter, placing it before Katiam and taking a seat across from her.

"I've a capricör roast I will start preparing shortly," Koel said. "Is there anything else you'd like with that?"

"I am afraid I do not eat meat," Katiam said. "But for Astrid's sake, please do make the roast."

Astrid was nodding wildly in agreement, her mouth full.

"Food has been a bit scarce these last few days on the road," Katiam added.

"What can I get for you, then?" Didus asked.

"I know vegetables can be harder to come by in winter," she said. "But root vegetables and nuts would make me very happy."

"I'll see it done. I believe a ground squash would be in order too."

"I'll admit, I find it odd that a Pater Minoris is cooking for a Primus," Katiam said, glancing over at Jined. "But then I remember who this Primus is—called by his god."

"Ha!" Didus said. "Chosen as he is, I wouldn't let Jined cook for me if he begged."

"Apparently," Jined said, "I burn perfect meat by looking at it, and the Brahz cuisine of boiling everything does not sit well in his sensitive belly."

"Before I took up the hammer," Didus said, "my parents ran a tavern in Hraldor. Visiting Paladins told my parents the food they served was the greatest meal they had ever had. Perhaps they were being generous, but it inspired me, and when I came of age I journeyed to Pariantür to become a cook for the Paladins. Even when Grissone showed he had other plans for me, I never lost my knack for the kitchen. When I ran the Bulwark in Birin, I still cooked for my men once a week, and I'll continue to feed whoever I can."

"The Paladins in Hraldor were not being generous," Astrid said. "You're very good."

"Thank you."

Astrid sat back with a sigh.

"Now," Katiam said to Jined, "tell us what happened and spare no detail."

Jined explained what happened after they left Precipice, from the journey to the lighthouse and the discovery of the Motean heretics, to the restoration and death of Pater Gladen; from the takeover of the Crysalas Convent and the deliverance of Didus Koel from the dominion of the coins, then finally to the threat from the Church of Aben and Jined calling down the full might of Grissone on Searn VeTurres and his cloak of darkness. He described the retreat to Boroni and his decision to stay at the chapel when his father revealed its history as an ancient Grissoni church.

"So Nichal continued on with the others?" Katiam said.

"He went as far as Donig," Jined said, "and sent word to us a month later. A select few continued on to Bortali, but it sounds like one of the worst snowfalls the Scapes have seen in a lifetime prevented him from following them through the pass. So he set up office in Donig, and has been there ever since."

"And you've remained here."

"To seek Grissone's will."

"Why?" Astrid asked.

"What do you mean, why? My god has granted me blessing. I've spent the winter learning how to live within this new Vow of Prayer under Didus's tutelage—seeking Grissone's will."

"You may think me presumptuous for saying this," Astrid said, "but you've twice taken an additional vow, and your god acknowledged both times with a miracle. I think it safe to say that you're an extension of his will. You've sequestered yourself here in this chapel, when you could have continued with the others and commanded the snow in the pass to clear away."

Didus shot Jined a look.

While Jined stared at Astrid Glass, he pursed his lips and furrowed his eyebrows. "Your family and your advice."

"What do you mean?" Astrid said.

"Your brother, may he rest in peace, was always an aggravatingly accurate voice of reason. I hated and loved him for it."

Katiam looked over at Astrid. Her eyes were brimming with unshed tears.

"I hated him for it too," Astrid said, "and it's what I miss about him most."

"Have I missed something?" Didus whispered across the table to Katiam.

"Astrid's brother, Killian, journeyed with us from Pariantür. He was killed by a vül in the mountains between Bortali and Nemen."

Didus nodded.

"We can wax nostalgic," Astrid said, "but we cannot bring back the dead. Mourn Killian and those who died in Mahn Fulhar and Precipice when this is all over. For now, your god has called you to act upon his will; Katiam and I have been called on our own journey."

"And what is that, exactly?" Jined asked.

"We bring word from our goddess for our sisters who have fled east. After we bring word to them, we must continue our journey."

"To where?"

"We're not at liberty to divulge that," Katiam said. "Our mission is to remain secret from that point on, for fear that the Thirteen-Limbed One will learn of it and undermine us. All the same, we would welcome your protection and guidance until we reach our sisters. We will simply have to leave you then."

"What do you think, Didus?"

"You've been waiting for a sign," Didus replied. "These two women need to be safely escorted east on a mission from their goddess. Who better to take them than you?"

Jined turned to Katiam. "We'll leave in the morning."

"I will show you both to your room," Didus said, rising.

Katiam and Astrid followed him to a side door and down the hall.

The room he led them into was cold, and the bed had no blankets.

"Give me a moment to gather up bedding," he said. "It's only been the two of us all this time, so there's been no reason to make all the rooms comfortable."

"If you'll tell me where to find firewood," Astrid said, "I'll get the fire going in the meantime."

"Pater Koel," Katiam said, as Didus turned to leave with Astrid.
"Yes?"

"Why have you and Jined not yet journeyed on? Do you really
think Astrid and I are some kind of sign?"

Didus shrugged. "Truthfully, Grissone has been silent these
past few months. I am of the Vow of Prayer, but in all my years,
Grissone has never responded to me. Who am I to assume he'd
answer my prayers, audibly or otherwise? But Jined has enjoyed
near constant companionship with Grissone until now, when our
god has gone silent with him as well. He hasn't taken it well."

"I imagine that would be discouraging," Katiam replied.

"He spends many nights wandering these halls, praying aloud.
At times I worry for his sanity, from the lack of sleep and
appetite."

"Did Grissone give him any direction before he stopped
appearing?"

"Only to head east, and that, for a time, Grissone would be
elsewhere."

"Then why is Jined upset?" Astrid asked. "It sounds as though
he has been given direction, and he's not following it. He needs to
travel east. Following the instructions given to him is the best way
to impress his god."

"I think he is an apprentice whose master wisely remains
silent," Didus said, "to allow the apprentice to make his own
mistakes."

"What do you mean?" Katiam said.

"I think I understand," Astrid said, after a moment of thought.
"My father is a glazier, and he hovered over his apprentices during
their early years, instructing their every move. But eventually he
would stop telling them what to do, and they would begin learning
from their mistakes. He was still there for them in a different way,
and they would draw on his wisdom and instructions when they
needed to. Eventually they would still come to him for his advice,
but it was more out of respect than need. At that point, they were
ready for their own glassworks. Still," she added, "it could be a
long road to that point."

Didus nodded. "You see to the heart of it. If your brother was
half as wise as you, I can see why Jined respected him so much."

"If anything," Astrid said, "it was I who was half as wise."

She turned to Katiam as Didus walked to the door. "I'll see
some dirt brought as well, to see our charge cared for."

"Thank you," Katiam said. "I'll open a window and sweep."

II

HOUSEGUEST

The first true deception of these two older men was feigning my lack of understanding. It was a continual frustration for Scepter as he explained over and over again the complex subtleties of social manipulation, all the while I did the same to him. Zephyr on the other hand adored oration. To kill time, and to allow myself my own thoughts, I'd often ask him to start a diatribe on the histories of Pan-Veldic cultures, and he'd gladly turn an hour lesson into three, in which I'd nod agreeably, having fully understood what he had said the first time.

—JOURNAL OF SEARN VETURRES, ENTRY TWELVE

T he old man next to her kept pulling on her arm, slowing her stride. The braid the tailor's daughter had put around her head was far too tight and hurt her scalp, and the dress she'd borrowed bunched uncomfortably around her middle. But the Voktorra guards who stood at each side of the entrance to the Stone paid them little attention, as they appeared like common denizens of the city. On entering the Stone, the old man and the girl moved to the right, where guest houses of the royal family sat in tight, tall rows of brick and stone. They walked passed the final house and into the King's Garden, open to the people of the city, and full of gardeners preparing the ground for the spring growth.

"Tell me of your childhood," the old man said.

"I'd rather not," Ophedia said. "It is my own story, and not something I wish to relive."

"I can understand a bit of that. I'm not even from Mahn Fulhar myself. I came from Düran, after serving in the Protectorate Wars."

"That was so long ago," Ophedia said.

"It was," Abgenas said. "A long, long time ago. Did you know I had another family, just after the wars?"

"Where are they?"

"My son left and traveled to Ikhala. I haven't heard from him since."

"It appears you are doing well now."

"I've always done well enough," the old man said. "A tailor can always find work. It was a blessing to find my current wife, and begin my life here in Mahn Fulhar."

"Will you stay here? In Mahn Fulhar, I mean?"

"I must do what is best for my wife," Abgenas said. "If she feels it is time to leave, then we will. What about you? I've heard what the Clouws think about the arrival of the Chalicians, but you've not spoken up."

"Because I don't know what to think," Ophedia said. "Nor do I much care for anything most religions have to say."

"Why is that?"

"They wish only to help those who will subscribe to their beliefs."

"And you disagree with their beliefs?"

"I don't believe in being forced into one."

"How would they do that?"

"I was an orphan, if you must continue to push. The Crysalas, the Nifarans, all have tried to take me in, and see that I did as they say."

"And you did not appreciate their sentiments."

Ophedia muttered in agreement.

"Then why are you willing to help these Clouws, to find and rescue the leader of the church of Grissone?"

"Because despite all we've been through, the Clouws accept me as I am."

"That seems to be a reasonable reason to stick with friends."

The old man stopped and took a seat on a bench.

"Sit with me, girl," he said.

Ophedia did as she was told.

"Now, my eyes may be going, but my daughters have told us to observe the window nearer the top. It has red curtains."

Ophedia lifted her gaze to the northern tower, which had broad windows that grew wider at each level. The topmost window was shadowed by red curtains, and she could vaguely see someone looking out over the expanse of parks toward the sea. The figure looked to be that of a small man with a bald head.

"And you think that may be the Prima Pater?" Ophedia asked.

"I don't know. I'm merely the decoy, aren't I?"

"Wave your hand," Ophedia said.

The old man glanced nearsightedly toward the castle and lifted his hand first to his chest, then raised it to the sky. Ophedia watched the man in the window lift both hands to his chest, making a motion she had seen several Paladins make when greeting one another.

"I think you're right," Ophedia said. "That must be where he's being kept."

"Have you noticed that there are few servants working, save the gardeners?" Abgenas said.

Ophedia looked around.

"Compared to yesterday, there are even fewer Voktorra."

Ophedia stood.

"Your loyalty to the Prima Pater," Ophedia said. "How far does it go?"

"Do you mean, young lady, how rebellious am I feeling?"

Instead of answering her question, he rose and took her arm, and they made their way through the garden to the door of the tower. Ophedia took hold of the latch for the servant's entrance and pushed her way through, the old tailor coming up behind her. The halls were nearly empty, save for a few errand boys running to and fro, and a young chambermaid who noticed them immediately.

"Are you staff?" she asked.

"No, just city-folk visiting the King's Gardens," Ophedia said. "We were hoping to get a view of the gardens from one of the towers."

"I..." the young girl gawked at them. "I really shouldn't let you in there."

"Do you know the tailor in the Grotto who makes the embroidered ribbons?" Abgenas asked.

"Oh..." the girl gasped. "Yes. His ribbons are the envy of the town!"

"If you would just give us a glimpse of the garden from the top of the tower, I think I can convince my granddaughter to part with one of her ribbons, for I am that tailor."

Ophedia reached under the whale boning and took out a green ribbon with blue embroidery. "Grandfather," Ophedia said, "will this work?"

"I love green," the girl said, eying the ribbon.

"Very well," the old man said, taking the ribbon from Ophedia. "If you show us the top of this tower, I'll give this ribbon to you. It must be worth at least a silver conta."

"At least," Ophedia agreed.

The girl turned and placed the pot in her hand behind a tapestry, then gestured for them to follow her.

"We'll need to be as quick as we can," the girl said. "The cook is in a good mood, but likely to sour as we near the servants' feast tonight."

They came to a wide set of stairs and began the climb to the top. The old man became gradually slower, and the girl more and more agitated at how long it was taking. Ophedia gauged they had come nearly to the top, when Abgenas dropped to the stairs.

"These are much higher than I thought," he said.

"I do apologize," the girl said. "But I cannot go any further without risking the wrath of my mistress."

"Very well," Abgenas said. "I shouldn't have asked you to disobey her." He held out the ribbon. "Take this. Perhaps I'll sit here for a time and rest, and then we can leave."

"Really?" the girl said, taking the finely-embroidered ribbon. "You can find your way out?"

"I think we can manage," Ophedia said.

The girl turned and fled back down the stairs.

"It seems we have the place to ourselves," Abgenas said.

"Are you as tired as you seem?"

"I am rather weary, but that light up ahead must be the battlements, which means the room we want is a level below us here."

The old man stood, steadying himself on Ophedia. They made their way down and entered the hallway beyond the tower stairwell, a short corridor with a single guard outside the door at the end.

"Who are you?" the guard asked.

"My grandfather," Ophedia said, "was making his way to the top of the tower and began to lose his breath."

Abgenas began breathing laboriously.

"You don't live in any of these rooms," the guard said. "You need to leave."

The old man gave Ophedia's arm a squeeze and suddenly collapsed to the ground.

"Please help!" Ophedia cried out.

The guard took a step forward then paused. "No, I am under orders."

"He's an old man, go and get help!" Ophedia screamed.

"You go, I'll stay with him," the guard said.

"In this dress?" Ophedia said.

The guard looked at her hesitantly.

"This is the king's private tailor. If he dies...."

The guard sighed and began moving down the stairs.

Abgenas smiled at Ophedia. "Go."

"What about you?" she said.

"I'll tell them you ran off to find help. I'll ask to be taken to the Abecinian medicae. Meanwhile, you bring the Prima Pater back to my home."

Ophedia walked over to the door. The guard had left the key in the lock.

"Almost too easy," she muttered as she turned it and pushed the door open.

It was a sparse room with a fleece-covered bed near the hearth and a desk with a few books stacked upon it. The old man was standing at the window wearing only a brown paladinial robe, but he turned and looked at Ophedia when she entered.

"What was that shouting outside?" he asked. Then he peered more closely at her. "You're the girl standing with the man who waved at me."

"Yes. We're here to rescue you, Dorian Mür," Ophedia said, looking back into the hall. "We must go now. I haven't time to explain."

"You have been guided by the Anka, no doubt," he muttered. "Let me gather my things."

"There's no time," said Ophedia flatly.

Dorian straightened up. "Very well. Lead the way."

She stepped back out into the hallway; Dorian followed just behind her.

"Prima Pater," Abgenas said, giving a bow of his head from the ground. "Ophedia, don't forget to lock the door."

She turned back and gave the key a turn.

"Ophedia?" Dorian said. "VeTurres' daughter?"

"Doesn't matter who I am," Ophedia said. "I'm here to see you safely away. Follow me."

"What of the old man?" Dorian asked.

"Don't worry about me," Abgenas said. "I served under you in the Protectorate Wars, and I'd give my life for you."

"I am no longer the Prima Pater," Dorian said. "I can't have you sacrificing yourself."

"Go," Abgenas said. "My wife was raised among the Crysalas. They still have a few women in their vaults. They'll see you safely away."

Dorian bowed his head. "Thank you for the honor you do me, then."

Ophedia and Dorian descended to the next level and peeked into the hall. No one was there, but they heard the sound of feet coming up the stairs and closed themselves into the corridor, waiting for the guards and the help to pass, after which they completed their descent. The Prima Pater was a faster mover than Abgenas, and they soon came to the garden door.

"We can't leave the castle complex by the front gate," Dorian said. "They'll recognize me. What about going over that wall there?" Dorian suggested, pointing to the south wall. The Crysalas Convent loomed overhead. Ophedia nodded, but still felt perplexed. No matter how agile the Prima Pater was compared to Abgenas, he could not scale the wall. As they came to it, he placed a hand on its stones.

"What do you plan to do now?" Ophedia asked.

"Pray."

"What good will that do?"

He took her arm and pulled her *into* the wall. Before she could flinch or gasp, they stood on the other side, in the side yard of the convent.

"How...?" she asked.

"By faith," he said. "Now, take me to that tunnel you and the Clouws used to bring Searn's body back to our bastion."

"The bastion is occupied by Chalicians now."

"Yes, I'm aware. We shall walk by the guidance of the Anka."

They found the long tunnel, which eventually led them out into the garden behind the Abecinian complex. A single monk stood there, staring in perfect surprise as they emerged from the mouth of the tunnel, right behind a leaf-budding rosebush.

"Brother," Dorian said, before the monk had a chance to say anything.

"How did you...?"

"Do you know if Father Ger is nearby?"

"He might be," the monk said, after recovering. "Shall I take you to him?"

The monk led them through a side door and into the back halls of the monastery.

"How does this go so easily?" Ophedia muttered.

"By faith, as I said," Dorian whispered. "If Grissone and the Anka willed us to leave the hospitality of the king, then we ought to follow his lead."

They came to a door just as an older monk opened it and emerged from his cell, his eyes widening in surprise. "Prima Pater?"

"Greetings, Father," Dorian said.

"Please come in," Father Ger said, reopening the door. He looked back at the monk who had escorted them. "Why don't you come with us, Brother Marn. What are you doing here, Dorian?" he asked, as soon as they were all inside. "We thought you were gone, after that night."

"I've been a guest of the king since then," Dorian replied.

"I do not understand."

"All I can say is the king is gone from his castle, and my god seems to have taken the opportunity to set me free."

"Albeit into the den of dræks," said Brother Marn, the monk who had escorted them.

"The Chalicians, you mean?" Dorian asked.

"Be careful what you say, Brother Marn," Father Ger said. "I believe I can count on your discretion here?"

"Father Ger," Brother Marn said, "I served the Paladins of the Hammer in Garrou for much of my life, and even took the daughter of a Paladin there as my second wife. My loyalty is almost stronger to them than to our order."

"That being the case," Father Ger said, "let us see if Brother Marn here can see you safely out of the monastery. Brother Marn, go and see about a few spare robes."

Soon Ophedia found herself looking out from under the gray hood of an Abecinian robe, the Prima Pater next to her wearing the same disguise. They patiently followed the figure of Brother

Marn out of the front entrance of the monastery, walking in the direction of town.

"You say you served the bastion in Garrou?" Dorian asked their guide.

"Yes. I spent many years there. I worked in the kitchen for the poor."

"Your name is Clouw, isn't it?"

The monk stopped. "Yes, it is. How did you know?"

"Your children traveled with us to Mahn Fulhar. Did they ask you to help me?"

"No. I haven't spoken to them since a couple weeks after the solstice."

Dorian looked puzzled. "I'd like to know why the gods keep dropping Clouws into my lap. What does it mean?"

"I'm sorry?" the monk asked.

"Your children. Now you. Why are you the ones to rescue me?"

"If what you say is true," Brother Marn said, "then be vigilant. My family is not blessed by the gods."

"What do you mean?"

"I mean that if the gods have a hand in all of this, be careful that the gods who assist you are right and good."

"I will bear that in mind."

They came to the Grotto. The smell of bakeries filled the space, and people were wafting in to find food. They came to the Dülar tailor, and Brother Marn knocked on the door.

"Two sets of monks in one day," the woman at the door said, showing them in.

As they entered, Ophedia glanced sideways to see the old man sitting in his usual place, pulling thread through the piece he was working on.

"You made it back!" she said, pulling back her hood.

He looked up and smiled. "What took you so long?"

"How did you return so quickly?" she countered.

"The Voktorra carried me to the gates of the castle, and my daughters were there to escort me home."

The Clouws came down the stairs together, staring at Ophedia and the Prima Pater.

"We couldn't believe it when Abgenas told us," Rallia said. "You just walked in and took him?"

"Luck," Ophedia shrugged.

"Faith," Dorian corrected.

Rallia turned and gave a respectful bow to Dorian, while Hanen nodded his head. Rallia's eyes grew wide as she looked past the Prima Pater to the monk standing behind him.

"Father?" she said in astonishment.

"Hello, Rallia," the monk, Marn Clouw, said. "Hello, Hanen."

12

Night Flight

Fill my cup, fill my cup.

With a drink, with a drink.

Hold my hand, hold my hand.

As we sink, as we sink.

—GRISDENI CHILDREN'S RHYME

Rallia counted loaves of bread as she lowered them into the cloth satchel. Ophedia checked the ceramic jars of preserves, sorting them into ten places designated on the table. Hanen held a sack open and Alodda and her mother scooped in a mix of oats and dried fruit. He tried to avoid the furtive glances Rallia gave him, while their father stood across the room with the two old men, Dorian and Abgenas. Three other monks sat in a corner in quiet prayer.

"Our neighbors," Abgenas was saying, "are getting suspicious, despite our attempts to keep you hidden. Whoever harbors you runs a great risk. I can't ask anyone else to keep this secret."

"Why are you helping us?" Dorian asked.

"Out of loyalty, I am trusting my daughters to you."

"You and your wife will not come with us?" Marn asked.

"I am too old to travel," Abgenas said. "My wife and I will work with her friends and allies in the Crysalas who remain in their vault, helping the people of the city."

"When do the women leave?" Marn asked, looking at Rallia and the others.

"A few of the Sisters have agreed to come and take the food," Eimeé said, coming to stand with her husband. "We cannot take men through the vault, even you, Prima Pater."

"I understand," Dorian said, "and I respect the sanctity of the vaults. I only wish I could convince the Crysalas to leave off and journey east."

"They will not leave the women of this city to despair. Nor shall I, especially now, with the Chalician Praetors occupying us."

A knock echoed up the back set of stairs. Eimeé turned and exited through the doorway. A few minutes later she re-emerged, with five women in black cloaks. They lowered their hoods, and one of the women stepped forward.

"Abbess Foi," Dorian said. "I expected you might have returned."

"Prima Pater," Foi said, giving a low and reverent bow.

"I owe you a great debt for agreeing to come on such short notice."

"Had we known you were held in the castle, we would have done what we could to help you long ago," she said.

"But Grissone and his mother had other plans," Dorian said. "So we are here."

"Is all in readiness?"

"Yes, Abbess," Eimeé said.

"Then don these," Foi said, motioning to another sister, who handed black cloaks to Eimeé, Alodda, Runah, Ophedia, and Rallia. "This will be a good practice run, as I'm sure we'll soon be helping others escape the confines of the city."

"Where will we meet?" Dorian asked.

"Two miles south of the city, there is an inn with a small lighthouse," Foi said. "The women will be there by tomorrow night at the latest. If they encounter no difficulty and make good time, they'll arrive before you."

"The innkeeper can be trusted?"

"Yes, it is owned by our vault," she said. "But the Chalicians have conveyed the desire to take control of it."

"Very well," Dorian said.

"Prima Pater," Foi said, drawing closer to the old man. "I must warn you that this Chalician, Zehan Otem, is very dangerous."

"I have heard he is quite an orator. His rank, Provost, means he has a great deal of authority."

"He's equivalent to your Pater Segundii," Foi said. "But, more importantly, he goes by another name among the Crysalas in Œron—the Enquêteur. He has made a name for himself by hunting down those who circumvent Chalician authority there."

"That is why they have sent him to Mahn Fulhar," Dorian suggested.

"He will work hard to seek out the vaults and bring them under his grip."

"Then," Dorian said, turning to the room, "we had best move quickly."

"We will leave in an hour," one of the monks said. "Most will be asleep then."

He and the two other monks, besides Marn Clouw, all had slight Œronzi accents. They had been sent by Father Ger. Two of them had fled Œron years ago, escaping church persecution. The third who now spoke was a known political enemy of the Chalicians.

"Thank you, Brother Guarin," Abbess Foi said. "I am sorry to see you go."

"Father Ger shall continue to be your ally. He'll gladly use your help to see those who wish to leave the city safely away under your guidance."

"Let us go," the Abbess said, turning.

Hanen stepped over to Rallia and Alodda.

"Be careful," Hanen said to his sister.

Rallia looked away.

"I'm sorry," he said.

"You knew Father was here," she said. "I could tell by the look in your eyes. You didn't want me to know."

"I..."

"Not now. We'll have time on the road for you to explain what other secrets you've been keeping from me."

Rallia turned and helped the Crysalas carry the sacks of food down the back stairs.

"You be careful yourself," Alodda said to Hanen. "The Crysalas have centuries of practice, moving women secretly from one place to another, including under curfew."

Hanen felt the eyes of the room falling on the two of them. Alodda gave the men a glance and then stood on her tiptoes and gave Hanen a quick kiss on the cheek.

"Don't do anything rash," she said. "Meet us at the inn."

She joined her mother, who waited at the top of the stairs, and they left. The others had taken seats at the table. Bread that would not keep on the road still sat there, with preserves already opened.

"Shall we discuss our route?" Dorian asked, motioning Hanen to join the men.

One of the monks rolled out a piece of parchment, weighing the corners down with jars. After pulling out an inkwell and quill, he quickly sketched out a rough form of the city. Dorian leaned forward as the monk noted the Grotto and the gates.

"We are not yet certain how the Chalicians are patrolling the city after curfew," Guarin said, "but they are using the Voktorra to help them do so."

"And no one," a younger monk, Nidian, said, "is safe from curfew. A few of our fellow monks have been out too late to visit an ailing widow—they were accosted by a Praetor, and kept for questioning for two days. We have all been made second-class members of the church."

"Those who see the truth with their eyes will do all they can to escape their control," Marn said, placing a comforting hand on the monk's shoulder.

"I question whether I should go," Nidian said, "or whether I ought to stay and help those who protest."

"Your hot blood," Guarin said, "will see you among the first martyred."

"And that is a bad thing? To die for our faith?"

"There are those that shall," Guarin said. "But we must first fight by the pen and word."

"We do not know how other cities fare," Dorian said. "Perhaps, in helping us leave, you can make other cities and countries aware of what has transpired here."

"Ought you not stay here and help?" Nidian asked. "The Prima Pater of the Hammer standing beside us would give us strength."

"I am an old and frail man," Dorian said. "I would gladly give my life to stand against these tyrants. But what good would that do? My death might light a fire, but it could also be used to further establish their authority over the weak. Let us continue with this plan, as the head of your own order has agreed to, and see you safely away, to build up resistance elsewhere."

A knock came to the front door of the shop. Two of the monks visibly startled, but Dorian held a hand up to calm them.

"I shall go down and see who it is," Abgenas said. "I'm old. It will take me some time. Hanen, hide our guests in the back."

The old man rose and walked to the set of stairs leading to the shop below, while Hanen, Dorian, and the monks moved into the back rooms. Two of the monks slipped quietly into Abgenas' room, hiding under the master bed there. Hanen and Marn made sure the blanket hung naturally, covering them. Then Guarin was placed into the storeroom behind barrels. Dorian and Marn followed Hanen into the last room, where two beds sat. The scent of Alodda's cedar and porumarian oil hung heavily in the air.

"I'll see myself under that one." Dorian lay down on the floor and scooted underneath one of the beds. Marn crouched down to look under the other.

"I'm not sure I'll fit," Marn said, patting his belly. "I've put on a few pounds since arriving at the monastery."

"Here," Hanen said, going to the end of the bed. He took hold of the frame and lifted. Marn shifted himself under it.

"Lower it," he whispered.

Hanen placed it back on the ground. Whisper, who had been considering what they did with interest, slunk under the bed next to Marn.

"Good boy," Marn said, patting the creature. Whisper's tail rattled in response.

Hanen returned to the dining room just as Abgenas came through the stairwell door and gave him a look of consternation. Two figures were behind him, men who wore vivid blue cloaks over armored frames and carried arrow spears. These men stood on either side of the door, and Hanen could hear another coming up behind them. Abgenas took a few steps to the side, lowering his eyes before the third man, who entered holding his helmet under his arm. He was a man of perhaps fifty, with a powerful jaw and thick hair—without a hint of gray—plastered back across his skull, his eyes taking in the room with a discerning air of suspicion.

"Only the two of you?" he said loudly. He spoke with a voice that knew only one volume, but was not falsely raised. "I understand you had a wife and two children."

"They are visiting my wife's sister across the city, Provost Otem. They must not have left before curfew."

"Where does this sister reside?"

"Near the northern wall. She and her husband have a

cobblerage there."

"That shall be verified. Who are you?" The Praetor asked.

"Hanen ... Marnson," Hanen said.

"Hesitance, and no reverence for the order," the Praetor said. "Have you received your *Book of the True Path?*"

"It is at the inn where I am staying."

"Yet it is after curfew. And you're here. What is your purpose?"

"Hanen is..." Abgenas said, stepping forward.

The Praetor raised his hand to silence him. "I asked him."

"I am courting Abgenas' daughter," Hanen said. "He asked me to help out around the shop, what with the women away. He is getting old and can only do so much."

"Your occupation?"

"Dock worker," Hanen said.

"Hardly built for it," the Praetor said.

"I am trained as a net mender," Hanen said. "I don't understand why you question this?"

"The responsibility for the safety of this city is on my shoulders, and so I have a duty to investigate any suspicious activity here. I was led to believe that several monks from the monastery have been seen coming and going from this shop today, and I want to know why."

"Provost," Abgenas said, "it is true that I've had guests from the monastery."

Zehan turned to consider him.

"My embroidery work is known across the city, and they asked me to make a vestment for the High Priest, as a gift for him."

"While an honorable thought," Zehan said, "only vestments provided by the Church of Œron are acceptable. I want to know what monks you worked with so that they can be chastised."

"I shall have to consult my wife. She wrote their names down in her personal ledger, which she keeps with her."

"Very well. As we do in all investigations, my Praetors are going to conduct a search of your house."

He made a motion, and the two Praetors moved to the back rooms.

"I hope you do not already have a date set for your wedding," Zehan said.

"Wedding?" Hanen replied.

"To our host's daughter."

"They've only just begun to court," Abgenas said.

"Good, because none of the priests in the city have been approved to conduct weddings. As the spring storms break, clerical administrators and judicators will be sent from the south. It will be some time before wedding bells are heard again."

"Spring is the time for weddings," Abgenas said. "There are many other couples who would like to be married in the near future."

"If they have gone down the path of sin over the winter and wish to legitimize their actions under the blanket of marriage, then perhaps it is better for their secrets to be uncovered. There are no children in Œron born outside of wedlock. If that is not the case here in Mahndür, examples must be made."

"What examples?"

"The children shall be given to the care of the Praetors, of course."

The two Praetors came out of the back rooms in a quick rush.

"Provost," one said.

Zehan perked up. A sinking feeling settled on Hanen.

"There was something under one of the beds. An ynfald. It was rustling nastily at us."

"Are you afraid of an ynfald?"

The two Praetors gave each other embarrassed looks.

A fourth Praetor came marching up the stairs.

"Provost," the new arrival said, "we've been called to another incident."

"What is it?"

"A meeting of men. In the Smokehouse district."

A wicked smile played across Zehan's face. "The insurrection we spoke of with the king?"

"We believe so."

"Speaking of ynfalds," Zehan said, turning to Abgenas, "I've a rebel who has been quick to give me trouble this week. Given your age, I doubt you'll leave the city. I should like to question you more about these illegal holy vestments, but it must wait for now."

He turned to Hanen.

"And you, boy, are to arrive at the monastery in three days' time, having memorized the thirtieth chapter of the *Book of the True Path*, which will instill in you a proper respect for our Holy Order. You're also to pay a fine of a silver dukt and a copper nit for each missed word when you recite the chapter for me—in Œronzi."

"I..." Hanen opened his mouth in protest.

Zehan silenced him with a raised hand. "My instructions shall see you safely on the path to Lomïn. It is my sole charge to see all safely on that path, lest you add to the brimming number of souls in Noccitan."

He turned and marched down the stairs, the other Praetors behind him.

Hanen and Abgenas sat in silence for some time. Then the old man stood and walked into the back room, where Hanen heard the him muttering the all clear to those in hiding.

"He looked me directly in the eye," Marn said as he walked into the room. "Had Whisper not been there, we would be on our way to prison now."

"There is much to do after you leave," Abgenas said to Dorian. "You were not in the room, but the Praetor declared he'll not allow the young to marry. Any children born out of wedlock are to be taken by the Chalicians."

Dorian scoffed. "The Crysalas Vaults shall be brimming with babies, then."

"Perhaps we can see some off to Morraine," Abgenas said.

Then he turned and placed a hand on the shoulder of Hanen, who looked up at him.

"See my girls safely from this Pantheon-forsaken city," Abgenas said. Abgenas was the most serious Hanen had ever seen him. The older man reached out and placed something on the table before the young man. Someone gasped. Hanen turned to see a heavy qavylli medallion.

"I paid you that," Hanen said.

"And I'm giving it back. To help with your escape."

Hanen stood and took the old man's hand.

"While I am glad to see my daughter take an interest in you, any fatherly threats I might make are a bit empty right now. I want to see her away and safe and you're the one to do it."

"I have only good intentions with your daughter."

"As you're traveling with monks and one of the highest authorities on Kallattai, I have no fear for her," Abgenas said. "Runah can be erratic," he added with a smile. "I don't doubt that she and your tall, black-haired friend will give you a good ribbing."

"I'd be surprised if they didn't."

Marn stood by the back door, holding Hanen's travel sack.

"Son," Marn said, holding out a gray monk's robe. Hanen pulled the robe on and then put the Black Sentinel cloak over it.

The others did the same with the cloaks Hanen had provided them from a stash of spare and disrepaired cloaks from Blackiron. Then they slipped down the stairs and into one of the halls behind the Grotto Market, where a few torches were lit. Hanen led the way toward the back of the Grotto, where the hall turned behind the fountain square. A short figure sat on a bench by a torch, wrapped in a cloak. When he glanced their way, Hanen signed for the others to pause, and when the figure stood and began to walk toward them, he turned toward the stairs that would lead up to the Smokers District.

"Wait," the figure said in a thick accent. "Azho! Hanen!"

Hanen paused, and turned. "Zhag?"

"Indeed," the hrelgren said, lowering his hood and revealing a gaunt face. "My friend," the hrelgren said, "you should not be out after curfew."

"The same could be said for you," Hanen said.

"Well, I have little choice."

"Where are the others?" Hanen asked.

"They left for home several weeks ago. I stayed to finish up some things, but got caught in the city when the Praetors arrived."

"Caught?"

"I am considered a lesser citizen even by those who live here. To the occupying Praetors, I am just a rodent locked in the ship's hold."

"I am sorry to hear that. They'll not let you leave?"

The hrelgren shook his head. "Where are you off to in black cloaks in the middle of the night?"

"Leaving," Hanen said.

"Perhaps you ought to come with us," Dorian said, stepping forward. "I seem to recall that you were among our company at the Solstice ceremony."

As Dorian lowered his hood, Zhag's face lit up in a smile.

"I never forget a face," Zhag said, "Holy Prima Pater. It is an honor to meet you. I am Zhag *rm* Tellis, of Tach'eyn." The hrelgren gave a flourishing bow.

"You are the only hrelgren in the city, then?" Dorian asked. Zhag nodded.

"Then you will come with us. We're leaving the city."

"I have little to offer," the hrelgren said.

"You have a bright smile and a sharp eye," Dorian said. "Your god has touched you, and I have no doubt his blessing lies upon you."

"One would hardly think so," Zhag said. "My luck has been poor of late."

"You find us here," Dorian said. "That is no luck. It is providence. Take hold of the offered escape."

Zhag's smile grew. "Gladly."

To their surprise, he turned and began walking away.

Then he looked back. "Come!"

The line of black-cloaked figures followed.

"Where are you taking us?" Hanen asked.

"Tell me first of your plan to leave the city."

"Only that we're to head west."

"I know of a way out," Zhag said.

"Why have you not taken it?"

"I would fare poorly in the cold chill of the surrounding countryside on my own. I've stayed here, begging. But now, with friendship promised on the road, I will survive."

"I don't understand."

"We hrelgren are social people. A hrelgren left in isolation will shrivel and die as a fruit forgotten on the vine. Imprisonment for being a foreigner in these lands would surely see me dead. Traveling the road alone in the early spring up north here, I would likely be arrested."

"I did not know the hrelgrens can't abide isolation."

"Few know this about us."

He came to another set of stairs and stopped.

"At the top of these stairs we'll come out to a row of inns, all owned by the Farrier Guild. They're chatty. But they've also conveyed, even to me, that they do not like the trouble the Praetors bring."

Hanen could hear laughter at the top of the stairs.

"They've little respect for the curfew and have set up a small barricade that they are claiming marks their 'homes' so they can stay out later than most."

"Show the way then, friend," Dorian said.

Whisper shot up the stairs ahead of them and out the open door at the top, into the torchlight. Hanen turned down the stairs.

"You're cloaked as Sentinels," he said. "Walk with purpose. We're Zhag's hired bodyguards tonight."

They crested the staircase and walked into the light. It was an uplifting surprise to see people out for an evening, moving between inns, with torchlight and bonfires in the town square. People cajoled each other and drank deeply of their ales.

"Why have the Praetors not come to clear this out?"

"There are a handful of other squares protesting in this way," Zhag said. "They've stopped two gatherings, but they've allowed this one and the one in the square before the City Guildhall, although they've posted Praetors to stand watch. Some suspect they're tolerating the protests so they can observe those who are pushing against their sanctions."

They came to the other end of the square. A Voktorra stood there, eying them.

"Where are you going, Coin Cloaks?" the young guard said.

"They are escorting me to my inn. In the Smokehouse District," Zhag said.

"Your name?"

The hrelgren hesitated.

"Name," the Voktorra demanded.

The hrelgren turned to Hanen and motioned him forward.

"Terlit ni Teth," Hanen lied, stepping forward. "And I am the Black Sentinel Kalle Bann."

The Voktorra took out a ledger and wrote down the names in charcoal.

"There is a fine for moving about the city after curfew."

"The Praetors have said nothing of fines," Hanen said, "only that it was disallowed. We'll take our chances."

"The fines are placed by the Voktorra Guild. Pay the fine, and we'll keep our knowledge of your passing a secret."

"So, a bribe then," Hanen said.

The young guard gaped. "I... No. It's a fine."

"A bribe to keep quiet," Hanen corrected again. "Listen, if you speak with Captain Navien just tell him that he can take what he owes me and use that for his bribe."

The young guard moved to block them from moving, but Hanen stepped forward, the other black cloaks coming up behind him.

"He knows where to find me," Hanen said. "He can take it up with me."

"Kalle Bann, was it?" the Voktorra asked.

Hanen nodded then began walking down the street.

Once he and his comrades turned a corner and were out of sight, he removed his cloak.

"Let's switch to being monks," Hanen said.

Thus, they began to move as a tight group of gray-clad brothers, the hrelgren hiding in the middle. The streets were empty, with only the rare curtain fluttering as nosy people peeked out at them. They came to the wall of the city, with a torchlit gate a hundred yards away, where several guards stood chatting.

"What now?" Marn asked.

"I doubt we can go directly through the gate," Dorian said.

"We won't need to," Zhag said. He walked over to the wall.

"They shut off the water from the reservoir at night, to stop it from freezing in the aqueduct, so the watercourse beneath the warehouse here is empty."

"How many know of this?" Dorian asked.

"I'm not sure, but I've seen a handful of washerwomen use it to leave the city at random times."

Zhag came to the door of the cold-storage warehouse and gave a light tap. No one came to the door. Hanen glanced toward the gate and saw one of the guards peering at them, trying to see in the dark.

"We need to get in quickly," he muttered.

His father glanced toward the gate and nodded.

Zhag knocked again.

"Hello?" the peering guard called. "Hey Norik, do you see something?"

Another guard came and stood by the first, holding a torch.

"Everyone close your eyes," Zhag said.

Whisper padded out from the group, standing twenty feet from the monks as they pressed up against the wall.

"It's too low," one guard said. "Probably a mongrel. Nothing to worry about."

The guards returned to their post, and Whisper came back to the monks.

"Good boy," Hanen said, patting the ynfald.

The door opened a crack.

"Who's calling at this time of the night?" a woman's voice asked. Dorian pressed himself to the door.

"By Grissone's grace, and the Mother's blessing," he said, "will you allow an old man to use your secret path to escape the city?"

"I... don't know you," the woman said.

"No," Dorian said. "But you knew my wife, the Matriarch Superioris."

The woman gasped. "Prima Pater?"

"Yes," he said.

She opened the door wider and let them all in.

"How did you know to come here? The others who left the city said you knew nothing of this way out."

"It seems," Dorian said, waving toward the hrelgren, "the gods had plans to help us escape this way."

The woman looked at the hrelgren.

"I inferred that there was a way to leave the city in the middle of the night," Zhag explained. "I've not given away your secret save to those who leave the city with me this night."

She sighed in relief and turned.

"Come this way. We've not got much time before the aqueduct begins to flow."

They followed her down a flight of stairs to a large pool of water. Barrels floated in the depths, tied up with ropes.

"What is this?" Dorian asked.

"The cold water keeps the contents of the barrels cool. Some merchants pay fees to store their perishable goods here."

"Even in the summer?"

"It stays cool here. We've also several icehouses in the city, where much riskier goods such as unsalted meat are kept. Here, it is mostly barrels of beer and wine."

She circled the pool and came to a grate. "You'll take the empty aqueduct for a half a mile without a torch, as there are guards at the top. That is all the help I can offer."

"Thank you," Dorian said.

He turned to the others. "Let's get out of this city."

13

SPRING ROAD

Treacherous path continued,

Across the muddy flow,

With each step he grew weary,

The weight of world and woe,

His constant mental foe.

—THE TRAVELER

Runoff from Crysania's Massif washed out parts of the road as they traveled on from the rendezvous point with the woman at the lighthouse inn. Everyone took turns riding the four sleipnirs they had acquired, and Marn and Rallia walked alongside one another most days, deep in conversation and in the joy of each other's company. The other monks spent the days walking with the Prima Pater, lost in theological conversation. Hanen often walked alongside Alodda, helping her and her sister over the fast and frigid streams cutting through the road.

"When we last passed this way, the road had been recently cared for," Hanen said as he helped Alodda over a large stone. "Of course, that was before the onset of winter."

"Maybe they repair it every year," Alodda offered.

"Most likely," Hanen replied. "Although I wonder whose

responsibility it is? We haven't seen many villages for the last three days."

"In Mahn Fulhar, a responsibility like this would be picked up by one of the guilds."

Hanen nodded. "Blackiron had agreed to help improve border crossings once spring came. Those responsibilities were abandoned with the contract."

"I'm sure a lot of things are going to change there. The Chalicians have forbidden the Guild Council to meet."

"I question whether the Paladins knew the Chalicians were coming," Hanen replied.

"If they did, what could they do?"

"Warn people, rather than just leave."

Hanen glanced over at Dorian, who was speaking with one of the monks.

"Do you know that I am from Œron?" the younger monk Nidian said to Hanen from atop a sleipnir. "From Ouiquimon, the theological center of the nation. I barely escaped the country with my life after I spoke up against the Chalician sect. I spent some time in Redot on the run, trying to warn people about the things the Calicians have done in Œron in the past two generations, but eventually I had to flee to Mahndür. There were rumors our High Priest, as head of the Abedürian branch of the church, was coming to an arrangement with the Chalicians, but we would never have believed that he would wholeheartedly give over the Abecinian church to them."

"What are you getting at?" Hanen asked.

"Only that no one could be ready for this."

Hanen turned to Dorian, who rode alongside Marn. "Why are we going south toward the Chalicians? We might have been out of the country faster traveling to Morraine."

"We are retracing our steps," Dorian said. "You'll recall the events at the Green Bastion. I believe they are connected to that night at the Crysalas Convent."

"The attack by Ghoré with his furies had nothing to do with Searn. Ghoré didn't have the cloak."

"And yet," Dorian said, "Searn used the cloak to try and attack Ghoré. At least that is what Brother Brazstein said."

"It is not far from here to Zebüdé," the monk Nidian said. "Some of us could journey there and catch a ship east."

"I travel south toward Limae," Dorian said. "It is better we travel together. There is safety in numbers, and I imagine the Clouws wish to honor their promise to Abgenas and see his girls to safety. It is said the early spring weather makes travel from Zebüdé difficult at times, and I'm sure the Chalicians have already secured the city. Düran is the most logical destination for us."

Hanen gave him a furtive look.

"Hanen," Dorian said. "The events at the Green Bastion and the events of that night when Searn died are seared in my mind, too. But we must face them, for they raise far too many questions. More importantly, the gods have their reasons for all of us to travel the same road—or else why would you have played such a role in my escape? I'll not question the Pantheon."

Hanen turned to look down the road. They were coming to a stream that flowed over the road from a heavy, rushing waterfall. Dorian and the others dismounted, and the latter directed the sleipnir one by one over the flood. Hanen and Dorian crossed last.

"Hanen," the old man said, putting a hand on his shoulder. "I am not pressuring you to continue with me. I'm only saying that it seems we were brought together for a reason. If a guided journey sees us safely away from the oppressive Chalicians, it is best to follow it. Fighting against the wills of the gods usually ends in tragedy."

"Why must they inflict their wills upon us?"

"Why question it in the first place?"

Hanen stared at Dorian for a long while. "I don't like that they use us, with little explanation. It is demeaning."

"If the king gives a command, do we question it? Or do as he says?"

"He is human. We can understand his motives. The gods, not so much."

"But they are greater than we. They have reasons for their actions. High above us, yes, but sometimes we do as our parents tell us, as children, without understanding. Looking back as older children or adults, we can see their reasoning."

"I suppose."

"I suspect you struggle with the same questions of faith we all do, at one time or another. We feel, as we grow in body and mind, we begin to the understand the world, becoming privy to the intentions of the gods. But we shall never reach that height, and we must come to understand that."

"What if the arrival of the Chalicians was ordained by the

Pantheon?"

"It is something I have wondered," admitted Dorian. "Yet we can compare the events of our history against the holy scriptures, and see that they are in opposition to the Pantheon, just as there is opposition that the Black Coterie brings against us."

"If such a dark sect rises now in the Abecinian Church, how is this not an even greater issue, questioning the validity of the entire church?"

"Aben is known for a general lack of interaction with his church. His is a path to discover and follow. If the path you follow leads to darkness, and you will not leave it, then you must assume that responsibility. The church itself, and the following of Aben, merely reveals who you are."

"What are you saying?"

"You follow a path set before you by a servant of the dark gods—Searn. This backtracking, this revisiting of events that occurred, is a way to find the original path you left. I welcome your company and hope we can learn from one another. Join me, and we'll shine light onto the dark corners together."

"What do you hope to uncover?" Hanen asked.

"The origin of this Motean cult."

"What do you think awaits us at the Green Bastion?"

"I have suspicions about Ghoré, the 'Deathless Beast' as he called himself. I need to see his remains."

Hanen held the reins of the last sleipnir for Dorian to mount and watched as he rode on ahead to join two monks singing a hymn. Rallia fell back alongside Hanen as they walked.

"What were you two talking about?"

"Why we're on this journey together. Apparently, he wants to go to the Green Bastion and exhume Ghoré's remains. He has some hunch he needs to follow up on."

"This is probably the safest path south," Rallia said.

"Why is that?"

"The Chalicians are more likely to use the coastal roads, not this inland route. It sounds like crossing the Lupinfang by boat is risky too."

"You mean with the war brewing there?"

Rallia nodded. "You'd have been pressed into service there, being from Garrou."

"Limae will always be a free country, since they refuse to side with anyone," Hanen conceded. "If the Chalicians try to take

Düran, it will cost them a lot of time. Of course, we'll have to go and report to the headquarters of the Black Sentinels in Limae."

"I hope none of the Sentinels who were at the battle with Searn have been there to spread bad rumors."

"I just want to get us somewhere safe, maybe back to Edi."

"Let's get back to Edi, then, and we can decide what's next for you and Alodda."

"What do you mean?" Hanen asked.

"You don't really think she came just to escape? She'd have stayed with her parents if it wasn't for you. They wanted to get her to safety, and you've proven to be a good man."

Hanen glanced up the road to Alodda and her sister as they joined in singing the refrain of the hymn. She glanced back and smiled. Hanen returned the smile then touched his satchel, feeling the bulge of the boneshroud and both journals hidden there, and grimaced internally to himself.

"I'm sorry I didn't tell you about Father," Hanen muttered.

"He said you had an argument when last you saw each other," Rallia replied. "So I understand why you haven't."

"Did he say what we argued about?"

"No. Apparently whatever you said to him gave him pause. He worries that you were right."

Hanen glanced at Rallia then back at the road.

"Were you right?" Rallia asked.

"I don't know," Hanen said. "I'm still working through that."

"But you'll share with me when you're ready?"

"Yes."

Rallia smiled, although Hanen didn't feel it was very genuine.

"I have my own secrets too," Rallia said.

"What do you mean?"

"I met someone out west, before I was arrested. I'm still processing what it meant."

Hanen just nodded in reply.

The following morning they rounded the curve of a mountain slope, looking south onto the valley of the Green Bastion. Both the burned and living trees were bare, but a few mountain flowers had begun to poke up.

"I hope this journey is not a burden for you," Marn said, coming to walk alongside Hanen.

"What do you mean?"

"You and I did not part on good terms when we spoke in

midwinter, and even on the road you've not said much to me."

"I've had a lot on my mind," Hanen replied with a sigh.

"I like Alodda," he offered. "You'd do well by her."

Hanen nodded.

"I... I'm proud of you," Marn said.

"Why?"

"I shared with you our family history, and not a few days later this incident at the Crysalas Convent occurred. I don't fully understand what happened, but Rallia says you stepped up and took charge."

"I still don't fully believe what that woman told you."

"It was my mother, whether or not you believe me," Marn said.

"It's hard to believe."

"The question is, what happened to that cloak of darkness. I suppose someone got it and is perhaps using it," Marn said.

Hanen looked away and shrugged. "You could be right."

Dorian had pulled up at the top of the final descent into the holdings of the Green Bastion. Everyone else, following behind him, drew to a halt.

"Before we descend, I'd like to ask you all a favor," Dorian said. "Please do not refer to me as Prima Pater or Dorian Mür. I know they will likely recognize me, but it is best that you refer to me by a different name."

"And what name is that?" The monk Guarin said.

"Brother Nethendel Unteel."

"Did you say Nethendel?" Marn asked. "My grandfather's name was Nethen."

"Was it?" Dorian said with a smile. "Another happy occurrence. It was the name of my wife's brother. He was my best friend in childhood and during the wars. You do remind me of him in some ways."

"Perhaps they are one and the same," Marn said.

"I like that thought," Dorian said, giving a broader smile.

Dorian turned and the two of them walked alongside one another.

"You've been quieter of late," Alodda said.

"I'm sorry," Hanen said.

"No need to apologize. You look as though you're struggling with something."

"This place we're going is the site of an attack on us by an ex-Sentinel who went mad. What's more, he was no longer the man who served with us."

"What do you mean?"

"He swears he was cursed by the Mad Gift-Giver, and had at his command wyloths and furies."

Alodda shivered. "I hate furies."

"I don't see many of them scurrying about in Mahn Fulhar."

"They hide away in the winter," she said. "I caught one or two of them toward the end of autumn. But in the summer, they're the worst. It's one reason I wear Porumarian oil, even if it is costly."

"Do they not like it?"

"That's the rumor, anyway."

They arrived on the valley floor, where a couple of Paladins watered the small saplings planted in the cleared, burned-out landscape. They wore only their gorgets and brown robes, and they looked up as the group approached them.

"Greetings in the name of Grissone," Dorian said.

"And his father, High King in Lomïn!" Marn added.

"Hello, Brother!" one of them replied, rising. He squinted, a hint of recognition washing over his face, and approached them with a broad smile.

"Pater Minoris Averin, I believe," Dorian said. "I am Primus Nethendel Unteel. I have arrived with several monks of Aben from Mahn Fulhar. We seek solace for a short time, then we'll be on our way."

"Of course," the Pater Minoris said. "Please come with me."

He ushered them to the barn the Sentinels were staying in the last time they were there.

"This will serve you well, I think? And keep you away from prying eyes?" he said as they all walked in and put their things down. "Of course, we can provide private quarters in the monastery for the women."

He closed the door and threw his arms around Dorian, a sob coming out.

"Prima Pater. I heard a rumor that you had died, and I know for a fact that Nichal Guess is now Prima Pater."

"He is the Acting Prima Pater until he can be elected by the brethren at Pariantür. I take it not all news has come to you, then, if you are not aware of these details. Did you receive a message to leave?"

"I don't understand."

"Nichal sent messages to all Bastions to leave our holdings and return to Pariantür."

"We received some information, but not that. Why would we leave?"

"Then you are not aware of the Motean Schism occurring?"

Averin pursed his lips. "I've not heard the word Motean since I was a lad. Has that heresy reared its head again?"

"You and I have much to speak about," Dorian said. "Away from the others."

"I am happy to arrange it. But first rest, enjoy a fire in the hearth while I see to it that you receive food from the kitchen, then you and I can speak."

The stable-like guesthouse was unchanged from their last visit. Hanen found the side room he and Rallia had shared, clean and ready for guests. Rallia left with Ophedia, Alodda, and her sister, while the monks found beds and laid down for a short rest. Marn came to stand at the entrance to Hanen's room, Whisper sitting next to him.

"I'm going to go and fellowship with the other monks. After a short rest we'll probably say midday prayers."

"That's fine, Hanen replied. "I need some time to myself, anyway."

Marn turned and walked away, Whisper following him. Hanen closed the door, dropping the wooden bar into place to lock himself in, after which he opened the satchel and pulled out the boneshroud. Taking a seat on the ground, he pulled the hood over his head and retrieved the journals; then he held the flat piece of bone to his lips and whispered into it.

"Searn."

A moment later words bloomed over the surface. *Why so long away?*

"Can you feel time?"

Of course. That hasn't changed. But I don't sleep, so I don't quite know how long it has been.

"A couple of weeks. We're at the Green Bastion now."

Why?

Hanen explained what had happened in Mahn Fulhar and their journey south.

The old man means to look at the skull of Ghoré, then. He will find what he is looking for.

"Which is?"

A hole in the middle of the skull, from which I pulled the chain link.

"Then you did incorporate Ghoré into the boneshroud? Is he in the shroud now?"

Very likely. It was his link that allowed me to have control over the Shades.

"What about the ability to see in the dark? Where did that come from?"

Found that one out, did you? It was a gift from the death of one of Wyv's Watchers. I didn't have the time to determine what ability the death of the Archimandrite gave the shroud.

"Were you behind his poisoning?" Hanen asked.

Happenstance.

Hanen got the niggling feeling that Searn had just lied.

"But you did kill him, in the end."

It was necessary.

Hanen knew that was the truth.

"Why?"

You'll reach that answer as you continue to read my journal. Suffice to say, just as the soldier agrees to die for his country, those that died to make the boneshroud did so for a greater good, even if they did not know it.

A knock came to the door. Hanen dropped the hood back off his head.

"Who is it?"

"Marn. The Prima Pater is back. They're bringing us food."

"I'll be a moment."

"Take your time, son."

Is this conversation at an end? the bloody words on the bone said.

Hanen ignored the words and put the bone into his satchel along with the boneshroud, and hid it all under the usual cloth. Then he opened the door and came out into the common area, where Dorian sat by the fire, his boots off and his feet up. The monks sat with him talking quietly. The door to the stables opened, and the women all entered, food in their hands, two Paladins joining them.

The smile on Dorian's face faded as a middle-aged Paladin with bags under his eyes entered at the rear of the group. The Paladin began to set the table without seeming to have noticed Dorian. Dorian rose from his seat and circled the room to stand behind him. Hanen watched this interplay curiously.

"Primus Loth," Dorian uttered.

The Paladin froze and slowly turned, wincing as Dorian took hold of his robe.

"Get the Pater Minoris," Dorian said to the room.

Rallia rushed out of the guest house.

Loth tried to put up a fight, but Dorian Mür was surprisingly strong. The other Paladin who helped set the table looked on in horror. He began to sign something Hanen could not understand.

"This Paladin," Dorian said, dragging Loth around the table to a chair by the fire, "is a heretic who somehow escaped imprisonment in Mahn Fulhar. He was part of the group of Paladins who killed several members of our order. Watch over him until your Pater Minoris arrives and we can discuss what to do with him."

14

GREEN BASTION

Zephyr and Scepter finally suspect me, and the Heptagrammaton has disappeared. I believe Zephyr has hidden it in the Veld, and I have not been able to enter that realm. It may be my one failing— that I have the imagination but not the skill to do so. I shall have to find another way to journey between realms.

— JOURNAL OF SEARN VETURRES, ENTRY FIFTEEN

The Pater Minoris entered the stables with two more Paladins, each in full-armored regalia, hammers held at attention. Dorian stood and gave them a nod as looks of recognition flashed across their faces and they dropped to their knees.

"Up," Dorian said. "I forfeited my authority. I'm merely another Paladin today."

They rose hesitantly.

"What is the trouble?" Averin asked, glancing over at Loth, bound in a chair with Hanen and Rallia's ropes.

"It seems you have not only a Motean heretic in your midst, but an escaped convict at that."

"Primus Loth?" Averin asked. "What do you mean?"

"When did he arrive at the bastion?"

"A month ago, perhaps. He came from Varea, assigned here by order from Haven."

"He did not come from Varea," Dorian said. "Do you know St. Nonn?"

"Of course. Excelsior Rann was raised here in the Green Bastion before he took up the hammer."

"Loth had killed him."

Averin's expression turned to horror. "Why?"

"Our order is at a crossroads. Fellow brothers are choosing whether to continue in the faith, or give their souls over to Moteanism. The Moteans, under the guidance of the now-deceased Pater Gladen, took the Rose Convent in Mahn Fulhar, declaring outright war against those of us who were stationed in the bastion across the field. During that conflict, the Moteans held in our cells, including Loth, escaped and joined in the fight."

"And in this..."Averin said with quavering voice, "Pater Gladen died?"

"No, he turned back to the light before he was killed, being visited by our god, Grissone."

Averin turned to Loth. "You brought encouragement and even insight to us, but now I realize that we have been deceived. I ought to have noticed the signs of Motean influence. My older brother was one of your number before he died long ago, or else I might not know what a Motean is."

"How little you truly understand," Loth said.

"No doubt he'll be more honest now," Dorian said, "betraying his spite of the gods, as he did when last we spoke."

"Spoke?" Loth replied coolly. "You put me in chains in the cold for days, with little chance to speak to you before I was dragged away. Besides, what authority do you have, Dorian Mür? You've given your authority away."

"You'll keep your insults to a minimum," Pater Averin said. "You submitted to my authority when you chose to be a member of this community."

Dorian added, "I've three Black Sentinels who have the authority to execute outlaws, so don't think I can't threaten you."

Hanen shot Rallia a look. She glanced at him in shock.

"I am open to a discourse with you," Dorian said to Loth, "but you must be reasonable."

Loth glowered at him.

Dorian waved to the table. "Let us sit. There is no point in talking on an empty stomach."

Marn walked around the table and pulled out a chair for

Dorian. Alodda guided her sister to the furthest end of the table, where they sat down and quietly filled their plates.

"Go sit with her," Rallia said. "I'm sure this is overwhelming for both of them."

He pulled up a chair next to Alodda.

"What is happening?" she asked him.

"That man, Loth, was involved in the incident at the Rose Convent."

"What incident?"

"I'll explain later."

"Admittedly," Dorian said as he took a piece of roasted bird and placed it on a trencher of dark bread, "you have much less rage than when last we spoke, although there is still spite in your tone and glare."

"You would have me executed."

"You are a murderer."

"You killed men as well, during the Protectorate Wars," Loth said. "You are no less guilty."

"Indeed," Dorian replied. "The faces of those who fell are burnt upon my mind and soul, and I will answer for them when I pass from this life. I openly admit that I have regret and guilt upon my conscience. Do you?"

"Those who fall do so for the cause, or because they oppose it. I have no guilt, only determination to do the right thing."

"That is what I thought," Dorian said, waving the meatless bone in his hand. He took a drink then looked at Pater Averin. No one else had taken a bite.

"Go on, then," Dorian said. "Eat. We will likely be at this discourse for some time. I also find that if we treat such proceedings with too much pomp, it sours the stomach."

He took a handful of dried berries and nuts and stood, beginning to pace the room.

"You'll note his lack of any shame for his actions," Dorian said. "This is the sign of a zealot, who either lacks conscience or feels that his ends justify the means."

"Dorian," Pater Averin said, "it could also be that his hatred masks his conscience."

"I agree," Dorian said.

"Primus Unteel," Marn said.

"Yes, Brother Clouw?"

"Is this why we fear the Chalicians?"

"All kinds of men give in to zeal, from the merchant who puts great weight upon his gold to the mercenary who, by dark means, creates a shroud from the bones of those he has killed. Indeed, the Chalicians who hail from a nation that has wholeheartedly given itself over to zeal of law-guided authority in those same Chalicians—all of these are equal. Humanity's covetousness and pride are the chief roots of all its evils."

"Yet you hold Pariantür as an ideal to attain," Loth said. "There is pride in that as well."

"As you can see, Pater Averin, he is no Paladin of the Hammer anymore. He is lost, and hiding as a predator in your flock. He can no longer see Pariantür for what is, nor see the vows for the voluntary humility that they are."

"I am appalled," Averin said, staring at Loth, "and ashamed, really."

"Don't be ashamed," Dorian said. "Be courageous, and let us discuss what we shall do next."

"What is it you need while you are here?" Averin said. "On the run as you are."

"I need to see the remains of the creature that commanded the Furies. I need to see the skull."

"I'll have it dug up. What shall we do with Loth?"

"Keep him sequestered. Send word to Nichal Guess in Boroni or Bortali, and ask what he would have you do. If you intend to remain here, know that our holdings are being made forfeit by the King of Mahndür and the High Priest Klent Rigal. I suspect this to be true in all countries that swear fealty to the Church of the Common Chalice. You may find yourself cast out by Praetors."

"Will you stay as our guest?"

"I cannot stay. I expect the Chalicians plan to take me captive. My death at their hands would not end in public martyrdom, but in a quiet event."

"We could see you off to Boroni, if you wish."

"It is best that I go south toward Limae, I think. I've another mission I am on that must be continued."

"Brothers," Averin motioned to two Paladins nearby. "Please imprison Loth. I'll decide what to do with him later."

The two Paladins grabbed Loth by the arms and took him out of the guest house.

"I hope you don't think me a Motean myself," Averin said.

"A Motean would more likely seek to change the subject,"

Dorian said. "Are you?"

"As I said, my own brother was one. I had hoped it a philosophy that died on the vine."

"Then know that you and your bastion here are an island in a sea of turmoil, and you, as its captain, must decide the best course to take."

"We shall remain here. The Green Bastion has stood and shall continue to stand. Even if I must pay an extorted fee, I'll negotiate our stay."

"We will not remain much longer, ourselves," Dorian said. "I intend to take my company to Limae and uncover the dark secrets kept there."

"What do you mean by 'dark secrets'?" Hanen asked.

"Do you all know the history of the Protectorate Wars?" Dorian asked those in the room.

Alodda and her sister shook their heads, along with Rallia and Ophedia.

"There was a figure known as the 'Warlord' who wore a suit of black armor that was supposedly impervious to damage. When he fell in the war, his famous armor vanished and I charged a group of Paladins to seek it out. Although they failed to discover the armor, it appears to have been found, or at least that's what the events in Mahn Fulhar would indicate. Rather than reporting it, its new owners have unlocked the secrets of the armor to use it for their own ambitions. I must therefore go to Limae and do what I ought to have done in the first place—seek it out and destroy it myself. But I am an old man, and I cannot do it alone."

He turned to Hanen. "I'd like you to help me—to exonerate your work as an honorable Black Sentinel. Do what Searn promised, but undermine his true intentions. Help me locate and destroy this dark armor."

Rallia nudged Hanen. Hanen looked at his sister.

"It will be dangerous," Dorian added.

Hanen glanced around the table. "I agreed to see you safely away from Mahndür. If what you're saying is true and Limae is dangerous, then we ought to decide a different route so we can guarantee the safety of Alodda and her sister, as I promised."

"We have some days to travel south for you to decide," Dorian said. "I am going to Limae, whether you accompany me or not. We can share the road until the Dead Pass, where we will either continue together or part."

Hanen awakened early the next morning, when it was still dark, and left the stables with Whisper at his heels. His mind was filled with the flames of that night, the night of Ghoré's attack. The rustle of a few budding leaves on the trees brought to mind the whip of furies flying around him. He pulled the Sentinel cloak over his shoulders tighter, to fight back against the cold. Rallia stood in the clearing where Ghoré had descended upon them and Searn had come to confront him, wearing the boneshroud. She stood holding her staff, not moving, until Whisper slunk by her feet and she visibly relaxed, crouching next to him.

"He's been such a comfort these past months," Rallia said. She stood and looked around, letting out a long sigh. "You know, I forget—or just didn't want to remember—that it was Searn who was there in that cloak, accosting Ghoré."

"He told me that it had been stolen from him. When he told me what it was in Mahn Fulhar."

"Why even believe him when he said what it was? A cloak made from chain links of bone is macabre. That he was wearing something he had made himself is even worse."

"He said it was made from animal bone."

"If someone has to make an excuse for even that, then it's already suspect." She reached out and put a hand on his shoulder. "Whatever happened, it's behind us. Are we going with Dorian? It sounds exciting."

"What do you mean?"

"An old Paladin offers a chance to go hunting for some mysterious artifact? Who wouldn't take the chance at the adventure?"

"I don't know if we can afford it."

"Oh, come on," Rallia said. "The Dülars gave back the qavylli gold. You know Alodda would follow you."

"No," Hanen said.

"What do you mean?"

"I'm not going to endanger her."

"So what will you do?"

"If I follow the Prima Pater, then she goes with the monks into Düran, where it's safe."

"And who will protect her on the way?"

"You and Ophedia."

"I'm not leaving you," Rallia said. "I'd love to continue with Father, but no. If you join Dorian, then so do I."

She put her arm through Hanen's and turned them back toward the bastion.

"You're not going to stay here and run through your practice?"

"Not this morning," she said. "Let's go and see if we can rummage up something to eat."

"Why does this sort of thing keep happening to us?" Hanen asked.

"What do you mean?"

"We lose our master to those brigands only to be taken in by Searn and the Black Sentinels. Then we're forced out on the road by Thadar only to be stuck behind enemy lines with fallen Paladins, and now the Chalicians."

"Yet we've made a good name for ourselves in Edi. We've made good friends in Mahndür. You found a loyal ynfald as a companion. You have a girl who cares for you. You're only focusing on the bad."

"You only offer the good. Not the why."

"Maybe the gods have simply blessed us with the good."

"And what if the dark gods brought about the bad?"

"We're not cursed," Rallia said.

"Aren't we?"

"No."

"Then what should we do?"

"The right thing."

"Which is?"

"Get down," Rallia muttered.

"What?" Hanen said as Rallia pulled him to the ground.

Three figures slunk out of the door of the bastion and made their way to the edge of the trees.

"Come with me," one of them whispered. "They're going to suspect that one of you let me out."

"We will continue to do what we can to turn the others to the way."

"And will you both remain quiet? Or will you turn each other in?"

"Never," one of them said. "Where will you go?"

"I cannot return to Haven yet. Knowing that the Prima Pater is nearly undefended and on the road, I've a mind to rally some of our number and finish what was started."

They clasped arms, and the other two turned back to the bastion.

"Come on," Rallia said.

"What?" Hanen asked.

"That's Loth. Apparently he is who defiled that bastion where I was arrested, so my imprisonment is partly his fault."

Rallia took off through the soft loam, staff held low. The figure of Loth was easy to follow through the trees. Hanen tried to follow Rallia's quiet steps, and Whisper lived up to his name. When Loth stopped for a moment at a tree, leaning into its shadow, Rallia came within fifteen feet of him. That's when he spun around to face them.

"I thought someone followed me," he said.

"Stand down, Loth," Rallia said.

"Or what? You think I'll go quietly?"

He threw off his cloak, brandishing a short sword in one hand and a knife in the other.

"You could come with me," he said, a hint of desperation in his voice. "I'll show you both a better way. We Moteans have so much more to offer than the Paladins do."

"We don't need what you offer," Rallia said. "We're better than that."

Loth made the first move, which was his mistake. Whisper was already underfoot and nipped at his heel, making Loth gasp and look behind him when Rallia charged forward and swung out with her staff, weighted on each end by the banded clubs mounted there. It took him behind the head and he tumbled toward Hanen, who now had his axes out. He took a swing as Loth regained his footing, but not quickly enough. The end of Rallia's staff shot out and took him again, this time behind the ear. He fell face-first into a tree and didn't move.

"Tie him up," Rallia said. "You're better with your knots."

Hanen took the rope Rallia offered and tied Loth's arms behind him, and together they dragged him to the front of the bastion and laid him out there.

"Should we take him in?" Hanen said.

"No, those two who set him free might act against us and set him free again. Let's sit here and wait for morning to arrive properly."

15

INTERLUDE

Seriah left the inn early and began to walk toward the end of town, the scent of Amston Forest washing over her and calling her to its cool paths. A familiar sound came to her—the tinkling of little bells and the clip-clip-clop of six-legged sleipnirs ridden by passing Paladins, in larger numbers than she might have expected. They were obviously in no rush to get where they were going and yet rode with enough purpose to suggest they had a destination.

"Brother Paladin?" she said, going up to a passing rider.

"Holy Nefer," the Paladin replied, pulling out of formation to consider her.

"You come from Piedala Fortress, do you not?" she asked.

"How did you know?"

"I recognize the sound of the bells. I've been a guest at your fortress twice. I've recently come from Mahn Fulhar, and I wondered if one of your number had safely returned from his journey. Pater Minoris Pellian Noss."

The Paladin's saddle creaked as he turned and beckoned to another rider, who left formation and trotted over to the two of them on his sleipnir.

"What do you want, Brother Adjutant?"

"This Nifaran says she met you in Mahn Fulhar."

There was a long pause.

Then the second man gasped. "Nefer Yaledít!"

Seriah smiled.

He dropped from his sleipnir and stood next to her.

"How are you so far south so soon? And before winter has truly given up its hold?"

"It was difficult," Seriah said, "but after the hardships of Mahn Fulhar, the Archimandrite felt it was important to return home."

"Now you're off on a pilgrimage once more. Where do you travel?"

"Aimlessly," Seriah admitted, "although I intended to head in the direction of Temblin."

"That would not be wise," Pater Noss said. "They've declared war on Hraldor, and Minor Hrelgreens will join in soon, I fear."

"But a Nifaran would still be welcome?"

"I do not know if that is the case. We've had some guests from Œron who insisted they'd be entering to bring swift solution to the situation. It appears the Church of the Common Chalice has decided to leave the borders of their diocese in search of establishing control."

"The word in Mahndür was that the High Priest of Aben and the Chalicians had made peace, and that they are unifying their holdings in the west."

"If they're declaring union there, then the authority they claimed over me may be founded."

"What do you mean?" Seriah asked.

"According to a Praetor who visited me, the Paladins of the Hammer are being expunged from the continent. The Praetors of the Chalice seek to take over our holdings before some supposed heresy does."

"The Moteans," Seriah sighed.

"Yes. What do you know of this?"

"I really ought to go," Seriah said.

"I am a scholar of history," Noss said. "I really would like to know."

"We are going in opposite directions," Seriah said.

"Then come as my guest," he said. "You can ride with me, and we can talk."

"Where do you journey to?"

"I intended to visit the Bulwark in Birin and then journey on to visit Brothers in Limae."

"I cannot return to Birin."

"Then some of us shall journey past and avoid the city. I can send others to retrieve what I need from there."

Seriah grimaced and considered what she should do.

"Please, Nefer. I'd like to hear what happened since I left Mahn Fulhar. I expect the Aerie in Limae may be one of the safest places we can journey to. If what the Praetors said is true, and we're to leave for Pariantür, then those of us who choose to stay and defend our holdings will need a place to do so. And the Aerie is the best place for it."

She stepped forward, holding out her hand, and Pater Noss helped her onto the sleipnir. He pulled himself up behind her and goaded the animal back into line with the others.

"Why not Ammar Citadel in Ormach, or St. Hamul in Setera? Doesn't Piedala Fortress answer to St. Hamul?"

"That is well reasoned," Noss said. "Both are agrarian and scholarly. Ammar is too near Œron and will fall to Chalician rule quickly. If the Paladins from Mahn Fulhar are to be sent away, then they will travel east, back through the Northern Scapes to St. Hamul. If we went there, I'm sure we'd all receive orders to join with them in the general retreat."

"When did you leave Mahn Fulhar?" Seriah asked.

"Not long after you and I met," Noss said.

"Then you do not know of what occurred there."

"I would if you told me."

"Dorian Mür is no longer Prima Pater," Seriah said.

"Then who is in charge? Pater Segundus Pír? Guess?"

"Prima Pater Guess sounded the retreat and left Mahn Fulhar, ordering all Sisters of the Crysalas to leave for safer havens."

"But why?"

"I was not able to gather much information before our order left for Birin, but there was an attack by some of your number."

"Our number?"

"Paladins. Under the command of..."

"You can tell me," Pater Noss said. "If there is trouble within our order, I need to know, or else how can I come to a solution?"

"There was a man who traveled with the Monks of Nifara, escorting them to Mahn Fulhar. He turned out to be a traitor."

"To whom?"

"To all. He sought to kill the gods."

"Ha!" Pater Noss said. "You can't kill the gods."

"I believe he might have if he hadn't been stopped," Seriah whispered.

"I'm sorry," Noss said. "I did not intend to make light of what you said. It is just such an audacious claim."

"It does sound foolish, I know. But the traitor Searn VeTurres had the ability to walk unseen by the gods."

"You say 'had.' Does he no longer have the means?"

"No. Because he is dead."

"How?"

"I am told he thrust something through his own eye when he faced defeat at the hands of the champion of Grissone."

"Interesting," Pellian said. "You also say he led a group of Paladins who had gone astray?"

"They called themselves the Order of the Gauntlet."

"That is an odd name. I believe you also said 'Motean'?"

"Yes. I do not understand exactly what that means, but others spoke of them almost as the same as the Order of the Gauntlet."

"Perhaps they are. There are some who even claim the Brothers of my own fortress follow the Motean philosophy, although we are not the zealots the Moteans are."

Seriah's heart sank in her chest. "What is the difference? What do you mean?"

"Motean is a very wide term. It refers to an old philosophical discussion between several Paladins, centuries ago, that explored the interactions between gods and mortals. It sought to answer just what occurs when a god answers a prayer—bestowing power on a mortal."

"Which is why you asked me if Nifara ever performed miracles."

"I did ask you that, didn't I?"

"Yes."

"And has your answer changed?"

"I am not sure," Seriah said.

"That sounds like hesitation," Noss asked. "Very well, I'll leave it at that. Now, the Moteans came to the conclusion that the gods bestowed power on their followers, seen most readily in miracles performed by we Paladins of Grissone. It was believed that once a connection to miraculous power was established, either a residual amount of power was left over and could be harnessed, or the connection was more permanent, and that a line of power established with a god could not be severed, save by death."

"With which line of thought does your own belief align?"

"I am a scholar. The bells we wear are forged from a special metal, imbued with the power of gods, known as skyfall metal. Those who came before me have sought to collect the metal, which is found across the world, but it became the means by which the Destruction came into existence."

"The Destruction?"

"Yes. A cataclysm that took place millennia ago, after the Deceiver betrayed everyone and sought to tear all down. The gods bent their wills and brought the skyfall down on Kallattai, to see the world reshaped and their people reduced in number."

"You say this sky metal is what was used to do so?"

"It is not explicit in any scripture. But 'the sky fell, and the world was shattered.' I have found studies from past millennia that suggest that many of our seas, and the bowls that many cities sit in, are far too round. At their epicenters, or scattered around, are small bits of this particular twisted metal. Thus it has been concluded that these perhaps fell from the sky, and delivered the blows that ruined our world."

"If you are not of the same mind as the Moteans in Mahn Fulhar, perhaps you ought to distance yourself from them. They are obviously a more violent sect."

"May I ask why you are so quick to perceive variations among the Moteans?"

"Because I met you before I ever knew what a Motean was, and you have been a perfectly civil person. Religious organizations are always rife with a variety of philosophies and ideas."

"All aiming at the same purpose," Pater Noss said.

"And what is that?"

"To understand the gods and the reason for our being here."

Seriah smiled to herself.

The sound of the tinny bells surrounded her, and each silvery tinkle that came to her ears touched her mind softly, offering solace in their drone.

PART 3

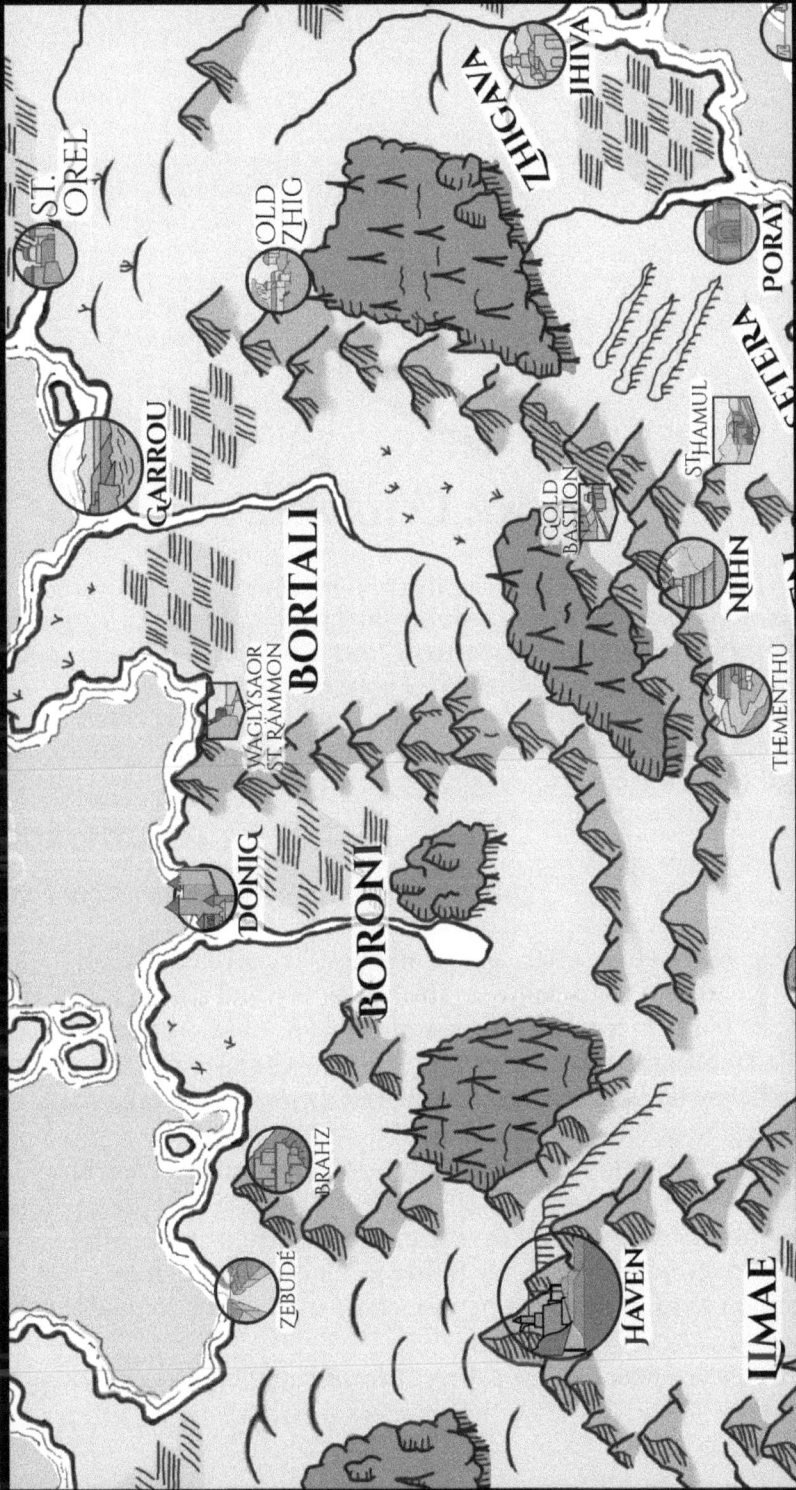

NORTHERN SCAPES

ZHIGAVA

JHIVA

ST. OREL

OLD ZHIG

PORAY

GARROU

ETCETERA

BORTALI

GOLD BASTION

S'THAMUL

WAGLYSAOR
ST. RAMMON

NIIHN

DONIQ

THEMENTHU

BORONI

BRAHZ

ZEBUDÉ

HAVEN

LLMAE

16

WAR COUNCIL

Each Jarl shall hold equal authority with the others. Upon the election of the High Duke, a single Jarl shall hold this title, which comes with respect and a status of first amongst equals. His voice ought to be the voice of fairness. Those Barons of the Lesser House ought to be heard by the duke, and his vote represents not only his interests but those of the Lesser Houses. As all monarchs ought to be, the Duke is a sacrifice for the people.

—*ON DUCAL AUTHORITY,*

FROM THE BORONII CODICES OF LAW

"I stayed here often as a young boy," Jined said, looking around the small inn. The innkeeper had placed tankards of ale in front of the four of them. Katiam's sat untouched, while Didus and Astrid were happy for the change from the muddy runoff they had been forced to boil and drink while on the road from Brahz to the outskirts of Donig.

"As a Jarl's son, why did you stay outside of town?" Astrid asked.

"When I was a young boy, my father was High Duke. After Toschbrecht was elected, my father felt it best not to draw attention to himself, and when we came to town for councils and other business, we stayed here."

"You were how old when Toschbrecht came to power?" Didus asked.

"Six."

"He's held the position since then?"

"Until Sturmguard's recent election, yes."

"That's longer than the reign of most kings," Astrid said, finishing off her ale, pouring half of Katiam's into her tankard, and pushing the rest to Didus. "Toschbrecht didn't do the same for Sturmguard, did he? Staying outside the city to allow Sturmguard pride of place?"

"I doubt it," Jined said. "Toschbrecht is not a humble man. As I understand it, he ruled with an iron fist in the years since I left the country. Sturmguard can be just as stern, but his austerity is tempered by his genuine good nature. "

"Why would that ensure it?" Didus asked.

"The jarls have always preferred a bit of freedom. What Sturmguard always promised to bring was structure. Having been under Toschbrecht for thirty years, especially these last ten years, prepared them for Sturmguard; and I think Sturmguard is what the country needs as it heads toward war."

"Should we arrange for rooms?" Astrid asked Didus. "In case it takes longer for the bastion to reply to us?"

"Probably a good idea," Didus said, rising with her to speak to the innkeeper.

Katiam toyed with the edge of her cloak, peeking underneath. She looked to Jined and offered a weak smile.

"You do that often," Jined said.

"Do what?" Katiam asked.

"Check on whatever it is you have hidden under your cloak. It pertains to the mission you are on, doesn't it?"

She gave a timid smile.

"There is no one near," he said. "Is there anything I ought to know?"

"Only that my goddess gifted something to my care, and our aim is to travel east with it—to speak to others who might have more answers."

"And to avoid the secret getting out."

Katiam nodded.

"It is a dangerous secret, then?"

"It is dangerous to those that know it," Katiam said, "and more important still that the Terrible Enemy not find out."

"You've no need to say anything more, then," Jined said. "I'll not bring it up again."

Astrid and Didus returned and took their seats.

"The innkeeper said he has two rooms available," Didus said. "If they do not send a message by midday, they're ours."

Two figures in brown cloaks entered the inn. They dropped back their hoods, and Jined smiled and stood.

"Over here!" he called.

The two men turned; an identical smile lit both of their dark Seteran faces. Loïc and Cävian, the two Paladins who had been his constant companions in Mahn Fulhar, crossed the room to stand by the table.

Greetings, Brother, Cävian signed. *It has been too long.*

"But I am here," Jined replied. He motioned to the table. "Will you join us?"

Loïc shook his head. *We need to return to the bastion and council. The Prima Pater knows you are coming. You're to be briefed at the bastion before you go yourself.*

"Is there trouble?" Jined asked.

Plenty, Cävian said. *We can tell you more on the way. It is good to see you, Didus,* he signed to the Pater Minoris.

"And you as well," Didus said.

Loïc's eyes started as he turned and saw the two women for the first time.

Cävian turned, his mouth gaping too.

We thought you were both dead! Loïc signed.

To Jined's astonishment, Astrid began signing fluently, almost faster than Jined could follow, saying more of her journey with Katiam than either had shared in the week they had all been together. The twins nodded as she signed, absorbing the tale and occasionally making remarks. When she was finished, they turned back to the table.

Let's go, Loïc said.

Jined and Didus rose.

"I didn't know you signed the Silent Language so well," Katiam said.

"I was, for a time, pursued by a Silent Brother at Pariantür," Astrid muttered. "So I spent a lot of time speaking it, a few years back."

"What happened?" Katiam asked.

"It didn't work out."

Jined eyed Loïc, who returned a furtive look.

It was a mutual friend of ours, Loïc signed. *Brother Feralon was his name.*

Was?

We're not as close any more, Loïc said. *He walked out the door behind Didus and the two women.*

Cävian fell into step with Jined.

We're not close with Feralon any more because of her, Cävian put a finger to his lips, and looked to make sure Loïc wasn't glancing back at them. *Feralon barely noticed her interest. She said he pursued her, but he didn't. She was more taken with him and his flippant wisdom and self-importance than anything.*

Arrogant?

Yes. Brother never liked how he treated her. Feralon broke it off with her when he realized how serious she was, but he didn't do it kindly. Brother hasn't forgiven him. Nor will he tell Astrid how he has always felt about her.

Because she chose Feralon over him?

Because she's never noticed him.

That hurts.

He'll never admit it, Cävian said, *touching his finger to his lips again.*

Loïc watched Astrid talk to Katiam as they walked up the cobbled road into the city. Although he was hanging on her every word, he was obviously resigned to being nothing more than an old friend. Cävian joined his brother and brought him into a conversation with Didus, the gregarious Pater Minoris always happy to have more friends to talk with.

Meanwhile, they wended their way into the city of Donig. Memories flooding Jined again as he walked past shops and homes that had remained unchanged since his youth. They passed the tavern where he'd been introduced to Ketiva by the very man he'd killed years later in a drunken argument, when the other man fell from a balcony and broke his neck. Jined turned away from the inn and moved back into the street over which the castle, Stoneliht, loomed. They passed through the arch in the wall and along the interior courtyard to the bastion.

Cävian spoke with the Paladin who ran the stable, giving him orders to return to the inn and retrieve the four sleipnirs they had ridden from Brahz.

This way, Loïc signed, leading them to the office Dorian Mür had once used, where a young man sat at a desk with an older man leaning over his shoulder, looking at figures. Both men looked up, smiled in recognition, and Jurgon Upona—the older one—crossed the room to them, while Silas Merun, the young Paladin Jined and the twins had rescued from St. Nonn, looked on shyly.

"It is good to see you," Jurgon said. "I got your message, and I've sent a message to Nichal. He's awaiting you at the council hall, but asked I speak with you first."

"Oh?"

"Come and sit," he said, inviting him to the table.

Katiam was already seated and voraciously eating from a bowl of nuts.

"She's been starving these past few days, with only bread to eat," Astrid was saying to Didus.

"Why didn't she say anything?" Didus replied.

"It's not in her nature."

"It is good to see you," Jined said, sitting across from Silas.

"Likewise," the young man replied. "Primus Upona has been training me to be Nichal's seneschal."

"Has he?"

"He has a good mind for organization," Jurgon said. "I'm still Nichal's seneschal officially, but it doesn't hurt to have two of us looking over the figures and documents, and it is time I took an apprentice anyway."

"You're not that old," Jined said.

"Old enough to know I've put it off too long. It keeps me distracted."

Jined took a handful of the nuts and tossed them into his mouth.

"You probably ought to eat a good bit of those," Jurgon said. "But don't fill yourself up."

"Why is that?"

"The council always ends each day with a feast, but Nichal has expressly asked you not to draw attention to yourself when you go. If you show up and start tearing into the food with the appetite I've seen you have on the road, it'll draw undue attention."

"What else did he want me to know?" Jined asked as he took one of the bowls and began snacking away.

"He wanted you to be fully informed on what the council has been speaking on, and where everyone stands."

"All right. Summarize away."

"Toschbrecht has a great deal of resentment for you and your father, it seems. He further resents no longer being High Duke. He and Donigar put up barriers to keep anything important from being passed, and he does all he can to bring attention to the war effort."

"What is new on that front? Some news has trickled to Brahz, but it sounds like Bortali has not yet committed."

"Not until now."

"Why now?"

"Winter kept troops from moving, and messages have only just now begun to arrive from Waglÿsaor and those we sent on ahead. Bortali has a camp set up across the mountains from Sturm, but diplomacy from Waglÿsaor has prevented it from becoming a theatre of war."

"Who was sent ahead to Waglÿsaor?"

"Marric, Polun, and the remaining provisioners all journeyed there on Beltran's last return trip. He arrived back here only three days ago, with word from Zoumerik."

"Dane is not here, then?" Jined said, sighing in relief.

"No," Jurgon said with a smile. "It's been a relief for all of us, to be honest."

"May Grissone bless him with wisdom," Jined said off-handedly.

"Let's see you off to the castle, then," Jurgon said. "Just keep your thoughts to yourself. Nichal hopes to use your presence to reinforce his position."

"And what is that to be?"

"With the passes clear, Nichal wants to head east and see if we can't stifle the war at the source—in Garrou."

"If Toschbrecht continues to play to character, though..." Jined said.

"Nichal is painfully aware that Ütol von Toschbrecht wants the war, if only to turn power back to himself."

The twins arrived with a bundle containing Jined's armor, unpacking it together and working to get him back into his leathers and plates. As they worked, Jined saw Katiam pull Jurgon aside for a quiet talk. She had been there when Jurgon's wife had died, losing the head of her order in the same incident. A tear came to Jurgon's eyes as she spoke, and then he took Katiam by her shoulders and pulled her into an embrace, sobbing, oddly enough, with a smile on his face.

What was that about? Cävian asked.

Loïc shrugged.

"Is there anything Jurgon isn't telling me about the situation there?" asked Jined.

The Jarls have drawn up obvious lines, Loïc signed. *Your father is trying to be the diplomat and bring them all together, but Toschbrecht's open disdain for him makes it difficult.*

"I'll keep that in mind."

They moved into the castle and entered the great hall, where servants were swiftly setting the tables with food. Jined had expected to see a council of jarls around the hearth in the center of the room. Instead, a hundred men stood around the room, all wearing the trappings of jarls and barons of the various smaller towns. Jined's father, Jaegür von Brazstein, stood at one end of a central table, lost in conversation with two barons, while on the other end a single baron spoke with Duke Sturmguard and his close ally, Jarl Gertigan. Sturmguard wore a fleece-lined blue velvet robe over his uniform, but he wore it open, brazenly exposing the gray uniform of his hometown.

Jined followed the twins across the room to where Nichal was speaking with someone he could not see until he was next to them. Nichal turned to the three Paladins, along with the man he was conversing with—Jarl Ütol von Toschbrecht.

"Primus," Nichal said. He had already looked burdened enough before this point, but the deeper shadows around his eyes spoke of a greater burden he was bearing—an entire church in crisis.

With fingers down by his side, he signed, Keep quiet.

Jined gave a salute.

"As you can see, we're in the middle of a council," Nichal said. "We just concluded for the morning, in fact, and we're going to eat before we enter the next session."

"I understand you've been cloistered away all winter," Toschbrecht said. He wore only the green hues of his home city now, but sapphire-studded beads in his beard spoke of the life he had lost and sought to regain. "Chosen champion of your god as you are, it would have been good to have you here in the council, to hear whether he'd bless our efforts."

He turned to Nichal. "I've said it before and I'll say it again, it is a shame we lost your mentor, Dorian. His council would have been welcome too, he having been through the greatest war modern history has known."

"And you've graciously allowed me to be his poor replacement."

"Hardly poor," Jined muttered.

"What is that?" Toschbrecht replied with a smile.

Jined shut his mouth and didn't say anything more.

The doors of the kitchen burst open and a train of servants entered carrying steaming trays of roast bird. The men all turned with light applause and then gathered around the tables, taking pieces of meat from the plates. Jarl Thommüs reached for a piece of meat just as the short, bald Jarl of Donig did. The shorter man gave him a cold look.

"Just arrived, have you?" a voice asked Jined. He had been watching the Jarls, and turned to a baron dressed in the red and blue stripes of the small town of Pluth, a slight man with harsh, angular features.

"Only just," Jined said. "What gave it away?"

"You seem surprised at the way Thommüs and Donigar act. But their petulant little feud has been going on all winter."

"As I understand it," Jined replied, "Donigar is loyal to Toschbrecht, and Thommüs has been stuck in between many of the factions."

"It is true. Thommüs and Clemmbäkker are close friends, but not nearly as close as the two southern jarls."

"You hail from Pluth. Do you still have fealty to Tosch yourself?"

"I got tired of Tosch and Brazh feuding over me and my mines. Out of spite I gave over my loyalty to Gerht, which has proven lucrative and kept me out of Brazstein's financial difficulties until recently."

The men began dividing into groups again, with the seven jarls all making their way to the head of the table along with Nichal. Duke Ragnut von Sturmguard took the head seat and called for order as the barons gathered around the other tables, just finishing up the first course. Another train of servants came out, this time with roasts, placing them all down in the center of each table. Sturmguard took up knives and began to carve his roast, doling out a piece to each jarl. Jined watched Toschbrecht eye the piece of meat before him and then take up a large flagon of fresh milk, drinking down a full tankard before he began cutting, but not yet eating the urswine ham. Jined's father dove in and finished his piece of meat, choking it down to keep his mouth open for discussion. After all the roasts had been doled out, Sturmguard made an overly dramatic move, pushing his plate away untouched.

"What is the meaning of this?" Jarl Donigar asked. "Are my cook's skills not to your liking?"

Sturmguard stood. "I should like to continue the discussion from this morning. Having wandered the hall and heard various thoughts on the matter, it is apparent that the Grand Council is still very much in disagreement. I am vowing not to take a bite of food until a decision has been made."

"Oh, come now," Toschbrecht said around the meat in his mouth. "You cannot discourse on an empty stomach."

"I have before and I will now," Sturm said.

"I'll eat it if you don't," Jaegür von Brazstein said, pulling the plate of food toward himself.

Sturmguard waved a hand dismissively, granting him permission. Jaegür dove in.

"As it stands," Sturmguard began, "we have an army gathering and camped across the pass from my own hometown, come from Ulev. Too few of you have committed to sending me more men, and I should like to avoid demanding it. Clemmbäkker? You've called for an alliance with the Isles of Bronue Jinre and their navy, but if we do that, we'll need to commit steel to the navy. Donigar, you have argued that this will take from the army, and that we can survive for a season without naval help. Regardless, we must come to a decision. Do we strengthen both army and navy? Or only one? I'll not have us sitting on our hands as spring arrives. We must commit."

"Strengthening our army," Gertigan said, "will not be a show of force until Bortali's army makes their way through the pass."

"But a strong naval push," Clemmbäkker said, standing, "would allow us to make an immediate show of force, which will give Bortali caution. It will also give us an ally in the form of Bronue Jinre."

"Who have long insulted us by trading with Bortali openly." Toschbrecht stood as well. "I will not have this council undo all I have worked for, an independent nation that does not rely on its neighbors!"

He slammed his tankard down and sat, sweat breaking out across his forehead.

"Not just neighbors," Clemmbäkker said. "Friends!"

Suddenly, Clemmbäkker fell over the side of his chair and became sick across the floor.

Thommüs and Gertigan lost their food, too.

Jined took a step forward as his father and Donigar both rolled out of their chairs; even Nichal and Toschbrecht lost their meals.

Sturmguard looked around at his colleagues in horror, then around to the guards at the door as someone shouted, "Poison!"

"Shut the gates to Stoneliht!" Sturmguard commanded.

The barons at the lower tables shoved their food away, though none looked the worse for wear.

It looks like only the main table, Loïc signed as he and his brother moved toward the front to help Nichal. Nichal was waving them back and standing to his feet.

"I think I'm all right," Nichal said as Jined came to him. "I only had one bite of the ham, but it had a bitter taste. See to the jarls."

Jined turned to the mess about him. The other jarls looked to be over the initial shock and were able to stand up weakly. All, that is, except for Jined's father, who was still on the floor.

Jined leapt over the table and sat his father up. The man's breath was staggered; his strong-rigid features were pale and ghostly.

"Help him!" Jined cried. "Grissone!"

17

SUBTERFUGE

There is a rigid fairness among the Boronii people. They hold the balance between the sexes as the highest virtue among their people, yet there is an unspoken strife between each Boronii citizen. In Boroni the Spirit of the Law is king. The duke, jarls, and barons, as well as their feminine counterparts, are only pawns in a bigger game.

—VITALI SABOMIFORE OF TASHAR, *ON BORONII LAW*

"The Prima Pater has summoned you," Didus said, coming to stand by Jined as they watched the wagon bearing his father's body roll out of the castle grounds.

"Not now, Koel," Jined said.

"He said it was urgent."

Jined sighed, set his jaw, and turned.

"Where?"

"His office."

Jined marched through the castle halls and out the courtyard to the bastion, Didus hot on his heels.

Loïc and Cävian stood at the door to the office, and each held up a hand to slow him. He ignored them and threw the door open with rising rage.

"What the Nocc do you want, Nichal?" Jined roared as he entered the room. "My father has died, and you still can't give me three mome..."

Nichal stood behind his desk, his face pale. Across from him sat two men, the calm and regal High Duke Sturmguard and the now sickly-looking Jarl Toschbrecht.

"Thank you for coming, Primus Brazstein," Nichal said, ignoring Jined's blatant ire.

Toschbrecht made to stand, then thought the better of it.

"My condolences," he said, dabbing at the sweat on his forehead, "to you and your family."

A wry smile sat at the edge of his lips as he said this.

"You're behind this," Jined said. "Aren't you?"

"Primus Brazstein, stand down," Nichal commanded.

"I take no offense," Toschbrecht said. "We have a history, Jined and I, which explains why he came to this conclusion. But the fact that we all were poisoned, myself included, speaks volumes."

"Yet only my father died."

Sturmguard rose to his feet. "All were poisoned, save myself, because I abstained from eating. Your father probably died from ingesting the additional helping of poisoned meat meant for me. I'd wager it was warning, sent by Bortali. Either it was intended only to weaken us, or perhaps my own portion was in some way more potent. Regardless, it has been done, and your father is a casualty of the war."

"Then you'll retaliate?" Jined asked.

"We'll do everything in our power to bring the poisoner to justice," Sturmguard said.

Jined sighed and turned to Toschbrecht.

"I've overstepped my authority and insulted you. For that, I am deeply sorry."

Toschbrecht held out a hand. "Bygones."

Jined shook his hand in acceptance.

"Will Arthoss be instated as Jarl then?"

"He will," Sturmguard replied. "Officially he is the Jarl right now. We just arrived here to confirm this with Nichal. It is important we understand Parianti Law, and whether we were incorrect."

"Why would that be incorrect?" Jined asked.

"It is not unheard of, albeit extremely rare," Nichal said, "for a Paladin to renounce the Hammer in order to take back the responsibility of a crown. You were Jaegür's eldest son. From what I can remember, without a lawyer here, there were two instances where a king's son, or brother, having become a Paladin, was asked to return to their country to take up the throne. Thus the precedent is set. However..."

"Because I took the vow of Poverty...." Jined offered.

"You forfeited your right," Nichal said with a nod.

"That doesn't mean there isn't the potential for others to raise the question among our fellows," Sturmguard said.

"I want nothing more than to ensure a smooth transition for Arthoss," Jined said.

"Good," Sturmguard said with a weak smile. "Then I think you'll understand if I ask you to leave the country."

Jined gave a curt nod. "So that Arthoss can take control easily."

"The death of a jarl, you may recall, comes with a shifting of loyalties in the barons. Those barons who claimed fealty to your father are free to choose Brahz again or switch allegiance to another jarl."

"I recall the tradition," Jined said. "Generally the other jarls also release a handful of barons, asking them to give fealty to the new jarl, as a goodwill gift."

"This is true," Sturmguard replied. "Unfortunately, since the barons only just declared their fealty, and with war looming, I doubt my fellow jarls will give up anything."

Nichal spoke up. "As Jined is not replacing his father as jarl, the matter is settled. The Paladins are heading east, and I will be making my way to Bortali within the week." He turned to Jined. "I'd like you to leave today and make for Clehm with the twins and Didus. As long as the pass has opened, you'll continue on to Waglÿsaor from there."

"I arrived with two companions," Jined said.

"I'm aware. You'll take them with you as well, and see them safely to Waglÿsaor."

"Prima Pater," Jurgon said from a side desk. He had been standing over Silas Merun, who scribbled away, taking notes on the meeting.

"Yes, Primus?"

"I'd like to go with them."

"I need you here, helping Silas."

"He no longer needs me, and I could go ahead and prepare a place for you."

"Very well. If you can be ready when Jined leaves, you may go with him." Nichal turned back to Jined. "You're dismissed."

Jined turned and left the room. Didus was waiting for him outside.

"Did you hear?" Jined said, hot tears of anger in his eyes.

Didus nodded. "I've already packed three days of trail supplies. I'll need to requisition enough for Jurgon as well, but that will be no problem. We leave as soon as the sleipnirs are saddled."

I'm very sorry for your loss, Loïc signed.

Jined gave a curt nod and marched to the stables.

Two men in purple stood there with saddled sleipnirs. One of them was Jarl Saedrick von Clemmbäkker.

"Primus Brazstein," said the Jarl.

He took the reins from him and led the animals to the door.

"I understand you mourn, and perhaps you do not wish to speak with anyone."

"I don't," Jined replied.

"I understand you ride for Waglÿsaor,"

"What of it?"

"My daughter is there, having run off to join the Crysalas despite my express orders to the contrary."

"I am not in a position to question those who choose to take up the Hammer or Rose. I have no authority over our sister church."

"You could at least ask her to write to me. "

"Why are you offended that she may have followed a higher calling?"

"If she has taken her vows, there is little you nor I could do. But if she journeyed to Waglÿsaor, thinking she could help with the war effort from Waglÿsaor... I can only stay the hands of the jarls from marching on that city for so long, and I cannot promise her safety in an invasion."

"If you fear for your daughter's life, then perhaps you ought to consider what this war means for everyone, including your daughter."

The man stopped in his tracks but Jined did not turn back. As he came out of the stables, he saw how dark it was and how road-weary the others looked.

"Jined," Didus said, "let us return to the inn. We can leave before morning and easily make Clehm with a hard ride."

"I... do not wish to face the memories there."

"It is too dark for the five of us to be traveling," Jurgon said, glancing at the two women. "Let's get a short night's sleep, away from the city, then we can journey east."

Jined mounted the sleipnir and rode out of the city without another word, forcing people to leap out of his way. The others had trouble keeping up, but he did not care; he rode to escape the country for the second time, but this time to flee not death but a broken heart.

When they came to the inn, Jined left his sleipnir in Didus's hands and fled to his room, slamming the door and sliding to the floor.

A light tap came behind him.

"What?" Jined barked.

No one answered.

"If it is Loïc or Cävian, I'm not in the mood."

The knock came again.

Jined sighed and lifted the bar, opening the door to both twins staring at him.

"Not now," he said, moving to close the door.

They both shouldered into the room, Cävian holding out a sealed letter to Jined as soon as he closed the door behind them.

"What is this?" Jined asked, taking the letter.

We were asked to give this to you only after we had some privacy, Cävian signed.

Jined took it and broke the seal, sitting on the bed as he opened the letter.

I apologize for the grief I've put you through. I am alive, and all is going according to plan.

Jined stopped reading and checked the signature. There was none.

"Who wrote this?" Jined asked.

Both brothers shrugged.

Sturmguard discovered there was going to be a poisoning attempt on his life. He shared this with me and we devised a plan that went off as expected. The food we were given was laced with an emetic in order to induce vomiting in all the Jarls, as a cover for who was behind the act. It is why you'll note that I quickly downed my portion, followed by Sturmguard's. The emetic on my piece allowed me to eat, then continue on with the poisoned piece intended for Ragnut. It was a calculated risk, but important in order to continue the subterfuge laid out. Please know that I intend to remain dead to the world until all of our plans come to fruition, helping your brother rule our domain well. We expect to lose many of the barons under our fealty. Indeed, we've personally asked some to switch to Toschbrecht in order to give a show of solidarity. Toschbrecht wants a war. And my death gives him what he wants: My death and a rally cry to bring troops to bear.

Please know that I love you, and everything is under control. Do what you're able to do in Bortali. But if it comes to all out war, when all this is over, Boroni will be the stronger for it.

Jined took up the piece of the seal he had not paid attention to once more. The imprint on the gray seal confirmed it had come from Sturmguard's desk.

Well? Loïc signed.

"My father lives," Jined said with a laugh. He held the letter over a candle and made sure it had set to burning, and then dropped it into a piss pot. "Tell Didus I want to leave before the sun rises. I'd rather no one in the city see the good mood this puts me in."

18

CONTRITION

Above all else, let everyone see your humility, for unseen humility is the only reward it receives.

— FROM *WORDS OF COMMON SENSIBILITIES FROM THE PHILOSOPHICAL FOOL, A BOOK OF COLLECTED SAYINGS THAT MANY SPEAK, BUT ALL KNOW TO BE FOLLY*

The walls of the canyon drew nearer as Katiam and the others approached the end of their trek from Donig. In the center of the road a single Paladin stood in a brown cloak of rough burlap, pulled over his shoulders. He was inconsequently small in the presence of two cliff walls rising above him. Loïc and Cävian rode out from the party at Nichal's command. Nichal and his new seneschal, Silas Merun, had joined them just before they entered the pass.

Astrid gave Katiam a glance of assurance.

The twins came within a hundred yards of the Paladin and one of them pulled up short, signaling the party to come forward. As they neared the lone Paladin, Katiam recognized him as Primus Beltran Cautese, the former and ever-serious organizer of the Prima Pater's entourage. He had left off in Donig the previous year, to travel back and forth between Boroni and Bortali until winter no longer allowed it.

"Prima Pater," Beltran said, saluting as Nichal drew near.

"How did you know to expect us?" Nichal asked.

"The city lookouts spotted you yesterday. I came here last night to await your arrival, although I may come to grief for it."

"Perhaps you ought to fill me in," Nichal said.

"That is why I'm here," Beltran said. "We can speak as we ride."

"Jurgon," Nichal said, "why don't you and Silas continue on to St. Rämmon and see to our lodgings. I'll take the guard and escort the sisters to a safe place."

Jurgon gave a salute and kicked his sleipnir into a trot, accompanied by Silas.

"Why the burlap?" Nichal asked Beltran.

"Pater Minoris Zoumerik has the entire city on a new 'diet of practices,' as he likes to call it. The use of burlap is a 'fasting of simplicity.'"

"I'm not sure I understand."

Beltran took a deep breath, considering his words wisely. "Do you know why no Bortalian army has gathered up at this pass? Why Garrou has not marched here to wrest control from Duke Ergis?"

"Tell me."

"Waglÿsaor has been declared a safe haven and thus people flocked here, including soldiers from all over the country. The place had descended to levels of debauchery I hadn't realized could exist. "

"Debauchery?"

"With the arrival of the refugees came coin—something Waglÿsaor has not seen for many months. And so the city turned to feast and celebration. At first Zoumerik allowed it, referring to those who arrived not as refugees but as pilgrims. But then he rode out into the city with the entire fortress at his heel, all of us in burlap cloaks and ash upon our heads to stand a night's long vigil at the iron monument, the Saor, in silence. By noon, Duke Ergis had come to stand before Zoumerik, confessing his sins and taking up burlap and ash of his own."

"I'm sure that was a sight to see," Nichal said with a chuckle. He turned to Astrid and Katiam. "Duke Ergis is a very arrogant man."

"Well," Beltran continued, "once the duke had concluded his confession, Zoumerik declared that the debauched soldiers were deserters, not refugees, and their actions were worthy of punishment. A long list of rules were decreed, and posted on every street corner."

Beltran handed Nichal a small pamphlet, which Nichal glanced over.

"Zoumerik has commanded all citizens to be servants of one another."

"They've followed along?"

Beltran nodded. "They are contrite, and seek the favor of any Paladin that rides by. They disdain ostentatiousness. They eat simple food. It was hard to watch for the first month. But over the past three weeks we started noticing that everyone began treating each other fairly and with care. Apparently, there is a precedent for this in Parianti law. We have spent many a reading in the evenings from selections of the Code of Commons."

"I forgot Zoumerik was an expert in law."

"He has used two incidents from recent history as examples, the first from a few years after the Protectorate Wars, when our beloved Dorian Mür—may he rest in the arms of Grissone and the Anka—put a similar set of Contrition Edicts over Pariantür."

"And the other?" Nichal asked.

"When Macena formed into a de facto nation, they requested legal aid from Pariantür, and Dorian once again posted a Contrition Edict."

"The edicts come from the Code of Commons, which is based on the Book of Common Life," Nichal said, "penned by Minu the Gentle, founder of the Vow of Pacifism. I would never consider enforcing these edicts upon a city outside Parianti Law. But if there is a precedent, I'll tread lightly."

They walked as they talked, winding through the narrow canyon to the gates of the city. Nichal waited while Beltran rode forward to speak with the guards. After some discussion, their captain gave a nod and the gates opened. Katiam noticed that the guards wore gray pieces of cloth tied over their heads.

"What is the meaning of the gray cloth?" she asked.

"It represents ash," Beltran said. "Soldiers ought to be clean, so they cannot wear ash."

"Ah, because of the general contrition."

"That, and today is the eighth and final day of the week, Velday. Brother Marric and Almoner Filip made a practice of walking through the city on Velday, with ash upon their heads, giving coin to those in need. After a few weeks, people began appearing before their homes as they walked by, wearing ash and with coin of their own to give."

As they rode down the main thoroughfare of the city, people came out of their homes to greet them. Some pointed to Nichal and the red slashed cape he wore, denoting him as Prima Pater. Others saw the Standard of Grissone, hoisted in the stirrup of Cävian, and made the winged sign of the Anka, averting their eyes. A light drizzle began to fall, and still people came out to watch them pass. As they neared the center of town, Katiam caught a faint whiff of rust in the air. Through a gathering mist, a chunk of jagged iron coalesced into view.

"What is that?" Katiam asked. "I don't recall it from my previous visit to this city."

"That is the Saor," Astrid said, "a sky-fallen slab of iron said to have formed the bowl of this city, long before anyone dwelt here."

"Why hasn't it rusted away? Or been mined?"

"Rumor is," Beltran said, "it can't be mined."

As they drew nearer the smell of the Saor grew stronger, and Katiam felt the Rotha begin to quiver against her. She clutched her chest.

"What's wrong?" Astrid whispered.

"The Rotha," Katiam replied. "It doesn't like that thing." She glanced up at the Saor as a procession of people entered from another street. Marric led them, in stoic manner, with the Almoner, Stevan Filip. They wore brown burlap robes, but their gorgets and hammers identified them as Paladins. Dane's eyes locked on them, first in a scowl of derision at the sight of Katiam and Astrid and then in awe as he saw what Cävian held aloft.

"The Standard of Grissone!" Dane's face contorted into a mask of mourning, and he drifted across the square toward them with his hands held aloft.

"What is the meaning of this?" Nichal said as Dane neared.

"Prima Pater," Dane said, "the people have asked for a Walk of Contrition, and by Pater Zoumerik's orders I lead it."

"How long will it take?" Nichal asked. "I think I'd rather go to St. Rämmon and speak with Zoumerik."

"He's not at the citadel," Dane said. "He is at the hospital, visiting the sick and ailing."

"Then get on with this, Brother Marric. We've had a long journey."

"Very well, Prima Pater, although hurrying contrition makes for sloppy faith."

Katiam thought she saw Nichal roll his eyes.

The throng drew close and several dropped to their knees before Cävian, who looked shocked.

"I'd wager this is why Valér Quéton was so quiet," Jined jested. "Always shaken by the attention that standard brought."

"From the Quatrodox," Dane orated. "As St. Maront confessed to Ikhail and joined the ranks of the brotherhood.

"'Cease thy strife!' Spake Ikhail. 'Cease thy wars and prideful arrogance. Seek contrition through pure humility.'

"'Don thy rags, and shake upon thee ashen countenance. Fast from excess and believe!'"

Several of the people tore the clothes they wore, revealing they already wore brown burlap underneath. Others took out jars, unstoppered them, and cast ash upon their heads. One old woman staggered forward, tears running down through the ash, and touched the brass tip of the shaft of the standard, set in the stirrup beside Cävian's boot.

She looked up at the Paladin, imploringly.

Cävian hesitantly made a sign of peace to her, and she backed up, mouthing her thanks.

This went on for several minutes, before Nichal finally held up a hand.

"Peace be with those of faith," he said, and without another word he pulled at the reins and turned his sleipnir northward.

Katiam quickly followed suit, the Rotha's vines rubbing at her collar.

A commotion arose behind them as they entered a north-running street. Katiam looked back to see that the crowd had followed them, and it was growing.

"This is absurd," Nichal muttered.

"It is," Jined said, "but unsurprising."

"Because Dane is feeding it?" Nichal asked.

"That may be true," Jined responded, "but I was thinking in terms of the people's fear of war. Wars are fought in the name of zeal, but zeal can also be appealed to, to avoid it."

Nichal gave a low sound. "I still don't like it."

They came out into the square before the hospital, which had been freshly whitewashed. Flags of burlap fluttered by the door, in front of which stood two more Paladins with hammers at attention, wearing only brown robes and gorgets. Although they remained frozen, their eyes followed Nichal's approach as he dismounted and ascended the steps.

"I'm seeking Pater Zoumerik," he said to the guards.

They did not respond.

"This is the Prima Pater," Beltran announced. "Nichal Guess."

One of the guards turned his head but did not change his stance.

"My apologies, Prima Pater," he said. "I did not recognize you."

"Why the rigidity?"

"Pater Minoris' orders," he said. "More so on Velday, as we lead by example."

"Is he within?"

"Visiting the ailing," the guard said.

"Are you going to stop me from entering?" Nichal asked.

"No, Prima Pater."

He entered, with Beltran, Jined, and the twins following quickly after him, along with Astrid and Katiam. It had once been a dilapidated building, full of hushed coughs and despair, but now light flooded the space. The floor's teal-veined marble tiles reflected the iridescent blue starblush lights that complemented the sunbeams from the windows at the top of the stairs. Not a mote of dust hung in the air, and in the corner a group of women scrubbed a white marble pillar. Pairs of women walked about wearing starched white robes and hooded head-dresses, which reminded Katiam of the garments of the Aspect of Solitude.

"I can't believe how changed it is in such a short time," she said.

"It is stiller than it was before," Astrid replied.

Katiam nodded. "At peace."

"Sister Astrid Glass?" a young voice said from behind. They both turned to see a girlish Paladame whose smile broadened as her eyes met Katiam's.

"Sister Borreau!" she cried.

"Hello, Sister Salnah."

"Please, you may call me Little Maeda again! Come!"

They followed her to a side room and closed the door behind them.

"It was rumored you had disappeared!" Little Maeda said.

"I had," Katiam said, "but I'm back."

"Are you stationed here as a guard?" Astrid asked

"I'm still the keeper of the vault," Little Maeda said. "Someone recognized you when you were traveling in the city, Sister Glass, and a message was sent to me. We assumed you would come here, and I came to escort you to the vault."

She turned to Katiam, her smile renewed. "I cannot tell you how glad I am to see you! When word arrived that you had disappeared at the death of the Matriarch... Oh, Esenath is going to be so glad to see you."

"Esenath is here?" Katiam replied.

"In the vault, yes. She's not yet moved on."

"When can we go to the vault?" Astrid asked.

Katiam placed a hand on her arm. "Shouldn't we see around the hospital first? I'm sure Captain Smith would like to see us."

The smile on Little Maeda's face faded to something less genuine. "If we were to go to the vault without letting Mother Smith know you had arrived, it would not be good."

"Mother Smith?"

"She was made the Mother Superioris over all of the Sister Superiorii in the Northern Scapes. She'd been declared Mother and Protector here only a few weeks ago, and word has been sent to the vaults in neighboring nations. She awaits their replies."

"Which nations' vaults are being asked to swear fealty to her?"

"Those around the Lupinfang, as well as Nemen, Eschenfurt, and Varea."

Astrid said, "Knowing Sigri Smith, she probably is looking to provide a unified leadership with the fall of the Oracles."

"Then the Dweol truly is gone?" Little Maeda asked.

Katiam took a hesitant breath.

"Yes," Astrid said sternly. "But we have news."

"Then let's visit Mother Smith."

She opened the door and walked into the main hall, where the Prima Pater stood with several more Paladins and with Sigri Smith.

Sigri was one of the tallest women Katiam had ever known; even Astrid came only to the woman's chin when she wasn't in boots. She had incorporated the starched white robes of the hospital nurses into her Paladame regalia, and her hair was completely obscured by a hood reminiscent of the leaves of a rose. Her face was framed by a chain that hung loosely from ear to ear, made of iron in the likeness of rose thorns.

A Paladin wearing a cape of brown burlap, and cordons across his chest of a Pater Minoris, noticed the three of them, and drew the attention of Sigri Smith who turned to them with a stern look on her face and made a motion, requesting they approach.

Little Maeda led the way and came to stand at attention before her.

"Sister Salnah," Sigri said.

"Mother Superioris," Little Maeda replied.

"Who do we have here?"

"Sisters Astrid Glass and Katiam Borreau, recently arrived from the west."

"I see that," Sigri said. "I'm sure you are both very tired."

"The road has been long, Captain Smith," Astrid said.

"Mother Superioris," Smith corrected.

"Mother Smith," Astrid replied.

"Little Maeda, please escort them to places unseen."

"I had hoped to see around the hospital," Katiam spoke up.

Smith gave her a stern look.

"It was all the talk when we last came through," Katiam said flatteringly.

"Sister Borreau," Sigri said, "you are no longer physician to the late Matriarch Superioris and are under my leadership, you'll follow protocol and show respect. You are to travel to the vaults and await my arrival, upon which you'll both give a full report of your travels and await my express commands."

Katiam opened her mouth to speak, but Sigri had already turned back to the others. Looking over Astrid's shoulder, she could see the twins giving her a look. The brother not holding the Standard of Grissone made a series of hand signals down by his waist.

Astrid turned, a look of determination in her eyes.

"What did he say to you?" Katiam whispered.

"Who?" Astrid asked.

"Loïc."

"I'll tell you later."

Little Maeda led the way to the eastern corridors.

"Is Mama Baker still making bread?" Katiam asked.

"She's Sister Baker now," Little Maeda said. "She and her Moon-Eyes are very busy today, since tomorrow is Kaltay, which is the weekly Day of Bread."

"This city is quite devout. We had a flock of pilgrims following us with Dane in the lead."

"That man," Maeda said, rolling her eyes.

Katiam laughed. "That's what I think!"

They came to a hall that was completely dark.

"The bakery is this way, isn't it?" Katiam asked.

"Yes, and it's the safest way to the vaults too."

"You say vaults in the plural," Astrid replied.

"Yes. You'll see what I mean."

She took a few steps and turned back. "Take hold of my shoulder, Sister Glass, and Katiam, you take hers."

They walked further into darkness, the smell of bread becoming overwhelming as they arrived at the door of the bakery.

"Permission to pass?" Little Maeda said.

"Is that you, Maeda?" came another young woman's voice.

"Hello Derah," Maeda said. "I've got two sisters to take through your bakery."

Through the glow from the hearth a figure approached.

"Who do we have here?"

Astrid stepped forward.

"Sister Baker, I am Astrid Glass."

"You guarded the Matriarch Superioris, I know. You've been spoken of all winter."

She turned to Katiam.

"Hello, Sister Baker," said Katiam.

The other woman smiled. "You're alive!"

"I am."

"Can we take some bread with us?" Little Maeda asked.

"I shouldn't let you, but I'm sure one loaf won't hurt," she said, putting a large loaf into Little Maeda's hands. "Go on. You know the way. I have a lot to do."

Little Maeda led them through a door behind the oven.

"She's grown up," Katiam said, "and she doesn't seem so angry."

"She almost slipped back into her anger when she heard that the Matriarch had died. It hasn't helped that her sight has become progressively worse. By high summer I expect she'll be completely blind. But she has kept her spirits despite the odds," Little Maeda said.

"Which of the vaults are we headed to?" Astrid asked.

"Not any one vault," Little Maeda said.

"What do you mean?"

"Remember when we first arrived, and we entered through the disrepaired buildings below the city?"

"Yes."

Maeda came to a door and gave a tight rhythmic knock.

A few moments later, the door opened into a candlelit space. A Paladame looked out, her head covered by a burlap veil.

"Sister Egrass, may we enter?"

The Paladame gave a nod and let the three of them in.

"Can you please ready two rooms off the Southern Hall?"

Little Maeda turned back to the two of them. "Is there anything else you'll require immediately?"

"An odd request, I know," Katiam said, "but can you please bring pots of fresh soil and rose water?"

The Paladame nearby nodded at their request and excused herself.

"All right," Little Maeda said. "Are you ready?"

"For what?" Astrid asked, following her to the door.

Little Maeda smiled and pushed the door open on the bright torchlight of a hidden city.

19

MISSION OF PEACE

*Though the forge be hot, enough to melt brick and stone, even
that shall not seal the veins upon its cracked surface. What made
it? By what means? In what year? No myth or legend speaks of it.*

—BROTHER SAILPIN

As they entered the ward, Jined could see Pater Minoris
Jamis Zoumerik at the other end, bent over the bed of one
of the patients. Behind him, his seneschal, Samul Haly,
took copious notes. Beltran marched through the room and came
to stand a few beds from Zoumerik. Unlike the other Paladins they
had encountered, Zoumerik was in full regalia, although he wore a
cape made of the brown burlap. He looked up and nodded, his
blond eyebrows as bushy as ever but his head freshly shaved, and
finished up with a man who smiled and gave thanks.

Zoumerik had words with Samul, then crossed the room to
Beltran.

"I see you've escorted our guests quickly through the city to
me," he said.

"Word was you were here, and I didn't want to keep you or the
Prima Pater waiting."

Zoumerik turned to Nichal, as though realizing he was standing
there for the first time, and gave a salute. "You honor me with your
presence."

"It appears there have been many changes here since last we

passed through," Nichal replied.

"Yes, many. I believe we'll have much to talk about."

"I've noticed that you don't wear the burlap the others have been ordered to don."

Zoumerik gave a sour smile. "I've worn this for the past five years." He stepped close and pulled back his leather gauntlet to reveal a modest burlap undershirt.

"There is method to my leadership," Zoumerik continued. "In this time of war I hope we can come to an understanding regarding my authority here."

"I am by no means here to undermine you," Nichal said.

"And I'm certain that, between the two of us, we can end this war and usher in a new era of faith."

"When do you expect to return to the citadel?"

"We can proceed back to the citadel now, if you'd like."

"I would," Nichal said.

Zoumerik nodded. As they returned to the main hall, he saw two Paladins speaking with a Paladame who was as tall as Jined. She wore a white nurse's robe under her armor, and a headdress that suggested a wilted rose. As she turned, he recognized the face of Sigri Smith, the former captain of the Matriarch Superioris's personal guard.

Across the front of her headdress, she had a loose ornamental chain of black iron. Jined was surprised he even recognized her, her features were so gaunt from the rigid rules of the past half year.

"Mother Superioris," Zoumerik said as they approached.

"Pater Minoris," she replied.

"Mother Superioris?" Nichal asked, stepping forward. "The last time I saw you, you were a Sister Captain."

"Greetings, Prima Pater Guess," she said. "With the loss of our Matriarch, it was apparent that these times called for the reintroduction of the historical position of Mothers Superioris—until a new Matriarch Superioris is chosen."

"What does that mean?" Jined muttered to Didus Koel.

"It means she holds much the same authority as Nichal does."

Zoumerik spun to look at the two of them, a broad smile across his face.

"Until you spoke, I hadn't recognized you, Didus!"

Didus took a step forward.

"I sent a message to you at the Bulwark after I was made Pater

Minoris here. I hadn't heard back."

"It's been a dark year, my friend," Didus said, clasping the arm of Zoumerik. "We have a lot of catching up to do."

Katiam and Astrid approached with another woman, and Sigri turned to speak with them.

Jined noticed Loïc and Cävian watching them with interest. Loïc's fingers fluttered a message to Astrid and she made furtive eye contact with him.

Things change rapidly. Be careful.

Thanks. You too, Astrid signed back as she and Katiam walked away with their guide.

"Mother Smith has done a fine job turning this place around," Zoumerik said. "She's provided help to those in need, training nurses who would banish sin-guided ailments, and establishing methods to prevent those same illnesses from infecting others."

"Sin-guided?" Nichal asked.

Zoumerik nodded. "First the sins of the flesh brought about by women losing their faith and selling themselves, and the number of deserters who, against their honor, escaped to the safety of our city. We welcome them, but we cannot stand idly by and let their sins make them spineless. We must ensure their pacifism is a matter of morality and not a lack of respect for authority."

"Then you do consider the decision made by Dorian Mür to return to Pariantür with any Paladins who will join us as an act of desertion?"

"I'll not question a decision made by Dorian Mür, but that decision was made after you became acting Prima Pater, and only after Dorian Mür supposedly perished. At least, that is what my investigation revealed."

"It appears you and I have much to discuss behind closed doors," Nichal said in a hushed tone.

"I've had my volumes of books of law brought to me over the winter. We can ensure that you have at your disposal the laws that back you up. Or perhaps I shall help you to revise your plans to match with Parianti law."

Nichal pursed his lips and gave a curt nod as Zoumerik walked toward the door. Coming out into the full light of day revealed a throng of people, both in the square before the hospital and on the stairs. Nearby, Dane Marric stood with the almoner, Stevan Filip, handing out the last of their coins. When he saw them come out, Dane approached them. Sigri Smith, who stood next to Zoumerik, did not even seem to notice him, but Jined caught Dane sending her subtle glances.

"What good has been wrought this day?" Zoumerik asked Dane loudly, so the crowd could hear.

"The city has been blessed by the giving of the week," Dane announced. "Lord Goleish gave ten silver dukt and begged boon upon his household."

A man wearing a shawl of sackcloth across his shoulders, along with a rich slashed tabard of mauve, stood nearby nodding wildly to this.

Zoumerik lifted a hand and made a gesture. "Let Lord Goleish approach."

The man came and fell to his knees before Zoumerik.

"What boon do you request?"

"Please, Pater. My son has been sent to the front. Let not his desire for war and its sins take his life, nor deliver a curse upon me and my household."

"For what reason does he serve? For self, or for honor?"

"He considers it a great honor."

"His name shall be added to those the citadel prays for."

"Thank you, Pater," the lord said. "Thank you."

"All who desire the prayers of the citadel shall have it," Zoumerik declared. "The prayers of the contrite, of those that humble themselves, shall be answered. A pittance given is a pittance earned."

Several people surged through the crowd toward Zoumerik.

He gave a nod and Dane descended the stairs, inviting the supplicants to come to him and Stevan.

"You would have them purchase their prayers?" Nichal asked as Zoumerik began to descend as well.

"Certainly not. I imply that acts of contrition have positive effects. Their guilt speaks to their souls, and they act upon it, feeding the poor. It benefits everyone."

"I question the method," Nichal muttered.

"There is little difference between what I preach and what Ikhail preached to those pilgrims who helped build Pariantür. He asked them to give, and blessings fell upon them."

"They journeyed from every country and every tribe," Nichal replied. "They had felt a nudge long before; seeds were planted in their hearts by Grissone. Ikhail was not the planter, but the harvester."

"Do I not harvest?"

"The people of this city were born here, not drawn here."

"But their ancestors were drawn here. Who are we to question his will? Perhaps this was intended long before you or I were born."

Zoumerik and Nichal led the way through the crowd with Cävian behind them, the crowd staring at the Standard in his arms and making signs of Grissone across their chests. They exited the city and returned to the crossroads, taking the precarious path around the edge of the slate mountains to the citadel of St. Rämmon, a black edifice buried in a black mountain and perpetually slicked with mist off the sea. The lighthouse glowed from high atop the mountain, now with the blue light of starblush powder, which was visible even in daylight.

As they rode through the vestibule into the ceilinged courtyard, Jined felt an overwhelming weight upon his shoulders. It was a return of the weight he had felt the previous autumn, which did not lift until he had taken the second vow. A third vow on his shoulders now did not relieve the burden.

Loïc shivered.

What is it, Loïc? Jined signed.

I didn't like this place when we were last here, and I don't like it now.

Me either, Cävian said.

"Perhaps the three of you would like to enjoy our baths," Zoumerik said. "It may relieve the stress of the road and the burden of the mountain."

"You saw what we said?" Jined replied.

Zoumerik smiled. "It is a feeling I am aware of myself, but my prayers, and the cleansing of my body and mind, washed the feeling away." He turned to Jined. "You bear the burden of the Vow of Poverty."

"I do," Jined said.

"I remember. I was there." He returned to Nichal and Didus. "There is one major change you'll find here. We ask everyone to contribute offerings for the poor. Chapel doors are locked, only to be opened by the dropping of a coin into the alms box. Obviously, those who have taken the Vow of Poverty will need someone to join them."

Zoumerik gestured for Nichal to follow him, and they both turned to go deeper into the citadel. Nichal gave a backward glance.

"Go ahead and enjoy the baths," he said.

"Make sure you do, too," Jined said.

Nichal nodded with a sigh, and followed Zoumerik.

Pay to pray? Loïc said, looking irritable.

Didus shrugged. "While uncommon, not unheard of."

They came to the door of the treasury; Cävian gave the Standard over for safekeeping to the Paladin who sat there.

"Then it is true?" the Paladin said. "Brother Quéton is gone?"

Cävian nodded.

"He died a hero," Jined said, "sacrificing himself to avenge the death of Pater Segundus Gallahan Pír."

"But they were both of the Vow of Pacifism..." the Paladin said.

Jined noticed the Pacifism bead upon the younger brother's red cordons.

"Sacrifice is sometimes called for," was all he said in reply.

"The Vow of Pacifism is a sacrifice of self. A sacrifice of your life, long before you lose it."

The young Paladin took the Standard and moved it to a corner. He did not return to speak to them.

"There is a frantic feeling here that wasn't here before," Jined said.

Better than the feeling of suspicion when we were last here, Loïc said.

"Why was there suspicion?" Didus asked.

Jined explained what had happened with the previous Pater Minoris, Saren Gui, who was sent along with most Paladins stationed in Bortali back to St. Hamul, and likely on to Pariantür itself.

"Now those here are newly stationed, and under Zoumerik's leadership," Jined concluded.

"He last held full leadership at the Bastion of Bremüm, over twelve years ago," Didus replied.

"It sounds as though you have experience working with him."

"All communiques and orders sent to me in Birin came from his desk and often included proverbs, exhortations, examples of scripture and law books to promote active faith, all written in red to denote the difference between himself and Pater Minoris Sachez and then when he passed, Pater Minoris Gage."

How long were you Pater Minoris at the Bulwark? Cävian asked.

"Three years. Before that, I was at Penoña in Morriego, both as Brother Adjutant and then Primus, for ten years and Pariantür before that."

"Then before I was there," Jined said.

But not before we two, Loïc said. *We took our vows when we were sixteen. And we've been full brothers ever since.*

"You're not much younger than me," Jined said.

Loïc rolled his eyes. *Are you saying we look old? You've got five years on us.*

"You're only thirty-two?" Jined asked.

Like brother said, we're not that old like you.

Both twins laughed silently.

"Why aren't you laughing?" Jined asked Didus.

"Because what does that make me?" he offered back. "I turned forty last year."

They all broke out into laughter as they arrived at the pools.

There was no one about. Didus touched the water with a hand and sighed happily. "It's very hot."

Cävian nodded. He walked over to a wooden display by the wall and began opening jars and sniffing.

"What is that?" Jined asked.

Cävian turned. *Salts, oils, flowers. The same sort of thing you find at the baths at Pariantür.*

"I never had much time to do more than wipe myself down."

That explains a lot, Loïc said, scrunching his nose.

"What's that supposed to mean?"

You're not the most pleasant man to stand next to after a battle. That's excusable. But the rest of the time?

Still not that great, Cävian added.

Jined grimaced. "Are you saying I stink?"

"Let's not jump to conclusions," Didus said, waving to the twins. "What is the bathing ritual of Boroni?"

"Oil and blade on occasion," Jined said.

Loïc slapped his head. *That explains so much.*

"What?"

Didus grimaced. "The people of Boroni. They dress nice, but they aren't the most fragrant people."

Except when they are, Cävian said. *When they wear more perfume than is reasonable.*

Cävian stepped forward and poured out the contents of the bottle into the water.

Go on, he said. *Get in.*

Jined had already slipped down into the water. It was hot. But his ears burned hotter.

"What's wrong?" Didus asked, slipping in across the pool.

"Now I'm self-conscious."

"Don't consider it an admonishment. It's a jest and a cultural marker as well. If you find it a problem, or wish to change it, then change it."

"I don't want to start dousing myself in scented oils. I don't much care for it."

"Well, we've not talked about it, but there is a practice among our Vow of Prayer to wear sachets of incense. They're often customized by each brother."

"To what purpose?"

"The sachets create a scent memory, often associated with prayer. If I smell a sachet in the air, I'm reminded to pray. I'll speak with the keeper of the chapel and prepare one for you. You can keep it in your gorget. Some wear one hanging from their cordons, in addition to their beads."

He took a phial of oil from Loïc, who waded over to give it to him, then returned to sit by his brother. Didus modestly took off his robe and began to scrub himself down.

Jined closed his eyes and sank under the water. As he came back up the scent of salts and oils washed over him. He rose out of the pool.

"Where are you going?" Didus asked.

"I need to go find a place to myself," he said. He donned another robe and left the baths, too embarrassed by what the three of them had said about him to stay. He walked past the rows of personal cells and on to the refectory. There he saw someone he wasn't interested in talking to, sitting at a table in the corner. He made to go when Dane turned and saw him there.

"Brazstein," Dane called.

Jined stopped in his tracks and turned.

Dane approached him.

"Brazstein," Dane said again. "Primus Brazstein."

"What is it, Marric?"

"I..." Dane faltered, then sighed. "I owe you an apology. Several in fact."

"What?" Jined replied incredulously.

"I've learned much over the past several weeks here, under

Zoumerik's guidance. Not least of which is that a clear conscience is greater than gold."

"What are you apologizing for?"

"Well, the looks I gave you. The haughty attitude, thinking myself better than you. The jealousy. The...hatred I bear for you. Bore for you."

"And you no longer do?" Jined asked.

"You have something I wish I had. Rather than being jealous, it's better to have the humility to ask how you acquired it."

"What do I have that you don't?"

"Your strong faith in Grissone. What am I missing?"

"I... don't know," Jined said. "but I suppose that is the point of faith. To feel your way slowly in the dark, with only the lantern of your hope held out."

"Those are good words. May I repeat them?"

"I suppose. Why?"

"I was challenged to collect words of faith from those who are blessed by Grissone. As much as I have disliked seeing you blessed by our god in the past, I will swallow my pride and ask you to absolve me of my offenses against you."

"Absolution is not mine to give," Jined said. "I am no chaplain."

"You are a Primus. You now outrank me twice. We can confess to anyone of higher rank."

"I'm not sure how."

"Apparently, a prayer said on my behalf."

"I'm not going to lie. This entire conversation is a shock to me."

"Imagine how I must feel," Dane said.

He bowed his head.

Jined tentatively reached out and touched the top of Dane's shaven head, as chaplains had done for him.

"Grissone, Lord of Faith," he began, "in prayer I accept my brother's plea for forgiveness, and ask you to absolve him of his guilt and transgressions. By your will, by the Anka, and by the vows taken upon the Pariantür, it is said and done."

Dane looked up, a smile playing across his lips.

"Thank you, Primus," he said, and turned to go.

Jined watched the man who had been a burr in his saddle for so long.

"Did that really happen?" Jined said to himself, half hoping Grissone might suddenly appear at that moment. He did not. Jined stood alone in the refectory. The scent of the bath oils still lingered in the air, and he wondered again how long his companions had turned up their noses at him and said nothing.

20

FORGOTTEN

There is a reference to three seeds—all that remain of an original five.

That even these remain is yet to be known.

—AVINE GELDIN

Torches guttered on every corner, and from sconces hung by those living in balconied apartments. In the middle of the square a flame burned in the center of a silver bowl, around which women stood in conversation, ran errands, or watched as the three women entered the market.

"You've moved the vaults into the under-city?" Astrid asked, staring about her in awe.

"Oh no," Little Maeda said, smiling. "The vaults of the Flowerwives and Alewives still continue to thrive. This is the 'City of the Forgotten.' Well, most here just call it 'Forgotten.' Especially those who live in the darker neighborhoods."

"This isn't all of it?" Katiam asked.

Little Maeda let out a laugh. "There are several thousand people living down here now. Some flee the burgeoning war, others are immigrants who had arrived in Bortali, and we have a whole neighborhood of Day Blind."

She pointed to the front of a large house. "That is where Mother Superioris Smith lives."

"Not in one of the vaults?" Astrid asked.

"Forgotten has the closest access to the hospital, and all three of the other vaults are easily accessed by this one."

A woman nearby suddenly cried out and ran toward them and threw her arms around Katiam.

"You're alive!" the woman cried. She had a veil down over her face.

"Who..." Katiam said.

The woman lifted her veil and Katiam gasped.

"Esenath?"

"Yes! It is you!"

She dropped the veil back down over her face.

"How are you alive?" Esenath asked.

"Why are you wearing a veil?" Katiam responded. "Did you take on another Aspect?"

"I wish that were so," Esenath said. "I contracted Day Blind, I'm afraid."

"Truly?" Katiam asked, her heart sinking.

"No need to worry about catching it. We have no reason to believe it's contagious."

"If it were," Little Maeda said, "the whole of the vault here would have caught it. This began as a place to sequester people who needed a dark place to live."

"How did you recognize me across the square, then?" Katiam asked.

"I'm not entirely blind," Esenath said. "I'm merely light sensitive. But it is true, I didn't recognize you across the square."

"I did," a younger woman said from behind Esenath.

Katiam and Astrid turned to see Onelie Clemmbäkker. She wore a white robe over the blush-pink undergarment of a Crysalas Novitiate.

"Onelie!" Katiam said with a smile.

"I'm known as Sister Pleasant here," she said. She scrunched her nose. "I didn't pick the name, but it serves well enough as a pseudonym to keep prying ears away."

"Ah," Katiam said. "Pleasant. I can see that."

"Let us find a place to talk privately," Esenath said. "I have so many questions."

"Fedelmina should have a room we can speak in," Sister Pleasant said.

Esenath nodded and led the way. They walked past Mother Smith's house at the other end of the square, where a tall, thin house stood. Esenath walked up to the door and knocked. After a long wait, the door opened and the form of a tall and large-boned woman, Fedelmina Barba, appeared. Esenath spoke with her in a low voice; Fedelmina glanced at the four women in the street and nodded for them to enter. She led them down a narrow hall to a sitting room, lit by bright blue starblush which she dimmed down by touching a sconce.

"Is it still too bright?" Fedelmina asked Esenath.

"I can grin and bear it," Esenath said. "I'm not missing this chat."

The women turned to Katiam and Astrid.

"Please have a seat, dears," Fedelmina said.

"Thank you for having us in," Katiam said.

"Of course, my dear. Oh my dear. Of course. We all thought you were dead." She turned to Astrid. "I feared you'd never be heard of nor seen again, when word came that you had stayed as sole occupant at Precipice."

"Why did you come to Waglÿsaor?" Esenath asked.

"How are you still alive?" Fedelmina added.

Katiam took a seat. "There is a lot to tell, and we're not sure how much we ought to share."

"You are among the most trusted women of the vaults," Fedelmina said. "Perhaps in sharing with us, we can help you know what you should and should not share with others."

"Others?" Astrid asked.

"As a leader in this vault," Fedelmina said, "I would be remiss to misspeak of others."

"There are a few of us," Onelie said, "who gather out of the sight of others, because we fear that there are those in the vault taken in by the teachings from St. Rämmon."

"I don't understand," Katiam said.

"We are getting ahead of ourselves," Esenath said. "Please, Katiam, tell us what happened. How did you disappear from Precipice, and what brought you here?"

"I have water on the fire," Fedelmina said. "Sister Pleasant, dear, please come with me and help me bring back tea." She turned back to the others. "Don't share anything until I'm back. I wish to hear it all."

"I'll go and help them as well," Little Maeda said, following after.

An awkward silence settled on the room.

"I am sorry to hear about your catching Day Blind," Katiam said to Esenath.

"In some ways I am glad it came to me," Esenath said. "I had been studying it, you know, and I have a feeling it is caused by something botanical in nature. Experiencing it first-hand better helps me to understand it."

"What makes you think it is related to botany?"

"I believe it arrives on a northern wind. Two weeks ago there was a gentle breeze, after which I awakened with blurry vision. Within a week, an entirely new outbreak occurred."

"And you know it is not contagious, how?"

"Because I would have contracted it much sooner, having been in close proximity with those who had it before."

A silence settled back on the room.

"When last I saw you," Esenath said to Astrid, "you swore you would never leave Precipice and the mountains around it. You swore you would be the protector of the Dweol. What changed your mind?"

"I am still its protector," Astrid said. "If we're in the company of women we can trust to keep a great secret, we'll share what we mean."

"I can think of no more trusted women than myself and the three of them."

As she said this, the others returned with trays. Fedelmina set the tea on a side table, while Little Maeda and Onelie placed trays with meat, cheese, and biscuits on a small table in the middle. Fedelmina resumed her seat with a wave of invitation to eat the food. "The tea shall be ready in a few minutes. Please, tell us everything."

"Well," Katiam started. "You know the Matriarch has passed on."

The others nodded.

"I was with her when she passed, and in my grief I fled the room. There I discovered a glowing Dweol petal, and when I touched it I awakened in another place entirely—the Veld."

Esenath gasped.

"I shall describe all I saw there another time. As it turned out, I had arrived in a protected pasture, and there I met another who had lost her way—Sabine Upona."

"Sabine lives?" Fedelmina said with a broad grin.

"She does, although no longer in our world but in the Veld.

"We traveled together and arrived at a Dweol that had not yet been destroyed like the one in Precipice. It sat at the bottom of a pool and I dove in to touch it, to return to our world, but instead it took me to yet another world—Lomïn itself."

"That is unheard of!" Esenath said.

"It seems I was called there, along with others of our order from across Kallattai. We were summoned there for one purpose—for our goddess to share a message."

"You met our goddess?" Little Maeda asked.

Katiam nodded. "We did not see her because we still lived, and seeing her would strike us down. But Maeda Mür was there, which confirmed the truth of what occurred."

"And what occurred, exactly?" Fedelmina said as she rose to prepare cups of tea.

"Our goddess shared the true purpose of the Crysalas. It has not been the protection of women—that is merely an outpouring of our seeking of purity. But our seeking of purity was a means to draw us closer to her will, and prepare us for the task now at hand."

"What is that task?" Esenath asked.

"To seek, discover, and restore the Warotha."

"Warotha?" Little Maeda asked.

"The Rotha, you mean?" Esenath added.

Katiam nodded.

"Oh Katiam," Esenath said. "I'm sorry. It was lost."

Katiam shook her head, a smile playing across her face.

She touched the front of her cloak, still pulled tightly around her, and began to open it, revealing the bundle within.

"Is that..." Esenath said.

Katiam opened the bundle to reveal the elongated brown bulb of a body within a tangle of vines, and atop it a closed bud. She placed it on her lap like a baby; the vines began to quiver, the five leaves at the end unfurling in a stretch. Fedelmina stopped what she was doing and watched.

"Wake, Little Rose," Katiam whispered.

The bud opened before their eyes, and a small rose-like flower bloomed.

"Hello, Little Rose," Katiam said tenderly.

"Laaaarozzzz," the little creature whistled from two thorns below the stem.

"Yes. Larozh," Katiam said.

"It's alive," Fedelmina said.

"Is it a thinking creature?" Onelie asked.

Katiam nodded. "More a creature like you or me than an animal, I think."

"But how?" Onelie said.

"We're not entirely sure," Katiam said. "Crysania made it clear it is important, so we're journeying east for more answers."

"It's adorable," Little Maeda said.

The Rotha, Larozh, seemed to look around the room, eyeless, and sniffing at everything through its flower. The leaves on the ends of the vines reached out to touch everything. It tried pulling itself up Katiam, and it took a firm hand to keep the little thing contained.

"It's like a baby," Little Maeda laughed. "Did you say its name is Larozh?"

"I was calling it Little Rose. After it ate a petal of loosetongue, it began to try whistling words through its thorns."

"It speaks?" Fedelmina said. "It truly speaks?"

Esenath had remained silent, utter amazement on her face.

She crossed the room and dropped to her knees before Katiam. She lifted her veil, blinking against the light, but unperturbed by the pain the light caused her.

"Would you like to hold her?" Katiam asked.

Esenath looked up at Katiam, tears welling in her eyes, clasping her hands before her. "May I?"

"You are the one I've most wished to share this with," Katiam said.

Esenath held out her hands as Katiam lifted Larozh forward, offering the little Rotha to her. Esenath took it up in her hands, holding it out awkwardly at first. The little leafy hands twisted and writhed, and at first the blossom pointed back toward Katiam.

"It is all right, Larozh," Esenath said. "Auntie Esenath is here."

"Annzzeeeenaaath," Larozh whistled.

Esenath burst out laughing through tears.

"It can hear? It can see?"

"I don't think it sees at all," Katiam said. "It smells and sees by that."

"What have you been feeding it?"

"It prefers flower petals, if you would believe it."

Esenath pulled the Rotha closer in an embrace that might comfort a babe.

It turned away from Katiam and began to sniff at Esenath. It sniffed at her collar, then sneezed.

The women all laughed fondly.

It continued to sniff, and made its way to Esenath's face and eyes.

"What is it doing?" Little Maeda asked.

"Getting to know me, I think," Esenath replied.

It came to Esenath's eyes, sniffed, and sneezed again, then began to snuffle at her eyes, more and more aggressively.

"Should it do that?" Astrid said. "If she has Day Blind?"

"It isn't hurting me," Esenath said, "if that's what you mea..."

Esenath suddenly gasped, then cried out loud

"What is it?" Katiam said, dropping on the ground next to Esenath.

"I..." Esenath said, holding out the Rotha to Katiam and rising to her feet. "I can see!"

"What?"

"It's gone! The film across my eyes is gone!"

The Rotha began to sneeze violently. The sneeze turned to a sort of cough, and out of the blossom a small pearl, not much larger than a grain of sand, fell onto Katiam's lap.

"What is that?" Onelie asked.

"I don't know," Katiam said. "There is so much we don't know or understand about Larozh."

"It doesn't seem bothered by it, though," Astrid said.

"You've brought a miracle with you," Fedelmina said, having pressed Esenath into a seat and examined her eyes with a candle.

"You've brought healing," Esenath said. "You could heal the city's Moon-Eyes."

A knock came to the door. Fedelmina rose and left, returning a few moments later.

"Mother Smith is at her home now. She's summoned the two of you to appear."

Katiam began to wrap the Rotha back up into its bundle.

"What are you doing?" Esenath asked. "She ought to know about this, too."

Astrid turned, a grave look on her face. "Katiam was given a mission and purpose by Crysania, but also a warning. The Rotha must be kept secret. If the gods of the Black Coterie were to discover it, they would seek its destruction."

"Then I agree," Fedelmina said. "Smith ought not to know."

"You said you had something to share about her," Katiam said.

"She took it very hard that the Dweol was destroyed and the

Matriarch dead. After the news came that the Paladins were retreating to Pariantür, she threw in her lot with Zoumerik. Together they seek to unite the Hammer and the Rose here as a new bastion of the faiths, but they have an interesting set of rules and thoughts on how to accomplish that. Stay agreeable, and we four women shall ensure you have what you need to continue your mission."

"And what mission is that?" Esenath said, turning to Katiam.

"We travel east," Katiam said.

"To Pariantür, and beyond. There are other Rotha, and we've been tasked to find them."

Another knock came to the door.

"You ought to go," Fedelmina said.

"I'll escort you," Little Maeda said. "Come on."

The atmosphere had changed in the secret city as they exited Fedelmina's house and came out into the street. Everyone watched them in quiet curiosity as they moved toward the house across the square, where a large torch guttered, perhaps denoting the occupant was home. As they came to the bottom of the stairs leading up to the door, Little Maeda bade Katiam and Astrid wait and proceeded to knock.

The low, commanding voice of Mother Sigri Smith came from somewhere deep within the house, calling them to enter. Little Maeda opened the door and led the way down the stark, unadorned hallway to a small waiting room. Several harsh wooden chairs sat along the wall. They did not take seats, but proceeded into the room beyond. Sigri sat on the other side of a wooden table with nothing else in the room but the parchment stretched out on the table, which she kept her eyes on even as she spoke to them.

"I understand you just arrived in town."

"Yes, Mother Superioris," Astrid replied. "We came directly to the hospital to report."

"And yet, when you were instructed to enter this secret city, you did not come here and await my arrival. Instead you went off to do as you please."

Astrid did not reply.

Sigri looked up. "You do not deny that you did so?"

"We were not instructed to come and await your arrival at your residence," Astrid started. "We instead bided our time, reacquainting ourselves with old friends."

"A Paladame committed to guarding the derelict Oracle, and a physician presumed dead, and rather than report this to me first, you have allowed rumors to circulate concerning your return."

"Not rumors," Katiam said. "Our arrival dispelled any rumors, I should think."

"It has been many long weeks, and now you show up here. What took you both so long to show up?"

"Weather did not permit us to journey past Zebüdé," Astrid said. "We helped out at the vault there, and proceeded as the weather cleared."

"Why did you abandon your post at the Oracle?"

"I am not at liberty to give a full disclosure," Astrid said.

"You answer to me as your superior and captain."

"I do not," Astrid said sternly. "I answer to the secret calling placed upon me by the goddess herself."

"A verified calling? Granted by a vision?" Sigri stood slowly, her eyes never leaving Astrid.

"I am not at liberty to say. Our road goes east. We shall meet with those at the Oracle near Pariantür and confer with the experts there."

"As you are under my authority here, you'll leave when the timing is right."

"We have no intention of leaving immediately, but would like the opportunity to prepare for our journey, as we may travel through war-torn lands."

"Not war-torn just yet," Sigri said. "If the diplomatic ministrations of St. Rämmon make the headway they intend, it may not come to that. But we leave that to the wisdom of the fortress's leadership."

"Until then, we can count on your hospitality?"

"In return for your duties," Sigri replied. She turned to Katiam. "You were thought dead, perhaps destroyed by the Dweol with Sister Sabine Upona."

"I passed through ways unknown and unseen, and returned by the goddess's will," answered Katiam.

"You speak in riddles. I do not appreciate it."

"If it makes you feel better, I spoke with Maeda Mür before she died, and it was she who had the oracular vision and told us the purpose of it. I beg you not hinder but help."

"I shall consult with Pater Zoumerik."

"Why defer to him when the vaults are under your command?" Astrid asked. "Are you not autonomous?"

"The Dweol crumbled," Sigri said, a dark look in her eyes. "The purpose of the vaults are in question now."

"This secret city stands," Astrid replied. "Your hospital stands. Dweol or not, your purpose holds true."

"To what end?" Sigri asked. "We are under St. Rämmon's sponsorship, and shall defer to them as it protects us and our purpose, then it is what I shall do. You'll do well to recall that you answer to me, not I to you."

"We answer to our calling, and to those leaders still at Pariantür and to the new Crysalas Matriarch Superioris elected by those there."

"You forfeited your calling and duty when you left the sacred Oracle you swore to protect."

Astrid opened her mouth to speak, but Sigri held up a hand.

"We are all tired," Sigri said, "and I'll not continue this circular argument when I hold authority. You may leave."

Katiam turned to see Little Maeda still standing there, a look of surprise stricken across her face.

"See they are given a place to stay, and that it is not far from here, Sister Salna," Sigri said, returning to her pen and parchment.

She ignored them as they left.

21

MONSTERS

It is with years of experience that I bring about this book for your perusal, codifying the kingdom of animals. I shall draw conclusions that contradict centuries of understanding, for I have compared and contrasted without tradition in mind. It is common enough to assume the ælerne and dwov, both four-winged birds, to be related, but this is false. The gryph and ælerne have more in common, while the faint glow of the dwov at night indicates a closer relationship to the forest will-of-wisps. Tradition teaches only proverbial explanations of the unknown. Observation is the true oracle of knowledge.

—INTRODUCTION IN *THE ANIMAL CODES* BY PROFESSOR GHINT ABENNA OF THE THEMENTHU COLLEGE OF NATURAL SCIENCES

"We'll not go to the Bastion in Bremüm," Dorian said. "Given what happened with Loth at the Green Bastion, I'm not sure we can trust anyone."

"It pains me to hear you say that," Marn said, "but I understand."

"Do we not think that Loth will escape again?" the monk Guarin asked.

"Given three more of the brothers disappeared from the bastion before the sun had passed its apex, I imagine they all knew Loth was untrustworthy and likely to turn them in. He'll remain there for a time under Averin's imprisonment."

"I fear for Pater Averin," Nidian said.

"He will not leave his bastion," Dorian said. "I spoke with him again before we left. He shall remain until they take it from him."

"Both admirable and saddening," Nidian said.

"It is. We all must choose the burdens we bear upon our souls. At times, we must answer for those choices."

"And what of the remains you sought to view?" Guarin asked.

"It bore a hole between the eyes, as though a circle of the bone had been removed by a precision tool. I'd wager it is the circumference of the individual links of chain incorporated into the mail worn by Searn VeTurres."

"That confirms a suspicion of yours?"

"Indeed," Dorian said. "I'll say no more for now. It has left me with much to think on."

They entered a dark stretch of evergreen forest, the bushes cut back from the edge. Signs of some forest work could be seen, though not done recently.

"These are very old woods," Marn offered.

"Indeed," Dorian said. "They were old when I was a lad and traveled this way."

"Are you from Mahndür?"

"I was born in Varea," Dorian said. "As was my wife, and, if my guess is correct, your grandfather, Nethendel."

"How did you come to be a Paladin?" Marn asked. Rallia fell in alongside her father, just as interested.

"Chasing my future wife, actually," Dorian chuckled. "She disappeared from our small community one night, seeking to visit the Oracle that sits in the mountains above the Green Bastion. I was asked by her brother Nethendel to go with him to seek her out, although I felt she had betrayed me, for I had every intention of marrying her and her leaving was an insult to my tender young pride. She refused to return home when we found her, having been ordained by her goddess at the Oracle. In the end, Grissone took hold of my soul, and I gave it to him."

"And then the Protectorate Wars happened," Marn said.

"Indeed," Dorian said.

Runah walked off into the woods with Rallia and Ophedia to look for firewood. Alodda took a seat on the log next to Hanen, reaching out to give Whisper a scratch.

"You seem lost in thought these last few days," she said.

"Do I?" Hanen asked.

"I suppose we all have a lot on our minds. I'm not sure how I'm going to support my sister and myself."

"I wasn't being flirtatious when I said you are a good embroiderer."

"Thank you," she said. "But finding work will still be hard."

"Can't you reach out through the church of Crysania?"

"They can be hard to find outside the cities, but you're right, that is the first step."

They sat in silence for some time. She poked the fire with a stick.

"What will you do?" she asked.

"What do you mean?"

"Rallia mentioned she's waiting to see what you decide to do."

"She didn't say what we were considering, did she?"

"Only that you were at a crossroads. What are your choices?"

"The most obvious one is to forget what happened in Mahn Fulhar and go back to Edi City. I'm sure we can find you some work there, and Rallia and I could return to our caravan. If we press hard enough, we might even arrive before the second one leaves the city."

"I hear it's quite hot in Edi. "

"In the summer. The winters rarely snow."

"I'm not sure I'd like that."

"The other road, helping Dorian seek out this armor he mentioned, leads me to face what happened in Mahn Fulhar."

"What did happen in Mahn Fulhar? None of you have actually said what happened."

"Our commander, Searn, made something—a cloak of sorts, but made of bone. Animal bones mostly, but some of the links were made from more macabre materials."

"Human bones, you mean."

"Yes. This cloak gave him some sort of power, which he used to try and bring down the Paladins of the Hammer, in league with the Moteans."

"But you somehow stopped him?"

Hanen nodded. "I inferred that the shades that came from the cloak were as afraid of fire as Wyloths, and we contained them with torches. Searn killed himself."

"And the bone cloak?"

"Went missing."

"I feel sorry for whoever has it now."

"Why?" Hanen asked, his ears burning.

"This Searn knew what he was doing when he made it. He had

already gone down that long road of his choosing. But what if whoever has it now doesn't know what it is? They could be forfeiting their soul without realizing it."

Hanen pulled his Sentinel cloak closer around his shoulders.

"So if those are your two choices, going home to Edi or taking this unknown road with Dorian, what do you think you'll do?" Alodda asked.

"What can I do? I feel frozen in indecision."

She put a comforting hand on his shoulder. "You'll do the right thing in the end. I'm sure of it."

"She has more confidence in me than I do," Hanen said to Whisper, as she walked away.

The Abecinian Monks came into the firelight carrying bundles of wood. They dropped them by the fire; Hanen reached out and ordered them into piles. Dorian and Marn came out of the woods as well, Marn holding a small cache of fish in a net.

"It looks like I still have the touch," Marn said. "It's been a while since I river fished."

He turned to Hanen. "Spread the coals out, and let's get these up over the flame."

Marn and Hanen soon had a fish hanging over the fire for each member of the party. One of the monks, with Marn's guidance, fed greener wood over the coals to keep a strong smoke rising into the calm forest air. As the group reassembled in the circle, they sat on the logs and ate. Zhag finished first, took out his small flute, and raised a beautiful but haunting tune. A warm breeze from the south meandered into the camp; stars blinked into view as the clouds above rolled away.

Then Zhag's melody faded and the wind with it.

One night," Marn said, dropping his voice into the cadence of a storyteller, "I sat upon the stairs of my home, and an old man passed by from the crossroad to town, humming a familiar tune. I was only a boy at the time, with my grandfather away. My bravery was green and untried.

He came to the gate that kept strangers at bay, if only by tradition—a child could have lept it; in fact I had, many a time— and asked, "Would you test that bravery within your chest?" I startled—for how had he known my thoughts? "What do you mean, stranger?" I asked. The old man chuckled. "I mean nothing by it," he said. "Only I just came from the crossroad and saw upon the signpost a zvolder web, a twelve-legged fiend at its center with brilliant color upon its armor. You seem a lad who might wish to see such a wonder."

"I thank you kindly," says I. "But I am charged by my mother's father to stay at my post."

The old man shrugged and away he walked.

Silver Umay rose and shed her glow, by which I could see the silver-threaded weave with the black of chitin at its center, turning web to eye as it bore its gaze upon me. And I was frightened. My bravery struck like a hammer upon the forge of fear. I found myself at my gate, watching that gaze, and pondering the fear within my gut that pushed back against my bravery.

After a time, the red glow of rising Norlok lit the eastern horizon as it followed its sister moon in the nightly dance across the starlit sky. The baleful stare of the web glinted in both lights. And the fear within me grew.

I saw then a languid form move into the light of the moons to the center of the crossroads. It was a small cör. I could not tell its color nor even its true size in the double shadows cast by the moons taking from its form, and adding fear within my gut. It sat in such a way that I could not tell if it was contemplating the zvolder and its web, or myself. I had no doubt that something was about to take place.

The night wore on and I leaned upon the gate, watching as the unmoving cör and the baleful web continued their vigil at the crossroads. Into the silver and red lights danced and capered a troupe of wyloths, performing for zvolder and cör a merry dance. A shiver ran down my spine, adding a rising dread to the fear that stood stoically in my gut.

But the troupe fell still upon the road, their dance upon the road complete, and exhaustion brought them low. And yet the cör only watched. The zvolder did not strike. The moons continued their slow procession, and I wondered at this. For by what means does a cör not take easy food? Nor zvolder the opportunity to capture prey? It was then the thought dawned on me. Perhaps they worked not their wiles upon each other, but instead upon another. Something, someone I could not see. Or perhaps, said the terror growing in my heart, they worked together against one I could only have seen in a mirror. Perhaps they sought to take me.

My bravery quavered and collapsed. I fled into my house, slamming the door, for fear, dread, and terror had conspired against me, and my bravery buckled.

The zvolder's web suddenly flashed with a consuming fire, and I felt the dark magic the Deceiver used to ensnare the souls of untoward men, and I shrank from that in fear. Moments later, the door I had just slammed began to rattle, the latch clicked, and I began to cry out to the gods to protect me. I prayed I did not fall to such agony as a zvolder, house-cör, and a troupe of wyloths might mete upon me.

Into the house stepped an answer to prayer, the form of one who always banished my fear, day in and out. My grandfather had returned. He took me into his arms and consoled me until I could see reason once more, and could describe what I had seen. The old man then carried me out the door, and fear, dread, and terror took hold of me again. I fell to crying and pleading to go back into the house. He carried me through the gate and down the path to the crossroads where zvolder, cör, and wyloth awaited me. "Look," he said, pointing to the ground. He kicked at leaves lying still on the road. "No troupe of wyloths, come to cavort." He put me down and pointed to a gap in the cobbles, the deep shadows cast by moons playing tricks upon the mind. "No cör come to guide you to a dark dream." He took my hand, and we walked back to our home, and sat together before the fire. "What of the zvolder and his deceitful web?" asked I? "Indeed, there was one. I saw it as I passed, coming from town. I touched my torch to his web, and it burned just as I saw you flee into the house."

"Then it was something to fear?"

"Fear is what you invited into your mind, when you let your imagination grow past what you had been told. The old man who gave you a warning only told you of a curiosity. It was your own mind that made the fear grow."

"But I had no bravery. I ran in fear."

"You ran because you were brave. What hope would you, a little boy, have against the machinations of darker gods? But I have the experience and knowledge to light the web aflame without burning the post, the crossroads, the world."

"I've never liked zvolders," Marn finished the tale, "especially after that night. But however much I still recoil, I do not flee at their sight."

They all sat quietly until Ophedia yawned loudly and stretched. Then she laughed. "Rallia, do you recall when the qavyl Ymbrys and you went into the abandoned zvolder nest, then tried to get the rest of us to eat the eggs?"

Rallia laughed. "They really weren't that bad."

"You ate zvolder eggs?" Dorian asked with disgust on his face.

Rallia nodded. "I was thinking about that story when I walked into the webbed nest. You told it over a few dark winters in Garrou."

"I forgot that Ymbrys traveled north with you," Marn said.

"Who is Ymbrys?" Alodda asked.

"A qavyl," Hanen said. "The one that gave me that gildpound in the first place."

There was a rustling in the tight branches of the pines, moving up the boughs, making its way higher. The monk Nidian stood, taking up a torch, and turned to face the trees.

"Put that torch back," Dorian said. "It'll only start a fire."

"I heard something," Nidian said.

"We all heard it," Dorian said, "and I don't like it either, but the sleipnir aren't spooked yet, and they're a good gauge for bad fauna."

"The story might have been a bit much, Father," Rallia said.

Marn chuckled. "Perhaps. I imagine they're used to lighter fare down south. Doesn't seem to bother you, though."

"We were both born in Bortali," Hanen said, "where the threat of vül is always a worry. You and the men who came into the poor kitchen always had a frightening story to tell."

"Where I was raised in Morraine," Marn said, "the tales were even more frightening, especially when told by storytellers from Nasun, hailing from that land of deep winters where they don't see the sun for months."

"What do you think it is?" Alodda said, pulling herself close to Hanen.

"Making that sound?" Hanen replied. "Could be a branch scraping. There are enough of us here to protect you, if that's what you're worried about."

"I'll take the first watch," Ophedia offered.

"I doubt I'll get much sleep," Nidian replied, eyeing the trees.

"Well," Dorian said, "just don't burn the trees down while we sleep."

Nidian laughed nervously.

The others found their sacks, pulling closer to each other and the fire. Hanen rolled over and fell asleep quickly, accustomed to odd sounds in the forest. In what seemed like an instant, however, he was awakened by nudges from Rallia, who crouched down and put a hand over his mouth. In the breaking dawn Whisper sat guard over Alodda, his scales rattling out caution.

"What is it?" Hanen whispered.

Rallia pointed first at the tree above the camp, then out into the woods.

Hanen eyed the tree boughs. There was something there. Like a long green vine, moving slowly but continuously through the branches.

He glanced across the glade to a form that was hunched over something. It had gray skin and a full mane of fur over its shoulders.

"It's sniffing at the remains of the fish I left there," Rallia said.

"Who else is awake?"

"No one yet."

"Wake Ophedia first, then Dorian. I'll wake Zhag."

Rallia dropped low and moved quietly across the camp to where Ophedia leaned against the tree. Hanen touched the hrelgren's shoulder and his eyes popped open. Hanen made a signal for him to be quiet, and then drew out his axes. The hrelgren rolled over and unsheathed two single bladed short swords.

"Then it is a dræc," he muttered, pointing to the thing in the trees.

"And something over there."

The hrelgren stood, his swords at the ready. Ophedia eyed the sinewy thing moving above the sleeping Marn. Dorian stood cautiously with Rallia's assistance, and then poked at the girls and monks. He motioned for them to rise and join him in moving the sleipnirs further into the woods.

The dræc in the tree did not seem too interested in them, but in the growing light Hanen saw it was easily twenty feet long, its body covered in sharply-tipped legs that rippled as it moved, its scaly segments flowing from branch to branch. Marn was just starting to rise when the creature decided to come down out of the branches. Its head was flat-nosed, marking it a less toxic breed, but the long whiskers, like the antennae of a myrm, felt around, and Hanen knew from the tales that those might numb what they touched.

The dræc suddenly halted and recoiled back up into the tree as the creature in the glade turned and began rummaging through the brush toward the camp.

"Should we bolt?" Ophedia hissed.

"No," the hrelgren said. "Now I see what it is."

"What is it?" Ophedia asked.

"Amyt," Zhag muttered. "They like to charge whatever runs."

It came into view, near-sighted and still unaware of them, its long, thin snout and two long tusks shoveling through the underbrush. Bristling like quills or feathers, its mane of thick hair covered its strong neck and shoulders, and a short, stout tail stuck out behind it. Although it stood no taller than Whisper, Hanen did not wish to risk its wrath. Marn slowly stood up and began to move toward the other monks. Dorian, Alodda, and her sister sat upon or next to the sleipnirs.

Suddenly the dræc fell from the tree, throwing its coils around Marn. Before anyone could react, the Amyt flew into a startled fury at the noise and charged into the camp. The dræc reared up, freeing Marn of its coils, and tried to climb the tree again as the Amyt charged toward it, seemingly unaware of the humans and hrelgren. Marn barely threw himself out of the way as the Amyt's tusks hit the wood, shaking the tree. Rallia took hold of one of the dræc's many legs and pulled it down as it tried to lunge at her. She swung forward, her axe chopping across its back. It hissed, and the Amyt near Rallia's feet spun in a fit of frenzy, its tusks trying to shovel and gore anything it could.

And then Whisper was there.

The little ynfald charged the Amyt, his scales protecting him from the Amyt's tusks, which merely lifted the little creature into the air and threw him in a curled ball across the space. Zhag caught him and set him down.

"Get him!" the hrelgren encouraged the ynfald.

The ynfald rustled his scales, the Amyt lowered its head, and they charged each other. The ynfald bounded over the Amyt's back and leapt into the open mouth of the dræc, which was baring its teeth at Rallia. The dræc clamped its mouth down on the impervious scales of the ynfald and recoiled. Rallia took a quick sidestep and brought the axe down behind its head, freeing it from its body.

Rallia kicked the head toward the Amyt as it fell to the ground.

Ophedia had both her clubs in her hands; she was working up

her courage as she watched the Amyt take the dræc head in its mouth and whip it around violently.

"Ophedia?" Hanen said. "Don't do anything rash."

Dorian approached Hanen and handed him a crossbow.

"It's mad and nearsighted. It doesn't really know what it's doing. Put the animal down."

Hanen nodded and lifted the crossbow, which Dorian had loaded for him. He took a deep breath and let loose the bolt. It shot true, through the mane, and sunk deep. That only angered it further.

"For Ozri!" Ophedia screamed, and threw herself forward.

She leapt on top of the creature, taking hold of the mane with one hand and wielding her axe against it with the other. The small but powerful creature spun, looking for a way to escape. When it tried to flee into the woods, she pulled the head back, forcing its tusks into the air. Taking hold of a tusk and planting her feet firmly on the ground, she got the axe bill under its throat and cut deep. The animal flailed about for a few moments as she backed away, blood spurting across the nearby bushes. Then, seemingly in the middle of its frenzy, it suddenly stopped and fell dead in a heap.

22

Bremüm

Scepter returned from the night of celebration drunker than usual, and I gave him another bottle of some of the stronger beer we had brewed the previous year, to get him to talking. Apparently, he and Zephyr have been working on something, and I recognized their little project as the beginnings of the boneshroud. He did not realize I knew how it could be done, from my reading of the Heptagrammaton. They had successfully made two links and bound them together with blood. He passed out before going any further, but not before saying the word that would lead me down a long road—shadebook.

—JOURNAL OF SEARN VETURRES, ENTRY TWENTY

T o Ophedia's eyes Bremüm sat unchanged. The same frost that covered the ground the autumn before had not yet retreated, despite sitting further south than Mahn Fulhar. They moved into the city in procession and came to one of the smaller inns bearing the image of an Amyt above the door. Ophedia followed Hanen, Marn, and Dorian as they entered and came to the bar.

"We're looking for two rooms," Dorian said. The bartender didn't give him his attention.

"Excuse me?" Marn said.

Again, no reaction. Hanen approached, placing his crossbow on the bar and dropping the Amyt tusks, both his axes, and his satchel on it as well. The bartender turned to him.

"Long day on the road?" he finally said.

Hanen paid him the same lack of attention. The bartender approached and placed a tankard of ale out in front of him.

"You look road weary," he said.

Hanen lifted the tankard, took a long pull, then pointed his elbow at Dorian and Marn.

"They were here first," Hanen said.

The bartender gave Marn and Dorian, in their gray monastic robes, a look. He glanced past the two older men, and gave a brief but leering glance at Ophedia before remembering his place, and turning back to Hanen.

"Are they with you?" he asked Hanen.

"Why?"

"We're not to serve monks. Them asking for help is a test, we're told."

"By whom?" Dorian asked, stepping toward Hanen.

"Them who come from the south. The Œronzi."

Hanen leaned in. "Are they still here?"

"Not sure I should say. "

"I'm a Black Sentinel. You think these monks need my protection if they're with the Œronzi?"

"What are you looking for?"

"Looking for? Rooms. Two of them."

"I've got two rooms off in the back, if you need."

"We're not looking to stay out of sight," Hanen said. "Just somewhere quiet. We had a bit of excitement this morning, and some of our members could use the calm."

"Oh?"

He pushed the two tusks across the bar.

"Fine Amyt tusks," the bartender said. "Not off a big one."

"Is the ivory worth anything?"

"Not in Bremüm. Not a day goes by where one of these isn't brought in by a forester. They're always out there looking for trouble. You run into one?"

"Almost got away without a scrap, if a dræc hadn't dropped out of a tree on Marn here."

"Probably good the Amyt was there then."

"Oh?"

"The Dræc and Amyt hate each other. They generally stay outta each other's way."

Hanen reached into his satchel and pulled out a gold royal.

"Will this do for bed, food, and drink?" Hanen asked. "We'll be on our way in the morning."

"Depends on how many of you there are."

"Ten," Hanen said.

The man sucked in on his teeth. "I ought not to," he said. "That'll be a lotta laundry my daughters'll be doing."

"Another royal," Hanen replied, "and that should also see to our five mounts."

The man took the coin and they shook.

Ophedia walked out the door. "They got a couple rooms," she said to Rallia. "I'll see to the sleipnirs."

She took two sets of reins from the monk Nidian. "Go on in."

He gave her a smile and left.

"I'll give you a hand," Zhag said, holding the other two reins in his hands.

"Have you felt as out of place as I have this entire journey?" Ophedia asked.

"I have, although I wonder why you feel so out of place."

"It's a familiar feeling, no matter who I'm with." Ophedia tied two of the sleipnirs off and led the last to a stall. "I'm not a Clouw. I'm not a priest. I'm not a girl that any of the men find themselves interested in. I'm the daughter, it turns out, of the man who tried to tear all my friends down."

"I have heard some of this information in passing, but I do not know the full story."

"Nor do I wish to go into detail," she said.

She guided the second sleipnir into the next stall. Zhag filled troughs with water from a cistern.

"You are not your father's daughter," he said.

"I am, even if he did not raise me."

"Then what I say next is even more true. You are not your father's daughter. You are Ophedia del Ishé."

She smiled, and felt a rushing flush in her face. "Why do you say that?"

"Because it is true of all of us."

"But I am still his daughter," she said.

"We've a philosophy among the hrelgrens—Tacheynian Thought. It focuses on the present. You are not your past, you are merely brought here by it. What purpose you make for yourself, what purpose you are destined for, is defined by who you are today and who you will be tomorrow. "

"How can I define who I am tomorrow by who I am tomorrow?"

"I did not say that," Zhag said. "I said your destiny is defined by today and by tomorrow. Your destiny does not come tomorrow. It comes at the end of your road. Stop dwelling on that which you cannot change. You can only change this moment and the next."

She led the third sleipnir to his stall and began brushing front toward the sleipnir's back end, a smile playing across her face.

The smile disappeared as someone sauntered past the stable.

"That look on your face," the hrelgren said.

She stepped out of the stall, took her black Sentinel cloak off, and hung it on a hook. She took up a sleipnir blanket and draped it over her shoulders.

"Come on," she said.

They walked into the street. The man who had passed by the stables was now in the square, approaching someone who leaned against a building on the opposite end. Neither figure was in uniform, but the man's neatly-trimmed beard and matching black hair were obvious. She turned to the hrelgren.

"You see that bearded man?" she asked.

He glanced past her and nodded.

"I don't know how good you are with human faces, but do you recognize him?"

"He does seem familiar, but I can't place it."

"He would normally have been seen in Mahn Fulhar wearing the gray uniform of the castle guards."

"He's Voktorra then," Zhag said. "Of rank, if I recall."

"Captain Abenard Navien," she said. "Likely looking for us."

"I suppose we ought to go and tell the others."

"I'd like to know who he has with him first. That man he's talking to, follow him for a while and see if he has anyone with him. I'll follow Navien."

"Navien is leaving as we speak."

"Good," she said. "If I'm not back by tonight, then I've probably been taken by him. Tell the others to continue. I'll be all right."

"If you're taken, then I'll take the city apart and find you. We all escaped Mahn Fulhar together. We all leave here together."

She put a hand on his shoulder. "Thank you, Zhag."

He smiled. "You'd better get going before you lose him."

She walked down the street and turned a corner to avoid making eye contact with the man Navien had been speaking to.

She recognized him as another Voktorra, who often stood watch over Blackiron.

Navien moved with purpose, stopping at another corner to observe the square in front of him.

She stepped up into a small smokehouse. The man behind the counter gave her a suspicious look.

"Can I help you?" he asked. The shelves looked scarce. Only three pipes were displayed for sale on the counter.

"I'm only browsing," she said.

"I am not allowed to sell my wares to women," he said.

"I was able to purchase smokeweed in Zebüdé a few weeks ago."

"I'd imagine much has changed there, too, since the arrival of the Cup Bearers from the south."

"The Chalicians are controlling who trades with whom, now?"

He gave her a look.

"It doesn't look like you have much to sell anyway."

"I'm fortunate that once the prohibitions went into place everyone came and purchased my stock quickly. But I get my wares from the south. I'd imagine it will be much harder to receive those goods while Mahndür is under consideration."

"I don't know what that means," she said, leaning toward the window to look at Navien, who still stood with his back to her.

"The Cup Bearers..."

"Chalicians," she corrected.

"Yes. Them. They informed everyone that we're to follow their dictates and prove our worthiness. Once that has been done, our leaders will be allowed to trade again."

"Since when does a church dictate who can trade what?"

"That's how it is done in Œron. The Œronzi can trade as they like, having been members of the Chalician church for so long."

She placed a silver baro on the counter.

"I cannot accept this," he said. "If the Chalicians find I have traded with you, I could have major trouble with them."

"I didn't leave any coin on your counter," Ophedia said. "That was there when I came in."

"I... Perhaps you're right," he said, pulling it off the counter. "I suppose, also, that the leather satchel I found here must belong to you."

He took out a small wallet of leather and placed it on the counter. She took it up with a smile and sniffed at it. "I'm not one to smoke the stuff myself. Perhaps it'll come in useful."

"Especially as it becomes more scarce in the coming weeks," he said.

"Perhaps you ought to make your way east. Macena has a flourishing smokehead trade."

"For new merchants?"

"Macena is new itself. Just don't get involved with the men who like to control the trade."

"Chalicians?"

"Nothing like that. Common criminals." She smiled. "Perhaps that is the same. Maybe Macena is no different."

Ophedia touched the leather wallet to her forehead and ducked out of the store—right into the arms of a soldier carrying a long, arrow-tipped spear. He wore a white tabard with the blue chalice across it.

"A woman in a smokeshop," he said, taking hold of her arm.

She feigned ignorance. "What do you mean?"

"The smoking of a pipe, while deplorable enough for a man, is forbidden to women under the tenets of the Church of the Common Chalice."

"First I've heard of it... What is your name?"

"Curate Basrien Whala. You will refer to me as Father Whala."

"Fine, fine," she said. "Father Whala. What is the trouble?"

"I have already stated it. Are you not from this slum?"

"I live out in the forest with my ailing grandfather."

"Then why are you alone in the town? And with such immodest clothing?"

"Immodest?" Ophedia asked, leaning forward and throwing her horse blanket back over her shoulders. "The season is turning. I was tired of the cold."

Whala squirmed uncomfortably. "You still have not answered my question."

"My grandfather is ailing" she said. "He ails," she insisted again. "He needs the pipe herb for his health."

He looked at her with suspicion.

"By the grace of Aben," she added.

"Did this merchant sell this to you?"

"Oh no, sir. We've an arrangement. I bring him eggs from our cottage and he gives this to my grandfather."

"Well," he said. "I suppose you did not know."

She shook her head innocently. "I hope you won't hold it against me, nor this fine merchant. He was hesitant to give this to me and made several warding signs of Aben as he did so."

"I'll have to confirm this."

"I think you ought to watch that man over there by the square," she said, pointing. "He's been leering at me. He stopped by my cottage for the night, and I wasn't able to sleep. I overheard him say something about escaping Mahn Fulhar after your brethren arrived in the city."

Curate Whala frowned. "That is very disturbing."

"And certainly frowned upon by the tenets, I don't doubt."

Ophedia watched as the Chalician left the merchant's door and entered the square, marching up to Navien and dropping a gauntleted hand on his shoulder. Navien visibly startled, then relaxed as they exchanged words. The Chalician pointed to Ophedia, but she turned before Navien glanced in her direction. She smiled at the merchant within the shop, and he gave her a wink. Then she walked back to the inn.

Zhag sat outside, a pipe in his hand. She tossed the leather pouch to him.

"Smokehead herb," he stated, sniffing the pouch.

"It's becoming very scarce, and now only men can purchase it."

"I've heard that is the case in Œron," he said. "The Chalician influence is traveling north."

"When you get back home, you ought to ship some up here. You'll make a killing."

"I do not understand that human idiom."

"It just means you'll make a lot of sales."

The hrelgren's eyes sparkled.

"What did you find out?" she asked.

"I followed the other Voktorra to an inn. He has four others with him, and they are anticipating the arrival of the last member of their company—that captain you followed, perhaps."

"Probably," Ophedia said. "We ought to tell the others."

Rallia was sitting at a table with Alodda and Runah in the inn.

"Where have you been?" Rallia asked.

"Buying some pipe-herb for our friend Zhag here. I discovered that the Chalicians are putting down harsh laws regarding how people conduct themselves. Oh, and I was following Navien and his goons."

"Navien?" Rallia started.

Ophedia had already emptied half the tankard in her hand; she held up a finger as she finished it off.

"He's looking for us, I think, and he brought help. I pointed him out to a Chalician who didn't like the cut of my vest. Well, not so much that he didn't like it as he didn't approve."

"I can see how he might take offense," Rallia said, raising an eyebrow.

"Regardless, we ought not to stay past tonight," Ophedia said.

"Let's go speak with the men," Rallia said, rising from her chair. The others followed her up the stairs to their rooms, in one of which Hanen was speaking quietly with Dorian.

"Hanen," Rallia said from the door. "A word?"

He nodded and came out onto the balcony.

"What is it?" Hanen asked.

"I took a quick jaunt through the town," Ophedia said. "No cloak on. And a good thing, too."

"Why?"

It appears the Chalicians have been here. They've got new rules and decrees posted pretty much everywhere. The forest workers of Bremüm don't seem to take kindly to those, but you never know who's a spy."

"And the other problem?"

"Our problems seem to follow us from Mahn Fulhar," Rallia said.

"One of the Sentinels from that night?" Hanen asked.

"Worse. Navien."

Hanen sighed.

"What should we do about him?" Ophedia asked.

"We're a few days across the plain from the pass," Hanen said.

"And no slow, blind monks, to guide along it," Ophedia said.

"One of us could lead Navien on a wild hunt," Rallia said.

"And, let's be honest," Ophedia said, "it's probably going to be me."

As evening came, the front door to the inn was closed and the windows shuttered. A few of the innkeeper's friends were seated with him at a back table, eyeing the monks who shared a table with the Sentinels until the innkeeper made hand motions indicating they were paying guests. Ophedia took a seat across from Hanen, who sat shoulder-to-shoulder with Alodda. Runah and Rallia sat with Marn by the Prima Pater and the monks.

"Why is everything shut up?" Runah asked.

"Apparently," Hanen said, "inns are only allowed to serve guests who have a bed in the establishment, so the innkeeper's friends really shouldn't be here."

"How do they intend to conduct any business?" Runah asked.

"Once you have earned the favor of the Chalicians, it changes what you can and cannot do," said Zhag. "At least, that is what another Hrelgren merchant said."

"Well, we won't be long for this country," Marn remarked.

"It is a sad state of affairs to watch this happen around us, nonetheless," Dorian said.

Rallia rose and asked something of the innkeeper, who guided her to a chest by the mantle. She came back with a bundle in her arms and a smile on her face as she unrolled a leather mat revealing a grid set into a circle.

Marn gasped. "Is that a six-sided Edi-Foz?"

"The owner mentioned he had one earlier," Rallia said, looking around the table. "Who's playing?"

Marn held his hand up. She handed him a satchel.

"I'll play," Ophedia said, taking one for herself.

"I don't know how," Alodda said.

"I'll sit this one out and teach you," Hanen offered. "It wouldn't be fair for Rallia, my father, and also me to play."

"You're confident," Dorian said. He looked at the smirks playing on Rallia's and Marn's faces. "Then it'll be a pleasure to show you how an expert with nearly a century of experience does."

"One more?" Rallia said, holding out the last two sacks. The monks all shook their heads.

"I'm not an expert," Zhag said, "but I understand how to play."

"Friendly game?" Hanen asked.

"Best not to toy with luck," Rallia said. "With the Chalicians around, I mean."

Hanen nodded. Everyone handed their satchel to the person on their right.

"Why do we do that?" Alodda asked.

"In case someone took a particular bag by intention. The colors drawn are important."

"All that really matters," Ophedia said, "is who draws white. They go first."

As they all poured their pieces out, Zhag revealed white. He began the game, placing a piece into a territory.

"Most games," Hanen said, leaning forward to Alodda's ear, "are won and lost during setup. It's important to start your aggressive placement, your feigning, and your bluffs now."

"I don't know what that means."

"Edi-Foz is territory control," Hanen said. "You can see that Ophedia has learned a trick or two since she played with us on our journey to Mahn Fulhar last autumn. She's setting herself up to build from the back."

Ophedia frowned. "It's not fair that you're helping her by exposing what I'm doing."

"I can be fair," Hanen said, sitting back. "Rallia is setting up a feign against Dorian. I expect my father Marn and Zhag are both using a bullying tactic against Zhag and Rallia respectively, as they see no threat in you yet."

"Then I am doing something wrong?" Alodda asked.

"Not at all. You're playing reactively. That's a wise move. Keep doing what you're doing."

"You haven't thrown me in front of an Auroch yet," Dorian said.

"No. Sitting between Rallia and Marn, I suspect you're questioning your life choices about now."

Dorian gave a quick smile.

"The advice you're giving me is more a way to get at them?" Alodda asked.

"I'm heckling, yes. Once everyone has placed their pieces, I'll shut up. This is fun! I'm usually the one playing."

"And Hanen is usually a very quiet player," Rallia said.

"But so is Zhag," Marn offered.

Ophedia glanced sideways at the hrelgren, who offered her a smile.

"When I first learned Edi-Foz, it was from a hrelgren. They consider silence during a game to be a sign of good playership. Just like their not asking questions."

"That is not always the case, though," Dorian said. "I had the opportunity to play Prince Gadulon di Gough during the Protectorate Wars. He was one of the greatest Thallat players I've ever known. He was quite verbal."

"Interesting," Zhag said. He made the first move, having placed all of his pieces. Ophedia waited her turn then reacted to his blatant invasion of her zone.

"Should I prepare for him to do the same to me?" Alodda asked.

"You should always prepare for everything," Hanen replied, "but don't let him get in the way of your own plans."

Ophedia noticed Marn retreating from Alodda's border, to give her an edge. She noticed Zhag eyeing the same thing. Ophedia began taking territories from Marn—setting up a wall that blocked Alodda from doing the same. Alodda began pressing hard into Zhag's territory. Marn, having built a strong bulwark of territories against Dorian's zone, suddenly moved aside, letting him come in, as he pressed into Rallia's. Ophedia braced for the worst, realizing Rallia and Dorian were circling into her territories, with Zhag and Alodda on the other side.

That was when she finally saw the opening and spread out across the back side of the board, taking Marn's original territories, then Alodda's, and sacrificing her own.

Marn stood up. "You've learned well, Rallia. And I can't compete with Dorian."

"Why is he leaving?" Alodda asked.

"He's considered a Dead Player because he no longer owns his original territories and hasn't taken someone else's. He's out."

"But Ophedia..." she offered.

"Took his home territories, and is inching in on yours."

The game became frantic. Ophedia was barely able to keep up as Rallia and Dorian pitted themselves against one another. Zhag played calmly and coolly, conceding territories to the women on both sides, and eventually conceded altogether.

Ophedia watched Rallia make a sudden move, ousting Dorian from the game in a few quick invasions, which left Ophedia and Alodda on the back foot.

"Is it possible to win at this point?" Alodda asked.

"No," Hanen said. "But you've learned a lot. To be honest, Zhag had you beat before he conceded. Because you didn't give up, and he did, you remain."

"To be honest, I'm not sure who is winning."

"Technically," Ophedia said, "Rallia is winning, but it appears pyrrhic?"

"What do you mean?" Alodda asked.

"Rallia's tokens are running thin," Hanen said. "It's the respectful thing to do, to concede now, but only out of cordiality. If you and Ophedia worked together, you could defeat her," Hanen explained. "But that would be poor sport at this point. She's earned her victory, as bitter as it is."

Alodda stood and held out a hand to Rallia. "Then I'll give this to you," she said.

Rallia smiled. "You play a good game. Six-sided Edi-Foz games are difficult to gauge and play."

"But you," Hanen said, pointing to Zhag. "Having seen you play, I'd love to play you again. But not for money."

"Why is that?" Ophedia asked.

"Because Zhag wasn't trying to win. He was reading everyone. I wouldn't trust anything he did if I played him right now."

"I think perhaps it may be some time before we play again," Zhag said.

"Why is that?"

"Because I've been thinking that Ophedia and I ought to be the bait tomorrow for our Voktorra friends."

"I was considering the same thing," Ophedia said.

"We can't let you go off on your own," Hanen said. "We should all get out of the country."

"I'm just a hrelgren," Zhag said. "I can make my way to a port and find a ship back to the Empire. It would be foolish to risk one of our monastic brethren, or our fair companions from Mahn Fulhar, and you Clouws need to guide them across the border. It has to be us."

Ophedia agreed with him.

"Ophedia," Hanen said.

"We're not so much asking as telling," Ophedia told him. "Zhag and I will lead them on a sleipnir chase come morning."

"You should take Whisper with you," Hanen said. "He can act as a lookout and get underfoot if your pursuers get too close."

23

PASS

By order of the Church of the Common Chalice, all travelers are to bear the words of the Book of the True Path *upon their tongue as they cross into other countries, granting blessings or curses to those they meet. Bless those that drink from the same cup as you, and let your curse be one of encouragement—a scathing indictment to bring the fallen into the true faith. Those that do not bear the words of the True Path upon their tongue, nor the book within reach, shall pay a gilded coin as payment for the debt of disobedience.*

— WORD OF ENCOURAGEMENT TO THE TRAVELER WHO GOES ABROAD

Mist rolled into the streets, obscuring the robes they wore as they filed out, leaving the sleipnirs in the stable as a gift to the innkeeper. Rallia led the company, with the monks walking in pairs and Alodda and her sister taking up the rear with Hanen. They left town and came to the first crossroads, where Rallia hesitated for a moment before taking the center road to the southeast. Ophedia had agreed to wait an hour to leave the city once the morning mist dissipated, heading west and passing Navien's inn to draw him off.

"Will Ophedia be alright?" Alodda asked.

"When we first met her she was a barmaid," Hanen replied. "She never confirmed it, but the inn she worked at was burned down by someone who didn't take too kindly to the owner getting handsy with her."

"Oh!"

"The next time she dropped in our life, Searn had helped her out of a tight situation, where she had been on the run from creditors. But she survived that for a long while, as I understand it."

"She sure is a free spirit."

Hanen noticed she hadn't made this remark with a smile.

"You don't care for her?" he asked.

Runah was shaking her head from behind Alodda, giving Hanen a look.

"Do you?" Alodda asked.

"I mean, she's a good companion to have by your side in a fight."

"Oh?"

"If you're asking whether I think she's attractive," Hanen said, "I mean... who wouldn't?"

"Wrong answer, Hanen Clouw," she said, turning away.

"Alodda," Hanen said.

She didn't respond.

"When we weren't on speaking terms in Mahn Fulhar, she did make a pretty blatant pass at me, but I turned her down because I was trying to make things right with you. She switched her interest away from me very quickly. It turned into her trying to figure out who you are."

Alodda smiled. "I like that answer a lot better."

She put her arm through his.

"That explains why Ophedia is always asking about you, Alodda," Runah said.

"What do you mean?"

"She seems genuinely curious what men see in you."

"She sounds lonely," Alodda said.

"I think she's been alone most of her life," Hanen said.

The fog took its time clearing up, and at midday they came to a rise. The town of Bremüm sat quietly on the other side of the woods they had just emerged from. Far to their left, Hanen could make out two sleipnirs on the western road leaving Bremüm. Several other figures on sleipnirs only just entered the stretch of forest the first had left.

"There's Ophedia and Zhag, and right on time," Dorian said, coming to stand next to Hanen. "Let us hope she is as tenacious as Captain Navien is ambitious."

"I don't doubt it," Rallia said.

"Let's just hope the hrelgren can keep up with her," Marn said. "He was having a little trouble on the big sleipnir."

"And that Whisper takes care of her," Hanen added.

"That black ynnie will bring her luck," Marn said.

They all continued on their road leading down to the plain, which stretched fifty miles to the mountains.

"If it was just you and me," Rallia said, falling in alongside Hanen, "we could make the pass by tomorrow."

"Really?" Alodda asked.

"When we left Edi City," Rallia said, "we left with Searn, Ophedia, and a handful of other Sentinels. Hanen thought to put them to the test, and we marched fifty miles to Suel. It was almost as fast as my fastest time."

"How?" Alodda asked.

"It's not easy," Hanen said. "You just have to press through. I hope Ophedia remembers that."

An hour before sunset, they took a road that avoided Mühndih then left the road as the light began to fade. Rallia spotted a trappers path that led up to the root of a mountain that rose straight up out of the earth.

It was the monks' turn to cook, and they quickly took control of the camp, bringing water to a boil over two campfires. Some root veg purchased in Bremüm was dropped into the pot, while Rallia made use of some of the hot water and shaved Marn's straight tonsure through the center of his hair. A sun-warmed mountain nearby and a southern breeze made for a pleasant evening, and Hanen walked through the forest after leaving his cloak and satchel by the fire. He came to a small spring the water had been drawn from, filling the little pond, if it could be called that, before tumbling over a channel cut over the top of a rock waist high, and then tumbling down the hillside.

He knelt over it, drinking the clean, sweet water.

Out of the corner of his eye he caught the movement of someone moving through the woods toward him. The twilight cast everything in gray, but the white blouse she wore made her easy to spot as she approached. She came to the small hill that surrounded the spring, and looked up with a smile.

"Help me up?" Alodda said, reaching out with a hand. She had over her shoulder the straps of several drinking bottles. He pulled her up to the edge of the pool, where she put the bottles down.

"It almost looks man-made," she said, looking at the perfect pool. Her hair was half down, with a braid crowning the top of her head.

"If it was made by a man, it happened a long time ago," Hanen replied.

"It's a wonder no town or village has grown up around it."

"Why?" Hanen asked.

"Dorian said he hasn't tasted sweeter water in his life. I suggested I go and fill up bottles for tonight, and we can replenish in the morning too."

"That's a good idea."

They each unstoppered bottles and began to fill them.

"If you weren't a Sentinel, what would you do?" Alodda asked.

"I don't intend to stop."

"I understand that," Alodda said, a note of irritation rising in her voice. "But if you did..."

"I'm not sure. All I've known is net-mending, moving goods, and acting as a Sentinel."

"You've an eye for logistics then. Maybe you could run a warehouse?"

"I suppose I could," Hanen conceded.

"Is there a lot of money to be made in Edi as a Sentinel?"

"Always," Hanen said. "But more to be made on the road. I didn't get a chance to look around, but Birin would also be a good place to live. It's busy, like Mahn Fulhar, but also feels like there is always something new happening. It's nice to see mountains."

"I love the mountains," Alodda said.

"What do you love about them?"

"The break in the horizon and hope of what lies in front of me. Have you ever been to the top of a mountain?"

"No," Hanen said, "but I imagine there must be a sense of accomplishment when you do."

"And humility," she replied.

"What do you mean?"

"My father tells a story of how, during his wandering days after the Protectorate Wars, he climbed to the top of a mountain. He said the beauty and sense of size of the world around him brought him to tears. Even after the wars he was a very proud man, but looking down from the mountain took that from him. He never raised his voice to another after that day."

"Did he?"

"Did he what?"

"Ever raise his voice?"

"Not once," she replied. "I've never known a kinder man. How far is it to the pass?"

"I'd wager three days."

"Then I suppose we had better make the most of it." She slipped her hand into his and sat down on a log, pulling him next to her.

"If you ask me to go with you to Düran, I will," Hanen said.

"I know. But I'm not going to do that."

"Why not?"

"You have to decide. Come with me and we'll forget everything behind us. But going with Dorian feels like a march toward the story of a lifetime."

She looked up through the trees as the first stars blinked into view.

"Both decisions will have their regrets," Hanen said.

"Every decision does," she replied, and leaned her head on his shoulder. "But I'll respect you whatever you decide."

"But what if...?"

"Shut up and kiss me," she interrupted.

"What?"

"You keep talking, and I keep giving you a chance to make the most of this beautiful night."

Hanen found he was holding his breath. She squeezed his hand encouragingly.

The last light fading from the day left her a mere silhouette. The stars multiplied. The campfires crackled. The rich smell of the cedars matched her cedar and porumarian perfume. And her lips were soft and sweet.

They came to the edge of the mountains three days later. The pass was a deep canyon a mile wide with mountains looming overhead and a few wisps of smoke rising from a stone fortress on their southern ridge.

"What's that place?" Alodda asked.

"That is Haven, my destination," Dorian said.

"Why is it called that?" Runah asked. "The name 'Haven' is usually reserved for seaside towns."

"I wouldn't be surprised if those that first founded the city didn't come from a Haven on the sea, as such."

"Runah," Alodda said. "Limae is the Land of Lawlessness."

"It certainly used to be," Dorian said. "Back when I was a lad, even. I've done what I could, along with leaders of nearby countries, to see them become truly legitimate in their governance. Although, I'd imagine a bit of that independent nature is still very rampant there."

"You intend to journey there?" Runah asked.

"I do. It has been thirty years since I've been there, though. I did not arrive from this direction. Hanen, what is the best way to reach it?"

"I've not been there myself," Hanen said, "but from the maps I've studied, I believe you can either journey south from here and take the roads up from Varea, or by the entrance to the pass there is a road we can take up."

"Very well. Let's proceed."

"I'll see Alodda and Runah safely to Birin," Marn said, falling in step with Hanen. "Or farther, if they prefer."

"What do you mean?"

"So that you and Rallia can go with Dorian."

"I hadn't decided that yet," Hanen said.

"Well," Marn replied, "you have an hour. And I don't doubt Rallia will go with him."

"Father, I..." Hanen faltered.

"Once you decide to go with him, I'll watch after the Dülars."

"We'll be alright," Alodda said, after Marn had walked away.

"Why has everyone decided for me?"

"What do you mean? You said you were going to Haven."

"No, I didn't," Hanen replied.

"You said there is a road 'we' can take. I assumed you meant you were going with Dorian."

"I promised your father and mother I'd get you safely out of Mahndür."

"And you have," Alodda said. "Now you need to go with Dorian, and get him safely to his destination. Help him find what he seeks."

"I'd...rather go east, with you."

"I know," she said, taking his hand and squeezing it. "But we both know you need to go with Dorian first. Then come find me."

"What if something goes wrong?"

"No need for 'what ifs.' Go. I'll be all right. Runah and I will find work. You can find that armor Dorian is looking for, and help him do what he needs to do."

They arrived at the edge of the pass. A guard stationed below the tower watched their approach.

"Business?" the captain asked.

"We monks," Marn replied, "are escorting these two sisters into Düran."

"Purpose?"

"To leave Mahndür."

"One royal a person."

"We're monks," Marn said.

"Doesn't change the orders we've been given. A gold royal if you'd like us not to record your names in our ledger."

Hanen stepped forward and took out his coin purse.

"Are you going with them, Coin Cloak?"

"No," Hanen said. "My sister and I are traveling to Haven, as escort to the scribe, Nethendel Unteel," he said, pointing to Dorian.

"It's a gold royal to Limae, too."

Hanen sighed and put nine coins in the soldier's hands.

The soldier nodded and turned back to his tower.

Rallia threw her arms around Marn, and they embraced. Alodda stood and waited for Hanen to come to her.

"I'll miss you," Alodda said.

"And I you," Hanen said.

She leaned forward. "You're supposed to kiss me goodbye now."

"I..."

She stood up on her toes and he leaned down to kiss her cheek. When she turned her face at the last moment, their lips locked. Runah giggled. It was a warm but far too short a kiss. Then Alodda turned, put her arm through her sister's, and walked away. Runah whispered something and Alodda glanced back, blushing, at Hanen.

"That's an absurd amount of money to cross a border," Dorian said as Hanen turned back.

"Not surprising, though," Hanen said. "I'd imagine it's gone up in the past few weeks, as others have fled Mahndür."

"I wonder how long this road has been here," Rallia asked, motioning to the wide switchbacks that zig-zagged up the mountainside next to the stairs they ascended.

"And, more importantly, how many stairs?" Hanen asked, motioning to Dorian, who ascended slowly behind them.

"This will take some time," Hanen added.

"Did you have somewhere to be?" Rallia asked.

Hanen shook his head and took the final steps to the next level of the road. A switchback began there, with a walled edge from which Hanen could look back at the plains, just making out the watchtower hundreds of feet below. Up above, the wall of another switchback would provide another vantage point to see down into the pass.

"Are you second-guessing following me?" Dorian asked as he huffed up next to Hanen.

"I don't know," Hanen said. "It's only been an hour."

"Only an hour?" Dorian protested.

"We can rest, if you like."

"I may need do. An old man my age was never meant to climb this many stairs, whether he be blessed by a god or not."

24

INDOCTRINATION

Cast aside thy desires; the path allows for none.

Cast aside ambition; thy fate has been sealed by the only ambition required—to reach for Lomïn.

Let all thou doest be justified by this.

—BOOK OF THE TRUE PATH 30:6

In other circumstances the port town of Wimdarf might have been a pleasant place to visit, but the blue pennants bearing white chalices upon their fields, newly hung at the gate and the corners of each square, told Ophedia and Zhag that this would not be a welcoming place. The peninsular country of Grisden across the water could be seen through the clear blue sky, but no ships came or went from there, and the wharf merchants hesitated to hawk wares. Women eyed Ophedia with fear as she walked down the street, guiding her recently lamed sleipnir by the reins. Another group of women moved to the other side of the road when they saw her coming, whispering to one another. Ophedia glanced at Zhag and then Whisper, trotting alongside them, both good companions on the road. She looked up at a passing man, who looked away and rushed down the street.

"A port town suspicious of newcomers can hardly survive," Ophedia said.

"I thought perhaps they were looking at me, but I think it is you that gives them pause."

"But why?" Ophedia asked.

"Come along," someone said from the other side of Ophedia's sleipnir. "We've got some stables you can take your mounts to." Ophedia gasped as she peeked around the sleipnirs and saw the familiar face of the tall, bulky-built Eunia Halla.

"Eunia!" she gasped.

"Words later," Eunia said, taking the sleipnir from Ophedia. "And close your cloak."

Ophedia looked down. The last several days had been warm and she only wore her leather vest. She closed her cloak, following Eunia across the street and into the stableyard of a small home, where Eunia handed the reins of the sleipnir to a young boy barely as tall as Zhag.

"Well," Eunia said, "what are you doing here, of all places?"

"We're on the run."

"I can see that," Eunia said flatly, "although why you walk so blatantly and immodestly in the face of the new Chalician authorities is beyond me."

"It was my heaving bosom, huh? That wasn't nearly so much of an issue in Bremüm."

"I'm sure every Chalician holds different sins higher than others."

"I didn't think that sort of thing mattered to you."

"It doesn't," Eunia said, "but last week the Chalicians put a woman in the stocks overnight for as much. She nearly died from the cold. We moved her out of town through secret paths."

"You're Crysalas now?"

Eunia gave her a look. "I didn't know you knew what that was."

"I'm not naive," Ophedia said. "I turned down their care as a girl, after all. And we've had a long road this winter. Speaking of which, what are you doing here?"

"I'm from here. I came here with Chös."

"Is Chös here?"

"He is, and he's probably making bread now. Night will fall soon, and we can't be out and about, nor working when the sun is down."

"What are you talking about?"

"Come on," Eunia said, walking to the door of the house. "Bring your two friends."

Ophedia glanced at Zhag and Whisper, who stood next to each other, un-introduced. Then she walked into the house, where a short man with thick arms worked dough on the counter. He glanced up and then back to his work. Eunia turned back to Ophedia.

"All right. Now that we're out of earshot of the street, introduce your friends."

Ophedia held a hand out toward Zhag. "This is Zhag em Tellis, a hrelgren merchant who left Mahn Fulhar with us. He's on his way back to the Empire. He and I, and the ynfald, Whisper, are all leading a man off the scent of the Clouws and those with them, and it brought us here."

"It sounds like you have quite a story, and it is a pleasure to have you as a guest, Zhag. My name is Eunia, and that is my husband, Chös Telmar. My apologies if he says little."

"Eunia and Chös journeyed with the Clouws and me on a journey from Edi to Birin last year," Ophedia explained to Zhag. "We had a run-in with a manticör, and Chös was saved from death by a qavyl."

"Did Ymbrys stay with you on the road much longer?" Eunia asked.

"Ymbrys Veronia?" Zhag asked.

Eunia nodded.

"He was in Mahn Fulhar all winter," the hrelgren said.

"He did not journey there with us. He came separately," Ophedia said. "I'm not sure why. Hanen never told me."

"It looks like you earned your cloak," Eunia said.

"Given to me at Birin," Ophedia said.

"And Searn?"

"Dead. But I'd rather not go into that."

"I should like to help," Zhag said, coming to the counter where Chös was working.

Chös wordlessly showed Zhag how he was rolling the dough into balls, and Zhag joined in.

"It's not common for a baker to be making dough in the middle of the day," Ophedia said. "And I didn't know either of you were bakers. You never mentioned it when Aurín spoke of his family's trade."

"We are not," Eunia said, "but the Chalicians took away several of the bakers when they arrived, so we picked up some of the work."

"What happened?"

"My parents own this place. We came here just before winter.

Chös has made himself invaluable and I settled back into this old life until the Chalicians arrived a month ago and posted their laws, which they call 'suggestions' for their 'better way to live.'"

"But they're more than that," Ophedia said.

"They didn't expect this quiet town to be so obstinate. Following the Chalician Codes didn't appeal to anyone, and so life proceeded as normal."

"The Chalicians didn't take too kindly to that, did they?" Ophedia asked.

"The local priest of Aben was cast from his small chapel for preaching against the Chalicians, and they carted him off to the south. Then Provost Zehan Otem arrived and added to the codes, demanding a new way of life to be adopted. After that point all coin transactions ceased."

"Otem came to Mahn Fulhar, applying the same rules to the capital."

"Well, our town here has fallen back on trade-and-barter. We adapted and life continued. Otem left us in the hands of one of his henchmen—a Chalician by the name of Curate Yanas Brodier. He's almost worse than the Provost."

"What did he do?"

"He started forcing changes to how business is conducted. No work is done at night. Immodesty is punished by a night in the stocks."

"I take it he's not been lenient against infractions?"

Eunia shook her head. "Given how long the nights are in winter, it cut severely into working hours."

"To what purpose?"

"To make us desire the approval of the Chalician church, to make us reliant on the new lord brought into town—a young Œronzian noble who by day is a civil and obedient member of the Church of the Common Chalice, but does as he pleases at night."

Ophedia took a seat at the table, and Eunia brought over a tankard of ale.

"Tell us about the rest of Mahndür," Eunia said. "We haven't had many visitors."

"It looks like it's about the same all over the country. The High Priest of Aben in Mahn Fulhar invited the Chalicians in, and the king allowed it. The king actually has very little power in the city itself. That power belongs to the guilds, but they didn't seem to put up much of a fight. I think they plan to wait it out like you are."

"Then they're in for a sore awakening," Eunia said.

Ophedia nodded and finished off her tankard.

"You finished that fast."

"It's a habit of mine," Ophedia said. "I spent this long winter working hard to develop that skill."

"So why are the Clouws on the run, and why are you the bait?"

"Because the king had the ex-Prima Pater of the Paladins of the Hammer as an involuntary houseguest and we helped him escape, and then left the city with several Œronzi expatriate monks who also wanted to leave the city, not looking forward to a life once more under the lash of the Chalicians."

"Then the Chalicians are now in control of all of Mahndür?"

"Every country this side of the mountains, I'd wager," Ophedia replied.

"Not all. Word from Grisden is that they've not been welcome there. And neither is their trade partner—Morraine. But it sounds like Redot has rolled over, as has Varea. Though there is talks of a rebellion forming—Old Alvaria rising again."

"Best not to blurt that to anyone," Ophedia said.

Eunia nodded.

"We were in Bremüm a few days ago, and the head guard from Mahn Fulhar showed up looking for us, so Zhag and I have drawn him away from the Prima Pater and those who are assisting him. And now we're here."

"Now you're here," Eunia finished her own tankard as a knock came to the door.

Chös stopped what he was doing and answered it.

"He has good days and bad days."

"And today?" Ophedia asked.

"Today is a good day," Eunia said. "He hears everything, but he says little."

Chös opened the door and a fully armored Chalician Praetor stepped in, shoving him out of the way. Eunia jumped to her feet.

"What is the meaning of this, Brodier?" she said.

"Silence, woman," the man said. He had a gaunt face and a broken nose, and rather than an arrow-topped spear he held a shorter version as a serviceable rod of office. He took in the room, his eyes falling on Zhag and then Ophedia.

"A hrelgren?" he said. "And another Black Sentinel."

Eunia opened her mouth to speak, but the Praetor held up a hand.

"Yes, I've found that much out. Both you and your husband are members of that organization. Your tax rate is increased by five points."

"Why would that be?"

"To show your devotion. You've not volunteered to act as guard. You've not offered your service to the Chalician church in fair trade. You pose as bakers, but you're to be taxed as soldiers who do not practice your true path."

He walked over to the table and eyed the dough. "You'll bake all this by nightfall? If that dough rises overnight, you'll pay a leavening tax."

He turned to the hrelgren.

"Only just arrived in town, green-skin?"

"To seek a ship south."

"Good. I hope you're not trading with this town. It has not earned the right to trade with others yet. It is still in religious detention."

"I have no goods to trade," Zhag said.

"Good. Then see yourself away by the end of tomorrow, or else there will be consequences."

He turned to Ophedia. "Who are you?"

"Ophedia del Ishé," Ophedia said. "I'm passing through."

"As what? A spy for Limae?"

"She is my bodyguard," Zhag said.

"I doubt that," the Praetor said, "as I have it on good authority that she is on the run."

"Whose authority?" Ophedia said.

"I'm not at liberty to say. At least, not here. Green-skin," he said, turning once more to the hrelgren, "I suspect you're complicit with this Coin Cloak, but I'd also rather have you out of my demesne. You're to find somewhere else to stay, and leave our city."

"You," he said, turning to Ophedia again. "You're coming with me."

"Why should I?"

He scoffed. "Have you not been in any town in Mahndür for the past month? You're under the ecclesiastical authority of the Praetors of the Chalice. Every lordling, baron, and duke has given us authority, to act as guards of the souls of all mankind. You'll do as we say, or forfeit your eternity."

"Ophedia," Eunia said, putting a calming hand out.

Ophedia unclenched her balled fists.

"Good!" the Praetor said. "Come along."

He walked to the door.

"As her hosts," Yanas Brodier said, "I expect the two of you to pay her imprisonment fees. You wouldn't want your friend to starve, would you?"

He led her out of the small house and onto the cobbles. Ophedia walked alongside the Chalician Praetor, glancing back at Eunia, who stood at the door. The tall woman spoke to the hrelgren next to her. Zhag was nodding, a dire look on his face.

"Now, tell me of your trip," the Praetor said to Ophedia. "I'd like to hear where you came from."

"I journeyed from Alnír."

"A nice lie," he said. "My guest said you journeyed from Bremüm."

"You don't seem offended that I might lie," Ophedia said.

"I'm not. I expect you to lie."

"Because I'm a Sentinel? Because I'm a woman?"

"Because you are not a member of my church. Because you are a soul bound for destruction and Noccitan. The least I can do is allow you your guilty sin, so that it can be brought to light."

"Is that what your taxes are for? To shed your light upon the people of this city?"

The man next to her laughed. "The taxes are a means to an end. Yes, this town doesn't seem to want the light. It continues on its path, unperturbed that we have even arrived. So we tax them to build up our authority and put pressure on them. We offer a pain, to sweeten the pasture we provide them. Eventually they'll be reliant on us, but until that point we take their coin to spend on those who have given their souls to the true path."

"To what end? Feeding your own ego? Lining your own pocket?"

"You assume me as sinfully debauched as you," Brodier said. "No. I wish to see the High King in Lomïn give me a kingdom, where those I have saved shall serve me in thankfulness for what I have done for them."

"Then it is pride that is your sin," Ophedia said.

She braced herself for him to lift his hand against her. He did not.

"It is a lesson from a scripture, penned by our High Missioner, and Benefactor, Abithu Omrab. I've brought it into your vulgar tongue so you can understand it. My pride and ego have nothing to do with it."

They came to a square, across which a large house stood, made of yellow bricks with whitewashed wood framing. The top was flat, and several Praetors stood guard there, viewing their empty surroundings.

"It's not much for a city lord's home, but the view from the upper room is a fine one."

He walked across the cobbles and through the door, opened by another Praetor.

"Apparently, you've been on the run after reneging on a contract you hold with the King of Mahn Fulhar," he said. "One of your pursuers has come to take you back, under the authority of Provost Zehan Otem."

"I have no such contract."

"But the heads of your guild do, and you have been asked for, by name, as the daughter of Searn VeTurres, who signed the contract. Shall we step into my office and discuss this with the Voktorra?"

"I can't say I missed the smug look of Captain Navien," she said as she pushed the door open.

The four Voktorra in the room turned to look at her. She didn't recognize any of them.

"Captain Navien," one of them said, "didn't leave with us from Bremüm. He informed us that he would be pursuing your captains on a different road."

Ophedia only stepped forward because the Praetor pushed her into the room.

"If my keen mind reads this situation correctly," Curate Brodier said, "you were meant to be the bait?"

Ophedia said nothing.

"Then your friends gain nothing from your days-long flight."

"And Captain Navien was not in the best of moods after you claimed to the Chalicians in Bremüm that he had ill-intentions for you."

"Lying to a Chalician?" Brodier said. "This seems to be a habit of yours. It is a difficult sin to break. Perhaps Provost Zehan Otem in Mahn Fulhar will find a way." He smiled. " Let's be honest. He will. I have no doubt he will."

"With your permission, Curate Brodier," one Voktorra said, "we'll leave tomorrow morning at first light."

"You have my permission," Brodier replied.

25

HAVEN

*It was with surprise and inevitable delight that I came upon the
city of Haven for the first time. This rube from Bortali had no
context. My journey had not prepared me for this city of desires.
All vices were fed here, but no sins were satisfied. For ever more
are new ones made. The false light it cast made for deeper
shadows than the Starblush of Bortali. Ever shall I recall with
fondness and shame those days spent upon the streets of Haven. I
lost myself there, and I've since wandered these roads to find my
path again.*

—JUREN LIEFSEN'S *JOURNAL OF GANTHIC ROADS*

The switchbacks spilled out before the western gate of the
city, before which stood a shanty town on a boulder field
that had been flattened into terraces over the centuries. The
walls of the city of Limae bore a few guards, and those few kept
watch disinterestedly. Behind them a few taller roofs could be
seen, but most remained out of view.

"More stairs?" Dorian wheezed, looking up the five terraces to
the gate.

Hanen forged ahead, with Rallia and Dorian taking up the rear
as they slowly came to the gate.

A young boy was sitting at the top. "More Black Sentinels?"

"Just come from below," Hanen said as Dorian caught his
breath.

"First time here?"

"It is," Hanen said. "We've had a trade route we escort through

Düran. We've not had an opportunity to come back here yet."

"You work for the Clouws in Edi?"

Hanen was surprised. "You've heard of them?"

"My cousin used to run that route. He's here in town himself."

"Who is your cousin?"

"Aurín Mateau."

"Aurín is here in Haven?" Rallia asked. "He worked for us."

"You're the Clouws?"

Hanen nodded.

"I'll let Aurín know you're in town," the boy said, and dashed off.

Inside the city gates, a wide square bustled with people. Beyond the houses and shops that lined the edge, the city rose to the north in additional tiers, and descended in longer tiers down to the main gate of the city.

"It's a lot bigger than I expected," Hanen said.

"It's a lot bigger than when I was last here, too," Dorian said. "This gate we entered used to be the front gate. All of that down there is new. The Aerie, though," he pointed up the city to the citadel at the top. "Just as imposing as it always was."

"Why is it called 'the Aerie'?" Rallia asked.

"They keep a menagerie of exotic birds, even griffins at one time. It was named such much farther back than that, though."

The streets led up city to the daunting walls of the citadel, all drawing the eye upward.

"For a country founded on independence, it's odd for a paladinial citadel to be the centerpiece," Hanen said.

"Limae goes back a long way to its foundation by Brase Turrian, who united the warring clans up here. The Aerie was established by the Hammer to mediate as the clans united under a new, more violent banner to repel other nations from their homeland. Pariantür negotiated a peace that permitted Limae to form around the Aerie—which, however, is not the government."

"Yet to an outsider, it looks like the center of power."

"Do you remember," Rallia asked, "how all of the buildings on Aritelo Hill are up against the grand estate, vying to be seen by their betters?"

"I do," Hanen said. "But this looks different." He pointed to several larger buildings, which all looked well-off and prominent. "I'd wager those belong to the city leaders. The personalities of their buildings don't seem to need the approval of the Aerie."

"A good summation of the politics of this city," Dorian said.

They came to an inn halfway up to the citadel, close to the western wall. It sat half-buried in the next level of the city.

"I'll go in and see if it's respectable," Rallia said.

"She's a good girl," Dorian said to Hanen, taking a seat on a bench.

"She is a good sister."

"You both come from good stock," Dorian said. "Your father. His grandfather."

"What do you mean?"

"Your great-grandfather, Nethendel Unteel, was my best friend in my younger years. In fact, do you recall my physician, who traveled to Mahn Fulhar with us? Shorter. Black hair. Rather curvy. Round, you might even call her."

"Yes," Hanen said, recalling the girl.

"Katiam is descended from the brother of both my wife Maeda and your great grandfather, Nethendel. Her own great grandfather probably didn't expect to inherit the farm we all grew up on. I was apprenticed to a redsmith. I had a rather awful distaste for that job. And a lot of resentment within me. After the Protectorate Wars, I turned back to it for a time. Or, I should say, I became an admirer and collector of copper pieces at Pariantür."

"Why do you mention this?"

"I'm nearly a century old," he said as he rose. "I was almost a copper tradesman before I became a Paladin and then the Prima Pater. It is never too late to change what you're doing. Especially at your age."

"Seems like a fine place," Rallia said, coming down the stairs. "What their serving girls do in their spare time, I couldn't say."

"You don't need to protect me," Dorian said. "If you don't think it's a brothel, that's good enough for me."

Rallia blushed. "It's not."

"Good. Then let's go see the rooms."

Hanen's eye was caught by a figure across the street. He stopped.

"You coming?" his sister said.

"I'll be along later."

Hanen walked across the street to the chandler and stepped inside. The heady smell of burning candles laced with herbs and tinctures filled his senses, and their dazzle added to the confusion. He moved through the multi-roomed shop to the main desk, where the merchant stood talking to a tall and languid figure—a qavyl with a leather-topped staff in his hand. He did not need to turn for Hanen to know it was Ymbrys Veronia.

The qavyl held a hand out for the chandler to shake; then the inhuman figure turned and smiled at Hanen, his flat tail shifting behind him.

"Hello, Hanen Clouw. What a surprise to see you here. "

"You mean because you didn't intend to be spotted? Or because, perhaps, you did."

The qavyl shrugged. "I am here because I must be. Shall we go for a walk?"

"Everywhere we turn, you're here," Hanen said as they stepped out into the street. "What is it you're after?"

"For the first time I feel I have aligned my path with the correct one. Although, while I believe I saw Dorian Mür with you, I did not see your father. "

"Did you expect to?"

I thought perhaps his path would follow yours."

"I saw him off to Düran with the Dülar sisters."

"Ah, good," Ymbrys said, clapping a long-fingered hand on Hanen's shoulder. "I had hoped you would follow that line as well."

"You are saying much, but at the same time, nothing. Could you be a bit more straightforward?"

Ymbrys nodded, smiling up at the sun. "Of course. It is only fair. What would you like to know?"

"What leads you on this path that runs along ours every step of the way? "

"That is the right question to ask. Although what I can say, I do not know."

"You said you were not surprised that Dorian is here. Did you know that his best friend was our great-grandfather? Nethendel Unteel?"

"Do you know, I did not know that? I knew that Dorian's wife, Maeda, was Unteel's sister, but I did not know that he was your great-grandfather. It was not your great-grandfather that interested me, however, but his wife."

"The daughter of the Apostate."

"Indeed. I have sought her and her offspring out since I began this quest."

"Quest?"

"I was placed on the path to seek out this mystery by the wisdom of the qavylli god."

"Lae'zeq?"

"The firstborn of Aben desires to understand the cause and effect of the Protectorate Wars. They were, after all, such meaningless wars, sparked in a country ignored by the gods. Yet so much has stemmed from these conflicts."

"What do you mean?"

"Hrelgrens, human nations, Paladins, vül, T'Akai...even a contingent of qavylli became involved. Even champions of dark gods. I rather think the Black Coterie, through their servants, sought to bring about the Great Imbalance. I'm convinced they are still doing so—through the boneshroud."

"How do you know about that?" Hanen stopped to consider the goods at a roadside stall, turning away from Ymbrys as a shiver ran down his spine.

"I have my ways."

"So you seek the boneshroud?" He pulled his hand from his satchel, realizing he had placed it there protectively.

"In due time. For now, I imagine I am here in Limae for the same reason Dorian is. To find the armor of the warlord. The Dreadplate."

"I think Dorian would like to hear what you know."

"Perhaps I ought to tell him. But first, before we find our way back, I'd like your opinion on something I saw, without the pomp and wrath Dorian might bring if he joined us."

"I doubt Dorian knows what wrath is," Hanen said, falling in step alongside Ymbrys.

"Then you are not as read up on the Protectorate Wars as you ought to be," Ymbrys said.

"You were there?"

"I was alive, but I did not go to the war. He was a capable leader and warrior, from what I hear, but I don't think he lacks anger."

They walked through the city.

"I was still in Mahn Fulhar on the night of the incident at the Rose Convent. I stood with Rallia when the new Prima Pater asked her what had happened to the corpse of Searn VeTurres."

"Rallia and I moved it with the twin Paladins."

"Apparently after you moved it, the cloak on his person went missing."

Hanen gasped, his heart beating in his chest. "It was on him when we left."

"Soon after that, a gauntlet also vanished. I followed the trail of the latter, first north of Mahn Fulhar and then here, to Haven. A long and meandering road."

"Then it was someone who survived that night? Someone who was there?"

"Yes."

They came to a long, short wall, and in the late afternoon sun the scent of lumber wafted from the yard beyond.

"Why are we here?"

"Because this is where Slate conducts his business."

"That's not a name I recognize."

"It's not necessary that you do," Ymbrys said. "He was once a Paladin, a Primus. He was there that night."

"It was my impression that the Aerie was ruled by Moteans. If you're implying he was one of those Moteans there that night, why not return to the citadel and lead from there?"

"Because while he is the highest ranking Motean of the Brotherhood of the Gauntlet, he is no natural-born leader. He fears what might become of him if someone were to betray him. Following him to the citadel has revealed several secret ways in. But he has chosen to cast off his armor and stay here in the lumberyard, with people he trusts more than Paladins: craftsman."

"Why craftsman?"

"He has connections with craftsmen across the city. He cannot hide away in his leather shop as he once was able, so now he hides here."

"And you think the Gauntlet is here?"

"I think there is more here than that," Ymbrys said. "Come, follow me as my bodyguard."

Ymbrys turned the corner into the busy yard.

Piles of neatly-stacked wood lay in rows while men with long wooden staves gauged the warp and length of several pieces. To the north, women leaned from the windows of tall homes and apartments with wash meant to dry. A large warehouse and office sat against the far wall of the yard, before which several men stood conferring with each other.

"You'd think this was a shipyard," Hanen said.

"A good guess," Ymbrys said. "My understanding is a shipwright emigrated here and founded it."

"Why so big though?" Hanen remarked.

"Most cities have a lumber yard like this. Although in my experience they are usually outside the city. Perhaps they benefit from the safety of the city. Or the owner doesn't like to travel to his holdings. I think it is the air here. The city is unusually dry for a mountain city. The forests of straight alpine wood are not far from here."

"You speak from experience, it sounds like."

"When I was younger I did do some work for a wood carver. It was not for me."

They moved around a large pile of lumber aging in the sun and came to a small workshop where several wooden coffins stood, and peeked through the window. A figure was visible, his back turned, working over a press, preparing a piece of metal. He gathered up and weighed out a portion of filings and clippings of some dark metal, and placed them into a tray, each compartment holding another weighed-out piece of metal. Then he walked out of the room into an adjacent one. Along the opposite wall a large coffin, too big for any man, perhaps for something more akin to a vül, stood on end.

"Where is he going?" Hanen whispered.

"I don't know," Ymbrys said. "This is the farthest I've come."

Hanen took another look into the room.

"Those look like the coins found on some of the people who died that night in Mahn Fulhar."

Ymbrys took something out of his pocket and held it out. It was a small coin, not a well-stamped one, bearing the symbol of a feather on one side and a tower on the other. Pocked with tiny folds, and made of a dark metal verging on black, it had a single hole for a leather thong to go through.

"Where did you get that?" Hanen asked him.

"From one of the fallen."

"So perhaps they're minting those here."

"I suspect so," Ymbrys said. "Shall we go in?"

"I don't think that's wise," Hanen said.

"I'll determine that." Ymbrys winked at him and walked in, pretending to examine the coffins while also circling the table and examining the bits of dark metal on the bench. Then he wandered over to the large coffin, giving it a push. It did not budge.

"What are you doing?" A man stepped into the room from the back with a sneer on his face. He stood as tall as Ymbrys, but only because his boots had wooden lifts under them.

"Ah! I wondered if the craftsman was in," Ymbrys said.

"You can't be in here," the man said.

"I understand you're Master Slate," Ymbrys said.

The man cringed. "My name is Morrin. Who said my name was Slate?"

"I am a qavyl librarian seeking an expert on the burial ceremonies of mankind, and I understood this to be a place where a Paladin by the name of Slate worked. He is an expert in both Limaean and paladinial burial techniques."

"Slate," the man said hesitantly, "is a cousin of mine. We're often mistaken for the same person."

"That must be it," Ymbrys said.

"What are you doing here?" Slate said to Hanen. "The lumberyard doesn't welcome Coin Cloaks. That was part of the arrangement."

"We've both just arrived in town," Ymbrys said.

"If you wish to speak with me, you'll need to wait until this evening. I meet with other craftsmen at the Gryph Crag Inn."

"And will we be able to speak on the subject of burial techniques?"

"If I can't answer your questions, there will be those that can."

"I see, too, that you're minting coins for paying the Three-Eyed god."

A chill ran down Hanen's spine at these words.

"What?" the carpenter said.

"The Three-Eyed god takes the payment of three coins, one for each eye. Minting coins would be an interesting side-business as a coffin maker. Perhaps it is a practice of Limae to use other metals for those—as symbolic representations of the payment."

The man said nothing, eyeing them with deeper suspicion.

"I shall seek out this Gryph Crag Inn," Ymbrys said, turning to the door, "and see you there."

"Of course," the man said, watching them walk away.

"I do not trust him," Hanen said.

"Nor I," Ymbrys said. "Would you like to accompany me to the Gryph Crag? I will fare better knowing you are there."

"That might be best. I can grab Rallia and we'll both join you."

"We've got about two hours before sundown. That is probably wise."

They arrived back at the inn, where Rallia was sitting in a comfortable chair by the fire. When she saw them enter she leapt to her feet, a broad smile on her face.

"Ymbrys!" she said, throwing her arms around him.

"I ... Leqaw y dis!" He returned the embrace awkwardly.

"What are you doing here?"

"Seeking answers to ancient questions, as I always am."

Rallia walked them both to the fire.

"Look who found us!" Rallia said. She indicated toward a man with a well-cared-for head of thick hair and a thin mustache upon his lips, sitting in the other chair.

"Hello Hanen, Ymbrys," Aurín Mateau said.

Hanen held out a hand and they shook. "I thought you might come here to Haven, after midwinter."

"Yes. My cousin came and found me an hour ago and told me you were here. I thought I ought to come and say hello."

"Where is Nethendel?" Hanen asked.

"Tired from the long day's climb," Rallia said. "He already went to bed."

"That's for the best," Hanen said. "I need you guard-ready."

"I always am," Rallia said. "What for?"

"Ymbrys and I just spoke with one of the Paladins who instigated the incident that night. He was minting coins, and asked to meet with Ymbrys at a tavern he frequents."

"Coins?" Aurín said, a dark look falling over his face.

"Yes. You were there that night, weren't you?"

"I believe we all were," Aurín said. "Although the details are hazy."

"I should very much like to speak to you about that," Ymbrys said.

"I'd rather not."

"Even if I paid you for your effort?"

"I'm more interested in knowing how I can help to stop the creation of more of those. Perhaps I should just leave town and go further afield."

"Aurín," Ymbrys said, putting a hand on his shoulder, "I should like to know if these odd coins are widespread. I should imagine you'd also like to know."

"What would I like to know?" Aurín asked.

"Whether we can uncover and stop the creation of these before more are minted, why they are made, and whether there are other places making them. If they are widespread, then there is nowhere you can hide where they will not haunt your dreams."

Aurín chewed on his lip.

Ymbrys reached into his pocket and produced three gold coins.

"I'll pay you each a gold royal for your trouble. Come as my guards. There is less likely to be trouble if I come escorted, and I trust the three of you."

"It won't matter," Hanen said, "if we're wildly outnumbered."

26

DOMINION

*The old fools could not see that the coin, the quill, and even the
bell were all the same. There was little left for me to learn from
them. Scepter was too taken up by his own conceit to be more
than what he already was—the heir of the Warlord, perhaps, but
only a child when the Warlord fell. Zephyr, as old and withered
as he was, did not have the wisdom of the other six who fell in the
Protectorate Wars. I would need to bide my time. When I was old
enough, I would do as Scepter did: become a Paladin of the
Hammer and enter the council of the Moteans hidden there.*

—JOURNAL OF SEARN VETURRES, ENTRY THIRTY

As they entered the Gryph Crag Inn, it was apparent that they
were wildly outnumbered. The room was crowded, with
more than half of its occupants wearing the black cloaks of
Sentinels. The inn served as a tavern only, despite its name, with
no doors leading off to private rooms. Instead, there were several
side rooms holding private meetings, visible through doorless
thresholds and guarded by a few Sentinels still on duty.

"There are a lot of Sentinels," Rallia said under her breath.

"Yes," Aurín said. "Each of the Sentinel Commanders owns an
establishment like this, where they hold court like a lord. This one
belongs to Yulan Vore, I believe."

"Should we leave?" Hanen asked.

"We merely look like a group of Sentinels joining their
comrades," Ymbrys said. "Hardly something to worry about."

A few of the Sentinels gave them disinterested glances as they followed Ymbrys to the back half of the bar, where he leaned up against it and held a hand to motion the barkeep over.

"What'll it be?" he asked the qavyl.

"Limaean Strong for me, and whatever they want."

"A bottle of pear brandy." Aurín said. "With three glasses."

The man nodded and soon came back with a tall, fluted ceramic drinking vessel for Ymbrys, and three smaller ones and a bottle for the others. Aurín took out the stopper and poured out the greenish yellow liquid. He handed one first to Rallia, then Hanen.

"To lighter days," he said, lifting his glass.

"Agreed!" Ymbrys said with a smile, and dropped back the thin glass in one go.

As Hanen finished his sip and Aurín poured again, a Sentinel approached. He was built like an auroch.

"Are you the qavyl who came to the lumber yard?" Though strongly built, he spoke eloquently.

"I am."

"Follow me."

Ymbrys and Aurín followed first, with the Clouws taking up the rear.

"He carries himself like a Paladin," Rallia whispered.

"I'd wager there are several here who have a similar past," Hanen muttered.

"Why hide as Sentinels?"

"We can travel anywhere, and not cause the stir a Paladin does, I'd imagine—even more so, west of here."

They moved past two large Sentinels standing beside an open threshold, beyond which five more men sat. Only two of them wore the black cloaks.

At the head of the table sat Slate, the man Hanen and Ymbrys had met earlier.

"Brought more guards, I see," he said.

"It is always best, when you are an outsider yourself," Ymbrys said. "The same could be said for you."

Slate nodded. "Always best to maintain a semblance of protection. You hoped to find out more about the coins I was minting. That a qavyl asks this intrigues me. That you brought with you three Sentinels who were in Mahn Fulhar a few short months ago causes that intrigue to become suspect."

Hanen touched the trigger of the crossbow held under his cloak.

"I did not realize that was an issue," Ymbrys said. He reached into one of the many pouches hanging from his staff and took out an ingot, holding it up for the man across the table to see. "It appears that you know more of this metal than I do. I thought perhaps it would be a good learning opportunity."

He tossed it across the table; it skidded to a halt in front of Slate. Everyone winced, but nothing happened.

"Based on your reaction, should I be more cautious when I come across this metal?"

"It is something found more readily in the Republic?"

Ymbrys smiled. "We come across it every once in a while. It's not something our sages have ever given much thought to."

"Where is it normally found?"

"If you're asking whether our scholars understand it is not of the world, but comes from the sky, then yes. We know this."

"Then it will come as no surprise that it is referred to by our own scholars as skyfall metal?"

"Descriptive," Ymbrys said.

"Do you also know that it cannot be smelted?"

"It is one of the reasons our people do not much care for it. It is not smeltable. It is not attractive."

"But," the man across the table said, "it is workable. And once it has cooled, it is all but impervious."

"Interesting."

"It has other applications, too. But that is not what I wish to speak of. Tell me, qavyl, would your people be willing to trade what skyfall they have found? I think a very lucrative business venture might be possible. You are, my sources tell me, a merchant."

"I trade in spices. Whether I could convince my fellow qavylli to part with the metal or not, I do not know."

"But you're willing to try?"

"I am willing to learn more about the metal. That will equip me with the knowledge I need to negotiate that trade."

"Or use that knowledge for your own smelters."

"Perhaps," Ymbrys said. "Convince me otherwise."

Slate considered him. "We can speak again at our next meeting."

"That was short," Ymbrys said.

"Yes. But it told me what I wished to know, that you possess something I would like to acquire. You're a merchant and you have means."

"But I would like to learn something as well."

"You have learned that the metal your people hoard is workable. That I know something an entire people does not is a position I am glad to find myself in."

"Add to that, you hold a piece of metal, freely given. It would seem you still have the upper hand."

"I would also not call for your death, so I think your momentary freedom is an even greater asset."

"Threatening me, when you know little about me, is not a good tactic," Ymbrys said.

Slate hesitated then said, "What do you wish to know?"

"Your name, and who you answer to."

"Easy enough," the man laughed. "I am Slate, as you surmised when first we met. I answer to no one."

"And what is your true name?" Ymbrys said, leveling his gaze at the man.

"Ingver Morrin."

"Third son of the ruler of Morraine. Presumed dead. Your uncle was executed for your death."

"How do you know that?"

"I have made it a practice to learn of the various houses and their kin. I have a memory for that sort of thing."

"Not many know of that," Slate said.

"And how many have died for knowing it?"

Slate's face darkened.

"I think we're now even," Ymbrys said.

"Leave," Slate said.

Ymbrys tipped his head and left with the Clouws and Aurín behind him.

They came out into the street.

Ymbrys said, "It appears I've made us an enemy."

"That seems to happen continually," Rallia said.

"Do you remember Slate?" Hanen asked Aurín.

"No," Aurín said. "Should I?"

"He was one of the Paladins at the event, and not on the side of the Paladins of the Hammer."

"I have little recollection of that night," Aurín said. "It felt like a bad dream, and when the next morning came, I just wanted to get out of the city as fast as possible."

They turned a corner toward the inn where they were staying, and at that moment a crowd of cloaked figures came out of an alley nearby and moved toward them.

"That was quicker than I expected," Ymbrys said. "Slate must be more soldier than plotter."

"I'm going to assume," a figure from the group called as they approached, "that you have more of that metal on you."

"If I did," Ymbrys said, "wouldn't it be better to follow me and find out where I stayed, rather than come with a contingent to bully me?"

"I don't have time to waste on long-term negotiations. And you're standing alone. Those three standing alongside you were there that night, which means they answer to me."

He held up a hand, enclosed in a gauntlet of black metal.

Aurín lurch forward and then froze.

"Aurín?" Rallia said. She put her hand on his shoulder.

"I can't seem to move," he muttered.

The men standing against them lurched toward them as one.

"It's the Gauntlet, isn't it?" Ymbrys said.

"I believe so," Hanen replied.

Rallia threw her cloak back over her shoulder and positioned herself with her staff out.

Slate twisted his wrist and Aurín turned toward Ymbrys.

"I'm sorry," Aurín groaned.

Ymbrys dodged Aurín's erratic rush at him.

"And I am sorry for you," Ymbrys said. He stepped forward and his staff shot down between Aurín's legs, toppling him. Three of the cloaked figures charged forward. Hanen raised the crossbow and let it fly, his arrow striking the first man in the shoulder and felling him with a roar. The second man raised his axe against Hanen, who deflected it with the body of his crossbow before dropping the weapon and drawing a knife. The man turned his shoulder as Hanen brought it down. It caught him on a heavy leather armored shoulder padding. The last man collided with the second one, practically lifting him up, giving Hanen an unexpected chance to knee the second man in the face and send him tumbling backward, dragging the last man with him.

"They're all working over each other," Ymbrys shouted.

"As though they're each taking the same command independently," Rallia added. She had two men on the ground around her, moaning.

"We must flee," Ymbrys said.

"Come on!" Rallia shouted.

Hanen took up the crossbow and ran down the street. Running footsteps on the cobbles behind him drove him forward.

"Go, Hanen!" he heard Rallia call from far behind. He glanced over his shoulder and saw five figures pursuing him through the torchlight. Rallia stood in the square, Ymbrys not far from her. She swung her staff, knocking another person down, and then took off in another direction.

Hanen turned and ran as hard as he could, juking into alleys and back out into streets, past raucous inns, and finally—when it sounded like no one was behind him—he ducked into a long, dark alley and hid behind a pile of broken crates, where he frantically pulled the boneshroud from his satchel. He took off his cloak, pulled the hood from the shroud over his head, then the Sentinel cloak once more.

A silence pervaded everything. All he could hear was the beating of his heart in his chest. He took deep, slow breaths until his heart slowed down. Then he stood, the dead calm within the hood washing over him, and he looked back down the alley, allowing him to see each cobble and brick even in the darkness. Then he turned and walked into the street, and caught the whiff of a familiar smell. The inviting scent of a lumberyard across a square from where he now stood, standing in derelict stoicism with no one guarding the gates. It was Slate's yard, empty for the night. So he slipped in the same way Ymbrys and he had come earlier that day, and entered the shop where the coffins were kept.

Again. No one was around. He slipped in resting his hand on the large coffin Ymbrys had tried to budge, and it still did not give way, although, unlike earlier, it appeared to have been recently opened. Hanen took hold of the edge and peeked within. When he saw a gauntlet of black metal—the opposite hand to the one that Slate carried—he shut it quickly. After a moment of getting over his shock, he opened the door again and revealed the figure wearing the glove. It stood as a large suit of armor, big enough to be donned by a vül. He reached up and touched the gauntlet, which was oddly warm and cold at the same time, with mesmerizing waves and ripples in the surface of the metal.

When his finger grazed the elbow of the gauntlet, a soft click sounded and it fell almost to the ground before he caught it. He quickly looked around, then shut the coffin and stepped away, the gauntlet in his arms, retreating into a back room, which was warmed by the heat of a forge. More of the skyfall metal coins lay next to a wooden chest, He took hold of the top, and pushed it back. It was well-made and the hinges were silent. Inside was not a wealth of coins but hundreds of bone-colored rings. He took hold of the rings and lifted them up to reveal a smaller and as-yet-incomplete boneshroud, not much smaller than the portion lost when the Paladin had ruined Searn's boneshroud at the Rose Convent. Much of it appeared newer and made of freshly bleached bone. Opening his satchel, he swept the bone rings and coins into it. Then he turned to leave, Slate was standing there, a crossbow leveled at him.

"I expected you might come back this way," he said. "Especially after I tried to use the gauntlet on you, and you didn't even budge."

"Why would I have budged?" Hanen asked.

Slate almost looked startled. "You're not who I thought you were. Your voice is much lower. Almost... like Shroud. Who are you?"

Hanen took a step back.

"I see you took some of my coins," Slate said. "You can have them. If our plans align I'm interested in knowing who you are."

Hanen didn't think his voice was low. But he was wearing the boneshroud over his head and under his hood.

"I am...Heir," he said.

"That's not a moniker I've heard used yet. Who sent you? Dusk? Or even the council at Pariantür?"

"I act on my own," Hanen said.

"What do you want with the coins?"

Hanen didn't answer.

"They won't do you much good. Not without a skyfall forge."

"It is the rings that interest me more," Hanen said.

"You... Wait. Rings? What do you want with that?" Slate's voice rose to a panic. The gauntlet under Hanen's arm, hidden within the cloak, weighed him down. With his other arm he raised his crossbow. The man across from him panicked and shot his own, wildly. Hanen ran out a side door and into the yard, where ten more of Slate's men began chasing him through rows of aging lumber. Crossbow bolts shot overhead into the wood nearby. Hanen raced around corner after corner, trying to find shadows to hide in, but the wood stood brightly even in the moonless, star-filled night. A twinge of pain shot through his shoulder as a bolt stuck true; thankfully it pierced his skin at an angle. He winced as he moved, his cloak now pinned to his flesh by the bolt. Every move, every waver of the cloak, pulled on the shaft that stuck out of him in excruciating detail.

He found a side alley, and ran toward it, only to discover a back access to another outbuilding. He kicked at the door, but it was barred from the inside, and then tried to escape, the silhouettes of Slate's men entered the alley. He was cornered.

Blood dribbled down from his soaked shoulder onto his hand. He felt something stir around him and looked down as the tattered edges of the cloak rustled. A small black tendril of smoke reached from the links, seeking a droplet of blood that had fallen on the shroud. The blood disappeared.

"No," he muttered to himself. "I don't want this."

But it was too late to take the cloak off. The figures moved toward him.

"Don't fire until you see him," the voice of Slate was saying from the mass of shadows.

Hanen reached into the satchel and felt around for something he could use, his bloody hand moving around and through the chain link folds of the new incomplete shroud. Then, to his startled surprise, the door next to him suddenly cracked open.

"What's going on out here?" a gruff voice said.

Hanen scrambled to his feet and forced the door open, bolting into the home of a man who stood dumbfounded. He could hear Slate's men rushing to enter.

"You're trailing blood into my house!" the man shouted.

Hanen flew up the stairs to a window looking out over the wall of the lumberyard and onto the rooftops of the houses beyond. He kicked the window out and leapt to the next roof, rushing across the ridgeline and down the opposite slope for another leap, barely making it as bolts began to fly after him again. He lost his footing on the ridgeline and slid down the other side of the roof, tumbling twenty feet through the darkness into a pile of refuse.

He had just finished shaking his head clear when a figure came into the alleyway.

"Hey!" the man shouted. "Stop!"

Hanen jumped out of the refuse but found himself cornered as a man entered the other end of the alley.

Little wisps of smoke were pouring from the hem of the boneshroud.

The second man leveled a crossbow at Hanen. His shot flew wide, striking the man at the other end of the alley. Hanen turned and tried to leap over his injured adversary, but the man still had the strength to pull Hanen down with him into a tangle of arms and legs. In the tussle, Hanen pulled on a strap of leather around the man's neck and a coin came free. Trying not to drop the gauntlet in his other arm, Hanen stumbled to his feet. The coin in his hand was vibrating. As he rounded the corner, the coin flew out of his palm and into the grasp of a wisp of smoke, which pulled it down into the chain links, making it another piece of the cloak.

Meanwhile, the edge of the shroud had found its way into his satchel and gotten stuck to something. When he pulled it free of the satchel, the second shroud came with it as an extension of the larger shroud. He kept trying to get away as Slate's men appeared and pursued him. Yet an energy buzzed through him, dulling the pain in his shoulder. He felt he could run all night.

He took another corner and sighed. It was another dead end. He didn't know the city, and would continue to get cornered by these men, who came around the corner armed with axes.

"Stop this!" He could hear the deepening of his voice this time, reverberating off the alley's walls. The tattered edge of the original boneshroud was now completed by the second shroud, and the coins, incorporated into the weave, and black smoke pouring off it. He pointed at the men, but the smoke didn't respond. The gauntlet under his other arm began to vibrate. It would fit his bloodied hand and protect it, perhaps, if it didn't have an adverse effect on him. He took up the boneshroud edges and covered his hand with it, then threw caution to the wind and thrust his hand down into the gauntlet.

Like the mouth of an ancient beast it consumed his arm to the wrist. He did not need to know what to do; he simply lifted the gauntlet at the men coming into the alley.

"Stop," he commanded.

They hesitated, each grabbing at their chests.

"Hot!" one of them howled.

Something flew from each of them into the gauntlet's palm. Hanen looked down. Ten coins of the same metal as the gauntlet glowed as though cooling from a forge. They seemed fused to the gauntlet. He tried to brush the coins away on the edge of the boneshroud; they came free and clicked into place, joining the cloak.

He looked up at the men, who all stood there looking confused.

"Go!" he shouted.

They startled and fled the alley.

Hanen shook the gauntlet free. It fell with a clang to the alley floor. His heart beat rapidly as he picked it up and walked out of the alley and down the street toward the distant torchlight of a nearby inn. When he was close enough to see by the light, he took off his Black Sentinel cloak and the boneshroud for examination. When Searn had been defeated, the boneshroud had been in tatters, but now, with the second boneshroud unnaturally, messily incorporated into it, along with fifty or so of the skyfall coins, it looked complete again.

The gauntlet sat dead, but there was no longer any blood on his arm. He reached up to touch the bolt that had struck him, and found nothing. His arm had healed.

"How?"

A search through his satchel told him that Searn's bone pin was missing.

Not missing. Incorporated into the Shroud itself.

"What does that mean?" he said to himself.

That was a lot of blood, words bloomed across the pin. And it looks like the boneshroud is complete again. How did you do that? Put the boneshroud on and tell me.

Hanen pulled both cloaks back on and walked down the street, hoping he could find his way to the inn he was staying at with Rallia and Ymbrys.

"That is better," Searn's voice said directly into this mind.

Hanen scrambled to pull the boneshroud off.

"Stop that," Searn said. *"I'm not going to harm you. This is better, really. For both of us."*

"How are you doing that?"

"I'm not sure. I'd wager some of your blood, and the blood of someone else, has fed the cloak. How is it completed again?"

"A man called Slate was making a Shroud of his own. It incorporated itself. Along with some weird coins."

"Interesting," Searn said. *"Very interesting."*

"How are you doing this?"

"It appears it took my bone pin into the cloak too. I'm part of the cloak now. I am the cloak. And it appears that everyone else is here too."

"What do you mean everyone else?"

"Those I captured into the cloak. Well...not everyone. It seems in the conflict in Mahn Fulhar, the bone ring from Ghoré didn't

make it. That's too bad. He was key to controlling the shades. I can probably assist with that."

"This is not good," Hanen said.

"What do you mean?"

"I don't like that I'm wearing a cloak that now talks to me with the voice of a dead man."

"A bit late for all that regret now," Searn said. *"I'd say this means you're now in a position to take the next step. We can put our minds together to unlock secrets in the other journal in your possession."*

"The Apostate's journal?"

"Of course. Now, tell me all that happened tonight to bring us to this point."

27

INTERLUDES

Despite its poorly-planned streets, Birin had been relatively easy to navigate over the past two weeks. Runah had gone to the east side of the city with the monk Nidian to seek out seamstresses, while Marn and Guarin had gone to speak to the monks of Nifara. There was no urgency this day. The money from her father would last some time yet. But there was still a desire to find work—to find a means to settling in. Hanen had mentioned it was even warmer down south, and the idea of heat that would wilt her hair in the summer, and require cotton or wool to soak up sweat did not fill her with excitement, although the exotic fabrics and accessories, which were more readily available and affordable there, did sound intriguing.

Alodda came to a long building, the upper level of which had finely colored drapes between the pillars. A woman stood behind a counter on this floor, counting bolts of cloth and only giving Alodda a momentary glance.

Alodda waited.

The woman made a mark in her ledger and then finally focused her attention on her.

"May I help you?"

"Yes, you might," Alodda replied. "I'm a seamstress who specializes in fine embroidery—trained in Mahn Fulhar and a member of the guild there."

"We have no work here."

"Yes, well, I'm not looking for work, per se. But perhaps you might know of a lady in the city looking for help."

"Have you been to the Templum?" the woman asked. "They provide for the needs of the less fortunate." She eyed Alodda and her northern clothes.

"Perhaps you've a mistress I may speak with?"

The woman scoffed. "Lady Emaine is away. She'll return in an hour."

"Way I look around?"

"So long as you don't make more work for me.

"That is never my intention for anyone."

The woman went back to her work, and Alodda walked into a room crowded with tables boasting messy but beautiful arrays of cloth and bolts and ribbons, filling her with awe. That a place like this existed, that there could be this much unused cloth just awaiting the touch of a seamstress! She made her way as a lone observer through aisles so busy with haphazard materials that the woman's admonition to Alodda made no sense. An out-of-place bolt would not have gone amiss here. But as her surprise wore off, she started to notice a pattern to the mess. Most tables displayed a single material, and generally the colors were grouped together, as though the mistress of the warehouse took pleasure in allowing her customers to hunt for hidden treasures.

After an hour Alodda found herself at a table of soft wool, dyed every shade of purple. The light wool was noted for being from the hrelgren empire, made of Drul wool. Her mind wandered as she took up a bolt of black wool dyed a deep purple.

"Considering the wool for a shawl?" a woman said, approaching from the back of the room. She wore a rich blue robe, and her long black hair hung freely behind her.

"Considering what shirt I might make for a beau. This wool looks to breathe well. It would serve in northern or southern climates."

"I agree," she said, touching the fabric. Then she gasped. "That is a finely embroidered ribbon you're wearing. It almost looks like an Abgenas Knot."

"It is," Alodda said.

"It may be like an Abgenas Knot, but it can't be unless you bought it from him directly."

"I did not buy it," Alodda said with a smile. "I embroidered it myself. He taught me, after all."

"Many have asked him to teach them, but few have succeeded.

How did you convince him?"

"He owed it to me." She held out her hand in the way she had seen other Dürani people greet. "I am Alodda Dülar, Abgenas' daughter."

The woman took her hand. "It is a pleasure," she said. "I am Lady Emaine."

"The pleasure is mine. I've been awaiting your return, in fact."

"What may I do for you?"

"I'm newly arrived in town and seeking work. My sister and I are both seamstresses and embroiderers. We can make dresses, and we wouldn't mind making home visits."

The woman shook her head with a smile growing on her face. "I'll hear nothing of it," she said. "I will offer you all the material you need to make your embroidered ribbons for me. What ribbons you do not sell directly to the women of this city I will personally buy from you. We can split the profits."

"Is my ribbon truly so unique?"

"Your work is astounding, yes. We've only just met, but I shall employ you as long as you are in town."

"Thank you."

"It is I who thank you. I cannot thank you enough. I ought to go make sure we have all the twist you need."

"What about this bolt of purple?"

"It is yours. Come back tomorrow and we'll discuss a work space for you."

"My sister and I might be able to help you organize things as well."

"Good, good! Abrelle!" she called to the front. "Come to my back room!"

The other woman hastily joined her mistress just as a couple walked through the door arm-in-arm, the man in a gray robe and the girl in a red cloak. They were talking amiably with one another; the girl was obviously flirting with him. Alodda made her way to leave, but halfway across the room she stopped in her tracks and stared at the girl. Runah, barely a woman at seventeen, was leaning on the arm of the monk Nidian. As soon as her sister made eye contact with her, she dropped her arm. Nidian looked up and blushed.

"I didn't expect you in this part of the city," Runah said.

"Obviously."

Runah and Alodda stepped away together.

"We thought we might come to see if they had work," her sister explained.

"And who is 'we'?"

"I…" Runah blushed, and glanced back at Nidian.

"You've known him for all of four weeks and he's a monk."

"Monks may have wives, especially out east in countries like Morriego."

"We're not in Morriego. He's a monk of the west."

"Marn was married," Runah said.

"Before he became a monk."

"You've gotten involved with that Coin Cloak."

"Hanen is not a man of the cloth." Alodda looked down and realized her fists were clenched.

"Runah," she said. "Let's start this conversation again."

"You sound like Mother."

"Someone needs to."

"But you're not her."

"That doesn't change the fact that we need to talk about this, but later please. I have good news and I don't want this…indiscretion…to get in the way."

"What is it?"

"This place wants us to work and sell our ribbons."

"We have a chance to start fresh and you want to make ribbons again?"

"The owner loves our work and doesn't have anyone doing what Father taught us."

"Fine," Runah sighed. "Can we go back to the inn?"

"Yes," Alodda said, "but we're talking about this later."

Runah gave Alodda a smile, but as she turned Alodda saw the broader grin she gave the man five years older than herself.

She needed to speak to Marn and Guarin to find out what kind of man Nidian had been before he took the cloth, and if she needed either to worriedly end it, or hurry up and embroider a wedding veil.

Ophedia sat on the edge of the bed. It was comfortable, but the room was cold even with the fire burning in the hearth. Navien was not trailing her. He was probably not far behind Hanen and

Rallia in Haven, or after the monks and the Dülars fleeing to Düran. Meanwhile she was stuck in this house with little chance of escape. A meager plate of food had been left for her, which she picked at while considering if she could remove the bars from the window and survive the jump to the ground.

The bell from the town chapel sounded, and she heard the scrape of guards changing shifts on the roof above.

She stood and paced the room a few times and jiggled the door handle.

A few moments later, the sounds changed to those of alarm. Someone was shouting "Fire!"

"Great. Locked in a room in burning a house. Just what I need."

There was a knock on the window.

She walked over and saw the smiling face of the hrelgren Zhag.

"Azho, Ophedia," he said, as she opened the casement.

"Are you the cause of the fire they're hollering about?"

"I think that's Eunia's doing. She's going to meet you on the road in an hour."

"What about Whisper? What about you?"

"Technically I'm on a ship in the harbor right now. Whisper is down below on the street. He refused to climb up the face of this wall. I'm not sure why."

"All right," Ophedia chuckled. "Well, how are you going to get me out of this room?"

He held up a bar of iron. "This was not easy to carry up here. But the guards are changing, and dealing with the fire. Give me a few moments to finish tying myself off, and then I can wrench the bolts in the stone free."

"Have you done this before?"

Zhag gave her a wink.

Tendrils of smoke came from underneath the door.

"It's a good thing that Eunia wants to go east with you. I fear to think how the Church of the Common Chalice would fare with her as an enemy."

"What do you mean?"

"You should have seen how she reacted when you were taken. She threatened to grab a bow and shoot your escort from behind."

"Why didn't she?"

"Chös stopped her. He is a calming influence on her."

"Is he coming too?"

"Yes. He prefers to stay near her."

He put the iron bar under a bolt and began wrenching back on it. The opposable digits on his hands and feet gave him the grip he needed. The bolt flew free.

"Let me get the opposite one out too, and you should be free."

A moment later he wrenched out another one.

"All right. Push."

He swung away as Ophedia kicked at the iron bar, wrenching the third bolt free. Then he swung down on the fourth and freed her.

"All right. Grab my waist," he said.

She put her arms around him and fought the urge to squeal as he jumped away from the building with her, the rope tied around his waist going taut as they swung down and landed on their feet. He swiftly cut himself free and threw the rope into the burning house.

"That ought to cover your tracks," he said. "Ophedia del Ishé, you're officially dead!"

"Thank you, Zhag," she said, throwing her arms around the small green creature. "I owe you one."

"If we ever meet again, you can buy me a meal and a night of drinks."

"Deal."

Whisper padded up to her, and she offered him a scratch. "I suppose you know where Eunia is?" she asked the ynfald.

Whisper turned and started walking away.

"You better get to the pier," Ophedia said to Zhag. "I need to go bail out those Clouws."

PART 4

MORIN

MORRAINE

MAHN
FULHAR

ALNIR

MAHNDÜR

PRECIPICE
ORACLE

GREEN
BASTION

ZEBUDÉ

BRAH

GRISDEN

HAVEN

ABINGEN

VAREA

LIMAE

RESDAM

REDOT

OUIQUIMON

LIBERTE

MAHNDÜR

28

CALLING

I finally had the courage to open Ollistan's journal. It is not something I shall do again until the day I complete this work and wear protection over my head. While I will not admit that evil exists, a darkness washed over me when I opened that book. Whether a god of the Black Coterie watches over it or a Shade resides within it, perhaps even the Shade of Ollistan Gœrnstadt, I will know when that day comes.

—JOURNAL OF SEARN VETURRES, ENTRY FORTY THREE

The Dræc Inn was smaller than most, built between two others and filling what was once an alley. Inside, the tables and chairs were small and cramped. But the back door was easy to slip through, out of sight of the wary owner, who constantly watched the entrance. Dorian Mür sat near the fire, the flames gleaming in his eyes as he stared off into nothingness. When Rallia Clouw approached and handed him a small ceramic cup of mead, he took a sip of the drink, smiled broadly, and ran a hand over his bald head. Rallia then poured out a mug of the mulled beer warmed by the mantel. The silver caps on the ends of her braids clinked, striking the studs on her vest as she took a seat between Dorian and Hanen.

Hanen kept an eye on the door with as much suspicion as the proprietor. He reached down below the table before remembering that Whisper had gone with Ophedia. He hoped the little ynfald was alright, and wondered if his not being there had brought the bad luck of the night before.

Ymbrys came down the narrow stairs carrying his staff in his hand. In his other hand he held his tail, keeping it close as he worked his way between the tight confines of the room. He had to duck below the bannister above, standing taller than most humans. The soft, skin-covered horns on his forehead almost brushed the rafters as he approached the table, smiling nervously, with the proprietor rushing up behind him carrying a tankard of beer. Ymbrys took the tankard with a thankful smile and sat down.

"The rooms are acceptable," he said, to the man and to the table. He took out a satchel from the folds of his silken layers and handed it to the eager man. "You'll need to acquire meat for me," he added, "and also whatever my friends require."

"Meat, good qavyl?" the owner asked. "What do you prefer?"

"Any meat is fine. I need only meat. No bread for me in the coming days."

"Do you think we'll be here that long?" Hanen asked.

"I believe we can remain relatively unknown here," Ymbrys replied as the proprietor left for his bar again. "It is respectable but relatively unknown. All the windows let out onto rooftops and the back door empties onto a wide street. We can leave at a moment's notice if we must."

"My good qavyl," Dorian said, "the sun is nearly setting. I have been very patient today, and it is time for you to explain what is going on, and why we are here at this inn."

"Of course," Ymbrys said. "We've no reason to wait any longer. It is important for you to know the fate to which these two Clouws, myself, and most certainly you, are inexorably tied.

"I met the Clouws in Edi City. It was not by accident, as much as I led them to believe, but tied instead to seeking their lineage out. I am a scholar of the Qavyl Republic seeking answers to a question our scholars have debated this whole century: what happened to the heirs of the man who instigated the Protectorate Wars?"

"Ollistan Gœrnstadt," Dorian replied.

"Correct," Ymbrys nodded. "He was defeated by your hand at the Battle of Desert Gate," Ymbrys said. "Yet there were rumors of his having a daughter by the woman he married in his early years, when he studied the Veld among the Oruche. Our scholars believe her name was…"

"Belivah," Dorian interrupted.

"Yes," Ymbrys said, smiling. "She disappeared shortly before the wars began."

"She went into hiding," Dorian corrected, "with her daughter. I only found out years later that she hid directly under our noses, amongst the Roses of Pariantür."

"That is what we surmised. After that she disappeared. Whether she survived or not, our auguries suggested her daughter lived."

"Auguries? I did not believe your people given to such superstitions."

"Indeed, we are not," Ymbrys said, "but our Librarian Priests have means of communicating with the Keepers of the Dead, and with permission granted by Lae'Zeq, they sought answers and discovered that the daughter did not die for some decades after this. "

"By what means?"

"By requesting the Watchers of Wyv consult their records. That is all they were able to tell us. I believe she fled Pariantür with a protector who fathered a daughter with her, and this daughter in turn birthed the father of these two." He gestured to the Clouws.

"And that protector," Dorian replied, "who helped the Apostate's daughter stay in hiding—it was Nethendel, wasn't it?"

"That you say his name," Ymbrys said, "confirms what I believe."

"I've never confirmed it but I believe my wife knew this. She was sworn not to reveal her brother's plans and whereabouts. I believe they kept up a correspondence for some time."

"And yet," Ymbrys said, "having discovered the heirs to Gœrnstadt, I realize it is not the full story, nor what my god has planned for me to uncover. The true heirs to the Apostate and his patron deity are not through his blood, but through his plan."

"What do you mean?" Hanen asked.

"The Apostate had followers who inherited his greater plan, and continued to enact it."

"You mean the Moteans?" Dorian asked.

"They are part of it," Ymbrys said, "since they follow the writings of those Gœrnstadt trusted, if he ever trusted anyone. The Protectorate Wars did not end with his defeat, but continue to this day ushering in the beginning of the Imbalance."

"The Imbalance?" Dorian asked.

Ymbrys sat back. "There truly is much to say," he said, shaking his head. "Alright. Let me submit it to you as briefly as possible so we can get to the matter at hand.

"The Deceiver, Achanerüt, was born from the mind of Sakharn. He was never supposed to be. His birth created the first Great Imbalance by working against the perfect harmony of the worlds, created by the Existence. The Deceiver brought down with him those who became the Black Coterie, and the Imbalance increased. It grew so wildly out of hand, until the Destruction occurred, sundering the world. Since that day, the White Pantheon has sought to unravel his work—to bring back the balance and proceed with the original plan of the Existence, but the balance of the universe is now like a ship of the sea, and the Deceiver and his Black Coterie are the waves that toss the ship. The appearance of the Apostate, and the war that followed was a swell and it set the ship to teetering once more. Yet a wave never crashes alone. While we passed through that storm, we still have the other half to weather. The Deceiver has brought a storm."

"The qavylli scholars think another storm is about to begin?" Dorian asked.

"No," Ymbrys said. "I alone think this. It is one of the two reasons I left."

"And the other reason?"

"They consider me a thief, having taken a treasure tied now to my fate."

"I should like to know more of that," Dorian said, "but let us not get side-tracked."

"Of course." Ymbrys nodded respectfully. "Given the events of that last year, I believe the Moteans are part of this new storm, especially those who inherited the relics of the Apostate's own dark coterie."

"The Warlord?" Dorian probed.

"And his council of Amethyst Magi," Ymbrys added.

"But they all perished."

"Five Magi died with the Apostate. But the seventh member, what of him?"

"Seventh?" Dorian asked. "The Amethyst Magi numbered six if you're including Gœrnstadt."

"Sakharn's holy number is seven," said Ymbrys. "I believe there was a seventh member, likely hiding in the Veld and acting as a channeler for the Revenants."

"Revenants?" Rallia asked.

"During the Protectorate Wars," Hanen explained, "men who died and came back to life, fighting on. They were called the Revenants."

Rallia shuddered.

"It was understood," Ymbrys said, "that the Warlord's armor disappeared. I believe this remaining member of the Coterie stole it through the Veld and returned it to Kallattai. In fact, I believe it is here in Haven."

"As do I," Dorian said

"You seek it out too, then?" Ymbrys asked.

"As I ought to have done sixty years ago. I can make excuses, that I had to reestablish Pariantür, that I needed to restore the imbalance caused by the wars... There was a time, when I felt that Grissone wanted me to go after the Warlord's armor, but I didn't. I fear that my failure's consequences are upon us all."

"That is much the same feeling the gods have had. Yes. Even the gods have regrets."

"How do you know this?" Dorian asked.

"My god has spoken to me directly," Ymbrys said. "He chose a liar and a thief to act as his scholar and prophet."

"It has been a long time since Lae'Zeq has spoken to anyone," Dorian said.

"That is what the qavylli believe," Ymbrys said, "but it is not entirely true. There are those who through the centuries have been chosen to carry the burden of his voice."

"You believe you are that voice now?"

"Providence has dictated it be so. I offered Lae'zeq an opportunity to leave behind the confines of his continent and search for answers abroad, to offset the regrets of an eon past."

"Why, then," Dorian asked, "are we here at this inn rather than the more comfortable one we stayed in last night?"

"I ran into Ymbrys as we arrived," Hanen said. "He's been here some weeks, and he found someone who was involved in what happened at Mahn Fulhar—a Paladin by the name of Slate. He is minting coins of an odd metal."

"Skyfall, he called it," Ymbrys said. "Hanen and I visited him, and he was under the impression that Hanen and Rallia possessed one of those coins. He recognized their faces from the event, but fled before discovering them to be those who foiled Searn's plans. He revealed he has the Gauntlet and tried to use it on them."

"We weren't affected," Hanen said, "but he has a large group of men and women under his control."

"Then it is good I've come here," Dorian said.

"Why?" Rallia asked.

"Because that means he knows where the armor is. I mean to find and destroy it."

"That is not going to be easy," Ymbrys said.

"But it must be done. If there is a means to take away a tool from the enemy, then we ought to. We can help restore the balance."

"Whether a balance can be achieved remains to be seen, even by the gods," Ymbrys said. "After all, they have not achieved it themselves. Who are we mortals to think we can help?"

"Who are we mortals," Dorian said, "to not answer their call and do all in our power to assist them?"

"Who are we mortals to think we can help?" Hanen said.

The three of them turned to look at him.

"What do you mean, Hanen?" Rallia asked.

"We... If the gods caused a problem, inviting the Deceiver among their company in the first place, then who do we think we are that our actions could help?"

"That's a very self-destructive attitude," Dorian replied.

"I should like to hear what he has to say," Ymbrys replied.

"I don't know what I'm saying," Hanen replied. "It's something that's been on my mind since Mahn Fulhar."

He lifted his tankard to drink, then put it back down and pushed it away.

"I was hesitant to fight against Searn at the Convent because, while he was a Sentinel, he had been a Paladin first. I wondered if he had been pushed down that road by the Paladins. Or else... or else why would he have stood against them? It was the Paladins' problem, not mine."

"That may be true," Dorian said, "and yet you did side with us and turned the balance in our favor. One might even say that providence offered your presence."

"Perhaps," Hanen continued. "But I didn't go looking to help. I just happened to be there."

"And you shifted the balance."

"So, to that same line of reasoning," Hanen continued, "it is presumptuous for us to say, 'Let's go defeat the the Deceiver.'"

"That's reductive, and hyperbole," Dorian said, crossing his arms.

"Is it?" Hanen asked. "Heroes of all the old stories fall because they seek to be heroes. Their desire for glory is what brings them low, and they become lessons in futility."

"I do not seek to be a hero," Dorian said. "I seek to save."

"You seek martyrdom," Hanen said.

Dorian glared at Hanen.

"What do you seek, Hanen?" Ymbrys asked.

"To live. To find my own balance."

"Hanen," Rallia said, placing a comforting hand on his arm, "you've exaggerated what he said. Dorian did not suggest we seek the destruction of the Deceiver. That is the responsibility of the gods. But, as he said, we can help shift the balance. Even a few grains can push a scale to balance. If we deal with problems at our own level, we are helping."

"But how?" Hanen asked.

"By doing what we know to be right," Rallia said. "By standing against what we know to be wrong. As you did in Mahn Fulhar."

"Because you forced me to," Hanen said.

"But you did it, and I stood alongside you. We were not alone."

"Nor would you stand alone now," Ymbrys said.

"So what do you propose we do?"

"I should imagine Slate has moved his location now," Ymbrys said, "or at least made it more difficult to enter his lumberyard. Dorian, as spry as he is, is old. I am a frail qavyl. Your help would be most welcome."

"I will help," Rallia said, giving Hanen a goading look.

Hanen took his tankard in his hand. "Fine. I'm in."

Hanen entered his room, shut the door behind him, and reached under the bed to grab the satchel he had stashed there. The gauntlet made it very heavy; he wondered whether he should move it to the bottom of his travel sack, except that Rallia often got into it when she repacked for the road. He took the gauntlet out and dropped it on the bed, followed by the boneshroud, which he dropped over his head, pulling his blankets up to his shoulders as the pervading silence flooded him. The light of his candle seemed to dim.

He reached over and pulled the two journals out. He pushed Searn's aside and touched the unopened journal of the Apostate, Ollistan Gœrnstadt, his great-great-grandfather

"Finally considering finally reading it?" Searn asked within his mind. He jumped.

"I...am."

"Have you finished reading mine?"

"Yes," Hanen replied. "And I have questions."

"Go on then," Searn said.

"Why can I only hear you? Why not the other shades? Why not Ghoré?"

"I'm the only true shade in here. The others are mere thoughts. Ghoré never moved on to Noccitan. After the events of that night, I suspect his ring was destroyed, or at least torn from the Shroud when that Paladin scathed it with his light. "

"Or he's in here biding his time."

"Would Ghoré remain silent?"

"No he would not."

"What is your next question?"

"Did you do what your mentors asked of you only because they had taken you in?"

"I did so, because I saw the truth of what they said. The world had shunned me. It had shunned them. So we made the boneshroud to protect ourselves from the other tools we sought."

"Such as the Armor of the Warlord?"

"The Dreadplate, it was called. There are others, but I think it important we first find the plate."

"Slate has it," Hanen said.

"What?" Searn replied.

"I saw it. He is keeping it in a giant coffin."

"And the gauntlet?"

"He has the one you used at Mahn Fulhar. "

"I expected as much."

"But he doesn't have the other."

Searn was silent.

"I have it," Hanen said. "I took it when it fell out of the coffin. It seems to have control over the coins, unlike what the other gauntlet does, which commands those who carry them. Instead it can...move the metal."

"That's the answer," Searn said.

"What is?"

"The two gauntlets. They control the metal, together."

"I'm not sure I understand."

"No one has been able to understand how the armor is used, but if the gauntlets are the key, then it means we need to gain control of both of them."

"That will be difficult," Hanen said, "since Slate has probably gone to ground."

"Then you have some studying to do while you make your plans to take it."

"What will we do, if we can use the armor?"

"We go into the next stage of the plan."

"And what is that?"

"Read the other journal. I'll leave it at that."

Hanen could feel Searn leave. He took up the journal of the Apostate and opened it.

I found myself upon a sea of sand.
And it seemed to follow my touch and command.

Nightly the vision came to me. It grew stronger as I sought answers in the Marches of the Oruche, where the path was laid for me and where I met her, giving myself to the fate I knew I could not escape. It was there I learned to command dream—walk between the worlds, creating machinations of my own, commanding the souls of the living and the no-longer-living, destroying what was raised up and seeking beauty in terror. It was there I became the vessel of the Black Coterie, and in the end I saw no victory, but instead an imperfect balance that would birth a new hope, despite the Deceits laid at the foundation of Kallattai.

I am Ollistan Gœrnstadt. If you read this, know that you choose to walk a path that shall surely lead to the destruction of you and those you love, for there is no armor that can stand against the Deceiver. So seek out a way to follow this path unseen, or you shall be exposed for all to mock.

29

HISTORY

Send a contingent of at least fifty to the father monastery. The Prima Pater shall not expect a squadron so large to ride in protest. But if we do not move on this opportunity, and insist upon diplomatic action against Ikhala, there shall be no Pariantür, and we citadels shall become islands. I've no doubt those that take up our stations after us may turn upon one another in argument, or worse, in schism.

— PATER MINORIS BLANDIS PORMAR OF THE AERIE TO

PATER MINORIS ARTH KELLIDOTH OF ST. HAMUL

AT THE OUTSET OF THE PROTECTORATE WARS

Hanen walked the streets wearing his brown traveler cloak to avoid the curiosity inspired by his Sentinel cloak. His hair hung freely around his face. He kept one hand on an axe on his belt and toyed with the whiskers with his other hand, considering the words he had read of Ollistan's harsh upbringing in northern Zhigava, near the Ikhalan border. Of his leaving home and eventually finding his way to studying with the magi of the Oruche Marches, who referred to themselves as the somnumancers. The other worlds had never meant anything to Hanen, and yet he had stood in Noccitan. Did that mean the Veld, the World of Dream, was real? And could it be so easily reached?

He considered the tales of the Üterk, told in Garrou, and their ties to Kos-Yran, who had been known as the Walker-Between-Worlds. Did the Üterk walk between worlds? Had Hanen's own mother, who came from one of their tribes, known of this?

The sweet smell of the smokeweed reached Hanen as he stood before a row of shops. A hrelgren sat on the stairs with a long pipe in his hand and smoke wafting from his bowl.

"What are you looking for?" the hrelgren asked.

"Not often you hear a hrelgren asking a question," Hanen replied. "*Azho.*"

"*Ashini.*" The hrelgren stood. "*Peglin-dor-gorun?*"

"I don't, I'm afraid," Hanen said. "Only the usual greetings."

"You ought to. It would open you up to a wider world. Speaking of wider worlds, I'm a map-seller."

Hanen perked up at that. "I love maps."

"All people do. Come on in."

Hanen followed the hrelgren into the shop. It was simple and neat, with the faint scent of smokeweed in the air. One wall was lined with map holes filled with scroll cases and boxes.

"Tell me about yourself," the hrelgren said, going to stand across the table in the middle of the room.

"First tell me your name."

The hrelgren laughed, his hands on his hips. "I am Zapas *yu* Caradadz."

"I am Hanen Clouw. My sister and I once ran a caravan from Edi City to Garrou."

"You are far from your path."

"I feel it at times," Hanen said.

"Perhaps," the hrelgren said, tapping his chin, "you could help me with something. I need information about the border of Bortali—for my maps."

The hrelgren found what he was looking for and pulled out a box. From it he took a piece of pulp paper showing a map of Garrou in charcoal. The coast and the mountains bordering Boroni were detailed, but the southern forests remained vague.

"I've been collecting information regarding Bortali, which I've been unable to visit myself. I would like to know what you can tell me of the border."

Hanen leaned over to look closer. Zapas held out a piece of charcoal.

"Here," he said, pointing to the edge of Düran. "This border crossing goes through a barracks between a gap of rocks, not far from which stand the stone landmarks called the Pantheon's Council. They sit in an endless field of griefdark. If this is for someone looking for an advantage against Bortali, this is the worst way to travel."

Zapas gave him a wink. "I could sell that kind of information, but it would have to be for a large quantity of gold. Thank you for telling me this. I can think of a few herbalists who would like to know of the griefdark. Now, what maps do you seek?"

"What kind of maps do you have?" Hanen asked.

"Human, hrelgren. I haven't come across any qavylli maps worth collecting."

"What about maps of odd things? Such as ancient tribal lands or places no one has seen, like what lies beyond the Protectorates?"

"No one has maps of those lands," Zapas said. "You'd be more likely to negotiate a map of the Veld from an Oruche than a map of the east."

"The Veld?" Hanen asked.

"The Dreamscape."

"There are maps?"

"No. Of course not. You can't map the unmappable; it's merely a saying. The Oruche tribesmen have their secrets, and they'd never part with them, I should say. Comes from an old tale of a hrelgren pirate who sought to take his ship into the Veld and seek treasure there."

"The hrelgrens have stories of the Veld?"

"Of course," Zapas said. "Not as many as men or the Minotyr do, but we have some. They've not been translated, but if you really want to learn about them, you ought to learn hrelgren. Then you can go and visit our library and read for yourself."

Hanen looked at the shelves. "I would be interested in a map of the ancient tribes of men. If it is an older map, even better."

"I think I can do that," Zapas said. "I might even have some from the Alvarian Age. The scholars of that era loved to map out the tribes and bloodlines."

He used a ladder to climb to the top of a shelf, where he removed a dust-covered scroll case.

"This one was copied from an older one. Alvaria was many, many centuries ago."

He opened the case and dropped the map into his hand, unrolling it on the table.

"What I like about this one is it is so very out of scale." He pointed out how small Düran was drawn and how short the southern end of Mahn Fulhar was. "All the mapmaker cared about was showing the people groups. See, the various Oruche tribes are named, and in the marshes between their baileys are the tribes of the Minotyr. Ormach didn't even exist. Just the old Pirate Coast up to the City States.

"What is that mark on Mahn Fulhar? There is a similar one in the center of the lake down by what is now Ormach."

"Those black squares?" Zapas said. "There is one on the Massif of Mahndür, too, and by Pariantür, and one by my people's capital. They aren't marked. The black square could mark our temples to our gods. That would seem to match with the holy sites, such as Mahn Fulhar for Aben, and the massif of the Mother."

"Then according to these marks, there are more black marks than gods in the Pantheon."

"It is not something I'm familiar with," Zapas said, "but intriguing nonetheless."

"How much for the map?" Hanen asked.

"Tell me why it interests you."

"My mother was Üterk," Hanen said. "This shows the old tribal borders of the Üterk in the north, as well as their cousins in the Oruche Marches. If I'm reading this correctly, there are even notations on the ocean of tribes gone elsewhere, off the map."

"I'd say you've got plenty to study here," Zapas responded.

He walked to another shelf and took out a small book with a wood cover.

"If you buy this primer on the hrelgren language, and this map, I'll sell you both for three gold royals."

Hanen whistled.

"If that sounds too much for their worth, then you'll have to counter me."

"Give me a box of hrelgren charcoal, a box of reed paper, and these three royals are yours," Hanen said, placing three royals on the map.

The hrelgren eyed the gold and his hand shot out.

"Deal."

Hanen shook the hrelgren's hand. Zapas took the gold and pocketed it, while he put the map back in the box, tying the primer, and boxes of charcoal and paper, and the map with a ribbon, and giving each over to Hanen with a broad grin on his face.

"When next we meet," Zapas said, "I hope you ask me about the weather and also offer me a proverb, all in my own native language."

"I will do what I can," Hanen said on his way out the door.

He walked down the stone steps, freezing for a moment as three men in gray cloaks passed in the street, headed by Abenard Navien.

"How are you here?" Hanen muttered to himself.

He watched Navien and his men march on for fifty feet before following them. He vaguely recognized the other two men, who had often watched Blackiron. They stopped in a square, perhaps to consider their next move. Hanen was afraid they were heading toward the neighborhood of the Dræc Inn, but to his relief they turned west, walking down the main thoroughfare toward the gate a mile away.

Hanen took an earlier street, and cut through to come out on the thoroughfare just as they passed, and he ducked back against a wall as they continued on. He crossed the street to a baker and bought a loaf of bread to pick at as he continued shadowing. They stopped at another corner and paused to look around the square before they turned and looked back the way they came. Hanen tried to hide in a stoop, only to startle when another figure pressed up into the space, and pushed him against the wall, his hand going over Hanen's mouth, a broad bladed sword held below his rib cage.

"You are terrible at following people," Navien said, "and just as bad at watching your back. I've had my eyes on you since Bremüm, and I haven't taken them off of you."

"Then Ophedia?" Hanen said as Navien took his hand from his mouth.

"Led chase for several of my men, by design. I imagine she'll be in shackles and headed back to Mahn Fulhar."

"Lower your weapon. I won't run."

Navien hesitated, and then pulled the sword back.

"What happens now?" Hanen asked.

"You return with me to Mahn Fulhar, along with your sister and the old man."

"We can't do that."

Navien laughed. "You're hardly in a position to negotiate."

"I am, though."

Navien frowned. "What do you mean?"

"I mean the king cleared my debts by asking me to seek out

answers for him outside of Mahn Fulhar. So, that I'm here should be no surprise to you. You were there when I last met with King Erdthal."

"I was not privy to your conversation," Navien said. "But he was very upset when you left the city."

Hanen sighed and pinched the bridge of his nose.

"The king," Hanen said, "told me that Searn possessed a cloak, and he wanted me to find it. I believed that coming to Searn's source of authority, here in Haven, was the wisest thing to do."

"You and your friends freed the old man the king kept in his castle."

"You mean the Prima Pater of the Paladins of the Hammer, kept against his will?"

"It doesn't matter who he is."

"It does," Hanen said. "Imprisoning a man with more authority than most kings is an act of war. That he held him in order to turn him over to the Chalicians as political prisoner, as potential martyr, is folly."

"Do not speak of the king like that," Navien said.

"He is not my king."

"He became your king when your guild gained its charter."

"A charter you treated with contempt and suspicion."

"Well-founded suspicion. You left the city under cover of night with an escaped prisoner, and several Œronzi monks who sought to escape the Chalician rule dictated by their high priest."

"The Abecinian church is known for its factions," Hanen said. "They wished to go somewhere they could live without the Chalician authority forcing them on a path against their beliefs."

"Who are they to decide? We each have a duty to follow those in authority. Such is the Way of Man. Such is the Path of Aben."

"That is your path, Navien. Not theirs. Not mine."

"You follow no path," Navien said. "I would see you back on the path. As an example."

"No one in Mahn Fulhar misses me," Hanen said. "Leave me be. Let me take the old man as far away from Mahn Fulhar as I can."

"So he can foment rebellion and deviant thoughts against Mahn Fulhar and King Erdthal?"

"So he can die," Hanen said. "He's an old man. How much longer can he live?"

Navien gave Hanen a look. "Why have you settled on Haven rather than moving on?"

"What do you mean?"

"Why stop? You've certainly not spoken to the leaders of the Sentinels. When will you?"

"As soon as we know no one is pursuing us."

"What interest does Dorian Mür have in the object you're seeking out?"

"He wishes to know what Searn did that night as much as King Erdthal does."

"You have ten days to find this object or produce verified proof of its location."

"And if we fail?"

"You return to Mahn Fulhar with me. If I have reason to doubt your commitment, I will take you back immediately. In chains."

"What about Alodda?"

"The girl? Your father? The other monks? They're truly no concern of mine, although I imagine their past will follow them, and they'll be continually fleeing the rise of the new, stronger Church of Aben."

"Do you truly believe the Chalicians are in the right?"

"I believe that authority is given from on high, and trickles down to each of us. The Chalician branch of the Abecinian Church does what the Church of Aben ought to have done millennia ago—stop providing parameters to reach Lomïn, and instead dictate and enforce those actions. Why should we be allowed to walk our own way into darkness, when their guidance can deliver us directly to the light?"

"Why be allowed the opportunity to choose the path in the first place?" Hanen asked.

"Exactly."

"No," Hanen said. "What I mean is, why did Aben provide us with a path and not just place us in Lomïn from the beginning?"

"Who are we to question his ways?"

Hanen sighed. "Your blindness will be your undoing."

"And your doubt will be your own," Navien said. "You have ten days."

The innkeeper placed another cup of Limacan Strong before Hanen. He dropped back half of it, wincing as it burned his throat.

"There you are." Rallia marched across the room.

Hanen dropped the rest back without looking at his sister.

"What are you doing here?" she asked.

"Trying not to draw attention." He said. He stood and misstepped, almost falling over.

"Poor job of that," she replied.

Hanen shook his head. "To the Dræc Inn."

"What?"

"I'm trying not to draw attention to the Dræc Inn," he said, louder than he intended.

"Come on," Rallia said.

The innkeeper came and stood across from them.

"Is he paid up?" Rallia asked.

The innkeeper shook his head.

"How many did he have?"

"Finished a bottle on his own," the man replied and held out a hand. "Silver conta."

Rallia whistled and gave him a coin.

With his arm over Rallia's shoulder Hanen stumbled out onto the street. It had grown dark.

"Why did you drink so much?" Rallia asked. "You never get drunk."

"I'm not," Hanen replied, stumbling out of Rallia's support and into a wall. He sighed and slid down on the cobbles. "All right, I might be."

Rallia sat next to him. "What is going on?"

"Ophedia rode off into a trap," he said.

"How do you know?"

"Because I found Navien," Hanen replied. "Or, he found me, I should say. He says we've never left his sight."

"There was no one coming up the pass behind us," Rallia replied. "I looked."

Maybe he watched from below and waited until night," Hanen said. "I don't know. I just know he's given us ten days to deliver."

"Deliver?"

"I told him we were here to find the cloak Searn wore because the king charged us to. Now he's given us ten days to find a cloak I'm not even sure exists."

"We'll have to tell Dorian," Rallia said.

"Why? He's given us ten days. That gives us ten days to figure out how to lose him."

"And what if Navien figures out that we're really here to help Dorian destroy that armor? That we've found an even greater prize?"

Hanen stood up carefully.

"Where are you going?"

"I'm regretting that bottle of strong beer," Hanen said, ducking into the alley.

A few minutes later he reemerged.

"Feel better now?" Rallia asked.

Hanen nodded, wiping his mouth with his sleeve and walking back toward the Dræc Inn.

"Are you going to go tell Dorian?" Rallia asked.

"No."

"Then what are we doing?"

"We're going to figure out how we can get Navien caught as a spy from Mahndür."

30

CUP BEARER

The Church of the Common Chalice started as a small sect of the Morriegan Church after the Morriegans refused to reform against the debauchery of the nations surrounding the Pyracene Sea. Conducting a pilgrimage to Œron, its dictates and philosophies quickly took root in the isolated people there, and through united culture and religion the nation rose quickly to prominence in the continental theatre of nations.

—*THEOLOGICAL HISTORIES*, IY 1785, UNKNOWN AUTHOR

Lake Alvaria stretched out to the slight rise of the eastern green hills and the mountains rising in the far distance. Abingen, capital of Varea, hugged the shoreline of the lake, and in the cool evening fleets of small fishing vessels were making their way home with their haul. Ophedia unstoppered the bottle hanging from her belt and took a pull. The leather corset she had been wearing over the loose white blouse lay over her shoulder.

"A stream to freshen up before we enter the city would be nice," she said.

"I wouldn't." Eunia ran her fingers through the few inches of hair on her head. "The smart washer women come out of the city to use streams rather than the lake water. You'd have no way of knowing if you were downstream of them."

Eunia's husband, Chös, knelt down and poured the last of his water into a bowl for the black ynfald, Whisper, who happily lapped up the offering. The ynfald shook and rattled, then nuzzled Chös, who smiled and gave the creature a scratch on the back of the skull.

"We'll find a rowdy inn tonight," Eunia said.

"Why rowdy?" Ophedia asked. "Not that I'm complaining. A brawl or two would make for a lively evening."

"If the inn is rowdy, then any ferrymen will be itchy for work. If it's not, then they'll eye us with suspicion."

"Ferrying across the lake would be obvious to any Chalicians or Voktorra trailing us," Chös said.

"We're not going directly across," Eunia replied. "We'll have the ferry take us down the coast and we'll hoof it from there toward the mountains."

"Doesn't seem the fastest way," Ophedia said.

"It's not," Eunia said. "But note the flags the city flies today."

Eunia was pointing to the pole above the gate they approached. Varea's silver fish on purple flew over a blue flag emblazoned with a silver chalice.

"Then they're here already?" Ophedia muttered.

"Abingen has always been loyal to the Church of Aben," Eunia said. "The fish they provide to the surrounding lands is blessed by the god of the sea. Or at least that's how they see it."

"You can hardly call the lake a sea," Ophedia said. "It smells like a river, not like the briny ocean."

"Don't be saying that out loud, or you'll be the cause of any brawls we encounter."

The city walls were short and the guards watched them pass into the streets with only mild curiosity. Whisper wandered into the crowd, nosing the stalls and falling into his old habit of nicking the odd roll or bit of dried fruit. Abingen was a wide and very shallow city, not unlike the lake beyond. The smell of dockyards and fish grew quickly. They soon came to a long row of inns and taverns, across a wide cobbled street from several piers. Small waves lapped the gravel shore where a few fishermen polished the bottoms of older boats.

"You're passing through," said a middle-aged woman sitting on a short wall overlooking the piers.

"How'd you make that out?" Eunia asked.

"You come marching down the street like a pantheon-forsaken Black Sentinel looking for a fight, eyeing every fisher, wharf, and tavern? You tell me."

287

"We three used to be Sentinels," Eunia said. "You got that right."

"Well, I wouldn't be spitting that fact out, if I were you."

"Why is that?" Ophedia asked.

"No one likes them here," the woman said. "Only thing that goes around here is coin, fish, and faith."

"Faith?"

"Are you Chalician? Or something else?"

"We'd prefer not to discuss that," Ophedia said.

"Then if you're not flaunting a Chalician verse, you better be paying out in coin and fish."

"What if we're just looking for a ship east?" Eunia asked.

"Better find it quick, I'd say," the woman said.

"Wind changing?"

"Always is, here."

"It doesn't seem," Ophedia said, "that Abingen is having the problems with the Chalicians that everyone else is."

"That's because we provide fish to peasants everywhere in Œron. If the Common Cup wants their people fed, they'll be coming to us."

"There is plenty of fishing in the sea," Ophedia said.

"Only fer nobs," the woman said.

"Oh?" Eunia pressed.

"A year ago, the Chalicians came in, touting their superiority, illegalized trades, such as my old trade, and in a fit of righteous zeal, everyone turned to the lake, or left the country. See, the only food that isn't regulated is fishing. It's a pantheon-given right, I guess. But those with rank and status have the rights to the sea, and the peasantry gets only freshwater fish. Abingen made promises, and put a cap on the prices of our fish, and the Chalicians liked that. They didn't account for the fact that every peasant began demanding our affordable and price-controlled catches, increasing demand. And anyone with a boat is set to make a guaranteed payday. Only now we have to meet that demand, or face the lash, as the Chalicians depend on us to feed their growing territory."

"Well, we're not looking to be another mouth to feed," Eunia said. "We'll be on our way. Do you know of anyone with a boat to hire?"

The woman pointed south. "Look for Gyle, and don't skimp on your pay. He'd just as soon alert you to the town militia, and he's a bitter ex-Sentinel too. So he hates the lot of you. Don't piss him off."

"Thank you," Ophedia said. "May we have your name?"

"Nope."

Ophedia flipped her a silver baro and proceeded down the pier.

Gyle was accommodating and said little, though he eyed Whisper suspiciously the entire trip. A few hours after dawn they came to the outlet of the lake. The crossing against the current made for a slow final hour, but with Chös lending an extra hand at the oars, they made the landing and their host was in good spirits as he rowed away. Several small towns and villages dotted this eastern shore between the water and swathes of ancient groves spreading to the foothills of the Limaean plain.

Eunia led the way, keeping an eye on Gyle as he rowed away.

"Worried he'll talk?" Ophedia asked.

"If he tells any authorities on this side, we'll be in trouble, but if he waits until he gets back to Abingen, I'm not worried."

The groves were well-cared-for, with little underbrush, and most trees were modified to make them climbable.

"Which way did you travel to Mahndür last year, after we parted?" Ophedia asked.

"We didn't go into Haven as we passed through Limae," Eunia said.

Whisper darted from tree to tree, and Chös followed slowly after him, digging at the soil when the small ynfald found something interesting.

"After Amstonhotten we crossed through the Lake District to the northern end of the Arbeswald, then up into the southern Limaean plain."

"From there," Ophedia said, "don't you have to go north or south?"

"There are some paths you can take through the western range if the weather hadn't turned."

"What about the wild animals? Like the griffins?"

"They're less desperate in autumn. We only saw one or two. One local mentioned something about a mating season elsewhere—only those too young to join in had stayed in the hunting grounds."

"And how did Chös do?" Ophedia asked.

"Chös has already markedly improved. Really, he's fine. He is just quieter now. He was a naturally quiet person in the first place."

Chös had been crouching near a tree. He looked back with a smile, dirt covering his face. He held in his hand a large white mushroom.

"He is also amused by the simplest things in life now. It's brought a calm and peace to me, as well."

They walked on and came to a grove of trees that were spaced in lines.

"Are we trespassing?" Ophedia asked.

"Why the extra caution?" Eunia asked.

"I worry the presence of the Chalicians have made people more suspicious."

"We're in Varea now, which has laws protecting people's well-being. We had discussed settling here instead. Maybe we will."

"If what you've said is true, though, Limae sounds even better. No one is looking to force laws down anyone's throat."

"It's true they have fewer laws, but that means every town, every street, every person, has their own ideas they enforce."

"Is that a problem?"

"I'm just saying, I prefer regular order rather than suggested order."

"I've lived enough years on the street," Ophedia said, "or at the mercy of someone's goodwill. I was forced to follow the rules of the house as a child would, but without any of the privilege of an actual child. The less inane rule I live under the better."

"Yet you are a bodyguard, who voluntarily works for people, suppressing your personality to meet their sensibilities."

"Yes," Ophedia said, winking at Eunia. "But they pay me."

They had lost sight of Chös and he suddenly cried out.

"Eunia! Eunia!"

The two women rushed forward. Eunia drew a short blade and stopped at a large tree just ahead of Ophedia. Chös was frantically tearing at the dirt with both hands, Whisper next to him pawing at the ground.

"Chös! Chös!" Eunia scolded. He stopped and looked up.

"What?" he asked innocently.

"I thought something was wrong!" Eunia said.

"Not at all," he grinned. "Come! See!"

They both approached; he reached into the dirt and held up a small black ball.

"The ynfald is a good mushroom hunter," he said. "Look what

he found here!"

Eunia took the ball from him and sniffed it.

"Truffle?"

"Not just one," he said, motioning to the ground.

Eunia gasped. There were dozens.

"Is this a good thing?" Ophedia asked.

Eunia gave Ophedia a look. "You've not heard of these? They'll go for a dukt or more at the right market."

Whisper soon stopped digging. Chös placed the mushrooms gingerly in his satchel, after which Chös walked with an energy in his step as they left the forest and crossed the plain to the foothills of the mountains. A few small villages were scattered around the idyllic valley, with a few shepherds watching lazy aurochs and capricör from large rocks. They gave the three of them a nod as they passed, but kept a wary eye on them.

"Should we sell our mushrooms at one of these villages?" Ophedia asked.

"No," Chös said. "We'll get top dollar in Haven. Those that would buy them here would only go to Haven themselves and reap the higher rewards."

They came to the greening trees of the lower slopes, and found an old fire circle as the sun began to set and soon had a blaze going. Chös heated up an iron pot on the coals.

"My father took me mushroom hunting as a boy," Chös said. "We only ever found one truffle, and we shared it rather than selling it."

He chopped the larger mushrooms into pieces along with some roots and grilled them together, mixing in handfuls of oats and some wine. Once those began to thicken, he washed one of the truffles, crushed it, and stirred it in. The earthy smell that burst into the air was overwhelming and decadent. Ophedia sighed and sat back, scratching Whisper on the back of the skull. A few minutes later, Chös served a scoop of the stuff into small wooden bowls and handed one to Ophedia. The scent of truffles delighted her as she lifted the spoon to her mouth. It was warm, salty, with a hint of moss amid the medley of mushroom flavors.

"I can see why people pay coin for this," she said. "You're a good cook."

Chös smiled. Then his face went flat. He took a jar of water and poured it over the flame. Steam hissed up into the air and he plunged their camp into twilit darkness.

"What is it?" Eunia hissed.

Ophedia peered beyond the sparse trees. A quarter of a mile off, torches guttered. Not a handful, but a long procession coming over a small hillock.

"Do you think they saw our fire?" Eunia asked.

"No," Chös said. "It was only embers. Quiet. Those are scouts."

Chös moved low to the ground to the woods' edge, accompanied by Whisper and followed by Ophedia and Eunia. The rider on a sleipnir cantered past them and pulled up fifty yards down the road. He was hard to see in the dark, but Ophedia knew he was comfortable in the saddle and that he was heavily cloaked. Another rider approached from the nearest village across the plain, and they conferred in low voices.

"Go back to the fire," Chös whispered to Eunia and Ophedia, "then move back toward the slopes. I'll stay and listen."

"No," Ophedia said. "Let me do it."

Chös hesitated for a moment then nodded, moving quietly back into the forest with Eunia. Ophedia pulled her Sentinel cloak around her so her white sleeves wouldn't be visible, and began creeping toward the two scouts. There was a tree with a large root system ten yards from her quarry, the perfect hiding place, but she almost yelped as Whisper came alongside her. They both dropped down into the roots and she pulled her cloak over them both, concealing them in the shadows.

"The village is short on supplies, but evidently they have paperwork to show they've paid their tithe."

"Provost Abrau will respect that, then," the other replied.

"They did, however, imply that tomorrow we'll reach the small town of Elliff, which sits at the foot of the pass up to northern Limae, and with stronger ties there than with Varea."

"Let us wait and see what Abrau says about proceeding."

They both sat in silence. Their sleipnirs pawed at the ground.

"Have you seen anything else on your patrol?" the first asked.

"No. It's a very quiet valley. I'd prefer a portion of this land rather than Limae when ransoms are given out."

"Would you bring your family here?"

"They've not earned enough favor to leave Redot, and they don't seem to care."

"But you do, Vathan?"

"Certainly," Vathan replied. "I wish health to our leaders, and I pay my tithe."

"Enough tithe to purchase a commission as a Chamberlain."

"You too, Aeler."

"I'm close," Aeler replied. "But I find it hard enough to pay the base tithe as well as maintain my dying mother."

"Then I'm jealous of you. You've had more time in Oiquimon, walking the Path as you help her, and positioning yourself in the Praeposit's Court."

"I'd rather be out here on the road myself."

"Will you take a ransom?" Vathan asked.

"I haven't seen anything I like, but I wouldn't take a ransom in Œron either, if I was offered it. I wouldn't take one here in Varea. I'm not a fan of the women I see, and I fear they'd ask me to take a Varean wife as a matter of duty to our beliefs."

"I have no complaints about that, if it means acquiring land I would never get in Redot."

"I forget you're Redotti at times."

The long train of riders and wagons was nearing. Several riders rode out from what was now obviously an army, and came to the two scouts.

"Provost Abrau," Aeler saluted.

"Report," the man said. He spoke with a firm voice, but did not bear contempt for the scouts.

They repeated much of what they'd said.

"Very well," Abrau said. "We march until dawn to this town of Elliff. Take a contingent of thirty Praetors ahead of us to ensure no one spreads the word to Limae. We may take a day or two respite in Elliff before the ascent. Prefect Gagnon," he called to someone else, "range out to the villages here and conscript foot soldiers with the usual promises. If they seek permission from their lords rather than following us in blind faith, note their names."

"What would you like me to do with their names?" another Praetor asked. "Prepare a stringent tithing method?"

"Of course not," Abrau said. "I'm not Zehan Otem. If they take their lord's permission and join us, they are to be commended as loyal to the law. But if their lords give them permission and they still balk, they are destined for a penal colony."

"Very well," Gagnon said. "I'll return in one week."

"You have eight days to arrive in Limae with them. I may need them at the walls by then."

"It shall be done, Provost."

The front of the caravan arrived and passed by in torchlight.

Ophedia could now see the arrow-styled spears in many of their hands, among which were groups of about six soldiers bearing the spears of the Praetors' office, wearing hip-length cloaks but without the cup-shaped helmets. She slowly backed away from the tree line and then ran deeper into the woods.

"What did you find out?" Eunia asked as she rejoined them.

"The Chalicians are marching on the town at the bottom of the pass, and they won't let anyone leave there while they ascend the plateau."

"They're marching on Haven?"

"It sounds like it. We can't take the pass now; it's too risky."

"We'll have to take the hunter's path," Chös said.

"Do you know of any?" Ophedia replied.

"No," Chös said. "We'll just have to start climbing."

31

GRIFFIN ROAD

Gryphs are fascinating creations, and wildly more mysterious than those ragged wyloths or flighty dwovs, and my fascination with them drew me to a life of study. From the Greater Griffin of the heights to the black and sleek gryph of the common lands. That they are categorized with birds makes some mote of sense, but little. In short, descriptions of the half-bird, half-felid creatures are better understood by their cunning, their spite, and their stunning looks. I know no creature that better reflects man.

—ARSTEDT GLAVVIN OF VAREA

Ophedia looked down the long meadow as the silver light of Umay reached its apex. Chös and Eunia walked a hundred yards behind, shoulder to shoulder, while Whisper zipped curiously from outcrop to rocky outcrop. Two mountains rose steeply to the north and south, with their path rising between them and beginning to level out. Ophedia refilled her water at a waterfall cascading down from snowy heights, and drank deep as she waited for her friends.

"I think we're nearing the top of the plateau," Eunia said as she approached.

Ophedia nodded. "Although whether we're near any road remains to be seen."

"Not too far," Chös said, pointing up the meadow. At the top, a steep-roofed chalet rose.

"Probably a good place to catch our bearings too," Eunia said.

After they had caught their breath and refilled their waters they continued up the hill. The chalet turned out to be one of several in a small mountain hamlet. A middle-aged woman came out of a roofed corral to watch their approach.

"Mighty courageous of you to be walking up the slope at dawn," she said.

"Why is that?" Eunia asked.

"The griffins like to hunt between night and morning, mostly for small vermin. But if they're especially hungry they'll work together and don't fear killing men."

Ophedia looked to the mountains. High above the snowy slopes she could see the outstretched wings of soaring griffins.

"We hadn't realized," she said.

"Well, a foolish thing," the woman said. "Come inside. It's best not to go out and about without others with you. We don't let the capricör into the meadows until after the sun has passed its height and the griffins have gone inland for hunting in the higher pastures."

She turned and walked toward her home, built on a rock above the piles of snow that still hadn't melted.

"Who you got there?" the woman's husband asked as they all came inside. He was broad of chest and worked at a bench, hewing wood shingles to replace the broken roofing from winter wear.

"Couldn't say," she said. "But they were foolish enough to be climbing the meadow all night."

"Smugglers or outlaws, then?" The man asked.

"If we were," Eunia said, "would we admit it?"

"In Limae no one cares as long as you don't bring trouble."

"We don't bring trouble," Ophedia said. "But we do bring news."

"You're a Sentinel," the man replied, pointing to the clubs on her belt.

"Ophedia del Ishé. And this is Eunia and Chös."

"Pleasure. The name is Avarr and my wife is Perrah. What news do you bring?"

"The Chalicians have forced Mahndür to join their church and have been working on Varea. As of last night, we came upon a small army marching on Haven. They're going to be starting up the Elliff pass in two days, so we decided to cut up mountain last night and warn people."

"You've got a long road ahead of you, for it's two days to Haven on foot."

"Does anyone have sleipnir we can borrow?"

"Only a fool rides the Griffin Road. You walk, or you'll draw the ire of the griffins and their starving bellies, especially this early in spring."

"I've seen a griffin or two on my journeys," Ophedia said. "They aren't so scary that I can't drive them off."

"Where'd you see them, girl?" Avarr asked.

"Macena. In the Eastern Foothills."

Avarr laughed. "No bigger than an ælern then? No bigger than your ynfald?"

Ophedia nodded.

"Then you're unprepared. We've two types in these mountains. The smaller gravons hunt in packs, and they're about yay high," he held his hand next to his hip. "All cords and muscles. They'll strip a body in moments and leave with what they can carry in their talons. Nasty business. But opportunistic."

He stood and crossed the room to a cabinet. "You ever see a slow falling star take its time across the night sky?"

They all shook their heads.

"If you ever see a black speck in the sky, in the light of day, slowly making its way across the sky, then it's already spotted you."

He came back with a large, rigid feather over a yard long.

"A griffin. A true griffin drops out of the sky like a black boulder the size of a draft sleipnir. I watched one throw a man fifty feet. Slashed the second in two. Lifted the final one into the sky, pack and all."

Ophedia stared at the feather. It was black but shone with a hint of purple, just as her own black hair was hued with the auburn of Macenan blood.

"How did you survive?" Eunia asked.

"I was in the trees nearby, and they don't like moving through trees. Their wings don't fold that well when they're attacking. It waited for one of the stretches of road that breaks out of the trees to attack. My brother never saw it coming, but I've not forgotten that moment all of my life."

"Why stay here, exposed to their attacks?" Chös asked.

"Because here," he said, "I'm a free man."

"You won't be free for long," Eunia said, "if the Chalicians have their way."

"Limae won't allow it," Avarr said. "They'll find each and every town and village will stand against them. They seem to believe if they force Haven to bow the rest of us will, too, but that is not the case."

"But will you all stand together?"

Avarr was silent.

"The southern cities might work together," Perrah said. "They could come to Haven's aid."

"But if Castenard gets word that Southern Limae has marched north," Avarr said, "he might take the opportunity to take a city or two."

"They have no love for Œron," Perrah said. "They might help."

"They might also choose to ally with Œron if it'll give them an advantage against the other City States."

"Regardless," Ophedia said, "we need to get to Haven. They need to know what's coming."

"Then go quickly, but keep to the trees. Make haste when passing through glades, and keep your eyes skyward. The leaves have only just begun to bud, so even among the branches the Griffins can see you. They will know you're there."

"Then we'll just have to make sure it knows we see it, as well."

"It looks like there is another stretch of forest around the corner," Chös said. He crouched low in the boulders that surrounded them with a wary eye to the sky.

"See anything up there?" Ophedia asked.

"I thought I did," Chös replied, "but I think my mind was playing tricks on me."

They rounded the corner and descended into what turned out to be tall bushes.

"This is stupid," Ophedia said, watching Whisper range in and out of them.

"We can duck down, but it wouldn't be hard for the griffins to get to us," Eunia agreed.

"What I mean is that moving this slowly and cautiously is stupid."

"Avarr said if we stay on this road and make a good pace, we'll make it to Haven by midday tomorrow."

"That's ten hours today and another five in the morning."

"If we don't stop," Chös said, "we could make it by midnight."

"Hopefully the gates are open," Ophedia said.

"Why wouldn't they be?" Eunia said. "They're said never to close."

"Unless the city has already seen the Chalicians approaching."

"Shh..." Chös said, holding up a hand.

They both crouched.

"There is a rider coming toward us. He just came around the corner ahead."

"What does he look like?" Ophedia asked.

"Traveler," Chös said. "He'll probably reach us in a few minutes."

"Let's melt into the bushes," Eunia said.

Ophedia nodded.

They moved off the main road and past several bushes before crouching down to watch the traveler pass. He was a tall rider on a lithe sleipnir with a satchel across his hip, and Ophedia thought she could just make out the hint of light blue.

He pulled on the reins and stopped near them, looking around. Then he took out a small leather-bound book and mouthed a prayer as he turned the pages, making several notations with charcoal. He squinted up at the sky, kicking his sleipnir into motion. Chös nudged Eunia and pointed to the sky. Two pairs of locked black wings circled a mile overhead. Meanwhile, the rider passed from their view, and Chös sidled across next to Ophedia.

"I think it was one of your Chalician scouts," he said.

"I agree," Ophedia replied. "He had his blue tabard in his satchel."

"He's moving in the opposite direction, though," Chös said. "I think we are safe."

"No," Eunia said. She pointed to the top of the rise they had come over, where the rider stood in a watchful position. "I think he suspects something."

"He's watching the sky, too," Chös said. "He knows how dangerous this road is."

"What should we do?" Ophedia asked.

Chös stood. "I'll draw him off."

"Like Noccitan you will," Eunia said. "I didn't nurse you back to health after that manticör only to have you die by spear or griffin."

Chös gave her a look.

"We're going together," Eunia finished.

He grinned.

"What about me?" Ophedia asked.

"Don't get eaten by a griffin," Eunia said.

"Shouldn't we talk about this?" Ophedia asked.

"Get to Haven, and if we're able we'll come with help."

"And if you're caught?"

"By a single scout? Nothing to worry about."

Eunia took off through the bushes, Chös close behind her.

Whisper looked up at Ophedia.

"What?"

The rider at the top of the hill stared at the sight of Eunia and Chös running through the shrubs, and took off after them.

Ophedia began moving quickly through the bushes as well, staying just off the path. Whisper darted from bush to bush alongside her. She heard shouts of fear and turned just in time to see a huge black figure dive out of the sky and knock the rider out of his saddle, the sleipnir screaming in alarm. Ophedia scrambled up out of the shallow valley, glancing back every so often to see Eunia and Chös charging in to help the man, while the flurry of wings tore at the sleipnir.

"Where is the other griffin?" she said aloud.

She almost screamed as huge wings beat against the rocks above. The second griffin soared overhead toward its partner. It had no doubt been watching Ophedia and decided the larger prey was more worth its time. It was easily the size of a sleipnir; the black wings had a blue and purple iridescence in the bright light of day. Its head was covered with a featherless purple skin, ending in a massive beak. The hind legs resembled a manticör's claws and were built for strong leaps, while the front claws were taloned, and designed for tearing prey to bits. The long, feathered tail helped it glide over the rocks and bushes right before it came down upon the sleipnir with all four claws outstretched. Ophedia could make out Chös and Eunia pulling the man away while he watched his mount get torn to shreds. She caught Eunia making a hand signal for her to go. After a quick salute, Ophedia took off north and disappeared over the rise.

There was a small lake on the floor of Haven's basin, a source of water for the city a mile beyond. The shore boasted a few small villages, not nearly so active on the water as the fishermen of Lake Alvaria were. As Ophedia walked the cobbled streets of the first village, she sensed a growing tension. It might have been her anticipation in trying to reach Haven, or perhaps it was the few mysterious men in gray cloaks, hard-nosed soldiers trying to hide in a crowd. While they did not wear their blue tabards, the cloth-wrapped spears they carried made them obvious. Whisper stayed close to her, avoiding the market stalls that would have provided easy pickings for quickly nabbed dried fruits and meats.

Having come so close to Haven, Ophedia ducked into an alley and pulled on her Sentinel cloak, after which people stopped giving her odd looks and instead averted their eyes as she passed, sometimes with holy warding signs at the sight of her black ynfald. Just as she left one village and entered a stretch of road lined with orchards, she nearly jumped out of her skin at the sound of a griffin's screech. A wagon bearing cages had stopped and several people gathered around to eye its contents, including the creature within the largest cage that fought weakly against the bars, tossing its head as someone threw an old fruit core at it. It wasn't the same breed as the huge griffins she had seen earlier that day, but a small rock gravon, twice the size of Whisper. Ophedia gazed at the pitiful creature, which had probably been caged for some time, its luster having faded and its black spots grayed. Unlike the massive mountain griffin, like the two that had attacked the Chalician scout, its head was not covered in featherless purple skin, but a tousle of rock-gray feathers and a hooked black beak.

The man in front of the cage was explaining how he was trying to tame the rock gravon for show or for hunting, but his audience was more interested in the beast than his speech. A small boy circled the cage, poking at the creature with a stick. The rock gravon was patient, but Ophedia caught a look in the creature's eye and knew it was biding its time. She approached the boy from behind and clapped a hand on his shoulder, making him drop the stick just as the gravon lunged at the side of the cage. A massive taloned claw reached through the bars, grazing the boy's cheek with a long slash that nearly cut out his eye before Ophedia pulled him from further harm.

The boy curled to the ground, holding his face.

"What have you done to my boy?!" a woman cried, rushing to his side. "Emrien!"

The beast-master circled the cage, and stood over them with a cudgel. The gravon pressed back against the far side of the cage.

"What did you do?!" the woman cried again, looking at Ophedia.

"Saved his eye, I'd wager," Ophedia said, standing tall and clenching the handle of her club. "Your stupid child was taunting the beast."

"Stupid chi..." the woman quickly became apoplectic. "How dare you?"

"You're right," Ophedia said, "I should have let it happen."

Ophedia pushed her way through the group and back out onto the road. She turned at the last moment to find everyone's attention on the screaming child and the mother. The gravon gave Ophedia a longing look. Ophedia reached out with the end of her club and gave the wooden dowel a testing tap. It looked like it would come free easily. She looked down at Whisper, whose tongue lolled out in humorous consent, and then gave the dowel another tap. It dropped free. The gravon didn't hesitate to burst out the door and fall in a tumble on the ground, its atrophied wings giving a weak flap. The beastmaster turned with a cry as Ophedia walked away backward, giving a bow. The creature recovered itself and leapt on top of the cage, flapping its wings again, and with a final leap glided out of sight over the trees as the mother and child flew into screaming hysterics.

"You stupid shunt!" the man called after Ophedia. He did not pursue her, but rushed to secure his cages of less interesting creatures.

"I hope he wasn't headed towards Haven," Ophedia muttered. "He probably won't forget my face."

Whisper nudged at her leg, and she looked down with a smile. "Yes, I know. Because I'm so beautiful. Not because I just cost him a lot of gold."

32

WARNINGS

It will only be in the years to come that our origins will come to light, for many lies within legalities are what formed our order. It was my own cunning that allowed me to stumble upon those archived copies of the original charters, absorbing the dissonant mercenary groups and bringing them under one banner, from which comes the mosaic of our new organization.

—EVON DARINCE, MARSHALL OF THE CITADEL LIBRARY

From the south, the city of Haven rose up the slope to its heights like a stew stuck to the inside of a bowl. The roofs were all of mismatched color and size, and there was no rhyme or reason to the city's layout, save a central thoroughfare that meandered from the southern gate to the black stones of the looming paladinial fortress. A second street ran, straighter than the others, from the western gate to the eastern wall. The only planning Ophedia observed were the terraced farms built south of the city, where farmers worked to break up the soil in the early spring, amending it in preparation for the late thaws of those alpine heights. To the east, the city paddocks of livestock were watched over by multiple guards, including some Black Sentinels. The slopes of the western mountains boasted only forests of spindly evergreens. She did not see any soldiers, although plumes of smoke rose from a smaller town far off in the distance.

Whisper trotted close to Ophedia as they approached the gate of the city, the sun casting a blush of orange and red over everything as it plunged under the horizon. Then it vanished. The cold washed over her just as suddenly as the dark. Without a torch of her own, she fumbled her way by the light of the city's torches ahead, moving along stone walls that kept travelers from tramping through the fields. Whisper kept redirecting her, as he was able to better see in the dark. Near the gate she could hear the sounds of carousing and loud singing, and one guard under the gate's arch held a large tankard of ale.

"Arrived a bit late," he said as she approached. "I'm supposed to ask your business, but you're wearing the Sentinel Black. So I suppose it is none of mine."

"I need to speak with your commander."

He sat up. "Why?"

"I bring news of trouble from Œron."

"That's a tough one, and what with the arguments between the city and the Sentinels, and what is left of the Pallies."

"I'm not familiar with the argument."

"They're all three looking for a bit of control. And more so than usual." He took another pull of the ale in his hand. "But again, none of mine, I suppose."

"My message will be important for all of them. Whom should I seek out at this moment?"

"The Sentinel commanders keep to themselves, especially at night. I don't know any of them personally, although one is barracked with his company at the Ynfald Arms Inn, which isn't too far from Captain Waller's place. But Waller doesn't like being bothered while it's dark."

"And the Pallies?"

"The citadel has been dark most days. No one really knows what's going on there."

"All right. Thanks."

"I suppose you'd like to know where the Ynfald Arms is," he surmised. "Just go to the Center Square and head north a few blocks, until you come to a crossroads with a nasty green fountain. Take the street east from the fountain and it'll bring you to a tight squatters' alley, which lets out across from the Ynfald."

"Should I go around that block and not through the alley?"

"That block of buildings is called the 'Slab' for a reason, and the alley is the only way through. Otherwise, you've got about a mile round trip to walk around it."

"No going through it by way of shops or inns?"

"None of them go through, on account of the seam of rock they were built around."

"Thanks for the help." She flipped him a silver baro, which he caught with a toothy smile.

Ophedia took out her clubs and pulled her Sentinel cloak closed. A few people glanced at her, but no one paid much attention. She was glad, for the last thing she needed was trouble. Walking up the middle of the street, she observed a Sentinel or two in the taverns she passed, but they were nobody she recognized.

"Where do you think the Clouws would stay?" she asked Whisper. "Would they go straight to the Sentinel leadership?"

The city rose easily. Her time on the road had made her limber, and she didn't mind climbing the stairs to the looming citadel and the mountains, which blocked out many of the stars in the clear sky. Norlock was rising, casting a red glint over the city.

"I hate that moon," she said. "It feeds on fear and gives courage to fools."

"I knew someone who had a black ynnie like that," a voice said.

Ophedia recognized the tight Œronzi accent of the man who spoke. He leaned against the wall of an inn, a pipe in his hand.

"I hoped I might run into you, Aurín," she said.

"Ophedia?" Aurín pulled his hood back and smiled as she threw her arms around his neck and gave him a hug.

He returned the embrace, then took hold of her arms.

"It's only been a few months, but it's good to see you," he said.

"And you. Especially now."

Aurín looked around. "You look like you're trying not to be seen," he said. "If I hadn't known Whisper, I wouldn't have looked closer at you. Is trouble following you?"

"No, but trouble is coming to this city. Eunia, Chös and I took a back road up into the mountains with a warning."

"Eunia and Chös? Are they here?"

"They're leading a chase away now. I'm bringing the warning, and the guard at the gate thought I'd find a Sentinel commander at the Ynfald Arms."

"Commander Deggar is there, yes. If your message is a warning, though, Commander Hardin is the better one to tell. What's the news?"

"Œronzi Chalicians are marching on Haven. They'll be here tomorrow or the day after."

"This is urgent, then. Come on."

He turned and began walking up the street. Whisper followed as Ophedia hurried alongside Aurín.

"Is anyone else I know here in Haven?" she asked.

"I saw the Clouws a couple days ago, though I don't know where they are staying. They disappeared with that qavyl, Ymbrys."

"Ymbrys is here too?"

Aurín nodded.

They arrived at the Slab. The buildings around it concealed the rock, but they leaned at a gentle angle, as if the slab wasn't propping them up quite as the builders planned.

"So that's the Slab?" Ophedia asked.

"Yes. How did you know?"

"The guard at the gate described it. We're supposed to take the dangerous alley through the heart of it."

"We could, but there is an inn with a passage up over the Slab into another..." he gave her a furtive look, "house."

"A brothel."

"They're connected, and no one causes any trouble there."

"Besides what they pay for," Ophedia said.

They walked past the alley. Ophedia noted the figures within the alley, eyeing them as they passed.

"I'm glad I didn't go through there."

"You might not have fared well."

"Neither would they," Ophedia added.

"But you'd still have ended up regretting your choices."

He walked past eight more businesses and inns, then stopped before the cleanest looking inn Ophedia had ever seen. Glancing around, she saw that most of the shops nearby had been scrubbed to within an inch of their lives.

"The good part of town, eh?"

"Over there is the embassy, if you can call it that, of Zhigava, and next to it the embassy of Ikhala. They don't get along."

"And this?" Ophedia asked, motioning to the inn before them.

"Owned by the ambassador for Macena."

"I believe it," Ophedia said, stepping into the small common room.

The man behind the bar had hair the same color as Ophedia's, black with auburn highlights.

"Freedom and Liberty," she said, nodding to him. He smiled.

"By our Pantheon-given rights," he replied. "You're Macenan."

"By blood and by the bounty charter I hold."

"Are you looking for someone?" he asked.

"Only stating my pedigree," she said, looking around the empty room.

"We're actually looking to cross over onto Black Street," Aurín said, "without passing through Cutthroat Alley."

"I'm not keen on taking the long way round," Ophedia added.

"Doesn't matter to me how you want to cross over," the man said. "Only that you pay the toll."

"Toll?" Ophedia asked. "Can I just buy a beer and call it a toll?"

"I'm afraid not, ma'am. Toll keeps my lips sealed. What you do on Black Street is up to you. But you pay a toll here with coin, in Cutthroat Alley with blood, or with the sweat you'll take to walk the two miles around."

Ophedia sighed. She put two silver baro down with three copper nits.

"What're those nits for?" The man asked. "It's just the baros."

"A baro for each of us, a nit for my ynfald, and two more nits to fill a short glass with Limaean Strong for each of us."

The man laughed. "I don't usually open a bottle. Not many that stay here. I'm just a gate keeper." He took down a very dusty bottle, popped the cork and poured out a glug each into three clay cups. He dropped one back himself and winced. Then he pushed the other two across to Ophedia and Aurín.

Ophedia took a sip. "Not bad. I hear they're making something out in Zhigava that'll give Limae a run for its money. It's stronger. Made with some sort of copper vat."

"I've heard of that. It's got the brewers in a tizzy here."

"I met a brewer up in Mahn Fulhar," Aurín said. "He was making ales almost as strong as this, and then accidentally left a barrel out back of his tavern. It half froze overnight. He fished out the ice and ended up with an ale twice as strong."

"Did he now?" the barkeep said. "I've got a barrel or two at home. Maybe I ought to leave it out. We still get plenty cold here at night."

"If I'm right," Aurín said, raising his cup in a toast, "and you make your fortune, you give me a barrel of it."

"Deal," the man said, and pointed to the back door. "Go on up the stairs there. What's your name?"

Aurín touched his nose. "How about I just come back another time."

The man winked and Ophedia and Aurín walked away.

"You come here often?" Ophedia said, following Aurín up the stairs.

Aurín laughed nervously. "Not on my own. But I did guard a merchant who came through here."

They came to the top of the stairs, which then crossed a long covered bridge over the rock. On the rooftops Ophedia could see the cherry-red glow of a pipe or two.

"Smokeweed is pretty popular here, is it?" she asked.

"Very."

"I traveled with a hrelgren who might be looking to import here and in Varea, although if the Chalicians get their way, no one is going to be using the stuff."

"I hadn't heard they didn't care for it."

"People smoked it when you were growing up in Œron?"

"Oh sure. A few. It's frowned upon by some but not preached against."

"I have a feeling," Ophedia said, "that might be changing."

"Not here. Limaeans love it too much. There are quite a few shops—they're built to look like the inside of ships and are often filled with people buying and trading small wooden barrels of it."

They came to the top of the next set of stairs.

"The common room is here. We'll have to leave by way of a window."

"Why not just hop down here and crawl down another face?" Ophedia asked. "That way, if the man back there made us, we won't get caught off guard."

"Not very trusting, are you?"

"Are you?"

"No," Aurín chuckled. "I suppose not."

Ophedia climbed out of the window and onto the stone of the Slab. Whisper scrambled up and leapt beside her, with Aurín gingerly following. Ophedia climbed across the stone and onto the roof of another shop. The narrow street below had lots of torches, but they burned dim.

"Black Street, huh?" she asked.

"Runs the length of the Slab on this side," Aurín said. "If Haven had a black market, if anything was illegal, it would be sold here. But nothing is, so it isn't."

"And where is the Ynfald Arms?"

"There," Aurín said, pointing to an inn across the street. It had no windows, just one door and two Sentinels standing guard.

"Not many go in or out without trouble, huh?"

Aurín shook his head.

"Then they probably won't let Whisper in."

"Can anyone actually stop Whisper from going where he wants?"

"This is true."

Aurín looked up and down the length of the building they stood on, then kicked a leg over the edge.

"Do you know what you're doing?" Ophedia asked.

Whisper began scaling down the face, leaping from ledge to overhang.

"No," Aurín said, "but he does."

Aurín followed Whisper and dropped the final ten feet to the cobblestones below.

Ophedia tossed her staff down to Aurín, then sat down on the ledge.

"I hate heights," she said to herself. "Why didn't I know this before?"

She took a deep breath, turned over on her belly, and lowered herself down to her elbows.

"Alright. What do I do now?" she muttered.

"Your toes are just out of reach of a ledge," Aurín hissed.

She felt down with the toe of her boot, found the ledge, and lowered herself until her hands suddenly lost their grip. The world disappeared for an interminable second. She closed her eyes, hoping she didn't end up before the Three-Eyed Judge. She struck cloth of some kind, which slowed her fall, and then hit the edge of a counter. Sheets tangled her as she tried to get free, but at last a hand took hold of her flailing one.

She looked up into Aurín's grinning face.

"Come on," he said through a stifled laugh. "Before the owner of the stall comes."

She looked back. A merchant's booth stood in a crumpled mess. A few people around them watched with waning interest. Whisper worriedly nuzzled Ophedia's other hand with his head.

"I'm ...fine," she said to the ynfald as she stood.

"That was spectacular," Aurín said, still laughing.

"Laugh about it later," she said, storming off across the street. He ran after her, holding the clubs. Ophedia was too embarrassed to look him in the eyes, but she noticed the smirk he was trying to drop and punched him in the arm.

"Ow!" Aurín said.

"Well, now you know how my back feels."

"Do you want me to take the lead in there?" he asked, motioning toward the inn.

"No," she said, marching to the stairs leading up to the Ynfald Arms. The two Sentinel guards glanced down.

"I'm here to speak to Commander Deggar."

"Should we know you?" one of them said.

"I've come up from Varea with an important message that can't wait until morning."

"But who are you?"

"Ophedia del Ishé."

They didn't respond.

"You probably knew my father," she said. "Searn VeTurres."

"Yeah right," one of them said.

"It's true," Aurín said, stepping up. "He admitted it right before he died."

One Sentinel leaned toward the other and muttered something, then disappeared into the inn.

"Fine weather we're having," Aurín said to the remaining Sentinel.

The Sentinel grunted.

The second Sentinel re-emerged.

"This way," he said.

Ophedia and Aurín followed him while Whisper darted ahead into the common room, which was well lit though boasting only four tables. Against the back wall sat a fifth table with papers strewn across it. A large double-headed axe hung on the wall above an empty chair. The Sentinel led them within ten feet of this table. A side door opened and a hulking figure came out, wiping his hands on the black cloak hanging over his shoulder. His whiskery face crowned a massive frame, and his thick eyebrows matched the coarse black growth on his face. His shirt was rolled up past his elbows. Taking the chair under the axe with a growl, he shuffled a few papers around then looked up.

"Who did you bring me today, Aurín?" the man said.

Aurín took a single step forward and bowed.

"Commander Deggar," Aurín said, "I'd like to introduce Ophedia del Ishé, Sentinel of two clubs and daughter of Searn VeTurres."

The commander at first looked incredulous, but then he leaned forward and examined Ophedia's face closely.

"I can see the resemblance," he admitted.

"Foolish no one else noticed," Ophedia said.

"You got the same wry mouth as your father," he remarked, after examining her again.

"I have my own mouth," she said. "And I speak with my own words."

"Then your answer is 'yes,'" he replied. "How is she in a scrap?"

"She holds her own," Aurín said.

"I've fought Manticör, bandit, drækis, and amyt," she said.

"A monster hunter, then?"

"Troublemaker," Ophedia replied.

"And risk-taker. My boys say they watched you fall from a roof to avoid paying a toll."

"It was important to get here with as few delays as possible," Ophedia said. "I'm here with a warning that can't wait until morning."

"Out with it," Deggar said.

"I just risked the Griffin Road to tell you that a large force of Chalician Praetors is marching up from Elliff. I have reason to believe they will do to Limae what they've done in Varea, Mahndür, and Redot."

"Which is?"

"Bring Haven under the same religious subjugation."

Deggar chuckled. "Haven answers to no one and no church."

"You will answer to them if they conquer you. Mahn Fulhar rolled over like a kicked ynfald."

"The guilds there will do anything to avoid conflict."

"That didn't stop them from doing everything to prevent Searn and the Clouws from establishing their guild office."

"And how did that end?" Deggar said. "My reports say that Searn died, and the Clouws, whom I only know from tales of their exploits, have gone missing—although rumor is they're here in town—and the investigator assigned to seek them out and take them back to Mahn Fulhar is here looking for them."

"I did not know that."

"I wouldn't expect you to. It sounds like every Sentinel who was in Mahndür over the winter ought to turn in their cloaks. You all made a real mess and harmed our reputation."

"The decisions made by one Sentinel does not reflect on the

others."

"Searn's words. And foolishness. He was a fool, or else he wouldn't be dead."

"Then you won't do anything about the Chalicians?"

The huge man sat back. "My second-hand man, Captain Stromm, has already left with a message for the captain of the guard. I'll have him on standby to close the gates at the city council's command, and I'll send scouts to confirm your suspicion. Until then, you will be my guests, and if we find you're wrong, you'll enjoy a nice life of sewer duty."

Ophedia lifted her chin. "I stand by what I said."

"I like you," Deggar said. "I like your attitude. It'll serve you well."

"It has so far."

"Then take your mangy ynfald and go up to room four. It's yours for the night. And don't go anywhere else."

33

PATHS UNSEEN

*There is something nagging in my mind, words thought but
unspoken. It is a call I must follow in the solitude of this edifice.
There is nothing left for me to do but heed that call.*

—FROM ST. RÄMMON'S FINAL TESTIMONY

T he weather finally cleared after five days of torrential rains,
and most people from the monastery took the opportunity
to go into the city, which gave Jined what he missed most
from his time at the chapel in Brahz—solitude. He found a door
opening onto a walkway circling the mountain and took the
winding path, cobbled with flat flagstones, through the shale. The
slope of the path would have been treacherous in the rain, but the
wind and sun rays breaking through the clouds had dried the black
slate. After several twists and turns he saw the entrance to the
original lighthouse, said to have been built by St. Iramus Rämmon,
the Sailor Paladin himself. The heavy door was bolted on the
outside. Jined attempted to slide the bolt back, but resorted to
tapping with his hammer. As the bolt was beat back, the door
swung open on its own as the wind shoved the door and Jined into
the space beyond.

Three chapels stood opposite the entrance, bearing what
appeared to be reliquaries. Rather than rug and tapestry, red
stones of a sort had been laid, and the alcoves were cut from the
rock itself. By the door, a stone basin full of candles, albeit slightly
rodent-nibbled, awaited use.

Jined took out a tinder box. He knelt down with flint and steel to make a flame, then lit a candle, which he placed in a sconce behind the door. He shoved the door closed against the wind, barely getting the latch in place, before lighting three more candles with the first one and approached the first chapel and its memorabilia. There was a painting at the back of the chapel of a Paladin wearing a robe and gorget, although he had a full head of hair and a beard. Jined recognized the likeness of the Grissoni mountains in the painting, rising above Lago Crysan by Pariantür. Pilgrims journeying up those mountains was a common enough image in art. Yet this picture showed them on an unfamiliar path, denoted by a strange landmark in the form of a hand. At the top of which was a small shrine showing the miniature likeness of a hairy hermit.

Jined turned his attention to a golden box sitting on a table, a reliquary, which bore the name of Brother Bulon Arrando. The box contained a dyed red woolen "pillow" upon which sat a long braid of hair, parts of which were already deteriorating. He closed the box and considered the unadorned wall to his right. Jined thought back to chapels he had seen, and remembered the shrine to Brother Pevon at Pariantür. His shrine lacked one of the three things required for sainthood: a relic or verified item of import to the ministry of the saint, an act of faith verified by Pariantür, and a recorded body of scripture-worthy text. Arrando's shrine appeared to lack text.

He left a single candle burning at the shrine and turned to the right, where another shrine, this time to St. Hamul, had been erected. He was a popular choice for many bastions and fortresses, and this particular shrine showed Hamul founding the port of Hamulon on the Lago Crysan, around which the largest Parianti city had been built.

Lastly, he turned to the central shrine, built to St. Rämmon himself. This one was thrice as large, with an elaborate painting representing all that Rämmon accomplished around the Lupinfang Sea, from the scouring of the vül from the ports of northern Zhigava, to the catching of a haul of fish in Nasun to feed those under a famine in Morraine. It was a copy of an older and more detailed painting in the main chapel of the fortress below.

On a pedestal lay an oar of steel. The paddle had been mounted to a hammer haft identical to the one all Paladins wore.

"He did not wear a hammer?" Jined said to himself, half hoping Grissone might appear and join in conversation. He did not.

With a sigh, he turned to a book sitting on the next pedestal, opening it to reveal the Rämmon Log, which had been inscribed in painstaking detail into steel leafs. He turned the plates, glancing through the dry, to-the-point entries, which detailed Rämmon's trip around the Lupinfang to the site of Waglÿsaor, where he noted the ominous sky-fallen slab of iron. The raising of the fortress had been fraught with difficulties. Rämmon persisted at the guidance of his god. It soon stopped being a line-by line-log, and became a summary of seemingly cursed events that surrounded his time at the monastery. He spent less time administrating and more time in the lighthouse in solitude, finally commanding his acolyte, Brother Arrando, to lock him in as a hermit until the lighthouse went out. As Jined recalled, the lighthouse, despite having no means to continue burning, went on for ten years, and when it was finally opened, they found only the Oar of St. Rämmon there, and no sign of the saint. The record in the log stopped abruptly after Rämmon detailed his request to be locked in, an unsolved mystery of the church.

Jined noticed that the back cover had a stylized engraving upon it, and brought a candle closer to inspect it. The style of embossing was common enough. He had seen it on many books in the library of Pariantür. But this engraving was different, composed of short and long lines of the Silent Language, and it continued the log for another untranslated plate. Some of the words were illegible, likely the copyist not realizing they copied words. But the new entries detailed ten years of additional dates.

Day one of my plunge into faith began. With that action my guest came to visit me. And confirmed my suspicion that there was a secret language, used now to continue my log. For I am now silent.

Week two. I am running low on supplies for the tower. My guest visited me and brought bread from town and fuel to keep the flame burning.

Week four. I followed my guest this time. I was unable to walk paths unseen, and yet the way had been there all along.

The log went on to describe a secret path by which the saint found driftwood and fish to eat from unreachable coves, eventually walking a path through a secret dreamlike place of darkness and candles, and arriving at the city, where he continued to do ministry as a pauper on the streets of Waglÿsaor. Throughout his ministry, he donned aspects of the vows of the Paladins as a Paladame adopts an aspect. He spent an entire year blind, and his mysterious and unnamed guest provided for him. The log ended with a single line:

I am called now to cease my hesitation, entering into deeper faith and walk another path not yet seen.

Jined took a step back, considering what he read.

"My god," Jined prayed. "Did you call St. Rämmon on the same path I walk?"

There was only silence.

A breath of wind caught the nape of his neck, and he turned and saw a ladder leading to a trap door. He climbed to the top to find it locked, but he pushed on it with his shoulders and it sprung open. It had not been locked, only rusted shut. Half of the circular room was exposed to the sky, the back wall carved from stone. Remnants of the silver that once covered the wall still glittered in spots. A stone basin sat in the center of the circular room.

From the unwalled side of the room, a view of the Lupinfang spread out before him, the waves choppy in the confused winds. Clouds raced along, sunlight breaking through in intermittent shafts and disappearing just as quickly.

A small masted fishing boat, tossed about by the waves, was sailing closer and closer to the rocky shore. He worried it would run hard aground, unable to escape the tide's pull.

"Grissone, guide them to safety," he muttered.

A series of light shafts appeared directly before the small boat. Another shaft broke on the mountain itself, a hundred yards from Jined. He could see a sheep path on the mountainside, just before the light vanished. He leaned out over the wall to look toward the sheep path. A crack in the bannister seemed the right size for the head of his hammer to fit. He took it up, and placed the hammer there, and considered whether it would give him the security he needed to go out over the ledge.

He sat down on the ledge and slowly lowered himself, searching for a foothold. When his hands lost their grip he fell, the leather of the old belt he wore snapped, and he tumbled unhurt to the stones not far below—the belt, chain, and hammer, still lodged in the crook above. He tugged to check it was secure, and nodded in satisfaction. He turned and scrambled down the path, which was merely a precarious ledge along the mountainside. He could see the little boat drawing nearer and nearer to the shoreline, moving less haphazardly.

Jined walked cautiously down the path, and came to a switchback. It reminded him of his home town, yet in dangerous mirroring, switching back all the way down to the coast, each narrow path a dangerous reminder of his own mortality. He followed until he was only fifty feet above the beach. The path led around the corner to another sight that Jined had not been ready for—a secret harbor and façade, carved into a rock face in an ancient style Jined had only seen in drawings. Derelict statues of the eleven gods were on display there; even the fallen gods were represented—Rionne, Kea'Rinoul, and Kos-Yran, in their original likenesses, before their corruption.

Meanwhile, the fishing boat had anchored and a group of women were disembarking. Jined crept closer. The sailors, all women, removed their cloaks, revealing clothing in the style of the Isles of Bronue Jinre. A woman in a white robe came out of the carved rock face. Dressed as Crysalas, she embraced the captain of the vessel and invited her to come in out of the weather.

The light was darkening, and Jined knew he'd have to return to the lighthouse soon.

"And yet..." he said to himself.

He stepped back up the path and stripped down to his brown robe, piling the armor carefully against the cliff wall. Taking up his satchel, he checked that he still had at least one candle, and then proceeded toward the now-empty harbor. He came to a deep cut where the path had washed out. He was not certain he could make the jump.

"Grissone, grant me the wings of the Anka," he muttered as he took the leap. He almost laughed out loud as he leapt much further than he intended, indeed further than should have been possible. After landing, he waited for his heart to stop pounding, and then proceeded to the façade as night plunged the harbor into darkness. He felt his way to the door and stared into what St. Rämmon had described—a secret dreamlike place of darkness and candles.

Within the rock face were several large storerooms, filled with various foodstuffs, and streets of derelict homes stacked three high. There were empty places of trade reached by dark passages sparsely lit by candles and emptying into a square with a dry fountain. He decided against continuing that route, instead venturing farther south into the city. As he approached the next square, a female voice coalesced. He slunk next to a wall and peered into the square. Two women sat on the edge of another dry fountain. One of them, dressed in full Paladame regalia, held a candle in her hand; the other sat quietly, listening to the other talk. Both looked very young.

Three figures came into the square, led by Astrid Glass, also bearing a candle.

"Thank you for waiting," Astrid said. "Mother Smith requisitioned us to help with the delivery from Bronue. The sailors thought they were going to be smashed on the cliffs, but the gods prevented that."

"Is it normal," the voice of Katiam asked, "for everyone to help with deliveries?"

"Is the weight too much for you?" the voice of Maeda Salna said. Now Jined recognized the younger-looking Paladame who sat on the fountain.

"Honestly, yes," Katiam said, "It feels as though Mother Smith has been targeting me specifically. As though she is angry about something. She has never brokered ill-will toward me before."

"She is a much sterner woman now than she was before she learned of the death of the Matriarch Superioris," the voice of the other young girl said. She had a decidedly Boronii accent.

"Shall we?" the last member of their group said. Jined immediately recognized the botanist, Esenath. She took the candle from Astrid and led the way down another dark corridor. Jined followed them until they came to another square, having put out one of their two candles. Ahead Jined heard sounds of coughing. An air of sadness pervaded.

"Is Sister Laven here?" Esenath asked loudly.

"I am she," the voice of an older woman said through the dark. "Is that Esenath?"

"It is. I've come to conduct a new test. "

"Your tests will only go so far," Laven said.

"This is something new. I ought not say much more than that. For I do not wish to give false hope. Will you please bring one of the Moon-Eyes who caught the blight when I did? Bring yourself, since you were one of the first."

"We can only take so much fleeting hope," Laven said.

"Please," Esenath said. "Trust me."

After a long while Sister Laven returned with a little one.

"This is a young girl by the name of Veras. She was stricken with Day Blind nine days ago."

Katiam, knelt and held a bundle up to the little girl, who took it as though handling a doll with a squeak of delight. There was a small sound like a baby sneezing, and the girl laughed in response. A moment later the girl gasped and began to cry.

"What is it, child?"

"Light!" the girl cried out. "I see the candle!"

"How did you do this?" Sister Laven said, dropping to her knees by the child.

Katiam moved the bundle from the little girl's hands to the older woman's.

"What is this?" Sister Laven asked. "I..."

She held the bundle close to her face, and after a moment, there was another sniff and sneeze. Then she too began to cry.

"Sister Laven, dear," Esenath said. "Was there a change?"

"I think so."

"May I look at your eyes with the candle? The light may hurt."

"Please," the woman said, a faint hope in her voice.

Esenath crouched next to her as Katiam took the bundle up again. She held the candle next to the woman's face, examining her eyes.

"The candlelight," Laven said. "It doesn't seem to hurt so much."

"But can you see better now?"

"I'm not sure. Perhaps."

"We should take her to the harbor," Astrid said. "To see if the daylight is any different."

"That is a good idea," Esenath said. "Although I don't know if it is still day."

They turned as a group and began to walk toward Jined. He fled as quietly as possible back toward the harbor, keeping well ahead of the candlelight and avoiding the light of the other candles as he passed. As he turned the corner of the square nearest to the harbor entrance, he heard the others coming up behind him more quickly than he anticipated, so he vanished quickly down a dark street.

"It looks like it is night now," Maeda Salna said as they emerged into the square and looked toward the entrance passage.

"We'll conduct this observation in the morning," Esenath said. "Sister Laven, please keep this to yourself. We need additional evidence, so we're not giving a false hope. I have my suspicions, but I must confirm."

"What are they?" Laven said.

"I'd rather remain scientific and not share them until it is obvious."

"Please. Give me hope or dash it. I cannot wait until morning."

"The thing Katiam offered healed me. This little girl was also cured, but you—you have had Day Blind longer—experienced only partial healing. Evidently, the longer you suffer, the more permanent the damage is. Tomorrow we'll treat more people and test this theory."

"Thank you," Laven said, a small note of defeat in her voice. "Perhaps I am not fully healed, but knowing that others will be gives me some hope. Perhaps I'll heal more with more treatment."

"Hold on to that hope."

Jined left having heard what he felt Grissone wanted him to. He exited through the harbor façade and made his way along the path, the storm having passed and the bright stars illuminating his way. He prayed and leapt once more over the washed-out part of the road, recovered his armor from its hiding place on the other side, and continued the difficult climb. It was even harder in the dark and with the cold pervading every inch of his body. When he came to the ledge of the lighthouse's open face, he warmed his hands as best he could and then took hold of the hammer chain, jumped, caught the ledge and pulled himself up. If he had been any shorter, such a feat would have been impossible.

The old lighthouse was serene; he sat on the edge for a moment and looked out on the sea.

"Grissone, I know the Pantheon works in mysterious ways, but your ways are what I follow and your miracles are what I pray for. Do others grant such miracles too? Did I witness a miracle by your mother?"

"Nichal has been looking for you," Dane said from the shadows nearby.

Jined jumped.

"You startled me!"

Dane stepped into the starlight. "Guilt is a heavy burden, and makes us all paranoid at times."

"What are you doing here?"

"You've been gone for hours," Dane said. "Nichal was worried. I happened upon the shrine below, saw the candles you lit, and came up here. I found your hammer over there and decided to wait until you returned."

"Why?"

"I've long suspected there are hidden ways to leave the citadel. It accounts for how the women are able to come and go unseen." Dane gave him a look.

"Are you leveling a claim against me?"

"Are you leveling one against yourself?" Dane replied. "I encourage you to remember your vow. Your first vow. New vows do not override the old ones."

"You think me guilty of some transgression?"

"I think all are guilty of transgression," Dane said. "The Day Blind afflicting this city is a sign of deeper sin."

"I believe there is a means to heal the city."

"Contrition."

"What?"

"You cannot heal from just punishment of sin except by contrition."

"I am going to tell Nichal what I have seen and heard. If he deems it appropriate, then it will be shared. But, I am a Primus now. I don't owe you an explanation."

"Primus Brazstein," Dane said, "I bear you no ill will. My request for forgiveness from you should be a sign of that. However, I take very seriously the sanctity of our order. Here at St. Rämmon, a life of stark simplicity could see a renaissance of our faith."

"It is at Pariantür that our order's fate will be decided."

"Who are you to decide that?"

"And who are you to question it when Nichal holds the rank of Prima Pater?"

"Acting Prima Pater," Dane corrected. "He may call, even order us, to return to Pariantür. But even the Crysalas stand their ground, here and in the cities we have left behind. Who are we if we do not do the same?"

"Let us go to Nichal, then. But Dane," Jined placed a hand on his shoulder, "please don't share this secret."

"Is that an order?"

"If it needs to be. If not because of my rank, then because of my ordination from Grissone."

"Put your armor and hammer back on," Dane said. "You look like a beggar rather than a Paladin of your station."

34

LEGALITIES

Take thy means to sacrifice yourself,

Drive it home, and enter bliss.

—FROM *HEAVY WEIGHS THE HEART, A TRAGEDY*

BY ELLAVON GAVALIN, DÜRANI PLAYWRIGHT

Jined entered the Prima Pater's office. Jurgon Upona and the young Silas Merun sat at a table by a window, poring over books. They had a pen and ink to take notes as they read. The twins sat next to each other, a stack of books between them, leafing through the texts. Nichal stood by another window, staring out at the sea, a book held open in his hands.

Dane crossed the room and gave Nichal a salute.

"I found Brazstein. I mean, Primus... Brazstein."

"Where were you?" Nichal asked.

"There is an old chapel at the site of the original lighthouse," Jined said, "dedicated to St. Rämmon and his disciple. I was praying there."

Unseen by Nichal, Dane narrowed his eyes.

"I've had need of you," said Nichal. "I need your prayers, your insight, and another brother poring over the law books."

"I am here to serve," Jined said. "What are we looking for?"

Nichal walked to his desk, rubbing his hand over his head as he saw the stacks of books. "We are reading through these books to find what legal claim I have over my title as acting Prima Pater. If we continue to declare Dorian dead, we will be establishing a new Prima Pater based on a lie, no matter who it is."

"Shall I seek out Pater Zoumerik?" Dane asked. "He would savor the opportunity to find entries in his own law books."

"He is more than aware of what I am doing and encouraging it, but he is not here."

"Then I will watch for his return," Dane said.

Nichal gave a nod and Dane left the room.

"I've been speaking with Zoumerik all these days we've been here," Nichal muttered after Dane left. "I suspect he knows that Dorian lives, but he has not said so. He is quick to bring up his own aims for the Northern Scapes, citing obscure law codes and making a strong case for his actions. But I fear he is seeking to establish something more permanent."

"What do you mean?"

"The lifestyle changes he is making to both the fortress here, as well as in the city, speak of deeper, longer lasting changes. He means to be an inspiration to others, from the fortress here, I suspect. Add to that, a ship arrived at a nearby port a few days ago. The first to come from Mahndür this spring. This means that the Lupinfang is clearing, and trade will begin."

"And with that, naval actions," Jined said.

"Yes. Even more dire is the news from Mahn Fulhar. Apparently the Chalicians arrived in full, and locked the city down, forbidding trade within or outside of the city. It is not dissimilar to what happens here, only it is with an iron fist, commanded by the authority of crown and holy arrow."

"And you fear the same here?"

"I fear I agree with him that establishing a Grissoni church of contrition here in this city would be the best defense against the Chalicians as they move this way across the Lupinfang, since they intend to convert nations to their authoritarian regime."

"But you have another fear," Jined discerned.

"Yes. If Zoumerik's changes get out of hand, it will reflect poorly on me."

"You want to remain Prima Pater, don't you?" Jined asked.

"I want unity," Nichal said. "With the possibility of Moteans in the brotherhood at Pariantür, they must have no reason to dispute my claim or my actions. If a better candidate presents himself, I am more than happy to step down, but I'll not be the cause of a schism."

"Do the stark demands of Zoumerik's teachings give you any pause?" Jined asked.

"They do," Nichal said. "However, as he pointed out, there is a precedent. We've discussed a course of long-term measures that would lighten the load but continue the tradition he is establishing. I've not spoken directly against his ideas, because I may have to do something similar at Pariantür if we discover the Moteans are a problem there."

"I hate the thought of enforcing these stringent measures at all," Jined said. "Not that I am in authority to say."

"Please speak. Grissone has blessed you twice, and I would not bring up this conversation with you if I did not want to hear what you have to say."

"Let us set aside the Northern Scapes as a talking point and use the example of Pariantür instead."

"Very well."

"Fasting and acts of humility are common enough," Jined said. "But they are traditional, and we already know when we must practice them. Harsh rules punish the faithful alongside the guilty, and may cause resentment, feeding the desires of those that seek to foment rebellion."

"I wish Dorian and Gallahan were here. I'd like to know how they dealt with the Moteans when Gallahan returned to the faith himself."

"There is no record here of that?"

"All of these law books predate the Protectorate Wars."

Jined touched the books on the desk and looked along the spines.

"Thank you for your insight, Jined," Nichal said.

"I'm not sure I did much more than share my own opinion. I've not felt Grissone respond to me these last several months."

"I asked Dorian if Grissone ever spoke with him when he prayed, and he made a point that the Vow of Prayer is directed more often at the Anka, which responds by nudges and goading rather than by words."

"But is it Grissone whom I have had this special relationship with? He is the one who called me to deeper faith and additional vows."

"Isn't praying to one the same as the other? They are same, but in different places and in different forms."

"What are we searching for now?" Jined asked, changing the subject.

"An answer to the claim of acting Prima Pater, while Dorian still lives."

"What about the era after which the Blind Prima Pater disappeared?"

Nichal gave a weak smile. "That is exactly what we look for. But we can't find any references, and between us, none of us can recall what year that happened."

"And we can't ask Zoumerik," Jined said.

"Because that might give away that Dorian still lives."

"Gallahan mentioned that the last Pater Segundus of the Blind may have been a mountain hermit. After he left, the Blind vow fell out of favor."

"Why did he leave?"

"I'm not sure," Jined said.

"He may have gone off to seek the blind Prima Pater, who had been declared dead after vanishing. That Pater Segundus left off to reclaim the armor of the Blind Prima Pater. That he never returned—it's been nagging at the corner of my mind. What if the Blind Prima Pater never died? What if the Pater Segundus who went to seek him didn't return because he found him? What if brothers stopped taking the vow for a reason?"

"So we're looking not for a particular date," Jined said, "but an era in which things shift— since it would surround several decades after these disappearances."

"And why for the life of me, as a Pater Segundus..."

"Prima Pater," Jined corrected.

"Yes. Prima Pater. Why can't I recall when the Vow of Blindness stopped being taken?" He motioned over to Loïc and Cävian. "Even they can't remember."

"Why should they? Because they're Silent brothers?"

"Because they're good scholars. They received top notches from the Pariantür schoolmasters."

Jined took a stack of books from Nichal's desk, found a bench, and began poring over the texts. A shaft of light lit the sleeping Silas Merun on the floor. He roused from his snore, which brought Jined to. He realized he had been staring at the page before him for some time.

Day had come.

The twins still worked, and Nichal stood with his hands behind his back as he stared at the embers in the massive hearth. Jurgon entered with a tray of bread and cheese, placed it on the Prima Pater's desk, sliced them up, and doled them out. Jined spread the softer cheese on a piece of bread as a knock came to the door.

"Come in," Nichal said.

A Paladin entered.

"Prima Pater," the man said, saluting. "Pater Didus Koel sent me from town."

"They're still there? It's morning."

"We stayed at the Ducal House," he replied.

"*We* being Zoumerik and those who joined him," Nichal confirmed.

The man nodded.

"What is the message?"

"He asked you come to the square outside the hospital immediately."

"Why?" Nichal said, approaching Jurgon and the sleepy Silas, who helped him into his armor.

"There is a crowd forming outside of it. He insists you come as fast as you can."

"Thank you. Please run to the stables and have six sleipnirs prepared."

The man bowed and left.

"Six?" Jined asked.

"Of course. The five men I trust the most will join me."

He turned to the twins. "Eat while you walk, and see that those sleipnirs are ready. And bring the standard, Cävian."

Jined went with Nichal and his two seneschals as they rode out of the fortress, Jined silently thanking Grissone for a dry road. They galloped around the curve of the mountain and arrived at the gates, with the guards calling for Nichal to halt.

"You know my face," Nichal said. "Open the gates."

They debated with each other for a moment, then did as he commanded. Nichal urged his mount to a canter and they passed the slab of iron in the center of town, and then took the last long street to the hospital. Before they came to it, they passed a long line of people, stretching into thousands leading up to the hospital. It looked to Jined as though the entire city had come. The doors to the hospital were closed and Didus Koel stood next to Zoumerik and a man who must have been Duke Ergis, the leader of the city.

He wore brown burlap and his beard was long and unkept, although Jined suspected it had been groomed to look that way. Zoumerik and the duke were mounted on sleipnirs.

"Prima Pater," Zoumerik said with a nod.

"Pater Zoumerik," Nichal replied. "What is going on?"

"Duke Ergis was summoned here not long after midnight, and, as I was a guest of his house, I came with him. A rumor has spread through the city that a little girl has been fully healed of Day Blind."

"Do we have proof?"

"The people don't need proof. They began marching on the hospital. Mother Superioris Smith gave us the little girl and she is now in the care of the duke. Mother Smith confirmed that she had indeed been afflicted with Moon-Eyes."

"But we don't know if this was an actual miracle or a natural recovery from the illness."

"We do not," Zoumerik said.

"Where is Mother Smith now?"

"She's looking into the situation, and has locked the hospital doors."

Nichal gave a few quick orders to all of the Paladins, calling everyone to formation. Cävian was positioned with the standard out front with the rest of the company on sleipnirs in a block.

Didus Koel came to stand next to Jined.

"The look on your face," Didus said, "tells me you're worried."

"Aren't you?"

"I am. But I'd like to hear what you're thinking first."

"It appears as though the entire city is here," Jined said. "If this is about Day Blind, and all of these people have Day Blind, then there is a bigger issue. If all of these people have gathered because they want any healing they can get, that is another. But people are never so formal. These people all stand in a long line rather than a mob filling this square."

"Isn't that good?" Koel asked. "It implies this isn't a dangerous situation."

"It's still uncanny that not one of these people steps out of line. And notice those whose faces we can actually see."

Jined pointed to the portion of the line closest to them.

"They're eyeing us with fear."

Zoumerik seems to have that effect, Loïc signed.

"Fear?" Didus said.

Not fear of him, Loïc said. *Fear of his disappointment.*

"When we arrived in town," Jined said to Didus, "you appeared to know him well."

"We know each other from the times he's brought messages to me, and when I've reported to the citadel. Why do you ask?"

"I don't know. I feel like there is something I must remember of him. But I can't."

"What do you mean?"

"I'm not sure. It's at the edge of my memory."

The doors to the hospital boomed open and several nurses filed out onto the steps, Mother Smith appearing before them. She stood at the top and held one hand up for the crowd to pause while summoning the Paladins with her other. Zoumerik urged his mount forward and the others followed suit. Jined noticed Cävian make a face as Loïc said something with one hand.

Jined raised an eyebrow.

Why did Z move first, and not Guess? Loïc repeated for Jined. Jined shrugged.

They came to the bottom of the stairs, and on Nichal's command they all turned their mounts to face out while he, Zoumerik, and the duke dismounted.

"What have you discovered, Mother Smith?" Zoumerik asked as they climbed the stairs.

"Little," Smith replied, "although the little we have discovered will change the situation irrevocably."

"Why is that?" Nichal asked.

"There is a group of Day Blind sufferers, isolated to avoid contagion, and every last one of them has been healed. Those afflicted longer do not have their sight entirely restored, but the disease is no longer hurting them."

"How is this a little thing?" Duke Ergis said, louder than he ought. "This is a day of miracles!"

A murmur rippled through the crowd.

"Duke Ergis," Zoumerik said. "Let us remain calm."

He turned back to Mother Smith and indicated she continue.

"I need more time to verify the source of the healing," she said. "Right now I have only a theory."

"If you've a means to heal the sickness of this city," Ergis said, a forced sound of panic in his voice, "then let no stone be left unturned to discover it!"

"Quiet," Nichal hissed.

"You'll not tell me to remain quiet," the duke replied. "I am the leader of this city. I have earned my place among the contrite. I barely know you. You are not the Prima Pater who came last year. You and your Paladins are merely refugees from the religious battle to the west."

He turned to the crowd, a hint of hysteria in his voice.

"My own daughter was struck with Day Blind. She was taken from me. If she is healed, where is she?" He approached the front of the line. "Lord Voris, where is your wife?"

The crowd surged toward the duke. The line began to fold in on itself.

The duke turned back to the Prima Pater.

"Where is your brown burlap?" he said to Nichal. "Where is your humility and contrition?"

"I am the Prima Pater of the Paladins," Nichal said, with a hint of doubt in his own voice.

"You are said to bear the Vow of Poverty," Ergis said, "and yet you wear a fine red satin cape."

Nichal stood taller. "I don't answer to you."

"Nor I to you."

Another commotion arose, this time from within the hospital. A man in a brown robe pressed his way out through the nurses and came to stand atop the stairs, his hand firmly gripping the arm of an armored Paladame as she struggled to break free, her wrists tied together with rope. It was the young-faced Maeda Salna. In their struggle, the man's hood fell and he was revealed to be Dane Marric.

"What are you doing, Marric?" Jined said, dismounting and marching up the stairs.

Nichal turned from his argument with the duke.

"Stand back, Brazstein," Dane said.

"Dane?" Nichal said.

"This has been a night of uncovered mysteries and dark dealings," Dane said.

"As we understand it, it has been a night of miracles."

"Miracles? Hardly. Grissone's hand was not at the bottom of this."

"The victims of Day Blind are said to be healed," Nichal said. "Unhand that sister."

"Moon-Eyes are healed," Dane said "But they were hidden below the streets of this city, their miasma no doubt poisoning the very heart of its people."

He turned to the crowd.

"Week in and week out you have been contrite, yet Day Blind continued to strike down young and old, rich and poor. Why? Not because you were not contrite but because the hospital has hidden Moon-Eyes away, in a secret city underneath this one. And their sickness has spread."

"Marric," Nichal hissed. "Stop."

Dane ignored him.

"I walked that secret city. I saw this so-called miracle of healing. I cannot explain it as anything other than a dark ceremony where the sick were given a bitter token, and brought back to the light of day."

The crowd had drawn up, no longer in a line at all. More continued to surge to the front.

"This woman knows how it is done. But she will not tell. She will not share. She holds the secret with avarice!"

"Paladins! To me!" Nichal said, surging toward Dane. Jined and Loïc rushed forward to tackle Dane, and wrest Little Maeda away.

In response the crowd rushed forward to try and tug her the other direction.

"Do not let them take her!" Nichal ordered.

"Cease this!" Zoumerik ordered in a booming voice.

The crowd stopped immediately.

Maeda was sobbing as she fell into Nichal's arms. Jined and the others formed a barrier between the crowd and Nichal. Dane stood on the side of the crowd.

"Explain, Brother Marric," Zoumerik ordered, coming to stand next to Nichal. "Calmly."

"There is a secret path," Dane said. "I followed it, by the grace of Grissone, and discovered that there is a city, an entire city, beneath this one."

"There have always been rumors that this is so," Zoumerik said. "Go on."

"In the secret city, those struck with Day Blind have been hidden away."

"Isolation of the sick is a common enough practice," Zoumerik replied.

"Leprosy camps are staged far away from others, not directly under carousing inns or under the clink of dining utensils as a family shares a meal."

"In this secret city, you saw the miracle?"

"I saw Day Blind healed. My hiding place was revealed, and I was accosted, as the sole man in that secret city. How many men with Day Blind are not healed? The healing is kept for the Crysalas, an order in as much disrepair as the Paladins."

"Harsh accusations," Zoumerik said.

"Dane, quiet yourself," Nichal said. "Do not betray the Crysalas like this. Do not."

"He will continue," Zoumerik said.

"As Prima Pater," Nichal commanded, "we will take this conversation away from the angry mob."

"As Pater Segundus, you mean," Zoumerik said.

"What?" Nichal replied.

"I have humored you long enough. I have offered you ample opportunity to confess your lie. You are not Prima Pater. I know Dorian Mür still lives. Your velvet cape is a deceit, and you break your own Vow of Poverty."

Nichal staggered, pulling Sister Salna with him.

"The Crysalas Societas no longer have an oracle. Their purity was sought for the sole purpose of supplicating that oracle. Without its guidance, they are nothing. That they now hold a miracle but will not give it up to heal the men of this city? What sin is this?"

"Give her to us!" the crowd began to murmur. "Give us the woman!"

"Mother Smith," Zoumerik said. "Come forward."

Sigri did as she was commanded, a cowed look on her face. Jined had never seen her defer to anyone in that manner.

"Explain," said Zoumerik. "So this may be a public confession."

"The secret city is like a makeshift Vault of the Crysalas."

"But it is not a true vault."

Sigri shook her head.

Zoumerik made a motion; the Paladins under his command marched forward.

"Sigri Smith, take this young Paladame into the hospital and keep her under guard. She will be questioned about the source of this miracle, and in the meantime you will show me this secret city."

"You have no right," Nichal said.

"I have every right. I will permit you to return to the citadel with your entourage, but you are merely my guest, not my Prima

Pater. Do not make me bring down full Parianti law upon you."

"Let me take Maeda Salna with me," Nichal said. "She will be safer."

"So you can let her escape? She will remain under Sigri Smith's protection."

Nichal relaxed his grip on Little Maeda's arm, an arm Dane took again, though she cringed at his touch.

Jined stepped forward.

"Dane," Jined said. "Don't do this."

"With Nichal's position in question, I make my stand among those who show themselves to be faithful. Let the legal proceedings continue under Zoumerik's command."

Jined turned to Nichal, who gave a defeated nod.

"If a hair on her head is harmed..." Jined said.

"The only harm that shall befall her is what she brings down on herself."

35

DAY SIGHT

The symbols of the Crysalas are plain and simple. The Rose Blossom is most recognized. Thorn, Leaf, Root, Purity—all of these are common themes. There is a rare instance where Vine is referenced. This is accepted by most scholars to reference the Dweol. What I found most interesting in my studies, both in Crysalas text as well as a rare mention in Abecinian texts are references to two lesser-used symbols, the Fruit and the Pearl. They are rare and obscure. A few commentaries write these off as mistranslations, interpreting them as Thorns attached to the Rose symbol. I thought this might be right, save for one passage that reads, "The Fruit which bears Thorns..." Following the previous logic, this would be retranslated as "The Thorn which bears Thorns," and in botany this is only found on sickly growths. I expect these obscurer symbols may be a secret, unlocked for millenia.

—AVINE GELDIN

Katiam watched with bated breath as Esenath examined Larohz. She checked each vine and leaf. She tenderly checked within the petals, then examined the thorns near the creature's stalk near the bloom.

"She doesn't seem damaged from healing the sickness. All of the petals look fresh and vibrant. Her leaves have no yellowing. She's flourished in your care."

"Thank you," Katiam replied with a smile.

"You say she always has five leaves?"

"Yes. As she's grown over the winter, the new ones will begin to form near the top, then the old ones will wilt."

"She grows from within, like an onion."

"Only she doesn't turn to paper, but wood."

"And the thorns?"

"She only had one to start. The second one formed over the winter, almost out of a will to say her name better."

"Can you say your name, Rotha?"

The Rotha didn't respond.

"Little Rose?" Katiam whispered. "Can you say your name?"

"Laaroohzz..." it whistled.

"Very good," she whispered.

"Can she say anything else?" Esenath asked.

"She tries other words, but they never make sense."

"And how did it start?"

"We gave her a treat. Sugared Loosetongue petals."

"Interesting," Esenath said. "And what of roses?"

"What do you mean?"

"Have you given her any other flowers?"

"She does prefer to sit in and soak up rose water over normal water."

Esenath turned to the apothecary cabinet, looked through it, turning back with several loose yellow petals in the palm of her hand.

"What are those from?" Katiam asked.

"Goldwealth. Tea made with these will supposedly help you find gold, I've spoken with prospectors. They actually grow over deposits of iron and fool's gold, so prospectors use them to know where gold isn't."

"Why keep it in the cabinet, then, if it does nothing?"

"It adds a nice bite to a tea," Esenath said.

"What will it do for Larohz?"

"No idea. But maybe she'll enjoy it."

The Rotha sniffed at the Goldwealth, and then with a whiff, the petals disappeared from Esenath's hand. It grew still, as though considering something, then began making a series of clicks, some short, some long. It touched Katiam's face and clicked once, then brushed her eyes and clicked twice.

"What is it doing?" Katiam asked as it began feeling around, clicking incessantly.

"I'm not sure." Esenath moved to the table. Katiam followed her, and took out a handful of grain from a jar.

"Put the Rotha on the table," she said.

Katiam did so, and the Rotha began to pull itself across the surface, exploring with its leaves and blossom, sniffing the air. It felt the grains and clicked several times, then took one up and dropped it into its blossom. It clicked once and the grain fell out.

"Well, it doesn't eat grain, it seems," Esenath said.

"No. We made some gruel on the road, it was disinterested. It was curious about mushroom soup. And of course, rose water."

"Mushrooms? Interesting. We'll explore that later."

Esenath reached for the container of grain, but the Rotha took hold of the jar and spilled the grain all over. The clicking from its thorns became a rattle as it felt through the grains and then held up a leaf, revealing five grains that Esenath took and examined.

"They have gone bad," Esenath said.

It clicked five times then whistled, "Ggggunbaaad."

"Yes," Esenath replied. "Gone bad."

The Rotha began feeling through the grain again, clicking as she did. She held up a single grain bigger than most and clicked once. "Bbbiigg."

"I think she's counting and identifying them."

"Why?"

"I don't know," Esenath said. "It seems on the nose that a flower with gold or wealth in the name would cause her to do so, but maybe there is a reason for that."

"Should we try something else?" Katiam asked.

Esenath turned back to her cabinet just as a knock came to the door.

"Who is it?"

"Astrid."

"Come on in."

The Paladame entered and stood there. "Katiam, we may need to hide elsewhere."

"Why?"

"The rumor is surging through Forgotten that Moon-Eyes are being healed."

"How did that get out?" Esenath asked, turning.

"Regardless of how," Astrid said, "it has. We have to discuss how we'll protect the Rotha."

"Why continue to hide?" Esenath said. "If the Rotha can heal, why not let it?"

"She must be kept a secret," Katiam said. "Those were Auntie

Maeda's directions."

Another knock came to the door and Little Maeda pushed in.

"Astrid, come quick," she said.

"What is it?" Esenath began following the two of them. "Katiam, stay here."

Katiam held the Rotha in tense silence, Larozh nestled close as she pulled her cloak about them both.

"It will be all right," Katiam said. "I've got you."

"Kkkatiim. Kaaateem." Larohz said, a single leaf touching her face. "Kateem."

"Katiam," she corrected.

"Kati...Kati-Am."

"Better, Little Rose."

After a commotion outside, the door burst open and a crowd of people surged into the small room. Katiam yelped and stood. The people who pressed in all blinked in the brighter light of the starblush lamp.

"What is the meaning of this?" Katiam yelled.

"Help us!" a woman replied.

"Stop where you are," Katiam shouted. Everyone froze. From over the heads of the crowd she could see Esenath's face.

"They're Day Blind!" Esenath said. "They all came from their isolation neighborhood as a crowd."

Katiam nodded and turned to the woman who had asked for help.

"Why did you all come at once?" Katiam asked calmly, trying her best to emulate the Matriarch Superioris' calm demeanor.

"If you can heal us, why should we wait?" the woman said.

Katiam took a deep breath then whispered to the Rotha, "Do you think you can try to help more?"

Katiam held Larohz up to the woman. There was a sniff, a sneeze, and the woman gasped.

"I can see!" she shouted, just as Little Maeda and Esenath came back into the room.

"Help me!" the next person said.

"Hold up," Astrid shouted, pulling the woman back as she pawed at Katiam. "Each in their time."

"Are you all right?" Esenath asked Katiam.

"Yes," she said. "How did this happen?"

"They came as a smiling mob, all begging for a miracle. Little Maeda and Astrid couldn't stop the press of the crowd."

"I only hope it's not too much for Larozh."

Esenath guided each person forward while Astrid kept everyone in line. The Rotha was presented to each woman, and each declared her sight markedly improved. Esenath recorded their names and how long they had been stricken with Day Blind, and then they left. It was well after midnight by the time the last woman, girl, and child left with a cry of joy. A small jar was filled with the little sand-like pearls that fell from the Rotha with each healing.

"We should get you back to Fedelmina's house," Astrid said. "You look exhausted, and I'm sure the Rotha would like water."

Katiam nodded, standing on wobbly feet. She stepped out into the square, which buzzed with activity even though the hour was late. Little Maeda stood at the foot of the stairs, smiling as they joined her and began walking together to Fedelmina's house. They stopped short only when they saw Mother Smith marching toward them accompanied by Onelie, who looked apologetic.

"What is going on?" Sigri Smith demanded.

"Mother Superioris?" Esenath replied, stepping forward.

"I've heard the Day Blind are being miraculously healed, and I've not been informed."

"It has all been rather sudden," Esenath said. "We had hoped to gather more evidence to give you in the morning."

"The murmuring has grown to a fever pitch. The noise down here will expose our city."

"Please, Mother Smith," Esenath said. "We can contain this, and choose the best way to reveal it to others."

"Reveal? By no means!"

"There are men in the city above who are stricken with Day Blind. They ought to be healed as well."

"I am going to go speak with Zoumerik. He will know how best to handle this."

Astrid stepped up to the Mother Superioris.

"When we left Pariantür, you answered only to Maeda Mür. Even then, with reverence and respect, as one of the Captains of the Crysalas Honoris, since when do you answer to a Paladin?"

"Since our Matriarch died and the Dweol collapsed. Since every Paladin that has come to town since the onset of winter comes with one thing in mind—the abandonment of their faith. And the allowance of war."

A tear budded in the Mother Superioris' eye. She blinked it

away.

"Sigri," Astrid said. "We still have a duty to the women of the vaults and to each other."

"To what purpose?" Sigri asked. "A march toward another generation come and gone? Or women cast aside and beaten into submission? At least Zoumerik teaches of a way that harbors mutual respect."

"We march toward hope," Astrid said, "not solitude and sadness."

"All is sadness," Sigri said.

"I thought so, too, when my brother died," Astrid said. "The thought of his smile will always bring a tear to my eye, sometimes in sorrow, other times in joy. That our beloved Matriarch is gone is something to mourn and find joy in."

"And what of those girls who die from diseases caused by the men who mistreat them?"

"You provide them comfort." Astrid placed a hand on Sigri's arm. "Otherwise they would have died alone in the street."

A woman approached wearing the whites of a hospital nurse.

"What is it, Sister Ellae?" Sigri asked.

"Dawn is breaking, and a crowd has formed outside the hospital. Zoumerik is there."

Sigri turned back to the others and gave a nod.

"For Rose and Thorn," Astrid said.

"For the women of Waglÿsaor," she replied.

Astrid watched her go and turned back to Katiam and Little Maeda.

"Can we trust her?" Katiam asked.

"What do you mean?" Astrid asked. "I reminded her of her true purpose. She'll not betray it."

"I agree," Maeda Salna said. "She is a Captain of the Rose first. She is rigidly dedicated to the Aspect of Honor and the protection of women. She'll not betray that."

"Still," Katiam said, "I wonder if we need to leave."

"Leave?" Esenath asked. "We have more to heal."

"Ellae mentioned a crowd," Katiam said. "If it threatens the Rotha, then I leave. Its safety matters more than anything."

"Half the city's blind have been healed, and the other half remain unhealed, and you speak of leaving?" Esenath replied.

Astrid turned to Esenath. "I don't like it either, but Katiam is right. She was given a holy purpose by our goddess. The Rotha must go east."

A cloaked figure suddenly burst from the nearby crowd and took Katiam's arm.

Katiam cried out as she looked into the face of Dane Marric.

"Dane?" Astrid cried.

"Silence, Glass."

Astrid, Esenath, and Little Maeda all drew their maces.

"No man is allowed to step foot here," Little Maeda said.

"You keep healing from the sick of the city. How dare you!"

"How dare you," Astrid said, "entering under a cover of cloak and darkness into our sacred domain. And touching a woman, no less."

Dane recoiled for half a moment. Katiam broke free and retreated to her friends, the crowd nearby watching in hesitation and fear.

"How did you get down here, Marric?" Astrid asked.

"A secret path was revealed to me by my god, and I have followed his guidance here in faith."

"What sign was that?"

"A secret path, revealed by the sin of another, brought me here to discover your people not only have a means to healing the city's blind, but that you plan to leave with that secret."

Little Maeda stepped boldly up to Dane, though she was a head shorter than him.

"I am the appointed guardian of this vault. You'll answer to your leadership for this infraction."

Dane scowled, but then a calm look came over his face.

"Very well." He lifted a stoic chin. "What I have done, I have done for my god, and I'll go with you for Grissone's glory."

"Esenath," Katiam said, handing her bundle to the botanist as Dane walked away with Little Maeda and Astrid. "Can you please take Larozh to Fedelmina's house? Keep her company?"

"Of course," Esenath said.

Katiam turned and followed the others to the vault's entrance, where Astrid was placing a cloth over Dane's eyes.

"What is this?" Dane asked.

"I do not know by how you came into this vault," she said, "but we'll not reveal all our secrets."

"A secret," Dane said, not struggling against her, "is a sign of guilt."

"So is your disdain for women," Astrid replied with a smirk only

Katiam could see.

Dane scoffed and made to say something, but Astrid shoved him forward. Little Maeda had just lifted the vault door's bar when Dane suddenly pushed Astrid sideways into a wall, ripped the binder from his eyes and charged forward, taking hold of Little Maeda's arm and pulling her through the door. Astrid recovered and charged the door as it slammed shut, a bar dropping audibly from the other side. They were locked in.

"No!" Astrid shouted, pounding against the door.

"Why did he do that?" Katiam asked.

"I thought he was too smug. He meant to do that—to take one of us as proof."

"Why?" Katiam asked.

"I don't know. Perhaps those were Zoumerik's orders. Come on."

"Where are we going?"

"We need to make sure Little Maeda is all right, and we need to find the Prima Pater and let him know what Dane has done."

"Not without the Rotha," Katiam said, marching to Fedelmina's house. Esenath sat at a table with Fedelmina while Onelie Clemmbäkker prepared tea.

"That was quick," Esenath said.

"Dane took Little Maeda," Astrid said, "and locked the vault door from the outside. The vault is compromised. We're leaving."

"You can't take the Rotha," Esenath said.

Astrid stepped up to Esenath. "Are you going to stop us?"

Katiam put herself between the two women. "Esenath, come with us. We can try and understand this on the road, but we have to leave."

"I do not know if the ship has left for Bronue Jinre," Fedelmina said. "You could take that."

"You'll not go with us?" Katiam asked.

"My true home was Precipice," the older woman said. "With the Dweol gone, I have no home to return to, and I am too old to weather the road."

"Speaking of storms," the young Onelie said. "I think one is coming outside. I doubt the boat at the hidden harbor is going anywhere."

"How do you know?" Katiam asked.

"I know it sounds silly, but when I was a little girl, I broke my leg horribly. When the weather gets bad, it still hurts."

"Regardless," Astrid said, "I am the sworn protector of the Rotha, and Katiam the caretaker. Esenath, you can go with us or you can stay, but the three of us are leaving after we ensure Little Maeda is safe."

"I know a couple less traveled ways out of Forgotten," Onelie said.

Fedelmina stood. "If you think you're going on the road, can we take a day to prepare you?"

"What are you proposing?" Astrid asked.

"I shall prepare things for the road," she said, "and have them taken to you. Go to the Alewives' Vault, where we stayed when we first came to the city. From there we can see you safely on the road."

Katiam gave the older woman an embrace. "Thank you, Sister Barba."

She gave them a warm smile, "when have I ever let you call me anything other than Fedelmina?"

Onelie led them by candlelight through streets Katiam had not seen. The only sound came from the Rotha, whistling nervously as Onelie brought them into a house where a ladder led up to a trap door, which she unlocked and pushed open with her shoulders. After climbing up into the space above, she reached down and helped the others into what appeared to be a storeroom in a mill house, with an exit onto a back alley.

"Where are we?" Astrid asked Onelie.

"The Saor is four blocks that way." Onelie pointed to the left.

"Then that is the way we go," Astrid said.

"Everyone is moving in the opposite direction," Esenath muttered as they entered a wide street, a family walking by, their children gamboling with each other while the parents chatted cheerily. The father had several burlap sacks over his arm. As they approached Astrid, the parents stopped.

"Where are you going?" the man asked.

Astrid opened her mouth to speak, and the wife interrupted. "We'd not want anyone to find themselves in trouble with the gospelers," the wife said.

"Did we miss some news?" Astrid asked.

"Where have you been all morning?" the man laughed.

"We were working late on a blanket for an ailing grandmother."

"If she's sick," the wife said, "you ought to retrieve her! Rumors say healings are happening at the hospital. The Day Blind have regained their sight. If that rumor is true, then others shall be healed too! Everyone has been summoned to the Saor square, to hear the word and to repent and ask for a miracle!"

"Then we had better hurry," Astrid said. "The old lady will want to come herself."

"Don't take too long," the man said. "You know how they can get."

"Who can get?"

"Oh, the gospelers," the woman said. "Just after the last bout of Day Blind came through, one gospeler was preaching the damnation of Noccitan. An old man arrived long after the others, not a clue anything was happening, and walked through the square with a smile on his face. The stern one gave him a talking to. What was his name?"

"Darric," the man said.

"Dane Marric?" Astrid corrected.

"That was it," the woman said.

"We'll make sure to hurry back to the square, then."

"If you're rushing to gather up family, you'd best bring your sanctioned sackcloth, too."

The family continued on, and the four women proceeded the opposite way.

"I don't understand," Katiam said.

"What do you mean?" Esenath replied.

"There is a relaxed acceptance to this madness."

"For some people, they have given into the frenzied desire to seek answers in contrition. Others, like that family, see it all as entertainment. I'd wager they were already a contented family, and to watch others give in amuses them."

"How can anyone find this all amusing?"

"It is the way of life in Œron," Esenath said. "That country has more holidays from work than any other country would find reasonable. Of course, half of those can hardly be called holidays. More are ashen days that call for confession, as it seems the fortress is calling for here."

"I cannot understand how Nichal can accept this."

"We don't know that he is."

They came to the alley leading to the Alewives' Vault. Astrid approached the door and gave a signal to her friends as the door opened, and they all entered. Abbess Krinna appeared from another door as they came to the main room of the vault.

"You're safe!" she said in relief, approaching each with an embrace. "We've received information that the Day Blind are healed and that Mother Smith has taken Sister Salna into custody at the command of Pater Zoumerik, for questioning."

"What?" Esenath cried.

"The square outside the hospital was taken by a mob not an hour ago. Little Maeda was escorted back into the hospital. Now you appear."

"We could not access the parts of the Hidden City connected to your vaults from that portion."

"And you need to?"

"We need to leave the city tomorrow morning," Astrid said. "We hoped you might have a way out, perhaps through the citadel."

"I'll not trust the citadel," Krinna said.

"Fedelmina is preparing provisions for us."

"Then she has a plan. Now, what of the healing?"

"The Day Blind of the hospital's vault are healed," Esenath said. "But there will not be any more healed."

"No!" Krinna cried.

"The means of the healing is threatened, and it must be taken away."

"My brother was stricken with the last fell wind. Is there no way to heal him?"

Esenath took something out of her satchel. "Come with me. I have an idea I'd like you to entertain."

Krinna and Esenath walked away together.

"We ought to get some rest," Onelie said to the others. "Tomorrow morning will come sooner than we think."

"I don't know that I can rest," Katiam said, "until we know that Little Maeda is safe."

"I'll speak with the Sisters here and see if we can't get some news from our friends at the fortress," Astrid offered.

"You mean Loïc and Cävian."

Astrid nodded. "You go rest, and make sure the Rotha is settled."

She turned and walked away.

"Are you sure you should leave the city?" Onelie asked.

"What do you mean?"

"It can heal Day Blind. What if it can help others too?"

"From my understanding," Katiam said, "it has an even greater purpose. I am commanded to follow that path."

"Then I'd like to go with you, too."

"But you were meant to be brought here to Waglÿsaor as a means for negotiating peace with your homeland."

"I've seen what the Rotha can do. I'm not only curious; I also feel called to help."

"You're not a member of the Crysalas," Katiam said.

"But I could be. I have skills. I can help."

"Oh?" Katiam asked.

"I can cook. I play the lute."

"Can you make bread?"

"I helped Sister Baker once," Onelie said. "She taught me some things."

"Astrid isn't so good at bread," Katiam said. "Let's find somewhere to rest, and I'll think about it. We can discuss it tomorrow morning."

Onelie smiled. "That's all I ask."

36

INTERLUDES

T he cries of the girl within the padded room were inaudible. Sigri stood at attention, gritting her teeth, trying not to picture Little Maeda's tear-streaked face as she shoved her in and locked the door.

"It was for the good of the city," Zoumerik said, giving her a half-smile and touching her shoulder. "She knows how the Day Blind were healed, and if she refuses to tell us, how can we trust her?"

"She is charged with protecting the secrets of the Crysalas," Sigri said.

"As we discussed, there can be no peace where there are secrets."

"I did not tell you of the vault below the hospital because I am sworn not to."

"It is not just a vault. I allowed you your vaults," Zoumerik said. "But an entire city underneath this one? What seditious cells are to be found there?"

"There is more to this underground city than you know," Sigri said.

"Tell me."

"Allow me to continue to explore those secrets," Sigri said, "and then I will tell you."

"Why not now?"

"Jamis," Sigri said, "I have come to respect your ways even as you have trusted me to advise you. I know your aim, and I would give you a gift to meet it."

"What aim is that?"

"To establish Waglȳsaor as a Holy City, separate from the world," Sigri said. "A lighthouse, as St. Rämmon is, but to the nations."

"Why help me? What of the Crysalas?"

"With the Dweol fallen, it seems we must forge a new destiny."

"You would abandon the Crysalas aspects?"

"No. I would see them continue."

"Because they give you access to a mote of power from your goddess."

"What do you mean?"

"Let us speak tomorrow evening. Over dinner."

"What would you have me do with Sister Salna?"

"She will be made an example," Zoumerik said. "For the good of the city."

"Do not harm her."

"Why should I wish to harm her? I want genuine contrition, not a pogrom."

Sigri winced at the word.

"Now, is our other guest here?" he asked.

"Yes. He's not said a word since he was locked away."

"Very well," Zoumerik said, unlocking and opening the door.

He nodded to the person inside and turned back to Sigri. "If you'll allow me our privacy, I have much to say for his ears alone."

She pursed her lips and stood taller.

"Sigri Smith," Zoumerik said sternly, "it is not a request."

She turned to go. Zoumerik re-entered the cell.

"You have overstepped your bounds, Dane," he said to the cell's sole inhabitant, "but I am interested in hearing how you found that vault."

The butcher finished killing the capricör. When it stopped moving, the foreleg came free at the joint with a swift chop. He nodded to his apprentice, who took the piece up and walked to the counter, placing it before the man.

"Not a normal request, a bloody leg as soon as the gentle creature dies," the apprentice said.

"Nor is it normal for a butcher to care about the use of meat."

"All of Pantheon's creatures ought to be respected. If you don't, you're only eating garbage and calling it pie."

The customer took up the hunk of meat and handed the apprentice a small satchel of coin. He walked around the block to a small rented room and closed the door behind him. Another butcher block stood there, stained from the work he had done with it over the winter. He cut the meat away from the bone and placed it in a cauldron of ale. The embers beneath the iron pot were stirred to flame when he shoved more wood in, lighting the room.

He took up the saw and began to cut the meat into even pieces, which was not so different from the wood and leather work he was so used to. He tossed the pieces into a small sack, which he'd dropped into the cauldron later to enrich the broth. Hunger gnawed at his gut. It had been three days since he had eaten.

With his poor woodworking tools he extracted the marrow and nodded to himself. The hole was the right size. He rinsed the bone off, dried it on a towel and filed it down to size with a coarse sanding block. Then he held up the ring and examined it.

It would do. So long as it took the blood, it would do.

He opened the wooden chest, revealing the only bone ring left after Shroud had stolen the fragment. It had taken all winter to repair the portions he had stolen from the Rose Convent, and it had cost him more gold and more blood than he cared to admit. But the obsession was overwhelming. It was all he could think about.

He took up the ring and placed it on the anvil. Then he placed the five new rings he had made from the capricör bone. Pulling back his sleeve, he unwrapped the bandage and winced as he touched the stitches there with a knife. The angry pain flared up once more and blood welled onto his skin. The hunger in his gut and the pain in his arm grew like a wildfire; his ears began ringing. He was losing time, and he had cut himself too deeply. Blood trickled down his hand and dripped onto the floor. Stepping to the butcher block, he let the blood dribble onto the new ring and then onto the old one.

Nothing happened.

He swore.

Then, something changed. The ring lapped up the blood. It was soon clean. He laughed and dribbled more onto it. It continued to drink it up, but did not bond with the other ring.

"How much blood do you need?" he croaked.

Minutes later and it continued to soak up the blood. The other ring still sat unchanged.

He screamed in anger and took up the ring with his bloody hand.

"Why won't you work?!" he yelled.

"More," a voice said directly into his mind.

"What? How?"

He held the single ring up and examined it. The fingers touching it were now clean of blood. The ring continued to lap up the red.

"More," the voice whimpered.

He turned to the sack of bone shards and bits of meat and set the ring atop the bloody mess. The bones quickly went white as the red soaked into the bone and disappeared.

"More," it continued to say, over and over in his mind.

He took up the ring and ran out the door and around the corner, the word filling his mind. He came to the butcher. The man and his apprentice looked up in astonishment as he entered, nearly as bloody as their arms as they continued the work of cleaning the capricör.

"What are you doing?" the butcher asked.

He leapt over the counter and ran to the drip bucket below the carcass. The butcher took hold of his shoulder, brandishing a knife, but he shoved him away and thrust the ring into the bucket.

"Yesssss!" the voice cried.

The ring glutted itself on the blood and within moments the bucket was empty.

"How did you do that?" the apprentice said.

He reached into his pocket, pulled out another satchel of coins, and handed it to the boy. Then he walked out into the street.

"Must I continue to find you more?" he muttered.

"I am full now."

"What are you?"

"Deathless. I was hungry, but now I am not. What are you?"

"You're only a ring of bone. How do you talk?"

"Because I cannot be killed. I am Deathless. I am one part of my whole. I am king. Where are we?"

"King? Shroud killed a king?"

"Then you knew him, did you? You knew the man who brought me to this sorry state? Who are you?"

"All we're doing is asking questions and getting no answers.

And I am starving."

"*Then eat.*"

"Will you allow me?"

"*Even a servant must eat. Go on. Find yourself food.*"

He returned to his room. The fire still burned and the ale now boiled with meat inside. It wasn't finished, and the meat was tough. He ladled out some of the hot ale and then reached for the sack of blanched bones, tied it off, and added it to the soup.

He sipped at the ale and sat back against the wall.

"*Have you eaten?*"

"It's cooking. You can't see or feel, can you?"

"*I am soul, I think. And nothing more.*"

"Shade, it is called, rather than soul," the man said.

"*How do you know this?*"

"I'm a member of a sect of Paladins. We study such things. I know less of what you are, being part of a separate group. It took me enough work to discover how to bond the rings to what was left of the portion of the bone cloak I took."

"*Why am I alone? Where is the rest of the bone cloak? And who are you?*"

"Why must you know?"

"*Because it is best that we speak frankly with one another. The loneliness of nothingness has given me a clarity I did not have when first I was given this gift.*"

"What gift?"

"*Deathlessness. Protection from the Judge. Now. Your name.*"

"I am known to most as Slate, but my name was Ingver Morrin."

"*I know you. But you do not know me.*"

"How?"

"*I hailed from a tribe of Üterk in Nasun. You hired my father to help you fake your death. It cost him his life.*"

"I am at a loss...your father. Was his name Kirth?"

"*That you remember his name is enough. I hated him. You did me a favor.*"

"You've not told me your name."

"*You shall call me Deathless. It is fitting. My mortal name means the same.*"

"I have always had a fondness for the Üterk people. My mother was one. She taught me the old tongue. Deathless. Ghoraz, then, if I remember my Üterk."

"That is close, yes. Perhaps with more trust I'll tell you my tribal name. It is interesting that a prince, dead to his old life, speaks the old tongue, brought to be only servant now to the lowest of the low, brought up by the hand of the Gift Giver to be king of those lower than himself."

"How did you come to be placed in a ring of bone?"

"Is that all I am? A ring of bone? Perhaps. Yes, that makes sense. I can feel things around and through me. Yet I also feel I am elsewhere. Now tell me about yourself, Ingver. And I shall tell you how I became only a ring. How I became Deathless."

Hundreds of tinny bells surrounded her, their sound washing over her every thought. It was getting on her nerves, but she could say nothing—not because she was too polite, nor because she had been told to remain silent, nor because they were anything but beautiful. She simply could not think straight. The noise seemed to take every thought and memory. She could not remember why she had even left the Templum. Something about ancient men and women, about a dark figure, a coldness she could almost feel once more. The image of a blue-clad being fleeing from her and the words she had spoken.

"Greetings, travelers," Pater Pellian Noss said to someone on the road. Her sleipnir halted as he pulled his up short.

"An interesting cavalcade," someone said. He spoke with a mouth full of rocks, as he over-pronounced everything, and his words were clear. "Fifty Paladins riding a road. Not something you see often."

"And yet," a second voice said, sharper, colder, perhaps muffled by fur, or a mouth-encasing beard, "and yet this is the third time we've seen this in the past months, first in the Northern Scapes and now here."

"You're well-traveled," Pellian said.

"The same could be said for you," the gravel-mouthed one said. "If I didn't know better, I'd say I saw you up in Mahn Fulhar as winter was settling in. Now, these many months later and we're traveling in the same direction."

She could almost place his voice. A dread rose within her.

"We ride to visit colleagues in Haven," Pellian said.

"I think that goes without saying," the muffled one said. "We're not ten miles from there now. Do you escort this monk?"

"Nefer Yaledít joins us as my guest, rather than we as her escort."

"Same thing in my book. Always a good idea to have a follower of the Physician."

"I've not heard Nifara called that," Pellian said.

"It's part of our trade, being storytellers. We speak in mysteries and sometimes forget what we've told to whom."

"Is there a tale of this?"

"Certainly. It was her first calling to be Messenger and Healer, but fate had other plans."

"Join us on this journey to Haven. Perhaps we can hear this story."

"I'll tell you the story if you tell me the story of those bells."

A wash of silvery sounds began to peal around her, seemingly synchronized to one another.

"I am not in a position to explain them to anyone outside the order," Pellian said.

"They're made of skyfall metal, are they not?" the gravel-mouthed storyteller asked.

"Why, yes," Pellian replied, "they are."

"They say that the skyfall metal was the cause of the Destruction."

"Who says this?"

"Scholars we have known. According to some, it continued falling in various places after the Destruction, to much less effect, or was it before. Same in our book. But it was the unceasing rain of metal sounding against the whole of Kallattai like a hollow gong."

"It is often found within craters," Noss replied thoughtfully. "Hence why it is thought to have fallen from the sky."

"And yet, it has been so long since it has last fallen," the muffled man said. "A wonder that none know why it does so, and why the gods know not its origin."

"Many believe the metal was sent by the Deceiver," the gravel-voiced man said. "After all, did not Rionne take the first fall of the metal and make his armor with it?"

"Yet according to the legend, the Thirteen-Legged god is also said to not be able to touch the armor," Noss said.

"Does a god need to touch anything if they are not of this

world?"

"The gods are as much a part of this world as anyone else. Their fate is tied to its survival or destruction."

"You stay so silent," the muffle-voiced one said to Seriah.

A cold shiver ran up her spine and her mind snapped to reality. A scream rose in her throat.

"No need for that," he said. The scream died. "I only wish to thank you for the service you rendered to me and my brother."

"Never again," she whimpered. "I'll speak for you never again."

"Nor shall you speak of it ever again."

She opened her mouth to speak, but no words came. The tinny bells washed away her thoughts. With Coldness now as her companion, she became blind, deaf, and mute. Her mind screamed to escape this living imprisonment; her soul sought a way out. But there seemed no escape. The grating sound, the cold presence, and the unspoken regret upon her tongue pained her with every tiny ring of those accursed bells.

ANDREW D MEREDITH

PART 5

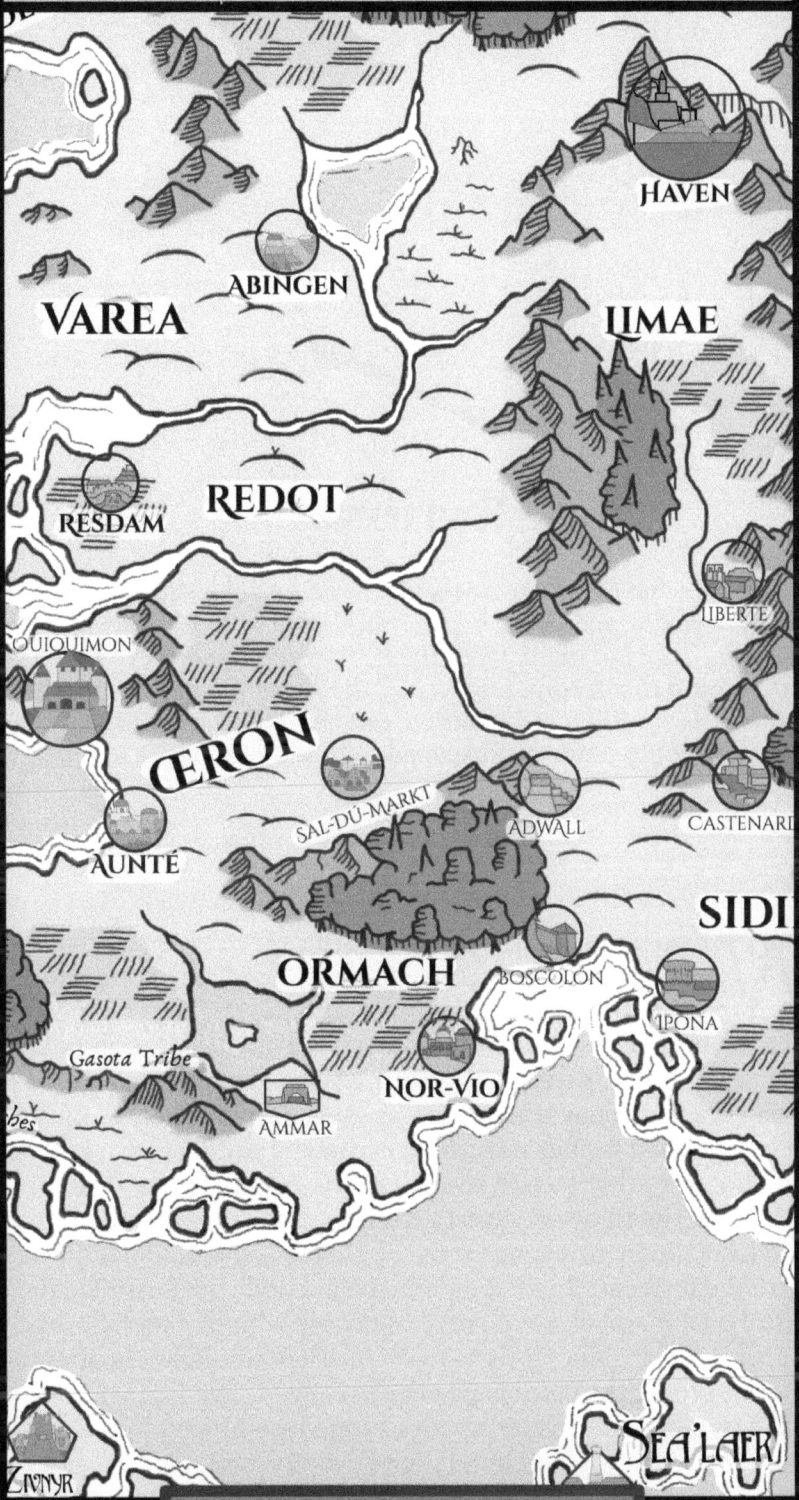

VAREA

ABINGEN

HAVEN

LIMAE

REDOT

RESDAM

LIBERTE

OUIQUIMON

ŒRON

SAL-DÛ-MARKT

ADWALL

CASTENARI

AUNTÉ

SIDI

ORMACH

BOSCOLON

IPONA

Gasota Tribe

NOR-VIO

AMMAR

ZIVINYR

SEA'LAER

SOUTHWESTERN
GANTHIC

37

RATIONS

Famine tore me from my mother's home, and the Riverfolk, in their generosity, provided hearth and home in trade for my freedom. I learned much from them. To twist the dice, to pull the card, to read the dream, and to boil the stone. I learned too much for their liking. I had out-cheated, out-deceived, and out-maneuvered my captors. I escaped with my life, into a tougher trap.

—JOURNAL OF OLLISTAN GŒRNSTADT

Whisper sat attentively at Ophedia's feet, his scales hackled and rattled against one another. Three cutpurses had already tried for her satchel, and the day prior someone had gone for her belt. Ophedia clutched the small leather binder holding her ration papers, regretting having given up on the line the day before. Today it was twice as long, and the chances of there still being bread for her were slim, especially with the man in front of her boasting that he had enough ration papers to buy food for two weeks. The line was close to the western wall, over which she could hear the hymns sung by the Chalician army, that had formed out on the terraces. Their song was melancholic but surprisingly uplifting. Ophedia observed several people with thicker hair, likely of Œronzi stock, making signs to Aben. They would be the first to roll over and let the Chalicians take the city.

The rustling of Whisper's scales suddenly whipped into a frenzy. Ophedia watched him lunge down the street after a pair of

Black Sentinels walking shoulder-to-shoulder away from her. One of them turned and saw the charging ynfald, bracing themselves for impact as Whisper leapt up into the air and hit the Sentinel squarely on the chest. The man cried out as he fell. Ophedia almost sacrificed her place in line until she realized the man's cries were actually laughter.

The other Sentinel helped their companion up, with Whisper circling and sniffing the man, his tail wagging in every direction at once. The two Sentinels looked around, made eye contact with Ophedia, and approached. They kept their hoods over their eyes, but it was unmistakably Hanen and Rallia Clouw. Hanen was letting his whiskers grow in, though it would be weeks before it might be considered a proper beard.

"Hello Ophedia," Rallia said with a smile.

"Rallia," Ophedia said. "Why the low hood?"

"We're not sure if we're being watched," Rallia said.

"Navien is in town, then?"

Hanen nodded.

"Seems like you're both all right, though," Ophedia said. "Did the old man come with you?"

"Not here," Hanen said in a hushed voice.

"Hey," someone behind Ophedia piped up. "Get to the back of the line."

"We're just talking with our friend," Rallia said.

"How do we know you won't just stick with her all the way to the front?"

"Just because that's something you might do doesn't mean others will," Ophedia snapped.

The man turned red and stepped forward.

Ophedia held a hand up to stop him. "You're going to risk your own place in line?"

The man halted and eyed those behind him suspiciously. Then he cowered back to his place.

"How long have you been standing here?" Hanen asked.

"I stood in line for two hours yesterday and gave up. Today this line is twice as long, but I'm waiting it out."

"From what I gather, this part of town is under Sentinel Commander Forenor. He's a hard-nosed businessman as far as Sentinels go, and he's the only one selling those ration papers. If you know the right people in other parts of the city, it's a lot easier to get food."

"Do you know the right people?" Ophedia asked. "I could use a bite."

Rallia handed her something cloth-wrapped. "Eat this. It'll help."

"How long have you been in town?" Hanen asked.

"I arrived in town just before the Chalicians," Ophedia said as she unwrapped the dense bar of nuts, honey, and spices. "What is this?" she asked, stuffing it into her mouth.

"Compliments of Ymbrys," Rallia said.

"He's with you?"

"He is."

"Well," Ophedia said between voracious bites, "I got here before the Chalicians. I was the one who warned the Sentinel Commanders they were coming."

"So this is your fault?" a woman in front of Ophedia said, spinning around.

"Fault?" Ophedia replied. "No. I merely brought this message."

"If we'd all had warning before the gates closed," the woman retorted, "I might have escaped to visit my family to the south. Now I'm stuck here."

"We're all stuck here," Hanen said. "Who knows if the army out there wasn't stalking the roads, anyway."

Ophedia ignored the glares of the others in line and turned to face the Clouws. "I made it to the coast with Zhag before we found out it wasn't Navien pursuing us, but several of his Voktorra. The Chalicians were already in control there. Before Zhag took the ship west to Grisden he helped Eunia and Chös break me out of the Chalician governor's house."

"Eunia and Chös?" Rallia responded. "Are they here, too?"

"They led off a chase with a Chalician scout a day south of here. We were in the woods down in Varea when the Chalicians passed by on their march to the pass. We climbed a mountain slope and cut them off and I arrived in time for warning."

"I'm sorry we weren't able to get out of here in time either," Hanen said. "It's been a very stressful couple of weeks."

"What happened?"

"Well, we brought the old man to town, ran into Ymbrys, and were attacked by Sentinels along with one of those Paladins with the black cloaks," Rallia said. "He was using the Gauntlet Searn used at the Rose Convent."

"Now Navien is in town, too," Hanen interrupted. "We've been trying to work out how to lose him, or maybe even convince someone he's a spy sent from Mahndür. He keeps moving inns. That makes it difficult."

"What could he do to you?" Ophedia said. "He certainly can't take you to Mahn Fulhar. No one is leaving the city."

"Navien might turn us in," Hanen said, "or turn the old man in, in trade for allowing him to take us back to Mahn Fulhar. I was able to make a deal with him, but it was a false one, and I don't have much time left to make good on it."

"What's that?" Ophedia asked.

"The King of Mahn Fulhar asked me to find the bone cloak that Searn wore. I lied to Navien, telling him I thought it was here in town and that I could find it."

"And he believed you?"

"He was there when King Erdthal told me to find it. If he showed up in Mahn Fulhar with me in shackles, and I told the king that he had not given me enough time to find it, well, he'd be in trouble with the king and his guild."

"Smart thinking, even if you can't fulfill the promise."

"Should we keep moving?" Rallia said to Hanen.

"Where are you two going?"

"We're trying to find Aurín," Rallia said. "We think he is still under the control of that gauntlet. He turned on us when we were attacked and we haven't seen him since. We're trying to figure out if there is a way to help him."

"He's staying at the same inn I am," Ophedia said.

"Really?" Hanen replied.

Ophedia nodded. "We moved there from our previous place when the owner turned cold."

"Come with us, then," Rallia said.

"I can't. I need to get some bread. I already bought some ration papers."

Hanen sighed. "We'll keep you fed; you can figure out how to turn those papers back in."

Ophedia looked up the line.

"How long since you moved?" Rallia asked.

"Half an hour," she replied.

"Then you're going to be here until after curfew. Come on."

Ophedia sighed and stepped out of line. Those behind her quickly took her place, the angry man with an evil smile of satisfaction. When Ophedia pulled back the edge of her cloak to reveal her clubs, however, the smile on his face disappeared.

"How does Ymbrys have so many of these?" Ophedia took another food bar from Rallia.

"He came back one morning with several large sacks of nuts, some honey, and some cheap meat cuts and began making them. The innkeeper helped him out."

"Well, if they start selling them, they're going to make a killing."

"They're stockpiling them right now. It's only been a week, but it could get worse."

They came to the Black Feather Inn, which was full of people drinking watered-down ale while sitting in silence.

"I moved here from another commander's inn after my story had been verified. His inn was too rowdy, even for me. This inn belongs to another commander," Ophedia said. "Bolla Elbay. Although since the closing of the gates, no one has seen her."

"From what we've gathered," Hanen said, "the Sentinel Council has moved up into the citadel along with the city leaders and hasn't left."

"What have they been talking about, these ten long days?" Ophedia asked.

"Who knows?" Rallia said. "We've unsuccessfully tried getting in."

The innkeeper motioned for Ophedia to come over.

"That friend of yours," he said.

"Aurín?"

"Yeah. He left a message for you. Something about a vok-something. He said you should stay put and he'd get word to you."

Ophedia turned to Hanen and Rallia. Hanen was crouched on the ground, scratching Whisper all over to the ynfald's delight.

"It sounds like Aurín spotted Navien, and he's following him."

Ophedia took three tankards from the keep and walked to the table. Rallia reached out to an unused smaller Edi-Foz board and began fiddling around with it. Ophedia placed a tankard in front of the two of them and took a seat.

"So, where are you staying?" she asked.

"The Drækis," Hanen said. "It's hard to find, over on the east side of town and north of the lumberyard by about ten blocks."

"The lumberyard north of Black Street?"

"You know it?"

"I know Black Street. It's where I finally met up with the commander to give them the news."

"When we get back, we'll make sure to set aside a satchel of food bars for you," Rallia said, pushing the board between Hanen and herself. They both started half-mindedly playing.

"I'd appreciate it," she said.

"Speaking of which," Hanen said, "we ought to get back. Could you send word, or come yourself, once you know more about what Aurín finds? Don't bring him, though. Unfortunately, he can't be trusted."

"I don't fully understand," Ophedia said. "Why can't he?"

"What did he do with the coin that was given in Mahn Fulhar, the day he helped Searn?"

"It was against his will," Ophedia said.

"We're not saying it wasn't," Rallia said. "But Slate used the gauntlet again with Aurín's help. Is he still under its power? Does he still have that coin?"

"I'll ask. And if he does have the coin?"

"See that he gets rid of it," Hanen said. "If he doesn't have it, it means there is some sort of long-lasting side effect, and we must figure out how to free him of it."

"You didn't seem to care much at the Rose Convent," Ophedia said.

"Well, I don't like the idea of anyone turning on me, whether friend or foe. If we can help Aurín, as a friend..."

"Then we can help others," Rallia finished.

Hanen rose. "Keep our location to yourself, though. We need to keep the old man's whereabouts a secret."

"What is he trying to accomplish?" Ophedia asked. "I can keep a lookout, too."

"He's looking for a large suit of black armor," Rallia whispered. "Both he and Ymbrys spend most days talking about it. They're trying to figure out where it's held so they can take it."

"To what end?" Ophedia asked.

"I'm not sure Dorian knows," Hanen said.

"Stay wary out there," Ophedia said as they left the inn and Whisper trotted after them.

"You're going, too?" she said. The ynfald stopped and considered her. "Not even a thank you?"

He lolled his mouth open and padded back over to her and licked her hand.

"Thank you, too." She patted his head before he turned and ran after the Clouws.

"Do you know those two?" a woman said from the next table. She wore plain brown leathers, a high-throated white blouse like a ranch hand, and a Morriegan-style, wide, black hat. She had black hair with a few grays growing in.

"We worked together on a job in Düran," Ophedia said. "Why?"

The woman didn't wear a Sentinel cloak, but she did wear a pair of Sentinel axes on her belt.

"The description of the two of them has been passed around from the commanders. Word is they'd like to speak with them. What are their names?"

"Chös and Eunia," Ophedia lied.

"Might not be them, then," the woman said.

"It's not often you see a ranked Sentinel without their cloak."

"I decide if and when I bring attention to myself," she said. "Speaking of which, you've been staying here this past week, but we haven't been introduced."

"Should we have been?" Ophedia asked.

"It's customary to introduce yourself to your hostess."

"You're Bolla Elbay?"

She nodded.

"I've been trying to speak with you for the past week, but everyone said you were at the Aerie Citadel."

"That's partly true. I've come and gone from here."

Ophedia took out her last gold royal and held it out. "People tell me I must pay a fee to you as a Sentinel Commander who is also my host."

Bolla held up a hand to stay her. "No need. You're Searn's daughter, as I understand it. I can see it in your face."

"Well, if that's the custom..."

"I have questions for you. Answer those, and I'll consider you paid up."

She signaled the innkeeper for a large loaf of seedy bread and two flagons of ale.

"Eat. Drink," Bolla said.

Ophedia tore the bread in two, gave half to Bolla, and pulled bread off her half and stuffed it in her mouth, washed down with frothy ale.

"What do you want to know?"

"How Searn died," Bolla said. "The Council needs to know if he's truly dead, and if we should begin the work of replacing him."

"Is that how he replaced the High Commander before him?"

"There was no High Commander before Searn."

"What do you mean?"

"Searn isn't just the High Commander of the Black Sentinels. He's the founder."

"Really?" Ophedia said. "I thought we had been around for much longer."

"There were a few other mercenary organizations, but twenty years ago he showed up and began purchasing their charters, uniting them as one."

"That's how you got involved?"

"No. I met Searn when I was about your age, and he took me in and made me a Sentinel. I've been building up my influence since."

"And the other commanders?"

"Two of them once led those other organizations, and I believe they're interested in taking control now. But, as Searn's daughter, you could throw a rock under the millstone. So, I ask again: Is Searn dead?"

"Yes. I watched him plunge a knife through his eye into his head."

Bolla sat back and sighed. "I'm sorry to hear that. He was a good man."

"He didn't reveal he was my father until just before he died. I wondered why he never made an advance on me, and why he was a bit protective."

"And now you're here in Haven. Why?"

"I came across the advancing Chalician army while journeying here, and I ran ahead with a warning."

"You're the Sentinel who told Deggar?"

Ophedia nodded and finished off the tankard.

"Deggar said he found out from one of his spies, but this makes more sense."

"Are his spies no good?"

"He has a few ruffians who are about as subtle as a bag of rocks." Bolla stood up. "I'd like you to come with me to the council posing as my bodyguard."

"I need to stay here."

"For that man you're staying with?"

"Aurín. He's following a man from Mahn Fulhar who has been hunting us."

"What does this hunter want with you?"

"Searn established a stronger charter with the city and formed

363

an official guild, and when he died, the king insisted our loyalty was to the throne and that we owed back pay on favors from Searn."

"I doubt that is true," Bolla said.

"It is," Ophedia said.

"I'm not doubting you," Bolla said. "I'm doubting what the king said. Searn is never indebted to anyone. He always makes sure the debt flows toward him, not away." She turned to the barkeep. "When Aurín Mateau arrives, have him come to the council at the Aerie."

"Yes, commander," the man replied

"Now we can go," Bolla said to Ophedia.

Ophedia followed her out the door. The woman walked west rather than north toward the citadel.

"Where are we going?" Ophedia asked.

"I walk the wall to the citadel so I can see the army for myself."

In the shadow of a long alley, beggars huddled together with blinds over their eyes.

"I hadn't realized Day Blind had reached this far south," Ophedia said.

"Day Blind?"

"Those people over there are covering their eyes like those with Day Blind up in Mahn Fulhar. Rumor has it people in the Northern Scapes are getting infected with it too."

"It's no surprise. We trade with both. What is Mahn Fulhar doing about it?"

"I'm not sure they are doing anything at all."

They came to a set of stairs just north of where they were exchanging bread for ration papers.

"I heard that it's only Commander Forenor that's selling ration papers," Ophedia said.

"That miser is going to be the first one the people string up if they turn ugly."

"What do you mean?"

"He's one of the Old Guard—a leader of another organization that Searn absorbed, and as soon as word came out that the gates were closing, he minted those ration papers and started selling them. Then he bullied the bakers who were under his thumb to only accept his ration papers, and turn them back into him for less than he sold them for. That's how he has always done business. He pays less in dues to the Sentinel Command and lives like a king."

"Why haven't the rest of you done anything about it?" Ophedia asked.

"Because he also has the farthest reach, with about twenty ships in the Kandar Sea and five more in the Lupinfang, at least half of which are privateers. They'd turn against the rest of the us if we tried to stand up to Forenor. Searn told me a few times, in private, that he thought about putting a crossbolt shaft between his shoulders."

They came to the top of the wall, looking over the army encampment.

"Did anyone know that Œron had formed their own group of Paladins?" Ophedia asked. "I've never been to Œron myself."

"I'd stay out of that country. They barely tolerate Sentinels. Even less so women."

"I think Searn wanted the Sentinels to become something equal to the Paladins," Ophedia remarked.

Bolla turned to Ophedia. "Did he say that to you?"

"In so many words," she said. "Why?"

"He said something similar to me, when we were younger. Do you know he had contacts among the Paladins of the Hammer?"

"I think he did," Ophedia said. "He didn't trust the Paladins, but he often met with men who carried themselves like Paladins, even if they didn't wear armor."

"Did you know that Searn was once a Paladin? That he somehow faked his death and became Searn the Sentinel?"

"That doesn't surprise me," said Ophedia.

They continued to walk up the wall, the guards giving Bolla a wide berth and the Sentinels saluting them.

"Have the Chalicians made any demands?" Ophedia asked.

"They've demanded that we give them the Aerie citadel, as they are, in their words, 'taking control of the forfeited fortresses of the Paladins of the Hammer.'"

"If they do that, they'll take control of the city as well."

"I doubt that. Haven values its liberty too much."

"The guilds of Mahn Fulhar probably thought the same thing before they rolled over."

"I think the guilds of Mahn Fulhar value their business over their liberty, but Limae will fight tooth and nail."

"I know people who may be heading south to rally the southern cities to our aid."

"Any troop movement from the south will be seen by

Castenard's spies, and the Doge of Castenard will move on those cities. He's been edging for an opportunity to expand his control."

"That's what Avarr said."

"Who is Avarr?"

"He has a ranch on the Griffin Road. By the look of him, he was once a soldier. He's one of those who may be heading south at this moment."

"You're intelligent," Bolla said, "but when we get to the citadel, keep your mouth shut unless I call on you. Deggar might remember you, but the others don't know who you are, and I'd like to keep it that way."

"Who should I say I am?"

"Tell a lie, like you did about your two friends Chös and Eunia. "

"I didn't lie," Ophedia said. "I worked with Chös and Eunia in Edi. We faced a Manticör together."

"See, the first part of your lie was better. I know those two are the Clouws, who established the Edi to Garrou escort. They were given Captaincy by Searn, and command of the Blackiron Guildhall in Mahn Fulhar. I'm very well-informed."

Ophedia bit her lip.

"That's a bad tell," she said. "Don't do that."

Ophedia stopped.

"I don't hold your secrets against you, but you should warn your friends that the council is looking for them. And if I find out that turning them in will benefit the Sentinels, I'll do it myself."

"Warn me first," Ophedia said. "Out of your loyalty to Searn."

"Convince me you're worth warning," Bolla said, "by being of service to the council."

38

HAVEN COUNCIL

The founding of the first Sentinel charter is shrouded in legal shadows. There are passing references to Sentinels during the Protectorate wars, but never explicitly as "Black Sentinels." It appears they may have only formed fifteen or twenty years ago, rapidly absorbing several other mercenary charters with authority and diplomacy.

—ON THE FORMATION OF MERCENARY CHARTERS

The Aerie Citadel was built in tiers like the city below it. According to legend, the whole of Haven had once been the tiered farmland of the citadel, until Pariantür gave the land to the people of Limae when they formed their nation. The Aerie rose twenty feet at each of its levels, and on each a castle was precariously perched with tall spires rising over the city and forming an awesome spectacle against the mountains behind it.

"What is up there?" Ophedia asked, following Bolla up the steps to a door that led into the lowest level.

"I'm not sure many have been to the top," the older woman replied. "Some levels have been abandoned, I've heard, and half the stairs have turned to dust with an abandoned griffin's nest moldering at the summit."

They both stepped into the hall barely warmed by a few torches burning on the walls.

"The Paladins just up and left?"

"Many did. Of those that remained, half of them have abandoned their hammers. Their leader died this winter, and if the rumors are to be believed, his replacement may be hiding in this city. I suspect this might be true, but I haven't been able to verify it."

They came to a large hall with black stone walls. "The council is through there," Bolla pointed to the door. "So keep quiet now."

Ophedia opened the door for Bolla and followed her into a large library where seventeen chairs were set around a long table, only five of which were occupied. One of the occupants was Deggar, the burly commander she had met on her arrival in the city. He didn't seem to notice her, as he was speaking to an older man when she walked past him following Bolla to her seat. The older man was distinguished by his white hair and beard, his bright crimson velvet doublet, and his black Sentinel cloak, which hung over the back of his chair.

Across from them a small middle-aged woman, clad completely in black leather, toyed with a long knife and ignored the gestures of the bald man sitting next to her, a man well-dressed and jeweled, with a heavy gold chain securing his cloak around his shoulders and several rings on his fingers. The last man was not a Sentinel, but wore the armor of a city guard. The helmet sitting on the table beside him was topped with a black crest.

"Captain Demaro," Bolla said, taking the seat next to him.

"Commander Elbay," the man returned.

Ophedia stood a few feet behind Bolla's seat. There were three other Sentinels standing guard behind the others. The wiry woman with the knife did not have one.

"Have I missed anything?" Bolla asked the guard captain.

"Deggar and Forenor got into a spitting match over who would take the midnight watch."

"Neither wanted it?"

"They both wanted it."

"I wonder why."

A side door opened and a contingent of ten city guards entered and stood at attention. The guard captain stood respectfully. Three men entered after the guards, the first wearing yellow and black, the same colors flying at the north of Black Street. This was likely Baronet Avis Drime, whose warehouses were responsible for importing foreign goods to the city. The second man was dressed as a ship's captain and entered with a limp, holding a pipe in one hand and a hard leather hat under the other. The third man was a thin, elderly gentleman, warding off the cold with a heavy brown coat, though his bald head was uncovered. They took three seats opposite the guard captain.

Demaro made a gesture of acknowledgement. "Baronets."

"Shall we begin?" the white-haired Sentinel asked.

"Commander Vore has not returned, Hardin," Deggar said.

"There are nine of us here, which is more than half of the seventeen seats. I motion to start."

"Seconded," the wiry woman said.

"Then I, Commander Lor Hardin, call this meeting to order. As the High Commander of Sentinels is not in residence, as there is no representative of the Paladins of the Aerie Citadel, and as the Duke of Baronets, Koll Durass, is not here to head the city leadership, we shall speak as equals, and a supermajority or six is required to pass all motions. All in favor?"

Everyone, including the guard captain, said "Aye."

"The Ayes have it."

"Has anyone had word from the army outside the walls?" Deggar asked.

No one raised a voice.

"Then, in response to our conversation this morning, I say we allow their envoy to address this council."

"I still call that foolishness," Hardin said.

"I agree," Bolla said. "If we invite them into this citadel, they'll not leave. Removing them forcibly will be the same as declaring war."

"I think we can all agree," Commander Hardin said, "that we are already at war, even if we don't know the terms."

The baronet dressed as a ship captain stood, softening his rough voice eloquently. "War with Limae requires a vote of the people, or else that a foreign nation declares war on us. Even when Castenard tried for Trémont three years ago, no one actually declared war."

"Well said, Baronet Gat," Baronet Drime said.

"If we had, though, or if Castenard had," Hardin said, "I still say Castenard would be Limaean by now."

"We're not discussing Castenard," Bolla said. "We're discussing the army that stands at our gates."

No one replied.

Bolla stood and continued. "It has only been one week, and yet they stand there and we allow it. We line our pockets with the sales of unofficial ration papers, and on my way here, I discovered a new malady has come to the city."

"Day Blind, you mean?" Baronet Drime asked.

"You know of it and have said nothing?" Bolla asked.

"It afflicts the poorest. A handful of prostitutes who refuse the protection of the bigger houses are said to have it."

"No doubt giving it to their lovers," the wiry woman said.

"Yet those of all ages have their eyes bound, not simply whoring men."

"What do you propose?" Hardin asked.

"We need to speak with the Chalicians and find out what they're doing here. We can't wait them out much longer."

Everyone startled as a discordant set of knocks came to two separate doors. Bolla motioned Ophedia to one of them, so Ophedia swiftly crossed the floor and opened it to reveal Aurín with three unfamiliar Sentinels and a gagged and bound Abenard Navien.

"I hoped I'd find you here," Aurín said. "I wasn't sure that innkeeper was telling the truth."

"Don't give me away," Ophedia muttered. "Come in, and keep your silence."

Aurín nodded.

"Who is it, Ishé?" Bolla called out.

"Sentinel Aurín Mateau with a Mahndürian spy," Ophedia announced. She could see Navien's eyes start in his head.

Meanwhile twenty Paladins of the Hammer marched in through the other door. Ophedia recognized the Paladin who walked in the lead, who was announced as Pater Minoris Pellian Noss. The commanders and baronets at the table stood awkwardly.

"No need to do that," the Paladin said, motioning them back to their seats. "It is good to know someone has been making good use of the citadel since the fall of my order in the west."

"Then," Hardin said, "it is true?"

"Is what true?" the Paladin asked.

"The Order of the Hammer has fallen?"

"Not entirely, but we've retreated to our primary Citadel-Monastery of Pariantür."

"Why?" someone else asked.

"There was a heresy among the Paladins, led by a former leader of this very citadel. Pater Minoris Jakis Gladen is now dead. The High Priest of Aben in Mahn Fulhar declared the Grissoni Church to be in schism, demanding that they forfeit their claims over their holdings in Mahndür, Varea, Grisden, Redot, and Œeron. I think it goes without saying, especially given the army camped outside your doorstep, that the Aerie was also abandoned."

"Where do you hail from?" Commander Hardin asked. "Are you here to claim the Aerie for yourself?"

"No," Noss said. "I am here to discuss a discourse with your organization, though. I hail from the Fortress of Piedala between Hraldor and Temblin, and I came to ensure that this Aerie library does not fall into the wrong hands. Now that I'm here, however, I see that the Black Sentinels have taken responsibility for the Aerie, and I'm filled with a different hope. I'd like to help."

"The Sentinel Command does not claim the Aerie," Baronet Drime said, standing. "You see at this table seventeen seats. Six belong to the Black Sentinels, six belong to the baronets and guard captains of this city, and five once belonged to the Paladins of this very citadel. If the Paladins of the Hammer are gone, then their seats are forfeit and neither a baronet nor a member of the Black Sentinels shall hold a majority."

"That is a wise arrangement," Noss said. "There are no Paladins who have claimed these seats, then?"

"Primus Slate may have returned to the city, but it is only a rumor."

"Slate lives?" Noss asked. "This is good. He ought to be found. While I mentioned that Pater Gladen was declared by the leadership of the Paladins to be a heretic, he still held command here, and Slate under him. I should like to speak to Slate."

He walked over to one of the empty chairs where the Paladins had once sat. "Will you allow me, and my second in command, to take up seats as representatives of the citadel?"

"And Slate?" Bolla asked.

Noss smiled. "I shall endeavor to seek him out and invite him to join us as well."

"You are not from this city," Drime said, "so how can we know you have our best interests at heart?"

"I may have a solution that will put you at ease. I came to the city with a Nifaran monk, and perhaps we can give her one of the forfeited paladinial seats. Both of your factions shall still hold six each, although I wonder at your empty chairs."

"We've only one empty space," Hardin said. "Commander Yulan Vore is erratic. He appears when he feels like it."

"By my count, that means the Sentinels had seven chairs. Did not Searn VeTurres hold High Command of the Sentinels?"

"When he was here each of us took turns giving him our chair."

Noss turned to the baronets. "And your empty seats?"

"Duke Koll Durass wintered in the south," Captain Demaro said. "He has not returned."

"I see," Noss said.

"If we allow you a place at our table," Hardin said, "should we adjourn until you produce this monk?"

"I will send for her. She'll be indispensable in this coming conflict."

"Then you think a conflict is coming?"

"A conflict is here," Noss said. "The Chalicians have all the western nations under their thumb, and I have reason to believe they've sent representatives into the Northern Scapes and into Sidierata too."

The Pater Minoris looked across the room to Ophedia and Navien.

"Do you know this man?" Bolla asked.

He studied Navien. "I spent early winter up in Mahn Fulhar, and I saw him skulking about your High Commander's compound there."

"Searn VeTurres?" Hardin asked. "You knew him?"

"I did," Noss said with a smile. "If you didn't know, he spent many of our younger years as a Paladin. I was a boon companion of his, before he left."

"The Nifaran," Hardin said. "What purpose would she serve? They all but shun the Nifarans in Œron."

"Even the Chalicians must acknowledge that a presiding Holy Nefer would deal only in fairness. But tell me more of the Chalicians," Noss said. "I only arrived today."

"May we ask how you entered the city?"

"We came with two itinerant storytellers who knew of an entrance on the eastern side of the city."

"A secret passage we do not know of?" Captain Demaro said. "You arrived with an entire contingent of Paladins, without anyone's knowledge!"

"I would be more than happy to share it," Noss said, "for the safety of the city."

This seemed to satisfy the guard captain.

"The Chalicians arrived seven days ago," Commander Deggar

said. "Tomorrow morning it will have been officially one week since they arrived. We were warned ahead of time and closed the gates."

"Then it is a siege?"

"There is an army camped at our door," Deggar said.

"They have stated terms?"

"They have not. They just sit there, like a bad dream gnawing at the edge of thought."

Noss turned back to Hardin. "I understand you closed the gates to them. Why?"

"We received a message that they were coming here to convince us to turn our country over to them and their religion."

"You made a wise decision," Noss said. "I would expect nothing less from their leaders."

"Yet you suggest we welcome their envoy. How do we know you are not like the heretic Pater Gladen?" Baronet Drime asked.

"What do you mean?"

"You mentioned," Bolla said, interrupting Drime before he could reply, "that there was heresy amongst the Paladins, yet you seem not to speak against them—merely speaking fact. Will you please explain yourself?"

"Pater Gladen is what the Paladins call a Motean. He believed that the gods impart power to their followers, and one can weaponize that power and control those around them."

"And are you a Motean?" Bolla asked.

Noss nodded. "From a different school of thought. I believe the gods' powers can be collected and used for the benefit of all. I am not a soldier as Gladen was; I am a scholar and diplomat. Hence why I was assigned to Piedala to continually negotiate peace between Hraldor and Temblin."

"You are here to claim the library of the Paladins and find out what the opposing school of Meteon knew?" Drime asked.

"Motean," Noss corrected. "And yes, I believe there is freedom to be had from the doctrines and dictates of priests and kings."

"You sound like a Limaean," Drime said.

"He sounds like Searn," Bolla added.

"Thank you for those compliments," Noss said. "So, may I join your company?"

There was a general murmur but no one consented.

He motioned to the chair again. "While I am here, I would welcome the opportunity to take this chair, and for my second in command, Primus Gowan Bosch, to take another seat among you. Gowan will admittedly defer to me, and when I am not here he will act in the best interests of the Paladins. We shall seek out Primus Slate who shall take a third chair, while the Nifaran takes the fourth."

"Are any opposed to this?" Commander Hardin said. No one raised a hand.

Hardin motioned for Noss to take a seat. Another Paladin took the seat next to him.

Bolla turned to Ophedia. "Please bring forward the spy."

Ophedia took hold of Navien's shackles and pulled him forward; Aurín pushed him from behind.

"Who is this?" Bolla asked. "For our records."

"This is Captain Abenard Navien. He is a known member of the Voktorra—the guard guild who keep safe the king's castle at Mahn Fulhar. Given that Mahn Fulhar has become allied with the Church of the Common Chalice, it is likely he is here to spy for Mahndür."

"What do you have to say for yourself?" Bolla said, motioning for Ophedia to take the gag from his mouth.

"I am no spy. I am here on official business from King Erdthal, seeking out several Sentinels who must return to their duties in Mahn Fulhar." He gestured toward Ophedia. "Including this woman here."

"By what right does the king make this demand? Especially given you are not in Mahndür?"

"I was arrested by this Sentinel," Navien motioned to Aurín, "at the inn where I was staying. I have paperwork concerning the charter signed by Searn VeTurres and the King of Mahndür. If I am allowed to retrieve it, I can show you that not only did Searn VeTurres personally owe King Erdthal fulfillment of his contract, but that upon his death those debts are passed to Hanen and Rallia Clouw, the verified heads of the Black Sentinel Guild in Mahn Fulhar. I know them to be here in this city."

"As you are being charged with espionage," Hardin said, "you will be placed in a holding cell in the citadel. Your things will be retrieved from your inn and gone through in order to establish whether what you say is true."

"This Sentinel served in Mahn Fulhar, too," he said, motioning to Aurín.

"Then you had better treat him with respect as he takes you to a holding cell. It would be sad if we were to forget you were there."

39

WAKENING

I walked alone in the woods, knowing the danger that lurked within the vül-infested darkness. Little did I know the web that drew about me. I came upon a man cloaked in gray, with coldness as his companion. At his fire I learned to make a proper stew, and the tales he told spoke volumes yet I saw through his deceits and saw him for who he was, the Deceiver. He intended to ensnare me in his ploys, but I gave him nothing, instead gleaning from him the knowledge of where to seek out his secrets for myself.

—JOURNAL OF OLLISTAN GŒRNSTADT

Rallia sat by herself at a table near the hearth, watching an older man and woman in front of the fire, he with a lute in his hand, she with a long pipe that touched the ground. Together they meandered their way through a low, sad song. There was no one else in the room except the barkeeper to entertain, so, with Rallia's coin in their plate, they helped the night wear on. Hanen took the chair opposite his sister, sipping at his ale.

"Do you think Ophedia will find her way here tonight?" Hanen asked.

Rallia didn't hear him, lost in her thoughts as she listened to the music.

The song ended, and Hanen half-heartedly joined Rallia in her applause.

"Is there something else the young lady would like to hear?" the old man asked.

"I just enjoy watching you play with one another."

"We've been playing with one another for many, many years," the old woman said, placing her hand tenderly on the man's forearm.

"Shall we play our song?" he asked.

"I suppose," she said with a quaint smile. She turned to Rallia. "This song is what Arrald played for me when he finally asked for my hand. It has changed a bit over the years, but the base melody remains the same."

The man began to pick at his lute, a light, tender affair that implied a walk through the woods. After a time, the woman on her reed instrument joined in, and their song came out of a forest and alongside a mountain pond. Their musical journey proceeded through many lands, wordlessly, effortlessly, and came finally back to where it began its theme. They fell to silence, placing their instruments across their laps and giving each other a fond look.

Hanen noticed a tear rolling down Rallia's cheek. Ymbrys had come to stand nearby, Whisper at his heels.

"A beautiful song," the qavyl said, sitting between the two of them.

"It is getting late for us." The man stood and gave a bow.

Rallia put another coin in their plate. "Thank you for playing."

"The pleasure has been ours," the woman said, putting the coins into a small purse.

"I've always wanted to learn to play something," Rallia said. "But I fear it's too late."

"It is never too late," the woman replied.

She took out a long satin purse and handed it to Rallia. "Try this," she said. "I carved it myself."

Rallia pulled a small rod from the satin, revealing a reedless pipe. Placing the tip in her mouth, she blew lightly. The note was shrill.

"Try softer," the woman directed, "Try sharper. Try covering the holes along its length, and see what it creates. Either fall in love with this little pipe, or seek out another instrument. Never stop learning."

Rallia gave the woman an embrace. "Thank you."

The woman smiled and left with her husband.

"Why did I never know this?" Hanen asked. "I'd have gotten one for you years ago."

"I never really told anyone," Rallia said. "And I've also never been so moved by a song."

"Enough to want to learn?" Hanen asked.

"I've heard many beautiful songs in my lifetime," Ymbrys said, "but even I cannot deny that song's beauty."

"See?" Rallia replied.

"Maybe I just don't have the ear for it," Hanen said.

"Nor the culture," Rallia winked, then looked past Hanen's shoulder to the stairs.

Hanen turned and watched as Dorian descended. He held a small cloth and approached them with furtive looks.

"We've been here together long enough, and spoken of many things," he said, sitting at the table and placing the cloth before him.

"What is that, Dorian?" Ymbrys asked.

Dorian took the end of the cloth and tipped out a wood-handled tool. A bone-colored ring fell out with it.

"It looks like skyfall metal," Ymbrys said.

"It is, and it was found on Searn's person when he died. Take a look at this."

The qavyl examined the tool, which was as long as a dagger, with a handle of black wood. The metal end was a tube. He looked down the length of it, then at the pommel.

"It appears to be made of a single piece. There is some wear on the pommel, as though it has been hit many times with a hammer."

Dorian pushed the bone ring across the table. "It was punched from the skull of Ghoré. I got the idea when I examined his skull on the way south. It had a hole between the eyes, and the metal tube-like tool fit the hole perfectly. I produced six other holes, and got this ring."

"To what end?" Ymbrys asked.

"I imagine it is how the rings of Searn's bone cloak were made. Searn bound thousands of rings, from countless victims, into the garment."

"As you described in our conversations, it appears to have command of dark shades," Ymbrys said. "They swarmed around him in a similar fashion to the wyloths and furies that harassed you under the command of Ghoré."

"Do you think it might be related?" Rallia asked.

Dorian looked at her. "What do you mean?"

"What if incorporating Ghoré's 'ring' into the cloak gave him control over shades the way Ghoré controlled the wyloths?"

"What if the cloak was destroyed and none of this matters?" Hanen asked.

The three of them turned and looked at him.

"What if we're disturbing ourselves for no reason?"

"I don't want to remember those days either," Dorian said. "But we have no reason to think it was destroyed, and just like the dreadplate, we need to find it."

"Why?" Hanen replied.

"Why not?" Ymbrys asked.

"You say you need to find this armor. Shouldn't we focus on one thing at a time?"

"They're related, though," Dorian said. "I'm sure of it."

"How?"

"Because both the bone cloak and gauntlet were stolen off Searn's body, likely by the same person, and it was taken for a reason. King Erdthal seems interested but doesn't know where to begin looking, which means more people know about them than I would like. I bear some blame for that because I didn't do anything about it sixty years ago."

"Tomorrow Hanen and I can go by the lumberyard again and look for signs of Slate," Rallia said.

"I shall go and speak with some of my own contacts," Ymbrys added.

"I suppose I'll just stay here hiding," Dorian muttered.

"A Motean will know who you are," Rallia said. "We have to assume that much."

Dorian sighed. "I know. I just don't like it."

Rallia laughed and placed a hand fondly on his arm.

"What is so funny?" Dorian asked.

"Seeing someone your age be disappointed like a petulant child."

Dorian scrunched his face and stuck his tongue out at her, and she broke into laughter.

After dinner, Hanen retreated to his room, leaving Rallia by the fire with Whisper beside her and Ymbrys in the chair next to her. Hanen shut himself in his room and eyed his satchel, considering then dismissing the idea of reading the journals. He sat down on the bed and stared at the wall before nearly jumping out of his skin when someone rapped on the window. He was just reaching for an axe as Ophedia's face appeared. Rolling his eyes, he opened the casement for her.

"Come on," Ophedia said as the cold night air crept in.

"You practically sent me to Noccitan," he said.

"Good. You'll need your wits about you," she said.

"Why?"

"I have Aurín nearby."

"I told you not to bring him."

"He doesn't know where you are. Bring your satchel."

"Why?"

"Because you have Searn's cloak."

Hanen gave her a look. "How did you know?"

"I didn't. But I had an idea, so I took a chance and called your bluff."

"What gave me away?"

"You go quiet whenever someone mentions it, and although you agreed when Erdthal told you to find it, you haven't actually tried. I assume you took it off Searn that night."

Hanen pursed his lips. "I don't like that you know that," he said hesitantly.

"Am I the only one that knows?"

Hanen nodded.

"I'm wondering if it'll help Aurín, if he has the coin still on him."

"If it doesn't, I might have something else," Hanen said.

He reached to the bed, grabbed his satchel, and handed it to Ophedia. She put it over her shoulder and climbed onto the roof above while Hanen slipped out and followed her. They stepped across to the next rooftop and descended a ladder to the alley below, which they weaved through before coming to several houses built around an outcropping of stone. The shadows of the mountains loomed above them, erasing the stars from view. Aurín stood against a wall and raised a knife in defense, relaxing only when Ophedia dropped back her hood.

"That took you long enough," Aurín said.

"By design," Ophedia said.

Aurín smiled as he recognized Hanen.

"Hello, Clouw," he said.

"Aurín."

"I have been looking for you."

"Because you were told to?"

"No. We went to speak to that man a week ago, then you disappeared."

"You don't recall what happened that night?"

"I..." Aurín furrowed his eyebrows. "Now that you mention it, no. I don't."

"Aurín and I just came from the citadel," Ophedia said. "You won't need to worry about Navien anymore."

"Why is that?" Hanen asked.

"Aurín arrested him. He's in custody of the city leaders and a Paladin named Pellian Noss."

"That name rings a bell," Hanen said.

"Funny you say bell," Ophedia said. "Noss and his followers all wear bells that are continually ringing. I can't explain why, but it's disturbing."

"I think I recognized him from Blackiron," Aurín said. "He met with Searn a couple of times, although he didn't wear paladinial armor then."

"I remember him now," Hanen said. "He did meet with Searn at least once."

"Then we can only assume," Ophedia said, "that they truly are, er, were, colleagues."

"Aurín," Hanen said, "do you remember much of what happened that night in Mahn Fulhar?"

Aurín gave him a questioning look.

"You say you don't remember the other night when I disappeared," Hanen added.

"I do. We were confronted by those Sentinels."

"What happened next?"

Aurín gave him a blank stare.

"You turned on me and Rallia," Hanen suggested.

"Why would I do that?" he asked, fear dawning in his eyes.

"Why would you attack Paladins in Mahn Fulhar?" Hanen pressed.

"I didn't," Aurín said, standing up. "But..."

"What?"

"I dreamed that I did," he said. "I wake up in a cold sweat."

"Did someone give you a coin?" Hanen asked.

Aurín glanced at Ophedia.

"Where is it?" Hanen asked.

Aurín touched the front of his shirt and looked at the two of them skeptically.

"Aurín," Ophedia said, "I think that coin is still affecting you. You need to get rid of it."

Aurín looked from Hanen to Ophedia and back several times, panic in his eyes.

Then he suddenly burst out crying.

"Shh," Ophedia said, placing a hand on his shoulder.

"I don't know," Aurín whimpered. "Those dreams I have. They seem so real. Like memories I can't shake, but I don't remember!"

"Do you still have the coin?" Hanen asked.

Aurín nodded weakly.

Hanen reached into his satchel, thrusting his hand through the boneshroud and into the heavy gauntlet, drawing it out.

"Hanen," Ophedia said, "you surprise me."

"This isn't what you think."

"Isn't it?"

"It's the other one."

He raised his hand, held out at Aurín.

Aurín didn't looked up, continued to cry, Ophedia's arm over his shoulder now.

Hanen felt something in his palm and saw Aurín's shirt move.

"What?" Aurín said, looking up suddenly. He saw Hanen's gauntlet-encased hand and stood up, looking for somewhere to flee.

"Stop, Aurín," Hanen said. "I'm going to help you."

He closed his fist and pulled back. Something tore through Aurín's shirt and flew toward Hanen, which he caught in his gauntleted palm. The coin sat there with the dull glow of cooling metal. Meanwhile, Aurín fell to his knees and clutched his chest, gasping for breath.

"Aurín?" Ophedia said, placing a hand on his back.

Aurín looked up, a huge grin on his face as tears streamed down his cheeks.

"I... I feel awake for the first time in months," he said. "What did you do?"

Hanen shoved the gauntlet into his satchel.

"Hanen?" Aurín asked. "I feel like I've been teetering on wakefulness and sleep for I don't know how long."

"It's passed now," Ophedia said, looking at Hanen's satchel with an arched eyebrow. "Do you remember coming here? After you arrested Navien?"

"I remember some things. Like, I know it's spring now. I know

I'm in Haven. But I can't remember why."

"Let me take Hanen back to his inn and I'll return and we can go to ours."

Hanen walked with Ophedia to the other side of the street.

"You know that gauntlet can undo everything Searn did," Ophedia said. "It could make up for the damage he caused."

"To what end?" Hanen asked.

"What do you mean?"

"If I do that, will I draw the attention of the dark gods? Will they come after me?"

"It's a bit late to be worrying about that, even if they exist. And I'm not so sure they do."

"They do," Hanen said, thinking of Wyv on his throne and the words he had for Hanen. "I think Ghoré is proof of that."

Ophedia turned to leave.

"Ophedia," Hanen said.

She turned back.

"Will you keep it quiet? What I have in my satchel?"

"I kept Searn's secret, but more out of fear of what he might do to me if I told. Do I need to worry about that?"

Hanen shook his head. "I'm still trying to figure this all out myself."

"Then you figure it out or get rid of it. The longer you take, the closer those dark gods you fear will come to finding you."

40

OBLIVION

Gird yourself against the cold, with truth over your shoulders to block the winds of deceit. Camaraderie shall be wood on the fires to stave away envy and strife.

— OLD NASUNIAN PROVERB

Seriah did not notice him enter. The chair she sat in chafed through her thick robes. The smell of the stew in the bowl before her gave off a rancid aroma. Even the blinder over her eyes seemed blacker. Over it all pealed the deep tone of the bell, set in the middle of the table, just out of reach.

"You've not touched your food," Pellian said.

She did not jump. She wasn't sure if she could. The ringing tone made her weak.

"You are free to move about the room, of course. You merely are asked not to leave."

She did not reply. That sound grated on her mind.

"I've just come from a council of sorts. The leaders of the city have asked my Paladins to join them. Their council includes wealthy businessmen, Black Sentinels, and us Paladins of the Hammer. They've asked that a Nifaran take a seat at the table, too—to act as mediator. Apparently you're the only Nifaran here, and so you shall join me and go to this council. They are hoping to invite a Chalician from outside the walls to hear what they have to say."

Seriah opened her mouth to speak but could not. She raised a weak finger and pointed toward the bell.

"Most do not remain so long under the bell's influence," Pellian said. "Perhaps it is because you are blinded by your vow as a monk. Still, while I could remove it, I encourage you to continue to push against it. If you can find the willpower to move and act normally while the bell tolls, you'll be all the better for it. All of the men under my command have overcome it. It provides us each a clarity over the noise of the world, and over our own little bells."

"Wwwwhy?"

"On the road up from Birin you seemed distracted. What you needed was relief, and that is what our tiny bells give us. I'm sure they have not sat well with you, but you have not thought of the thing that makes you flee your own order. Is that not a gift?"

She felt him rise from his seat, after which the bell stopped pulsing and every sound in the room returned. She took a sudden gasp for air.

"We're leaving in an hour," he shouted. Then he cleared his throat. "I apologize. I seem to have been hollering over the bell's peal. We're leaving for the council in an hour. Our other guests have asked to say goodbye to you before they leave the inn."

He walked to the door.

"She is in here," she heard Pellian mutter.

The temperature of the room plummeted. Seriah tried to rise in panic, but her muscles were still too weak.

"Stop that, Kash," the gravel-filled voice said. "You're scaring her."

The cold suddenly stopped.

They both dragged chairs out from the table and sat across from her.

"What an interesting couple of days," one of them said.

"What do you want?" Seriah drawled.

"Only to formally say goodbye, and to say thank you."

"As you said several times on the hour-long ride into the city," she replied.

"Because we can't thank you enough for what you did for us. We'd have come in here earlier, but that bell..."

"It grates on our minds, Nair," the other said.

"I do not wish to speak to you. Ever again," Seriah said, courage rising up through the fear.

"We cannot promise that we shall never speak to you again," Nair said. "But we can give you a word of advice—as a recompense for your trouble."

"I will not accept it," Seriah said. "I cannot. My soul is forfeit enough from that message you made me deliver in Mahn Fulhar."

"Leave behind this supposed Paladin," Kash said. "He bears no goodwill for you."

"Knowing that these bells keep you from me," Seriah said, "I would stay in this prison for the rest of my life."

She felt cold creep back into the room.

"Kash, control yourself," Nair said.

Seriah reached out and found the bell, which stood in a small wooden stand with a mallet next to it.

"Leave me be," she said, raising the mallet.

"Do not do this to yourself," Nair said. "You do not know what you do."

"I know that I can cast you from this room with the strike of this bell," Seriah said, a rising confidence coming into her heart. "If I had the ability, I would make a bell large enough to cast you from this world entirely."

"You foolish girl," Kash said. The temperature continued to drop.

"I deny you, as Nifara did," Seriah said.

A low growl came from Kash, and she felt the same from Nair. She struck the bell. The sudden wash of sound killed the cold, and the two of them ran from the room. She dropped the mallet as feeling left her body once more. The memory of their meeting in Mahn Fulhar and the message she had delivered to her goddess fled from her mind as fast as the two dark gods had left the room.

"Where did they rush off to so quickly?" Pellian said, re-entering the room and extinguishing the bell's sound again.

"Will we be taking this bell with us to the council?"

"I should think not. We'll all have things to discuss."

"Will the tiny bells you wear beside my ears do the same?"

"Do what?"

"Keep darkness from my mind. Numb me against the pain."

"Are you asking me for bells of your own?"

Seriah nodded. She would do whatever she must to keep away the uncomfortable and unclean memories of the dark gods addressing her as a friend.

41

SHADES

Power is a fleeting thing, but the gifted power from the gods is permanent. Only by experiencing such power can one truly understand.

—PATER STEEL OF ORMACH

Nichal lay on his face, arms outstretched, legs straight behind in the traditional pose of deep prayer at the St. Rämmon chapel. The Standard of the Anka had been placed in front of the ælerne and hammer hanging from the wall. Jined sat in the back pew, staring at Nichal and pondering the words of Zoumerik.

"Do you think Zoumerik might be right?" Didus asked, taking a seat next to Jined.

"I'm not sure," Jined said. "I worry that there has been some misstep—that Grissone has in some way abandoned this cause."

"By what reasoning?"

"He has not appeared to me since that night in Mahn Fulhar. I wonder if I said something wrong."

"I highly doubt that," Didus said. "Do you think that the choice Dorian made, along with Nichal, was too hasty?"

"To fall back toward Pariantür?"

"To leave our holdings in the west. Did Grissone say anything to you after the incident at the Crysalas Convent?"

"He didn't," Jined said. Then he gasped. "That was after the decision had been made. He had been there in my mind, watching from my eyes when they came to that decision. He would have said something. Right?"

"There you go," Didus said. "Then why is there a hesitation?"

"You feel it, too?"

Didus nodded. "Ever since we arrived at Waglÿsaor."

"Ever since we came to the center of town," Jined corrected.

They both grew quiet for a moment.

"It's the same feeling I had before this, but left behind in Mahn Fulhar," Jined said.

"Or similar to the feeling that weighed on me when I was under the influence of the gauntlet," Didus added.

The door behind them boomed open and Zoumerik marched in with several Paladins behind him. He walked past Jined and Didus, giving them a commanding glare, and approached the prostrated Nichal.

"It is time we discuss the future of our order, Pater Guess," Zoumerik said.

Nichal continued to pray.

"As I said at the square before the hospital, you'll answer for your actions."

Jined stood, but three of Zoumerik's Paladins blocked him from leaving the pew.

"You're to be put on pillory," Zoumerik said, his voice rising in timbre. "You must answer to the higher authority."

"What authority?" Nichal rose to his knees without looking up at Zoumerik.

In response, the Pater Minoris stepped between Nichal and the Standard of Grissone.

"By the authority given to me by the Order of the Hammer."

"Not by our god? Grissone?"

"Of course," Zoumerik said. "And that authority trickles down the order to me."

Nichal rose and stood nose to nose with Zoumerik.

"You forget yourself," Nichal said. "You forget whom you speak to. I am acting Prima Pater, besides which I still hold twice the authority you do as Pater Segundus of your Vow of Poverty. You have no right to put me on pillory. I can take your station away as quickly as Dorian Mür gave it to you."

"Not if you have been deemed unfit."

"I was deemed fit by Dorian Mür when he put me on this pillory I pilgrimage to now."

"What do you mean?"

"When Dorian forfeited his position and granted me the title of acting Prima Pater, he granted it to all remaining Pater Segundii. Each shall stand in Pillory-Judgement at Pariantür, and all of our actions shall be weighted against one another to determine who among us shall lead—just as it was when he became Prima Pater. If you hadn't removed the book of law from your collection that would justify the Act of Living Authority, my men and I would not have pored through all of the books and found the Accords of Pater Velitab, the silent Prima Pater who forfeited his title in the Imperial Year 1764. You cannot put me on a Pillory, while I am already on one."

"More reason to place you under arrest and march you back to Pariantür."

"You'll not do that," Nichal said calmly. "And you and I shall have no more need to fight once you've been freed."

"Freed?" Zoumerik said.

"When we tore apart your personal library of law books, we also went through the entire library of this fortress. We found something, covered in ages of dust, which is probably the source of this contention between you and I."

Nichal glanced at a side door that hung ajar. It opened to allow Jurgon to enter with Silas, each holding two dusty books.

"Do you recognize these at all?" Nichal asked.

Zoumerik shook his head.

"Within these covers are pages and pages of scrawling madness," Nichal said. "I think these are shadebooks."

Jined caught his breath to keep from gasping.

Jurgon gave the book in his hand to Nichal and brought over a brazier.

"Do you know what a shadebook is?" Nichal asked.

Zoumerik shook his head again.

"There is a secret sect of Paladins who have delved into dark mysteries. Some dominate the minds of others with the use of coins made from an accursed metal, while others create these books, in which the shades of those who have died are held in a half-life and denied the Judgement of Noccitan. These fallen heretics are known as Moteans."

Zoumerik gave no indication he had ever heard the word.

"They're destroyed only by flame."

He put the book into the bronze bowl, and Silas placed the second one on top.

Nichal took a candle and set the second book aflame.

"Dorian has ordered me to return to Pariantür under the guise of acting Prima Pater for the sake of our order, to root out the Motean philosophy. You would be wise to help rather than hinder me."

"Was this show meant to convince me of something?"

"My friend, and the chosen champion of Grissone, Jined Brazstein, was given a shadebook at St. Hamul to deliver to Mahn Fulhar, which influenced him against warning us about the destruction of the Crysalas Dweol. The shadebook was discovered only after the Dweol's destruction, and the death of the man he was meant to deliver it to. That man, Primus Melit, spoke with me on several occasions, asking whether a parcel had been given to one of my Paladins, to deliver to him. I had no knowledge of it. He continued to press, indicating that the parcel would be coming from you in particular."

A memory suddenly snapped into Jined's mind. He recalled who it was who had given him the Shadebook.

"I..." Zoumerik said, "cannot remember giving it to Brazstein."

Zoumerik fell to Nichal's feet and began to sob. "Why can't I remember?"

"Open your satchel," Nichal said.

Zoumerik fumbled to take the satchel off his shoulders, and rummaged through it. "What is this?" he cried out, finding a black cloth-wrapped square at the bottom.

"You've not seen this before?" Nichal asked.

"I have. It...has always been there. Yet... Why can't I remember?"

"Because you have been under the same influence," Nichal said.

"How?"

"We do not know, but I wager this is not the only shadebook carried by an unwilling brother. I've noticed your countenance change when you are here in the fortress wearing that satchel, or dressed in sackcloth and preaching in the city with clarity and a discerning mind. And yet, its influence somewhat affects you even then. You were drawn to don this satchel when you returned to the fortress?"

Zoumerik nodded, his head hung low.

"Then let us free you," Nichal said, placing the shadebook into the brazier along with the burning books. The cloth binding took flame and a howling scream exploded from the brazier accompanied by black smoke. Zoumerik gasped, now on his hands and knees, as though he might retch.

Then he began to laugh in relief.

"You're free now, Pater Zoumerik," Nichal said, reaching down to help him to his feet.

Zoumerik rose and gave a weak smile.

"I feel free."

"Then why don't I?" Jined said. "There is still something hanging over the fortress."

"I feel it, too," Didus muttered.

Zoumerik turned to the chapel of Paladins. "Who else among us is under the same oppression?" he inquired.

Five of the Paladins took a step backward.

"Seize them," Zoumerik said.

The others took hold of them and extracted five more shadebooks from their satchels. These too were cast into the flame, although they did not burn with the same effects. The men fell on their knees only to stagger to their feet again, with looks of relief on their faces.

"This calls for a day of confession," Zoumerik said, turning back to Nichal once more. "To realign myself with the faith. With Grissone."

He turned and marched out with a smile on his face, accompanied by the other Paladins. Meanwhile, Jined and Didus walked to the front of the chapel.

"How did you know?" Jined asked.

"I realized that since we arrived Zoumerik has not once said 'Grissone.' It led me to believe that he was not following our god's will, but the will of something else."

"That I did not remember who gave me that shadebook in St. Hamul may have been an effect of carrying the book for so long."

"Now that it is destroyed, perhaps a semblance of normalcy will come to the fortress now," Nichal said.

"Then why don't I feel like this is over?" Jined asked.

The twins walked into the chapel, a determined look on their faces.

"What is it?" Nichal asked.

We just passed Zoumerik in the halls, Loïc signed. *He was shouting orders to those of the fortress.*

"Saying what?"

To some he ordered they join him on his journey to town,

Cävian said. To others, that they lock down the fortress until he orders otherwise.

There was a sudden wave of supernatural relief that washed over Jined. The others had similar reactions.

Jined looked around. "What was that?"

"You felt that?" Nichal said.

"I think we all did," Jurgon said.

Nichal turned. "To the gates."

They marched out of the chapel and through the halls. Primus Beltran Cautese appeared around the corner.

"What is happening, Prima Pater?" Beltran said.

"Where is Zoumerik?"

"He just left the fortress with a cart bearing what looked like our entire library, leaving a complement of Paladins behind under orders to let no one else leave."

"So nothing changed," Nichal said.

"Something changed," Jined said. "I think the remaining shadebooks were just taken away by Zoumerik."

"If he's taking the entire library," Nichal said, "and the city is demanding more miracles, then the city is on the verge of becoming a zealous mob."

"And nothing sparks a mob more than a book burning," Jurgon said. "It is the next logical step."

"What makes you think that is happening, Jurgon?" Nichal asked.

"It has been mere moments since we burned those shadebooks," Jurgon said. "There is no way Zoumerik had time to gather all of the books from the library. This is all playing according to his plan."

"Plan?" Nichal replied.

"When the shadebook Jined carried was destroyed," Jurgon said, "it knocked him out for days. If Zoumerik was carrying one for even longer than that, why didn't he pass out himself?"

"We need to get to Waglÿsaor," Nichal said, his face darkening.

"There are twenty Paladins stationed at the door."

Cävian and Loïc looked at one another, then to Nichal.

Fight our way out? they both signed.

"I know another way," Jined said.

42

REASON'S PYRE

To hunt the heretic does not bear the fruit of their forgiven soul. It is a means of proving your control over their salvation. The heretic is hunted so that, by their destruction, others will know there is no hope for those who take even a single step down that path.

— UPDATED CHALICIAN CODEX, WORDS OF

PRAEPOSIT ANHOUIL CHÉTAIN

"Regardless of what happens," Astrid said, "the Rotha must be taken east."

Onelie stood alongside the Sister Superioris, now in full regalia.

"What is out east?" Onelie asked.

"Hopefully friends and allies," Katiam said, "who can help to unravel Larozh's secrets."

"Everyone is on edge throughout the city," Fedelmina said. "Anyone may suspect our movements, no matter how careful they are. However, people say an event of some sort is taking place at the Saor this evening, and we will use the distraction to move you out of the city and to free Little Maeda at the hospital."

"I pray she is safe," Onelie said.

"Sigri Smith and I have not seen eye-to-eye at times,"

Fedelmina said, "but she has never had anything but the safety of the vaults in her heart. She will not betray that."

"She does seem to consider Zoumerik her authority, despite the title she's taken," Astrid said.

"She believes in structure," Fedelmina said, "as I do. I couldn't balance the exchequer if I didn't. But I believe she still has much to learn, too."

A door at the end of the vault opened and Esenath appeared, leading someone whose eyes were covered in a blinder.

"What is this, Esenath?" Katiam asked.

Esenath led the blind girl forward, and guided her to sit in a chair.

"You'll remember that last night I left to go and conduct an experiment. Several, in fact. They seemed to have worked. I wanted to try one more time, in everyone's presence, to confirm I've not gone completely mad."

"And who is this?" Astrid asked.

"This is Sister Derah Baker," Esenath said.

Katiam stepped forward and dropped to one knee. "Sister Baker, I didn't see you in the vault last night. You of all people I had hoped to bring sight to."

Katiam began to open the bundle.

"Actually, Katiam," Esenath said, "I have something else we're going to try."

She turned to a table, took out a small ceramic jar, and tipped something out. Then she returned to Sister Baker's side.

"Sister Baker was one of the first in the city to be stricken with Day Blind. It's gotten bad enough to affect her work at the bakery."

"I've taught the others as much as I could," she said, "but I can't bake much myself."

The edge in her voice had gone. She had the care of a mother in her voice now.

"Sister Baker," Esenath said, "if you'll open your mouth and put out your tongue..."

Esenath placed a small gray pearl on her tongue, which Sister Baker swallowed.

"What was that?" Katiam asked.

"One of the little pearly pebbles the Rotha made after taking away the Day Blind. I tried it out last night on several Day Blind children who had been blind the longest. It takes effect after an hour."

"What does it do?"

"The same thing the Rotha does. It heals."

"How?"

Esenath held the jar up to Katiam. "Smell."

Katiam did, and wrinkled her nose.

"What does it smell like?"

"Mushrooms. Or mold."

"I think that is what Day Blind is, a fungus carried on the wind from somewhere to the far north. When the Rotha takes it in, it converts it into an antidote."

"But how?"

"How does grain turn to beer? How do we eat and gain energy? Because we are meant to."

"You don't want to know how?"

"Of course I do. But for now, I'm going to accept this for what it is. A miracle."

They worked together preparing the last satchels of food. A sack of nuts and parched grains went into each one, and when a woman came and announced the setting of the sun, they all gathered near the entrance.

Fedelmina would walk with Esenath, Astrid with Onelie.

"Who am I to go with?" Katiam asked.

"Me," Sister Baker said, rising.

Esenath approached her and touched her elbow. "Are you ready?"

The younger girl nodded. Esenath reached up and untied the wrapping and removed it. Sister Baker had her eyes closed, and Katiam held her breath as the girl opened them, blinking against the light of the torches. Then she collapsed to her knees, sobbing.

"Shhhh," Esenath said. "It's all right. There is hope. Maybe it will just take longer."

"No," Sister Baker sobbed. "It worked. It actually worked."

Katiam began crying as the others joined in.

"Then you can see?" Esenath asked in confirmation.

"Not fully," Sister Baker said. "But yes, it is better. And the light doesn't hurt!"

Esenath pulled the girl into a hug. "Then there is hope. For everyone."

"What do you mean?" Katiam asked.

"I have an idea. I'll consult with Fedelmina on the way. Let's go. I'll tell you once we escape the city."

ANDREW D MEREDITH

Katiam helped Sister Baker to her feet. "Are you all right to walk through the city?"

"Yes," the girl said, her face streaked with tears. "Of course."

Esenath and Fedelmina took the lead, followed by Katiam and Sister Baker. Astrid and Onelie took up the rear, and the guardian of the vault closed the door behind them.

"The pebble healed me," Sister Baker whispered as they walked arm-in-arm down the street.

"Heeeeel," the Rotha whistled from within the bundle at Katiam's chest.

"What was that?"

"A secret I cannot share right now," Katiam said. "But perhaps on the road east."

"Oh, I'll not be going," she replied. "I'm only here to see you out of the city, and to help Fedelmina."

"But she is going too," Katiam said.

"I don't think so," Sister Baker said. "She won't leave knowing Little Maeda is in trouble. She dotes on her like a daughter, the way the Matriarch Superioris doted on you."

"And you won't leave because of the children."

Sister Baker nodded. "There are more Moon-Eyes in hiding than anyone realizes. I'll continue to help them as best I can. If things get too bad in this city, I'll take them by cover of night to someplace safer."

"The college in Thementhu."

"I don't know what that is. But if that is where you think I should take them, I will."

"The college is in the country of Nemen. It is friendly to the Crysalas. They would protect you."

"Thank you," Sister Baker said.

As the light of the setting sun dimmed in the west, a new light lit the city several blocks ahead.

"What is that?" Katiam asked. "Where is that?"

"That is near the Saor, I think," Sister Baker said.

"We aren't heading that way."

"If we're going the direction I think Fedelmina is leading, we'll pass near but not through that square."

"I don't like the look of that. It takes a big fire to make a blaze that bright."

The pairs up ahead turned a corner and disappeared from view. Katiam and Baker came around the same corner to find three

Paladins on sleipnir blocking Fedelmina and Esenath.

"And as I said," one of the Paladins was remarking, "we're under strict orders to ensure all go to the center of the city."

"We're imploring you, in the name of the Rose, to allow us passage."

"Not tonight, Sister," the Paladin said.

Fedelmina and Esenath turned and began to walk away. They passed Astrid and Onelie, unseen in the shadow of an alley. One of the Paladins urged his sleipnir into a walk behind the two women, ushering them toward the central square.

"Gather those two as well, Brother Varib," the lead Paladin called. He pointed to Katiam.

Katiam sighed and crossed the street to walk alongside Fedelmina.

"Will Astrid follow us?" Esenath whispered. "I do not think she has been spotted."

"She'll not abandon us," Katiam said. "But how well she'll follow in secret remains to be seen."

The sound of the crowd ahead grew; their figures cast dancing shadows upon the wall by the flame.

"What are they doing?" Katiam asked.

"Oh no," Sister Baker said.

"What?"

"None of you are from here," Sister Baker said. "But there are old tales from back when Waglÿsaor was no more than a place where tribes of Üterk gathered. They'd gather from the forests surrounding the Saor, stack up the wood, and set it alight. Most of the city's moral stories are from those dark days past. Tales of creatures who moved in the night to steal away naughty children. Tales of vül. Tales of the Moon Eyes."

"Moon Eyes?" Katiam asked. "Like those with Day Blind?"

"We took that name as a joke at first," Sister Baker said. "But the old stories of the Moon Eyes are those who spent too much time in Dream. In the Purple Veld. Their eyes were said to glow when they returned to the light of day. Supposedly, the Veld was closest when all of this city was a vale of trees."

"And the Saor?"

"The legends of the Üterk say that it fell from the sky, long before the trees rose and were burned in sacrifice."

"Now people are doing it again," Katiam said as the crowd nearby swallowed them up, pressing them forward with those who danced and marched in a parade spiraling toward the center. Katiam could make out the massive form of black iron reaching up into the sky, with a fire burning around its circumference. The people spiraling toward it brought more fuel in the form of broken furniture from their homes and even fine cloth.

"Why are they doing this?" Esenath said.

"That's why," Astrid said, appearing next to them with Onelie at her side. She was pointing to where a wagon had been set up as a stage, atop which stood Pater Minoris Zoumerik with the Almoner Stevan Filip and Dane Marric. Below the cart, Sigri Smith and several of her nurses stood at attention, with a burlap-robed Sister Maeda Salna.

"Little Maeda," Katiam muttered.

"Mmmaaaeedaaah," Larohz whistled.

"I don't like this," Astrid muttered to Katiam.

Zoumerik stepped up to the banister of the wagon and held up a hand. After a few moments the noise and movements stopped, and only the roaring fire made a sound.

"Penitent people of Waglÿsaor!" he began. "My brothers and sisters seeking the faith. Your cries for mercy, for healing, are legitimized with continual acts of contrition. The sickness that has befallen you is but a symptom of greater transgression, and by your sacrifice shall it be forgiven! But a rumor of false healing has brought a falser hope—as proven by the other maladies that continue to fall upon you."

"What is he going on about?" Esenath muttered. "The healing of the Day Blind should be a good thing."

"Shhh," someone nearby hissed. "Don't draw the ire of the Gospelers. If someone speaks against them, a fine is paid."

"Your secrets," Zoumerik boomed, "fester and burrow, laying the foundations for hidden crypts. Not the vaults of protection, offered by the long and much respected societies of women. I am not here to condemn them. I instead speak of the secrets kept for long centuries, of insurrectionist cells, of homes and cellars deeper than any basement. This city has at its very heart a spirit of malice, a curse upon those born under its shadow. I speak of that abomination."

He pointed to the towering black iron.

"Tonight, we light the fire to burn it to the ground. Too long has it stood in mocking defiance. Too long is it the cancerous symptom of a heart of hate. And so, I say unto you—throw in whatever can make this flame hotter, and let the flames fan our hearts toward true contrition. Let tomorrow dawn with a new people, neither Bortalian nor Boronii, who shall bring the flame of contrition to the ends of Kallattai!"

"He's spouting madness," Astrid said.

"He's inciting the people to fanaticism," Esenath said.

"Well, that too," Astrid said. "But I was more referring to that slab of iron. If it is iron, you can't melt it with wood fire. It would need to be torn down and smelted."

"I don't think that's his true aim," Onelie said. "I think he's doing what my father does with new soldiers, breaking them down and building them back up in the way he wants. If he wasn't a Paladin preaching contrition, I'd have said his words were seditious to both Bortali and Boroni."

"Paladin or not," Astrid said, "that's exactly what he's doing. I think he means to establish Waglÿsaor as a city state on its own."

"All are called to bring sacrifice," Zoumerik continued. "If not wood or cloth, then a contrite heart, or knowledge of the false healing of the Day Blind. As the heat burns away and purifies, so your admittance shall do the same."

"Oh no..." Fedelmina said.

The crowd parted, and through the gap a new cart appeared. A Paladin rode atop it and began passing objects from the back to people nearby. They began to cast the objects into the flames.

"No!" Fedelmina said, surging forward.

"What is it?" Katiam asked.

"They're burning books," Astrid said.

Katiam saw Esenath's hand go to the satchel at her side.

People began tossing books and wood into the fire. Boys cavorted nearby, breaking pieces of furniture up to feed to the flames. A man punched the man next to him, tore a sack free from the other's shoulder and tossed it in, the crowd laughing as the first man cried out in protest. Esenath could barely hold Fedelmina back as she tried to charge through the flying debris to gather up the precious books being burned.

"So much knowledge," the old woman cried, falling to her knees, unable to approach the blasting heat of the flames. Esenath fell beside her. Their tears were dried up in the heat.

"We cannot let this happen!" Fedelmina said. "Are we not scholars?"

Katiam helped pull Fedelmina back into the crowd, away from

the bright flames.

"Hhhheeeet," Larohz whistled.

"What have you here?" a man said, taking hold of Esenath's satchel. "Brought something else to burn?"

"No!" Esenath cried as the man tore it free and shoved a filthy hand down into the bag, bringing out *The Chloïs Book of Flowers and Their Uses.*

"A book!" he said, holding it up and letting it fall open. The images Esenath had illuminated by hand glinted in the light of the flame.

"What kind of evil is this?" the man said.

"You!" Zoumerik called from twenty yards away.

The man turned toward the wagon.

"What have you there?" Zoumerik asked.

"A book with flowers in it!" the man called. "Looks like dark evils."

"Bring this offering," Zoumerik said.

The man marched toward the wagon, the crowd coming behind the women and pressing them toward Zoumerik. Dane leaned forward and said something in Zoumerik's ear. Sigri stood unflinching as she watched them approach.

The man handed the book up to Zoumerik then dropped to his knees.

"Will this offering pay for my freedom?" the man asked.

"Freedom?" Zoumerik replied.

"You sentenced me to street cleaning for a transgression against the law."

"What was that transgression?"

"I took a whore into my home."

"Consider yourself forgiven," Zoumerik said with a flippant wave of his hand. "Go and do not do it again."

The man fled into the crowd.

"You are the botanist," Zoumerik said to Esenath. "Why are you here?"

"It appears I have little choice."

"I mean why are you here in this city? Are you not a member of the college at Thementhu?"

"I was."

"I've sought you out all this day and the last."

"Why?"

"I heard you may be able to explain the healing of the Day

Blind. Sister Salna has not been forthcoming."

"If Day Blind were healed, why the need for these flames? For the destruction of people's homes and means of warmth? Of the knowledge contained in books?"

"I do not care what burns. I care about answers. I care about that thing that permeates this city with its stink. And it is a metaphor for the hidden cities I did not know lie underneath this one."

"Why should you care if there are secrets under this city you do not know of?" Astrid said.

"I am the spiritual leader of this city and Sigri Smith is its physician. To heal the body, one must know its workings, inside and out. Don't you agree, Sister Borreau?" he looked directly at Katiam.

"So you try to scare the people of this city with fear and terror?" Astrid asked.

"I lead with the firm hand of a father."

"What of Prima Pater Guess?"

"He'll be leaving soon enough. That has already been seen to."

He held the book up once more. "Now, will you help me, Esenath? Or will you be cast out along with all others who question my authority?"

Katiam looked at Esenath, and then at Sigri, who returned her glance briefly. Little Maeda watched Zoumerik with a hint of rebellion in her eyes.

"I think Maeda is going to make a move," Katiam muttered to Astrid.

"I left my city in Tranu in Sidierata," Esenath said, "for the rise of the despot whose corrupt descendants continue to rule in his stead after killing their own father. Chaos and destruction shall never bring about order."

"Very well," Zoumerik replied.

He cast the book into the fire.

Esenath screamed; Astrid and Onelie prevented her from rushing to save her book, but someone else pushed past the three women and walked confidently toward the flames. It was Fedelmina Barba, and she walked into the fire to retrieve the book, clutching it to her chest before taking a step forward and collapsing. A cry of horror rose from the crowd as another figure broke free, this time from near the wagon. Little Maeda rushed to the fallen woman and began dragging her from the edge of the inferno, a portion of which collapsed, throwing burning embers onto the still form of Fedelmina and setting Little Maeda's burlap aflame. Sigri Smith surged forward with Onelie and Astrid and pulled Little Maeda back, slapping at the flames on her clothing until they were extinguished. But it appeared to be too late. Her skin and hair were blackened; she did not breathe.

"Take her away from here," Zoumerik said with disgust and a wave of his hand.

Sigri looked up at him. "How dare you."

"You and I can have words later, Smith. Take her to where you can heal her. Begone."

Sigri looked up at Astrid who stood over them. Katiam had crouched down next to the still form of Little Maeda.

"Is she..." Sigri said.

"Let's get her back to your hospital," Katiam said. "We'll not know until then."

Someone appeared with a wheelbarrow full of debris. Astrid shoved her way to the owner, tipped the contents out, and they placed Maeda into it.

"What of Fedelmina?" Sister Baker murmured.

"She is gone," Astrid said, putting a hand on the girl's shoulders.

They came to the edge of the crowd as it continued to grow.

"Take her to the hospital," Astrid ordered Sigri.

"You do not tell me what to do," Sigri said, stepping up to Astrid. "You answered to me in the entourage, and you'll defer to me in this city."

"You forfeited your authority over me long ago, Sigri. Take her. See your nurses heal her. But I'm leaving this city tonight with anyone who will leave this Pantheon-forsaken place."

"I'm not leaving," Esenath said.

Katiam looked around. "What?"

"I have work to do with Sister Baker."

"Me?" Baker said.

"We'll discuss it later. For now I have something I need to do, if only for the memory of Fedelmina and for the knowledge lost today."

Onelie stepped forward and revealed a burlap-covered bundle, which she presented to Esenath.

"What is this?"

"Little Maeda rescued it from the arms of Fedelmina. I took it from her while no one was looking."

"Oh..." Esenath said, clutching it to her chest.

"Now will you go with us?" Katiam asked.

"No," Esenath said. "I will see Little Maeda to the hospital. You leave now, and I promise I will see you soon. Sister Baker, please come and help me. We have Moon-Eyes to find."

Esenath turned to the wheelbarrow which Sigri now pushed.

"Consider who you throw your lot in with," Astrid called after them as they moved away toward the hospital.

Astrid turned back to Katiam and Onelie.

"Well?"

"It appears that Zoumerik could care less whether we leave the city," Katiam said.

"Will you leave with us?" Astrid said to Onelie.

"Waglÿsaor has become unsafe. I can't stay here. Maybe my road takes me with you, or maybe I find Shieldmaidens and journey to the Isles of Bronue Jinre."

"I thought I recognized you," a snide voice called from the darkness.

From an alley a Paladin stepped out. The fire lit his face just enough for Katiam to recognize Dane Marric.

"You're the daughter of Jarl Clemmbäkker," Dane said. "Word is you had disappeared."

"What do you want, Dane?" Astrid asked.

"I want this city to be brought to humility, not to this inflammatory zeal." He waved in the direction of the crowd. "I want the three of you away from this city."

Katiam was curious. "Why?"

"Because you've brought strife here, and because I want the daughter of a jarl far away from this city if we're to gain what we seek."

"What do you seek, Dane?" Astrid asked. "Power? Worship?"

"I want what I always have. Fealty to Grissone."

"How is it you are talking to us?" Katiam asked. "I thought you were not allowed to speak to women."

"I've come to realize that I cannot reach the lofty goals of this new faith if I do not allow myself to change."

"It appears we've all learned lessons in the last year," Katiam said. "If you're going to help us, can we be going?"

Dane nodded and turned, leading the way.

They came to the front gate, with two guards atop it.

"Open," Dane demanded.

"By whose order?"

"Gospeler Dane Marric."

The door cracked open.

"Leave now. But do not go to St. Rämmon," Dane said. "If you are there when we return from the city, I cannot promise you'll ever leave."

Katiam, Astrid, and Onelie turned and walked out of the city. The gate boomed closed behind them.

"Vvvbooom," Larohz whistled.

43

SLAB OF HERESY

You have cast your sins unto the sky,

And in response it showers ash upon your head.

Made hot by furnace unknown, it rains upon the land.

None can know its origin. None can make it bend or break.

All is brought low. And it shall stand a testament for ages to come.

—BOOK OF VYRIAB 5:7

Jined came to the gap in the path before the others, motioning for them to stop.

"I'll make this leap first so you can see how far it is," he said. "I only achieved it on prayer."

Nichal pushed past him and made the leap without hesitation. Loïc threw his hand over his mouth to stifle a laugh of surprise.

Nichal looked back across the twenty-foot gap.

"Jined?"

The big Paladin whispered a prayer and made the leap. Nichal knelt against the cliff, lighting another torch. Jurgon jumped next and almost missed the landing, but Jined caught his gorget and pulled him the rest of the way. Silas followed and would have fallen into the waves if Jined and Jurgon hadn't caught him. Beltran leapt, then Koel, and finally the twins made the jump, hand in hand, landing further than anyone else.

"Do I have the least faith?" Silas asked Beltran.

"If you're to compare yourself to Loïc and Cävian, you're in for a lifetime of disappointment. I know no one with more faith than those two."

"Even Dorian Mür?"

"Löic and Cävian together have a compounded faith. I doubt there is a man alive who can equal the power and knowledge those two bear."

"Beltran," Jined said, and then corrected himself. "Primus."

"No need for formalities, Jined. You're a Primus now yourself, officially in the Order Leadership—and I prefer you to call me Beltran, honestly."

"Very well. Beltran."

"What is it?"

"I have a rather awkward question to ask."

Beltran gave him a look of interest as they walked down the path.

"What do you know of the Moteans?"

Beltran nodded. "More than I ought to, I'm sure. Is this because I mentioned the power the twins bear?"

"I think it's important to know where you stand."

"I came upon the beliefs of the Moteans in my youthful research," he said. "Gallahan Pír was my mentor then, and I brought the subject up. When he explained his past as a Motean, I acquired a lifelong obsession with the philosophy, and after studying the subject with him I came to the conclusion that their theories contain valid ideas."

"And you subscribe to those theories?"

"If you're getting at whether I follow the Motean beliefs, I do not. I think they are like toxic mushrooms wrapped in bacon, tossed to anyone that will eat them. But I do think they are onto something."

"What do you mean?"

"In short, they believe that power is bestowed by the gods. When the gods part with that power, our mortal frames can use up that power if we have the ability to hold onto it. But I think the hubris of that belief is the falsehood."

They came to the lookout over the hidden harbor. The little ship was gone, and the harbor was derelict.

"Follow my lead," Jined said, "although I don't know where we'll go once we're in."

Nichal nodded and they followed him to the façade of the underground city. Within, the sparse candles lit enough of the place for them to avoid tripping, and they quietly moved through dark streets and alleys. Suddenly light bloomed ahead from a fountain-like feature, around which a few women and children talked amongst themselves.

Jined crouched behind a corner.

"Do we stop and ask directions?" Nichal said.

"Until we must, let's not reveal we're here."

"A bit too late for that," a woman's voice said, and they turned to see an unfamiliar Paladame standing there.

"If you weren't the acting Prima Pater," she said to Nichal, "I'd be turning you in to yourself. I am Sister Loban. Explain your trespass."

"Sister Loban," Nichal said, offering a salute. "Pater Minoris Zoumerik, in a breach of authority, locked us away in the fortress. We sought a means to escape our confines and the pathway led through here. For that I am sorry."

"How did you reach the harbor?"

"In a leap of faith," he said.

"Sounds like we'll need to widen that gulf in the path," she said.

Nichal chuckled. "It won't take much. It was not an easy leap, even by Grissone-ordained miracle."

"Wait here while I fetch help—and blindfolds."

A few minutes later they walked in a line, eyes covered, hands over the shoulder of the next man. Jined could hear those around him murmuring as they watched the procession. After an interminable time they came to a stop; their hostess spoke to someone ahead, and a door boomed open for them to proceed.

"You're approaching a set of stairs," a woman said as they passed.

"Thank you, Sister," Nichal said. "You'll not see us come this way again."

"Promise us that," a woman said.

"I swear it."

Someone fumbled at the head of the stairs, but their steps soon led into an even rhythm as they climbed a spiraling staircase, were guided around some turns, and finally came to a stop.

"You may remove your blinders," sister Loban said.

Jined blinked in the brightness of the room.

"We're in the hospital?" Nichal said.

"We are," Loban said. "Now go. There is word that a gathering is happening at the Saor."

"Thank you for your trust, Sister Loban."

She merely nodded and watched them leave. No one guarded the hospital doors, and the square outside was empty except for several women entering with a wheelbarrow.

"To the south," Jurgon said.

He was pointing toward the women, two of whom brandished their maces as they saw the Paladins.

"Mother Smith?" Nichal called out as they crossed the square.

"How did you recognize her in the dark?" Jined asked.

"I know her figure and manner," Nichal said.

"Prima Pater," she said, approaching.

"You recognize my authority now?" he asked.

"I have made a mistake."

"What happened?" Nichal asked, looking at the body in the wheelbarrow.

"A tragedy," Mother Smith said. "She threw herself into the flames to try and save Fedelmina Barba, who had gone in to rescue a book."

"Who is it?"

"Little Maeda," Esenath said with a sob.

The twins stepped forward and crouched next to the wheelbarrow. One of them placed a hand on the girl's head. Brittle hair broke free at his touch. Loïc looked to Nichal.

She is not dead, he signed.

Jined dropped to his knees beside the twins.

"Paladins," Nichal called, drawing closer with Didus, Beltran, Jurgon, and Silas, all of them placing their hands on the girl.

"Grissone and Anka, twin-souled and connected, by your grace, bring your power to bear."

"Let not this woman leave her mission unfinished," Nichal continued. "By your will, let her be healed; cause her to smile on others once more."

Little Maeda suddenly gasped and began to whimper against the pain of her burned flesh.

"Be a balm to her wounds," Jurgon muttered. "Let her sleep in restful dreams of healing."

The soft crying of the woman subsided.

"I am always amazed by this," Mother Smith said, looking to her nurse attendants. "Bring her to the hospital, apply griefdark and gauze, and see that the physicians do all in their power for her. I'll be along shortly."

When the nurses had left with Little Maeda, Smith then explained what had happened at the fire, with apologies for the part she had played. Nearby, Jurgon spoke quietly with Esenath. Jined split his attention and listened to them speak.

"Then they are gone?" Jurgon said.

"They just left," Esenath said. "I imagine they'll be well along the road tonight."

"They were to take me with them," Jurgon said. "They had news of my wife."

"I'm going after them, but I need a couple days to prepare. If you help, you can go with me."

Jurgon nodded.

"I have been in error," Smith was saying meanwhile to Nichal, "and I humbly beg your forgiveness."

"Consider it given," Nichal said. "Will you join us on our march east?"

"No," Smith said. "I must continue my work here, no matter what. This city is likely to enter an even darker time, and someone must see it through."

"I will not be returning to the fortress," Nichal said. "I am abandoning it to apostasy."

"I shall see that those who speak against you are brought to justice," Smith said. "There are enough Paladames here that we can take them by surprise, although it saddens me that it has come to this, a war between Rose and the Hammer."

"There is no war," Nichal said. "I'm going to that bonfire to kill the drækis."

"Be careful," Smith said.

Nichal turned to the others. "Let's go."

"Not me," Jurgon said. "It is time I said goodbye as well, although our roads may yet cross. I am going with Esenath after Katiam and Astrid, who has news of my wife."

"What news?" Nichal asked. "The report is that she died with the World Rose."

"Apparently she did not, and she asked me to find her when my mission was concluded. I've taught Silas what he needs to know, and it is time for me to go."

"Very well," Nichal said. "But not before I give you your reward."

He walked up to Jurgon and placed a hand on his shoulder. "By my authority, take with you the blessing of the Order of the Hammer, Primus Upona."

"Primus?"

"I don't have cordons to give you, but you are Primus now. Dorian had long meant to give you that promotion."

Beltran stepped forward, removing his cordons.

"Take mine," he said. "I second that you deserve this for your service. I'm sure we'll find new cordons for me later."

Nichal nodded in approval, taking the cordons and attaching them to Jurgon. Then he handed him a ring. "Take Dorian's signet ring as your mark of authority. Go and find your wife, wherever she may be."

Jurgon nodded and turned to go with Esenath and Mother Smith.

Nichal looked at the twins and Jined. "Cävian, unveil that standard and follow me into battle again."

The twins gave him a grim smile.

"Jined?" Nichal said. "Lead the way."

The inferno lapped up the massive slab of iron, heating the square like a full sun in a desert. People danced around the flames in a frenzy, and Zoumerik stood atop the wagon, barking out commands to bring more fuel for the fire. He glanced at the Paladins entering the square and faltered. Then he held up a book in his hand.

"See now as we continue to burn away the evils of the past," he said. "I found this book, known as a shadebook, in the office of the man who calls himself Prima Pater!"

He leveled his hammer at Nichal; the crowd turned to face the Paladins.

"Let us burn this book, and with it the sins of Nichal Guess!"

Jined and the twins stepped forward before Nichal as a shield.

"Seize them!" Zoumerik ordered.

The crowd surged forward.

"Grissone, offer us protection," Jined muttered. "Burn bright a light of hope."

A sudden flash rippled out from Jined and the twins. The people took a step back.

"Where did they go?" someone shouted.

"Come on," Jined said, pressing forward. "We need to take this fight to that man."

The crowd jolted in surprise, unable to see him as he pushed past them.

He broke out into the center of the square, Zoumerik glaring at him.

"How did you escape the confines of the fortress?" he called. "This city humbles itself, and you shall humble yourself before this night is done."

"To what aim?" Nichal came through the crowd, which was still dumbfounded by the flashing light.

"The aim of bringing about a new era for man," Zoumerik said. "One where we take our fate into our own hands."

"You're a Motean," Nichal said. "The book you hold is testimony of that."

Zoumerik tossed it into the flames, where it caught fire. But no black shade exploded from it.

"It is nothing. You are nothing. You stand in the way of this city's true repentance."

He gave a command and ten of his Paladins charged forward.

"Eagle formation," Nichal ordered.

Jined leapt forward and attacked the first heretic Paladin as the twins rushed in from his sides, their three strikes taking him down. The second heretic charged at Jined, but he counter rushed and lifted the man up with his shoulder, throwing him back several yards. The twins took down a third Paladin together while Nichal and Beltran rushed to take out the fourth. The defeat of half their number gave the remaining heretics pause.

"Do you not see how his actions against us speak, Stevan?" Nichal shouted at Stevan, who stood next to Zoumerik with a look of horror on his face.

"Do not listen to him," Zoumerik said. "We act in humility, for the soul of this city."

"But in whose name?" Nichal shouted, striking down another heretic.

Zoumerik did not reply.

"Ask him who he serves," Nichal called out. "Ask yourself who you serve."

"I serve the city in the name of Grissone," Stevan called.

"Then why are you blinded by the actions of Zoumerik—a Motean and a heretic. When did he last speak a blessing in Grissone's name?"

There was hesitation in Stevan's eyes.

"Do not listen," Zoumerik said. "They seek to lead you astray."

"Whom do you serve?" Stevan asked.

"I serve this city," Zoumerik said.

"Then this is all a lie?" Stevan asked, crying out in horror. "You had only to call upon Grissone. But you do not!"

Zoumerik backhanded him. He toppled off the cart head first. His neck snapped and he did not move.

"No!" someone shouted, diving into the cart. It was Dane Marric. "You heretic!" Dane swung his hammer, striking Zoumerik across the chest and throwing him off the cart. "You killed him! You were a pacifist, and now you're a vowbreaker."

He leapt off the cart.

"Jined, go!" Nichal shouted.

Jined charged forward to stand next to Dane.

"This is my fight," Dane said to Jined. "Stand down."

"It belongs to all of us."

"He misled me."

"He misled all of us," Jined replied.

Zoumerik stood to his feet. "I brought truth no one wanted to acknowledge."

"Shut up," Jined said. "No truth comes wrapped in lies."

"What about that?" Zoumerik said, pointing to the Saor.

"What about it?"

"Can you feel what hides within? A metal from the sky. We Moteans have sought out its secrets. It is our primary purpose."

"At the cost of your souls."

"To understand the secrets the gods keep from us."

"How dare you assume you know better than the gods," Dane hissed. "That you know more than Grissone."

Jined gave Dane a wry smile.

"What?" Dane snapped.

"I had worried about your belief," Jined said. "That perhaps the Moteans had their claws in you long ago."

"Even the faithful can be led astray by silken tongues of draekis."

"I don't recognize that verse."

"It isn't a verse," Dane said. "It's something Amal Yollis often said."

Dane turned back to Zoumerik. "I'll offer you one final chance. Confess and show your contrition."

"Hah!" Zoumerik said. "To what purpose? Being marched off to the penitent Fortress of Durance?"

He reached into his satchel and took out a long pin. Jined gasped.

"You've seen this before," Zoumerik observed.

"Searn VeTurres used it."

"Searn was not always his name. I knew him as the silent Paladin Roderig. He was the one who brought me into the fold, and now I'll do as he did. Why prevent me?"

"There is still the opportunity to pay for your actions in this life," Jined said. "Please. You saved my life as a young man. Do not throw it all away."

"The secrets I know are enough to anger the gods against the souls of a hundred men." He sighed. "I have the secret to cheating death at my fingertips, and it comes to this."

"Drop it, Zoumerik."

"I took the name Dusk among the brothers because I thought I'd bring about the dusk of the order, the dawning of a new one. But I see now that it fulfilled its own prophecy. I'll not see the dawn."

He unlatched his hammer, and held it toward Jined.

Dane stepped forward to take it.

"That's not a Parianti hammer," Dane said. In the light of the flame, Jined could see it was made from the skyfall metal they had seen in Mahn Fulhar.

Zoumerik looked at Jined, then sneered. "If I die, let the miserable rabble join me."

He swung around and threw the hammer with great force toward the flames and the Saor. It struck the metal with a dull clang, then a pulse throbbed out from the hammer. The flames at the base guttered, the metal groaned, and the Saor began to lean toward them.

"Away. Away!" Jined shouted as people began to scream and flee.

Zoumerik stood his ground and laughed as the rusted metal tower fell upon him. When it hit the ground, Jined was thrown a hundred feet, rolling to a hard stop. The pain in his arm, broken the year before, flared up again. After the dust settled, he forced himself to his feet and looked around. Dane was fifty feet away, pulling himself up out of the rubble. The twins helped Nichal out from under a pile of debris, and then the three of them lifted a piece of twisted metal off Silas Merun, his left arm mangled. In the middle of the fallen Saor stood a giant orb of twisted metal like a broken egg, twenty feet tall.

"What is that?" Dane said, coming to stand next to Jined.

"I don't know. But I'd imagine it is what Zoumerik sought."

Nichal hobbled up, holding his bruised hip.

"Dane," Nichal said. "I am sorry if I ever doubted you."

"You ought to have doubted me," Dane said. "I was led astray, and now I cannot leave these people who have given themselves wholly to his lies, in good conscience. I cannot abandon these holdings of the Hammer while Zoumerik's work must be undone."

"The Chalicians will come and demand you give the holdings over," Nichal said.

"Then we shall stand against them," Beltran said, "with older laws still. Parianti Law was adopted as a basis for the foundation of the Chalician sect."

"Are you sure what you do is not infected by Motean thought?" Nichal asked Dane.

"I will see that it is not," Beltran said. "As I said, I knew Motean thought and I ought to have seen it in Zoumerik."

"We shall work with the Crysalas as well," Dane said.

Nichal gave Dane an odd look. "Not words I thought would come from you, Dane."

"I was foolish in my youth," he said.

"You're in your forties," Nichal said. "Six months ago is hardly your youth."

"But I've lived under that pretense since I took my vows, and it has held me back."

"Reconsidering the benefits of women?" Nichal said, with a wry smile.

"I shall never break that vow," Dane said. "But I cannot deny that the Hammer and Rose must stand together or fall together."

"Then I give you and Beltran the Fortress of St. Rämmon," Nichal said.

"There is another problem," Beltran said.

"What is that?"

"Rumor of this night is going out. It will provide reason for Bortali and Boroni to move on Waglÿsaor and take it under their strong arm."

"Then set yourself 'free' of the Hammer," Nichal said, "and take matters into your own hands. Zoumerik sought to free this city from all other nations. Push harder. Make Waglÿsaor a free city under this Grissoni faith."

"I shall see it done," Dane said.

413

44

APPEAL

Gather unto yourself the power required. Store it up with avarice for the future.

—BROTHER DOUBT

Aurín now stood alongside Ophedia. The last Sentinel commander, Yulan Vore, sat not far from Pater Noss' second-in-command. Both looked to be cut from the same cloth—suspicious of those around them, yet seeking to be seen and respected by colleagues. They were half-heartedly talking with one another. Captain Demaro had been replaced by another city guard captain while he stood on watch at the wall and arranged for a Chalician representative to join the council. At the head of the table sat the Nifaran monk. Ophedia knew her from the trip north to Mahn Fulhar, although she did not mention this to anyone, nor did she speak to the monk.

The monk, Seriah, now had two small bells hanging from her eye blinder. They chimed quietly and in synchronization with the bells on Noss, his second, and the other Paladins standing at attention. The more Ophedia thought of the bells, the more she realized that the Paladins wore not one or two, but several on their persons. She wondered at their significance, and why the monk now wore them as well. There was a loud knock at the door and two more Paladins walked in and stood at attention.

"Announcing Provost Weskar Abrau, of the Order of the Chalice, requesting the opportunity to speak."

Commander Hardin looked around the table as the others

nodded, then gestured solemnly to Baronet Drime, who stood and placed both hands on the table.

"Let the Chalician Praetor enter," he said.

The man who entered practically charged into the room, wearing a sleeveless coat of light blue over full armor. He removed his flat-topped helmet and placed it under one arm, holding a short Chalician spear with a sleipnir hair tassle at the end. Five other Praetors marched in behind him, long spears held at attention, their helmets strapped tightly under their chins. One of them broke rank and came forward with a book. Standing just behind the Provost, he unclasped it with a flip of his hand.

"Greetings, Provost Abrau," Baronet Drime said. "Welcome to the council of Haven. As you can see, we are made up of representatives of power, authority, and mutual respect." He pointed to his baronets, then the Sentinels, and finally to the Paladins of the Hammer.

"I am honored to have been invited. It is with trepidation that I do come after so many days left unwelcome at your gate."

"It is not our custom," Drime said, "to host armies that march upon us."

"You did not receive our message, then?"

Drime shook his head.

"It appears there has been a miscommunication. We sent a cordial message stating our intentions, and we were angry when we arrived at the closed gate. I shall endeavor to call off those who are coming to help our cause."

"What cause is this that requires a show of force, accompanied by reinforcements?" Commander Hardin asked, turning to face the Praetor.

"Show of force?" Abrau replied. "We come in peace, hoping that we might use this city as a base before proceeding to Düran."

"Then you did intend to occupy this city?" Drime asked.

"Of course not," Abrau said. "We've come to take what has been lawfully given to us—this citadel—to live in peacefully."

"By what legal means?"

"The High Priest of Aben and the King of Mahndür declared the holdings of the Hammer forfeit to the High Priest and his ally the High Missioner, who gave the various bastions, fortresses, and citadels over to the Praetors of the Chalice. Those countries that belong to the Chalician and Abedürian sects of the Abecinian church are now united."

"Then why do you need access to the citadel and free rein to continue to Düran?" Drime asked.

"Düran is a country under both Abedürian and Morrig church sects. It is important that those loyal to the Abedürian church work together to ensure our entire church is united."

"I think you can safely assume that none of us are informed on the politics of religious sects. To what end is this done?"

"The Abecinian church is made up of four sects. Three now, if you take into account the uniting of the Chalicians and Abedürians. The other two sects are the Morrig Church, and the much smaller Luzoran Hermits. The latter is likely to be easily absorbed, and the Morrig Church shall capitulate to us eventually, after which the Church of Aben shall stand united."

"Then you mean to enter Düran," Drime said, "and force the country under your authority."

Abrau shook his head. "We mean to envelop the Morrig sect into our embrace."

"What part does Limae have to play in this?"

"Your country is under the authority of the Abecinian church."

This produced light laughter among several of the people at the table.

Abrau gave the council a quizzical look.

"Your country does not give allegiance to the Grissoni church, or else you would answer to the citadel. Instead you hold an alliance with it. All men who have no allegiance to another deity have fealty to Aben, by divine right."

"This is the first I've heard that," Commander Hardin said. "Anyone else?"

The others all gave a shake of their head.

Abrau made a motion and the Chalician holding the book opened the cover, leafing through the heavy parchment. Finding his place, he held the book out to Abrau.

"Book of Morrig, 5:24," Abrau began. "Spake Grissone then unto his father,'They hath forsaken me, and thus I them. For if they'll have not their creator, then I shall bide my time, and allow only those that seek me in faith to come under our wings.'

'And yet they came unto my throne,' spake the Father of the gods, 'and begged that I, people-less, shall be their god, providing the means by which they might come into my kingdom.'

'Give them the words and speak scripture they can follow, and let them choose for themselves whether they seek your path or my faith, for I shall never again force them to my will.'

'So be it,' Aben said, 'that all men who do not subject themselves to your faith shall be beholden to my path. They drink their own judgment from my cup, and shall give their testimony before the judge.'

And with that Grissone departed."

Abrau closed the book and gave it back to the other Praetor.

"And so you can see, you are under the authority of the church."

"That is an interesting interpretation," Pater Noss said.

Abrau did not look at the Paladin but continued to look at the Sentinels and baronets.

"If that passage is to be taken at its value," Noss continued, "that conversation between Grissone and Aben intended to show the free choice of man, not to place man under Aben's authority."

"Who are you," Abrau said, "to interpret the scripture of a god you call not your own?"

"I am a Pater Minoris of the Paladins of the Hammer. I bear an authority earned by blood and sweat and not a commission purchased, as the authority of the Chalice is."

"And yet," Abrau said, "my authority is granted, purchased or not, by the head of our church. Your own church has no leader. Your former Prima Pater is dead, and his replacement is only temporary."

"You are well informed," Noss said. "Regardless, your assumed authority over the men and women of this council is unfounded."

Bolla stood from her chair. Noss and Abrau turned to consider her.

"You can have a theological debate later," Bolla said. "It is more important to the rest of us what your intentions are."

"Peace," Abrau replied. "By whatever means."

"You'll have to give us more than that barely veiled threat. What role would the citadel play in this council? What would be done with the Paladins still in this country?"

"We grant the Paladins time to pack up their belongings and leave, although we would like the opportunity to negotiate retaining some of those belongings."

No one responded.

"The Paladins of Ormach have been granted a year to remove themselves, which they capitulated to at the beginning of last summer."

"Strange that they would not say anything," Pellian said.

The Praetor did not respond or look in the direction of the Paladin

"To answer your previous question," Abrau said, "members of our own order would take the seats. We would be granted freedom to travel within the city. Trade would improve with western nations."

"What is that supposed to mean?" Baronet Drime asked.

Ophedia dropped to one knee next to Bolla. Several eyes turned to watch her, including the Praetor.

"Citizens newly brought under the Chalician church," Ophedia muttered to Bolla, "have no rights to trade, even with one another, but are first required to take part in the Chalician religion to show their allegiance. They're second class 'citizens' to any Œronzi."

"It's not permitted that junior members speak in this council without being first addressed," Commander Deggar said.

Praetor Abrau's eyes bored into Ophedia as she returned to her place.

"Apparently," Bolla said, looking around the table, "other countries brought under the protection of the Chalicians are treated as second-class citizens."

"Second class to whom?" Commander Deggar asked.

"Œronzi," Bolla said.

"What is the reasoning behind this?" Baronet Drime asked Abrau.

"Varea and Mahndür have been brought under our protective wings by two colleagues of mine who are not nearly as reasonable as me. I am thankful, for your sake, that Provost Zehan Otem was not sent to your city. He is a determined man, but he does not understand the intricacies of your government. He believes only in tiered authority, and that those of lower tiers are meant to be ruled."

"And you, as a military entity in your order, do not?" The diminutive, black-clad Commander Domic looked around the table. "While known to hold the title of 'Catechist' among the Praetors, Provost Abrau is third son of Œronzi General Armain Abrau. He was only turned over to the Praetors at the request of the head of the order."

"You are well informed," Abrau said. "My mother, however, was Limaean. Not many know this, as she died when I was very young. When the decision to begin the expansion of our church took place, I begged for the opportunity to ensure that Limae was given an offer by myself—because I have long studied the laws and customs of Limae, and desire to see them continue to flourish."

"Then you're proposing the council continue to act as it does?"

"I'm proposing nothing change in this country, save that the holdings of the Paladins be turned over to the Praetors."

"The monk has remained silent on this," Baronet Drime said, turning to look at Seriah.

The monk leaned forward. "There...has been nothing to say. Nor has there been means yet to negotiate a peace."

"Then I think it best to thank you for coming to this council," Drime said, turning back to the Praetor, "and ask you leave so we can confer in private."

"You would allow this Paladin from Piedala to have a say on this council, but not myself?" Abrau said.

Noss said, "I fill a traditional role to ensure the Sentinels and baronets remain fair to the people."

"The seats the Praetors take would not get in your way," Abrau said, looking at the Sentinels and the baronets. "We would give our input in regards to dealings with other nations, but we would abstain from all decisions regarding the citizenry of this nation. The Sentinels and land-holders would be free to do as they choose." The Praetor gave a curt bow. "If you will excuse me, I shall now return to my camp."

He walked to the door, the other Praetors following him, but then he stopped suddenly and turned back to the table.

"I will, however, ask that you come to a decision quickly. I promised the heads of my order that I would deliver the citadel to the control of the Chalice three days from now. If I do not, Inquisitor Otem or one of his lackeys will arrive to take control of the situation. And as I said, they have a very different approach to authority and proselytization than I do."

He turned and left.

"If we give the Praetors this citadel," Deggar said, "he promises not to interfere with this council's decisions."

"That does not mean they will not try to influence us," Noss said. "They would most certainly be a thorn in our side." Noss turned to Drime. "Imagine a year from now, when the Chalicians offer you swathes of land in Varea if you'll give up your holdings in this city and your seat on the council." He turned to Commander Forenor. "He could grant your ships tariff-free entry in Œronzi harbors, if only you would join the Church of the Common Cup."

He then addressed the entire table. "The Chalicians have power to give, and the more they take, the more they will be able to offer. But where does it stop? Who will stand against them when the entire world bows to them?"

"If we stand against them," Drime said, "our country may be wiped off the face of Kallattai."

"What army can erase the memory of Limae?" Noss said. "What power could wipe out the tenacity of Limaean liberty?"

"You suggest war," Seriah spoke up. "I was not called here to stand in judgment over a war."

"But what of standing up against injustice?" Noss said.

Seriah hesitated, then sat back.

"What are you proposing, Paladin?" Drime asked.

"I meant to take the library and leave, but now I wonder if it's not better to stay and see this through."

"We have much to think upon," Drime replied. "My colleagues are welcome to join me at my home, and I imagine the commanders would like to confer amongst themselves."

"May I send Primus Vade to join you?" Noss asked with a smile. "I also ask to stay with the Sentinel Commanders, to ensure our order is doing everything it can to reach a mutual agreement. Limae will stand as one, for or against the Praetors."

"I believe we can agree to that," Drime said. The baronets and the guard captain left with their entourages.

Commander Domic nodded to one of the last guards, and Ophedia saw him wink in reply.

The door closed. Noss walked to the other end of the table and looked at one of his Paladins. "Brother Meinshül, will you please see our Nifaran guest back to her chambers?"

The Paladin helped the monk to her feet, and they walked out of the room. The other Paladins left, leaving only Noss standing there with the Sentinel Commanders.

"Was the monk only a pretense?" Commander Deggar asked.

"You see through me," Noss said. "She was here to legitimize the meeting, and set the Chalician at a relative ease. But now we can talk freely, I should like to propose an even better plan, which will not only free Haven of Praetor dominion, but also place this council of Sentinel Commanders in control, just as it always sought to be."

45

DARK TOOLS

The Archive sat at the edge of a dry basin overlooking the desert below. Tales had been told of the secrets kept there, and what happened to intruders, so it was only out of desperation for food and water that I crept within those halls. I lived almost as a rodent for two years, gleaning knowledge and stealing provisions, and I might have continued on there had I not begun my journey of discovery, first in my homeland of Ikhala, then wherever there was hunger, thirst and ignorance in the world.

—JOURNAL OF OLLISTAN GŒRNSTADT

"The Chalicians aim to move quickly into Düran," Noss said, "to play their hand against the Morrig church. If Limae falls to their control, Düran's resolve will be weak. I am here to offer an alliance."

"Between Pariantür and Limae?" Hardin asked.

Noss shook his head. "Between the Black Sentinels and Moteans."

No one responded.

"I'm proposing for you to do what Searn VeTurres intended to do from the beginning, peaceably creating a new order of knights by uniting my Paladins here with you commanders."

"You've already made it clear that the Moteans are the reason the Paladins of the Hammer are in schism," Hardin said.

"Because of the choice of one faction out of four," Noss said. "Those that are now under Slate were the fools that revealed themselves in Mahndür. My small but tight-knit faction was stationed at Piedala. I have taken a risk in traveling here to Limae, not only to save this country from ideological destruction, but to absorb the knowledge and men under the command of Slate."

"What exactly are you offering us Sentinels?"

"A new order, with a new rank for each of you and a seat at this council in the name of the new order. You would have a controlling majority of seats."

"What of the women among us?" Bolla asked.

"What of you?" Noss replied.

"The Paladins of the Hammer are an exclusively male order."

"And I've never seen a woman hold any position of power in Œron," Domic said.

"You would not be the Paladins of the Hammer, but something new entirely. All would be welcome."

"You'll have to give us more than just your word," Commander Forenor said.

Noss made a motion and several of his Paladins stepped forward, each laying out silk-wrapped objects before their leader.

"My men and I are scholars and ambassadors. We've kept the nations of Hraldor and Temblin from each other's throats for a very long time. When we are not doing so, we are studying. And we have made a study of the tools of each Motean faction our primary purpose."

He opened the first one, revealing several bells of various sizes.

"These are called Resonant Bells, made from a metal that falls from the sky and, until a few years ago, considered unworkable. These bells ring with a tone you may have noticed on my fellow Paladins. The smaller bells, once you grow accustomed to them, help scholars concentrate. The bigger ones, though..."

He took up a larger handbell, and tapped it with a hammer, producing a sound that rang suddenly, violently. The nearest commanders grabbed their ears.

Noss placed it back on the cloth, smiling.

"Noccitan!" Deggar said, checking his ear for blood.

"Had it continued," Noss said, "your ears would have bled. But I am not here to harm, I am here to enlighten."

He opened up another cloth. Within lay a featherless quill and a small book.

"The brothers in the north call themselves the 'Order of the Feather,' and they use these quills to place the souls of the dead within the pages of books like this one. They have other skills at their beck and call, but this is the most important."

Deggar, then several others, began to laugh out loud.

Noss opened the book, touching the quill to his wrist and then to the paper. A moment later words bloomed on the page. Deggar started back, no longer laughing. Noss glanced around the table, then touched the third cloth; within lay a pile of coins.

Ophedia saw Aurín take a step back, gripping his axe tightly.

"I see by the look on your face that some of you recognize these," Noss said. "From what I've gathered, these coins are able to command the wills of others. When we find Slate and absorb his people into our own, he'll share with us by what means he does this, and by what means he makes his other tools."

"Other tools?" Deggar asked.

Two more Paladins came forward and placed down a sledgehammer and a pair of axes. The hammer head was made of a single piece of dark, twisted black metal. The axes were edged with the stuff.

"I believe Slate has more of these and possibly the means to make more. While the first items I showed you are the most powerful, I have no doubt that these weapons are much more suited to your desires."

"What do they do?" Hardin asked.

"If I struck a hammer head and dropped it to the floor, everyone in this room would die, and these axes have unbreakable blades. I have seen one of them shear through stone and steel. If we could make more of these, they could be a symbol of our new order."

Bolla stood.

"All you say is tempting," she said, "I'll not deny that. But why tell us this? Why offer this to us? Why not just take power from us entirely?"

"I certainly could have," Noss said. "But I am not Pater Gladen. I am not a commandeering general who seeks conquest. I am a scholar. I seek to have at my disposal the opportunity to study, and I believe the library here holds many secrets gathered by the Moteans, and by Searn VeTurres himself. That is vastly more important."

"What of Searn?" Bolla asked. "He betrayed the Paladins and it cost him his life."

"He made a move to take over Gladen's order by force, and got the manticör's sting. He was the highest ranking Motean, yet he chose to work from the shadows. I intend to lead from the top of this citadel by the legitimacy of my hierarchical organization allied with this council."

"What of your god?" Deggar asked.

"What do you mean?"

"The Paladins of the east follow a god, Grissone. You are a Paladin yourself."

"This new order would not," Noss said.

"You forsake your god?"

Noss shook his head. "I seek a new path. One of human learning and understanding."

"You deny that he exists then?"

"Certainly not," Noss said. "I merely choose to align my goals away from his guidance. We use the tools made of a metal unknown to the gods, nor indeed even referenced in history."

"Metal greater than the gods?" someone else said.

"Unknown, rather. Whether it is greater or not remains to be seen."

"What must one do, to join this new cause?" Bolla asked.

"That is open to negotiation, but just as your organization acknowledges ranks by the tools they carry, those that elevate into these higher ranks shall be known by the secrets they hold."

A Paladin entered the room and knelt before Noss, whispering something before quickly departing again. Noss looked around the table, and his eyes fell on one Sentinel Commander.

"What is your name?" Noss asked.

"Vore," the seedy man said.

"It appears you've been holding out on us. We've all been seeking Primus Slate, and you've had him at your inn for weeks now."

"What?"

"One of my men found him there and followed him to this very room. No one likes a surprise attack. I shall allow you to walk to that door over there and bring Slate out so he may address us cordially."

"I don't know what you're talking about," Vore said.

"You do," Noss said with no emotion in his voice. "And if he follows through with the plan you've already agreed to, I'll see to it that you're dead before the day is out."

Vore sighed and he pushed his chair out. Several of the others gasped, but Bolla and Domic only gave each other knowing looks.

Vore walked to the door, opened it, and left. An awkward silence descended.

Noss addressed those that remained. "We shall hear what Slate says, but I want each of you to note—he is his master's pupil. He shall not hesitate to take advantage of this opportunity and bring you all to heel."

The door opened and Vore re-entered with twenty men wearing black cloaks slashed to look like wings. At their head, back in his full armor, the Paladin Slate strode—his boots built on the thick soles to give him height. He looked like a thin carrion bird. From his belt hung one of the skyfall hammers, and from his neck hung a leather strap with a single ring the color of bone. He stood twenty feet from Noss.

"Did the new Prima Pater send you to bring the citadel back under Pariantür's control?" Slate said.

"You must be Primus Slate," Noss said. "Although it was my understanding that you had taken the Vow of Silence."

Slate sneered. "I have no need of that now. It was a millstone around my throat."

"Liberated, yet you fled back to Haven once you were defeated. An army at the gates, sent from Œron, and you still lurk in shadows and don't even bother to come and take what was yours by right?"

"I know better than to paint a target on my chest."

"A target for whom?"

"Anyone who might seek me. Whoever it is that now wears Shroud's cloak, or his apostles who march from Piedala to pillage our library—although it will be hard to pillage without the key."

"And what must I give you to relinquish that key?" Noss asked.

"Tell me why you are here."

"To liberate."

"A savior then?"

"Enabler."

"I don't understand."

"Nor would I expect you to. You were Gladen's lapcör. I expect you to understand little aside from authority and subservience. Instead, I have offered up a sharing of the secrets in the library here—for the Sentinels who shall become our equals."

Slate looked around with a sneer playing upon his lips. "You cannot give them our secrets. We've worked long and hard for them."

"We've all an axe and crossbow," Deggar said, pulling his out from under the table. "We could turn on you and take your key from your corpse."

"And my Paladins," Slate said, "trained in battle, could see you all dead." He pulled out the large piece of metal from his belt and held it out. "Or I could merely drop this and kill every one of you."

Several other commanders pulled out crossbows and trained them on Slate.

"Or we shoot you first," Deggar said. "Your piece of metal might hurt some of us, but we'll make sure you precede us before the Judge."

Slate took a faltering step backward, his head cocked as though listening to someone speak.

"Dropping that to the floor will do little more than give us all a headache," Noss said. "And no one wants that."

"What then..." Slate said and sighed, offering a weak smile. "Shall we start over?"

"I think that is a wise decision," Noss said. "Give your weapons to my Paladins and sit."

Slate surrendered the piece of metal. "And my colleagues?"

"I assume they are, or were once, Paladins? Perhaps some are Sentinels under Vore's command? They can stay and listen."

Slate slunk to a seat at the table.

"Humanity is rife with intrigue," Noss said. "We all have our hopes and plans. Align yours with mine—past the end of this siege, for one year—and together we'll forge something new and powerful."

"And what is that?" Slate asked.

"A new order. One founded upon the gifts of the skyfall metal."

"You want to unite my Motean order, the Brotherhood of the Gauntlet, with your bells?"

"I wish to establish a new paladinial order entirely. The Order of..."

"The Axe?" Bolla interrupted.

"Why the Axe?"

"We commanders carry a great axe, and you offer us these skyfall blades. It goes without saying a symbol of our status should be our icon, just as the Hammer, Rose, Staff, and Chalice represent the other orders."

"All in favor of the Axe?" Noss asked the table.

A few hands went up, and none protested.

"And what of those who do not wish to join?" Commander Hardin asked.

"You once commanded a mercenary company in Morriego, didn't you? The Red Banner?"

Hardin nodded.

"Return to that life, if you will, and you may take any who wish to join you. But those that leave will no longer wear the Black Sentinel cloak."

"What incentive do you offer those Sentinels who join, yet do not have the rank to be a Black Axe?"

"I don't see why we can't offer a boost in rank. Anyone about to make Captain can have it."

"You've given us a lot to think on," Hardin said. "Allow us all to reconvene tomorrow."

"Let's meet here at dawn either to part ways or formalize our union."

Hardin gave Noss a bow of his head. Chairs were pushed back as everyone rose.

Bolla turned to Ophedia. "Will you follow me back to my inn?"

They proceeded together to the hall. Ophedia glanced over her shoulder to see the Paladins and the black-cloaked Moteans pulling up chairs, with Noss at the head. He cut a commanding presence, opposite the suspicious-looking Slate, who sat petulantly with his arms crossed.

Bolla and Ophedia walked through the citadel to the door opening onto the western wall. A Sentinel stood on the wall outside the door, in the dying light of day, a petite girl who watched their approach from under her hood.

"You always move so quickly," Bolla said.

The petite Sentinel was Commander Domic.

"I had been wanting to get out of that meeting since Slate showed up. So this is Searn's girl?"

"Ophedia del Ishé," Bolla said. "His daughter."

Domic gave a low whistle, but it felt disingenuous.

"And you trust her?" Domic asked.

"Can any Sentinel trust any other Sentinel?" Ophedia offered.

Domic laughed. "All right. I like you."

They came to the wall at the edge of the city, looking over the gathering Chalician forces.

"They're going to force their way in soon enough," Bolla said.

"Who do you think will sell us out?" Domic said.

"Can you specify?"

"Who is going to open the gates for them?"

"Initially I assumed that one of the baronets would. They'll want to secure their power."

"But now?"

"Forenor. He's been gone more and more from the country. His ships are meeting with great success, and he knows everyone in every port. The promise of an alliance with Œron will be too good to pass up."

"Not if you and your council choose to side with Noss," Ophedia said.

They turned to look at her.

"What do you mean?"

"I'd imagine that Noss will look to the south next, to Ormach. If he does that, Limae gains a port on the Kandar Sea. When he allies with this faction he says is in the Northern Scapes, and Limae gains access to the Lupinfang. This country already relies on imported goods."

"Financial incentives will be much stronger influences on Limaeans," Bolla agreed. "As the Chalicians grow, we can be a haven for those that flee."

"Forenor ought to be reminded of that," Domic said.

"The bigger issue we face now is Vore," Bolla said.

Domic nodded. "He's been lying through his teeth the whole time. I personally went and searched his tavern. It appeared Slate had moved on."

"Why protect him?"

"He may be under Slate's control entirely," Ophedia offered. "In Mahn Fulhar there was a gauntlet, made of the same metal as the tools Noss showed us, which controlled people who held or otherwise possessed on their bodies a particular kind of coin, minted of the same metal. It sounds far-fetched, but I saw it with my own eyes, right before Searn died. He wore the gauntlet that night."

"You think Slate has it in his possession now?"

"I have it on good authority."

"I think I'd suggest bringing that 'good authority' in for a conversation," Bolla said.

"I'll see if they're willing," Ophedia said. "And if you're offered a coin made of the mysterious metal, don't accept it."

"What would you like to do about Vore, then?" Bolla asked

Domic.

"I'll have my network look into these coins; then I might pay a visit to Vore."

"Don't do anything that will harm our council numbers," Bolla said. "Not yet, anyway."

"Would I?" Domic asked with a smirk.

46

CITADEL

I was drawn to the Aerie's grandeur, shrouded in political intrigue. I knew then that Haven was where the Charter House would be built. The city lords were fighting incessantly, and the Paladins wanted the city as a plaything. It was easy to establish the first inn, and then I took up the Red Banner's charter and they joined me, many others followed. Admittedly many were washed up and out of work, but even the drunken sot, given a purpose, can be bent to my will.

—JOURNAL OF SEARN VETURRES ENTRY SEVENTY-FIVE

From her seat by the fire in the otherwise quiet inn, Rallia blew softly but unmusically on her pipe, starting and stopping in a way that grated on everyone's nerves. Ymbrys scratched figures in a ledger with a dry quill, muttering to himself. Had Hanen seen the scrawling and not known they were qavylli numbers, he'd have thought the creature ranted insanities in two voices. Dorian nursed a tankard and stared through Hanen, unaware of anyone around him. The innkeeper had polished all his drinking vessels three times over. The coin they paid him quieted his complaints, but he made up for it by clattering his tankards and dragging a cask loudly across the room. Whisper sat on Hanen's feet, his normally comforting weight burdening Hanen as he searched his friends' faces, his thoughts returning to the satchel hidden upstairs, wondering when Ophedia or Aurín would expose its contents.

As though summoned by the thought, Ophedia entered the inn,

the others looking up as she entered. Rallia smiled and rose to her feet, closing the distance between them and falling into a warm embrace.

"Where have you been?" Rallia asked. "I thought you'd have come to visit by now."

"I tried," Ophedia said, casting a sideways glance at Hanen. "But I've been busy up at the citadel working for one of the commanders."

"Come and sit," Ymbrys said, gesturing to the largest table. He made a motion to the innkeeper for drinks and took a seat himself.

"I understand you've been in town for some time," Dorian said, "and that you brought the warning of the Chalicians, too."

"It's true," Ophedia said. "It would be nice if a bit of coin came from the city in recognition. We can't all work merely for the goodness of others."

"What brings you here now?" Dorian asked.

"Hanen and Rallia, actually."

Hanen felt his ears grow hot.

"The members of the council have been asking after you," she said, turning to Rallia. "You've done a good job of staying out of sight, but you keep creeping up in conversation. The commander who hired me has suggested on several occasions that you ought to present yourselves before the council."

"What do they want with us?"

"I think they'd like you to corroborate what happened in Mahn Fulhar. I'm sure your work in Edi City means something to them, too."

"They've got your word," Hanen said, "and probably Aurín's. They don't need ours. And we don't need to expose our location and risk Dorian's presence being revealed, either."

"Well," Ophedia said, "I'm just the messenger."

"Better a message that comes from a friend," Ymbrys said, "rather than someone who would be less considerate."

Five men walked in and looked around, gray cloaks over their heads. Hanen saw Rallia's hands tense on her tankard before she slipped them under the table. Ophedia cocked an eyebrow and turned just as the five men dropped their cloaks and leveled crossbows at them.

"Hold!" the leader shouted.

They had tightly trimmed beards and well-combed hair, but it was their signature crossbows that gave them away as Voktorra.

Hanen held both hands up and slowly rose.

"Sit back down!" the lead Voktorra ordered.

"Let's all calm down," Hanen said. "The fact that I haven't raised my voice is the only reason my ynfald hasn't attacked you yet."

There was a hesitance in the Voktorra's eyes; the crossbow lowered an inch.

"Perhaps you should tell us why you're here," Dorian asked, "and we can discuss what it is you intend to do."

"Our captain, Navien," the man said. "He's held hostage in the citadel."

Rallia glanced at Ophedia. She gave a slight but confirming nod.

"As I understand it, the city's council meets at the citadel," Hanen said. "They probably have a good reason to detain him."

"He's an agent of Mahn Fulhar, sent by the king to bring you all back."

Hanen clicked his tongue. "I wouldn't use the word 'agent.' It might confirm the council's suspicion concerning Navien."

"What do you mean?"

"Your captain's been arrested as a Chalician spy," Ophedia said. "If you go to the citadel and demand his freedom as an 'agent,' I imagine you'll be arrested as well."

"Chalician?" the Voktorra responded. "Spy?"

"It makes sense," Hanen said. "You've come to rescue a political prisoner, which is something a spy ring would do."

"We could just kill you all and return with your heads, proving you'll no longer be a threat to Mahndür. Or we could burn the inn down so the old man receives no martyrdom, since no one would know."

"And yet," Dorian said, "you came here with the sole purpose of getting our help to rescue Navien, I take it."

The Voktorra didn't respond, but looked from person to person.

"Asking for help is not usually done at the end of a crossbow," added Dorian.

"We're not asking," the Voktorra said. "We're demanding."

"That's better," Hanen said. "But how do you know you're up to the task?"

"A weak qavyl, an old man, and three cowards, against five hardened soldiers."

Hanen smirked. "A creature with centuries of experience, a chosen champion of a god, and three bodyguards who have stood against monsters, bandits, and defeated a man wearing a cloak made of darkness. Hardly an even match for you."

"And an ynfald," Ymbrys offered with a smile.

"And an ynfald," Hanen parroted. "I'd say you're in over your head."

"We'll kill the old man first, and he'll never fulfill his plan," the Voktorra said. "He'll never find the armor."

"You know where it is?" Dorian asked.

The Voktorra nodded.

"Not much of a bargaining chip," Ophedia offered. "I know where Slate is myself."

"But not where he moved the armor," the Voktorra said.

"What is it you want, exactly?" Dorian asked. "And what are you offering in return?"

"Two of you Sentinels are going to rescue Navien from the citadel while we stay here holding the others as ransom. When we're satisfied that you've gotten him safely out of the city, we'll release our captives and tell them where to find the armor."

"How do we know you won't kill those here and leave once you're certain Navien is free?"

"Because we're honorable, and loyal to the crown of Mahn Fulhar."

"And if your orders from King Erdthal were to bring us back or kill us?"

"We would kill you now and leave Navien as an acceptable loss."

"We are not their goal," Dorian muttered to the others.

"Quiet," the Voktorra ordered.

"If you want our help," Ophedia said, "you must let us discuss this matter."

The man took a step back. "Go on then."

"If Navien leaves the city, he'll report back to Erdthal," Dorian continued, "which may see Mahndür joining the fray and marching on this city."

"That would be a very long time from now," Ymbrys said. "We'll be long gone."

"And if Navien is a spy for the Chalicians?" Ophedia asked.

"Then us freeing him makes us complicit," Rallia said.

"They're offering the armor, though," Dorian said.

"Is it worth the risk?" Hanen asked.

"We're not really in a position to refuse them," Rallia said.

"Ymbrys, I have a gut feeling they'll kill you first. You don't play into their plans."

"You need not worry about me," Ymbrys said. "I'm better equipped to defend myself than you think."

"Then should we turn on them now and risk the chance?"

"I think we have an opportunity to avoid violence," Dorian replied. "And if they are truly honorable, we could find the armor and leave the city."

"Who is going with me?" Hanen asked.

"You're going?" Rallia asked.

"If I free Navien, he'll owe me," Hanen nodded. "I like the sound of that."

"Then I'm going too," Rallia said.

"No," Ophedia said. "It has to be me."

"Why?"

"Because I've been to the citadel several times now, and they know me."

"Besides," Hanen said to Rallia, "you're the best fighter here. If anyone can defend Dorian, it's you."

Hanen turned to the men. "We'll do it."

The leader smiled. "I thought you'd see reason."

"This is hardly reasonable, but Ophedia and I will see if it can be done."

"See if it can be done? You're going to do it."

"We're going to try. And if we don't accomplish it tonight, then we'll try again tomorrow."

"You'll do it tonight, or else."

"Or else what?" Rallia said, standing up.

The crossbows all turned to her.

"Or else we kill you first."

Hanen held up a hand. "We've agreed to your request," he said.

The Voktorra sighed and motioned for the others to lower their crossbows.

"I have to grab a few things from my room," Hanen said to Ophedia. "I'll meet you outside."

She nodded and walked past the Voktorra out the door.

Rallia followed Hanen to the foot of the stairs.

"If we have a chance, we'll take these men down," she said.

"Don't."

"Why not?"

"If we can accomplish this without violence, we may be rid of

434

Navien forever."

"He's already under arrest by the Sentinels. That puts him out of the picture."

"If the Chalicians invade the city, he'll be free, and he'll come and find us. But if we set him free, he'll owe me. Secondly, we can release him to the Chalicians, and then leave town by another way and get separated in the confusion."

"And thirdly?"

Hanen smiled and began going up the stairs.

"Be careful," she called after him.

Once in his room, Hanen put on his cloak and pulled his satchel from under the bed, slinging it over his shoulder. Then he walked to the window, slipped out, and nearly jumped out of his boots when he saw Ophedia there.

"What in Noccitan?!" he hissed.

Ophedia laughed. "I figured you'd like a chance to don your other cloak before we went through the city."

Hanen sighed and pulled the boneshroud out of his satchel. "I really hate that you know I have this."

"Well, better you than someone else. We know Slate has the other gauntlet, but if he or Pater Noss had the Shroud, I don't think I'd stay in this city. Or even on the continent."

"Who is Pater Noss?" Hanen asked, pulling on the boneshroud and donning the Sentinel Cloak over it.

"He's a Paladin who came to town recently. He's been negotiating with the Sentinel Council to form an alliance."

"What kind of alliance?"

"He's offering the Sentinel Commanders an opportunity to become members of his new paladinial organization. Paladins of the Axe."

"That's not how Paladins work."

"Well, he's not really a Paladin of the Hammer anymore. Nor is Slate. They came to an arrangement today."

"So they're Moteans?"

Ophedia nodded.

"And how do the Sentinel Commanders play into this?"

"All Sentinel captains and the ranks above become what they're calling 'Black Axes.' With that title they'll gain access to Motean secrets. This also means the Order of the Axe obtains a majority on the council, giving them control of the city. Noss was a follower of Searn, and this was Searn's plan all along."

"Noss will eventually betray Slate," Searn's voice said in Hanen's head. *"Before Slate has the opportunity to do so himself."*

"Shhh," Hanen said quietly.

"What is it?" Ophedia asked.

"Nothing," Hanen said. "I thought I heard something."

"I can almost hear something myself," Searn said. *"I'm starting to hear through your ears."*

They came to the roof's edge and Ophedia climbed down, waiting at the bottom as he scrambled down after her.

"So what can the cloak do?" she asked as they started walking down the street.

"What do you mean?"

"Today I watched Noss show what the tools he brought can do, but I also once witnessed Searn incorporating the ring of the Wyloth king into the boneshroud; it was what allowed him to control those black shades. I can only assume that the boneshroud has more power than anything else."

"Why assume that?"

"Because you and I know Searn would never settle for a lesser tool."

"She's right," Searn said.

"Um..." Hanen said. "It keeps me hidden from certain people. I can see better in the dark."

"That sounds fun," Ophedia replied.

"I haven't confirmed it yet, but I think I can also tell when truths are spoken."

"Should we test it out? I killed a man when I was twelve."

"She's not lying," Searn said.

Hanen ignored him. "Somehow I doubt that."

"Well," Ophedia said, glancing sideways at Hanen, "maybe it doesn't work."

"Wait. So you did kill a man when you were twelve?" he asked.

"He tried to take advantage of me. I shoved him away and he fell on his own weapon. I ran away and found out the next day he had died."

"So it wasn't your fault," Hanen said.

"No, but the twelve-year-old me didn't understand that. It set the course of my life."

"What about the inn in Suel? Did you actually burn that down?"

"The innkeeper had been trying to take advantage of me, but I never gave in. It was his wife who set fire to my room and burned the whole place down. I wasn't there, and neither was the innkeeper. He was with his actual mistress after having beaten me, and I fled to Father Diono's chapel. The only person who actually died was the innkeeper's wife.

"And the innkeeper?"

"He's a drunken sot in Macena now. I became a bounty hunter to get in with the criminal elements there and try to ruin him. Instead I ended up stuck in debt myself, but fate saw that he ruined himself anyway. He has drinking debts with three different crime lords."

"Macena doesn't sound as nice as everyone seems to think it is."

"It's pretty lawless. Which is fun. It's still figuring itself out, I think."

"Why were you so willing to accept that Searn had this cloak? That I have his cloak?"

"I've known men who have the façade of goodness but every evil intention in their hearts. But Searn treated me with kindness."

"Because you're his daughter, it turns out."

"Perhaps for that reason. He has done things that are certainly on the wrong side of a morally gray area, but not out of spite." Then she stopped and considered Hanen. "As for you, you're a bit cold and calculating, but I can't think of anything that makes me think you're not a good person."

"Even using this cloak?"

"It seems to have fallen into the right hands. If Searn left it to me, I don't know that I'd use it for good."

"I'm not sure I've used it for good myself."

"A sword kills, but can it be used for good? Is a sword good?"

"It's a tool. It can't be good or evil in itself."

"Exactly. That cloak has been made by questionable means, but it's yours now. So put it to good use."

They came to the outer wall of the city.

"This is where we'll bring Navien once we get out," Ophedia said. "I think we can lower him down over the wall and he can run free."

"You've really gotten to know the city, haven't you?"

"Well, this part of the city, anyway. Commander Elbay travels this way to the council every day."

"So you're not worried we'll run into someone you know?"

"It seems that everyone left the citadel after the meeting. There might be a Paladin or two, or a few Sentinels."

"Last time," Hanen said, "It was a bastion. Now we're sneaking into a citadel."

"We are making a habit of this, aren't we?"

They approached the door to the citadel, which Ophedia opened.

"Put your hood up like me," she said.

As he did, the darkness beyond the door lightened. The utter silence fell over him.

"Do you want me to lead?" he asked.

Ophedia shivered and shot him a look.

"What?"

"Your voice changed," she said. "It sounds like Searn did that night. Like...I can't even describe it."

"It's the shroud," Hanen said. "It blocks out noise to me, but also makes voices clearer."

"Maybe keep quiet, for my own peace of mind."

They entered the citadel and came to a large, empty stone hall where a couple of candles burned. The carpet running down the middle of the room muffled their footfalls, but Hanen still felt they were being too risky.

"Do you know where you're going?" he asked.

"The council room is that way," Ophedia pointed down another side hall, "but they took Navien this way."

They turned into a long corridor lined with doors.

"Paladins live in their monastic cells," Hanen said, "and their holding cells for detained brothers are little different from normal ones, save that they can be locked from the outside."

"How do you know that?" Ophedia asked, testing a cell next to her. It opened easily, but she shut it again after finding nothing.

"Rallia and I grew up next to the Bastion in Garrou. They had a single holding cell there, often used for town drunks who needed somewhere to stay."

They took turns checking for locked doors among the rows of empty cells, until Hanen saw a light far behind them.

"Someone is coming," he said. Ophedia nodded and they hid in a cell.

"What do you think Alodda would say if she knew about the boneshroud?"

"Why would you ask me that?" Hanen hissed.

"Because you probably don't like that question."

"No, I don't. It's been on my mind from time to time. I'd like to hope that when this is all done I won't have to figure that out."

"You're living under a delusion that things will go back to normal after this?"

"Why shouldn't they?" Hanen asked.

"You took the cloak from a man bent on killing the gods. We've seen some weird things before and since then. Nothing is going to be the same after this, and if you think you haven't changed already, you're wrong."

"What do you mean?"

"You wanted to leave town before you were convinced to fight Searn. This time you're the first volunteer for the hard work."

"Because I'm tired of Navien always being there. I'd like to get him out of my life forever."

"Quiet. I think they're approaching."

The sound of voices came closer and the light under the door glowed brighter. After a moment, however, both faded away. Ophedia cracked the door open and peeked out.

"They're far enough ahead," she said.

They resumed their search until they came to a break in the hall. Far away Hanen could make out the two figures. A Paladin carrying a torch allowed a hooded Sentinel to precede him through a door, which shut behind them. Ophedia grabbed Hanen's cloak and pulled him into another room, closing the door behind her.

"What?" he hissed.

"More Paladins," she whispered.

Torchlight glowed under the door from the direction they were heading. After another wait, Ophedia cracked the door open and stuck her head out for a moment.

"I think we're nearing whatever area those Paladins are bunking."

"There have been Paladins in these halls this whole time? Then we need to stop talking and search more quietly."

"I have a better idea," Ophedia said. "You drop the temperature in the room with that cloak on. If you forge ahead, it'll probably startle anyone in a given room, and if it's a Paladin, they'll peek out. We'll be invisible in our dark Sentinel cloaks, as long as they don't bring torches."

"But if the person within is locked up..." Hanen offered.

"Then Navien cries out, perhaps, and we find him."

"All right," Hanen said. "We'll try that."

He ducked out the door and moved down the hallway. There

was someone muttering in one of the cells as he swiftly passed, but he didn't stop until he heard the creak of a door opening behind him. He pressed up against the wall and looked back the way he came, but he could see neither the door that he had opened nor Ophedia in her cloak. He heard the door close, and he continued down the corridor.

"So you're going to help the man who has been harassing us for months?" Searn's voice said in his head.

"I'm going to escort him out of our lives forever."

"You honestly think he'll stop?"

"I have to try."

"He's a man of conviction. He'll stop when he's dead."

"Well, I'm not you. I'm not killing him."

"You think me a murderer."

"You've killed enough."

"I'm a soldier for the cause. There is a difference."

"Your own cause," Hanen muttered.

"Well, in the end, it worked. So it appears I was right."

"I'm not so sure about that," Hanen said.

He moved past a door and heard the quick drag of a chain over stone.

"We need only find a god now. You'll find that they do not see you. Nifara didn't see me…"

"Quiet," Hanen whispered. He reached out and tested the door before him. It was locked.

The rustle of Ophedia's cloak approached and he crouched down, pulling his hood off his head.

She sighed in relief. "Thank you for taking that off."

"Why?"

"Honestly, it's taken a lot of self-control not to flee from you when you wear it."

"Who's there?" came the voice from the cell. Hanen recognized it as Navien's.

Hanen took hold of Ophedia's arm and pulled her further down the hall.

"I could leave my hood on so he doesn't recognize me."

"That won't help," she said. "If he sees you wearing that cloak, he'll know. You're supposed to be hunting it down, right?"

"All right, no cloak."

He took off both cloaks and placed the boneshroud in his satchel.

"Give me your clubs," he said.

"Why?"

"I'm your apprentice now. Navien will wear my cloak."

"That's a fantastic idea."

"I'm full of them. Well, full of something, anyway," he replied with a smirk.

Hanen followed her as she crouched beside Navien's door, taking out a pair of picks.

"Can you do that without a torch?" he asked.

"It's by feel, anyway," she said. An interminable minute later, and there was a click. Ophedia opened the door and entered the dark cell.

"Who are you?" Navien asked.

"The last person you probably thought would bust you out," Ophedia offered.

"Del Ishé?" he replied.

"Don't you wish we had a candle so we could see his face when I say your name, Hanen?"

Navien shuffled in the dark—hid from them, by the sound of it.

"Calm down," Ophedia said.

"You're here to kill me," Navien said with spite in his voice.

"We're here to get you out of the city," Hanen replied.

"Then the city is about to fall," Navien said.

"What do you mean?" Ophedia asked.

"I ordered my men to break me out when word came through the underground that the Chalicians will take the city by force. I want to be on the other side of the wall when it happens. The last thing I need is to be killed by Paladins or considered a traitor to the church."

"You're very trusting with your plans," Hanen said.

"I don't trust you. But I trust you to serve yourself. See me out of the city, and I'll make sure the Chalicians are lenient with you."

"Maybe we should just kill him," Ophedia said.

Navien scoffed. "And risk your sister's life?"

"How do you know Rallia is in danger?" Hanen asked.

"Because you wouldn't have come otherwise."

"How are his chains coming?" Hanen said.

"They're twist keys. I can't break them."

"Check the wall then," Hanen said.

He heard her follow the chain to the wall.

"You'll escort me out disguised as a Sentinel?" Navien asked.

"Good guess," Hanen replied.

"And a good guess by you, Hanen," Ophedia said. "There is a lock here."

After few moments of fiddling, Hanen heard a click.

"Are you going to give us trouble?" he asked his old enemy.

"Why should I? This was a plan I put in place myself."

Navien stood, and Hanen put a cloak over his head.

"Don't make us regret helping you," Hanen said.

"I want away from this Pantheon-forsaken city," Navien said. "If you end up regretting your actions, it'll be your own conscience."

47

INTERLUDE

"So you were there then, Sentinel Mateau?" Noss asked the Sentinel before him.

"I was," Aurín replied. "I accepted the coin, but I don't recall much after that until the incident was over."

"You rid yourself of the coin?" Noss asked.

"I thought I had, but it appeared around my neck a few weeks ago. I don't recall putting it on."

"Where is the coin now?" Noss asked.

"It was removed from me."

"How?"

"By...Shroud."

"Searn died."

"I know. Or at least, that's what I was told."

"His cloak went missing, though, along with the gauntlet that commanded the coins."

The Sentinel hesitated.

"You know who freed you?"

Aurín nodded.

"But you are loyal to them and won't say?"

The man nodded again.

"Then why come to me?" asked Noss.

"I was in the room when you showed those other tools of your sect."

"And?"

"And if your bells, if your tools, if your teachings will protect me from being controlled like that again, then I want them."

"What do you mean?"

"You offered the Sentinel Commanders a place in the new order, and captains too. I do not have a captaincy, but if no one else has yet stepped forward, then please accept me as your first volunteer."

"You're no Paladin."

"According to yourself, neither are you anymore."

"Is this your ambition talking?"

"Of course it is," Aurìn said with a laugh. "Show me a man who doesn't have ambition. Even a coward is ambitious."

"And what are you?"

"Determined. I marched with Searn. He told me stories of men who commanded griffins. I wonder now if it was done by those coins."

"It is one possible use, I think."

"Then accept me into your order. Make me a Black Axe."

"How far are you willing to go?"

"As far as it takes."

"Then follow me," Noss said, rising.

They wended their way through the citadel, Aurìn moving behind Noss quietly and without complaint. They passed through the dormitory halls, and Noss felt an odd chill pass by him. Part of him wanted to flee, yet another part pondered the source of this mysterious cold. But the willingness of the volunteer behind him was more important.

They came to the hall he was looking for. He walked down the hallway to the tower door, which he pulled open, allowing the Œronzi man to go through first. Then they continued up the curving steps and finally came to a boarded-up section.

"We've climbed high," Aurìn said.

"Do you know the decrepit tower above the citadel?"

"Yes. Half of it is missing."

"Past this wooden barrier is the break. There is a rope ladder to the top, but few are willing to climb it."

"And you want me to go up there?"

"I'm wildly curious what is up there. Go and look. Tell me what you see. If I determine you're worthy, then I'll accept you into our order."

"How do I know you won't betray me?"

"You don't. But I wager your curiosity will outweigh your

hesitation."

"What is said to be up there?"

"The griffin from Searn's story. His remains are said to lie there."

Aurìn hesitated for only a moment. "I'll do it."

Together they tore away the wood, creating a space for them to climb to the other side, exposed to the elements. The entire wall of the tower was missing, and the city could be seen below, the fires of the Chalician encampment lighting the eaves of the forest just beyond the boulder field. An untrustworthy rope ladder hung from somewhere fifty feet above.

"That's a very old ladder," Aurín said, giving it a tug. "But if I fall, I won't fall all the way to the city below."

"Do you have tinder and a candle?" Noss asked.

The Sentinel nodded and began to climb.

Noss bit his lip as anxiety washed over him. The man was considerably slighter than he was. If he couldn't make it up, no one could. One of the rungs snapped under Aurìn's foot and he yelped, scrambling to recover. Noss almost dropped his torch so he could catch him if he fell, but Aurìn managed to finish his climb and disappeared over the edge.

"Is something wrong?" Noss called after a long silence.

"I cut my hand. Let me light a candle."

After a moment, tinder was struck and Aurìn lit a candle.

"Woah," he muttered.

"What is it?"

There was no reply.

"Sentinel Mateau, what is it?"

"I... I thought I cut my hand on a nail or something, but it's an axe made of your sky metal. It's lying with the remains of a man."

Noss's heart beat hard in his chest.

"Noccitan," Mateau yelped.

"What is it?"

"I found the griffin. It's just a skeleton now, but it was chained up, and here is an old satchel moldering away. It contains those orbs you showed the council."

"Be careful with those!"

Aurín's smiling face appeared over the edge. He held one of the orbs up. "I shouldn't drop this, right?"

"NO!"

Aurín laughed. "Just give me a minute to gather everything up."

A rope soon fell from above.

"Hold the other end so I'm not flailing around."

Noss did as he was told, and the slight man descended, his cloak tied around him.

"Look here," he said, opening the cloak to reveal some of the most perfectly-formed skyfall orbs Noss had ever seen, along with a battle axe of the same metal, a book of some kind, and lastly the griffin skull.

"Well done," Noss said. "You've earned your place."

"Take the rest," Mateau said. "But I'd like to keep the skull."

"It's yours."

"When do I join your order?"

"We'll conduct the ceremony tomorrow. Welcome to the Axes, Aurín Mateau."

ANDREW D MEREDITH

PART 6

VAREA

ABINGEN

HAVEN

LIMAE

RESDAM

REDOT

LIBERTE

OUIOUIMON

ŒRON

SAL-DÜ-MARKT

ADWALL

CASTENARI

AUNTÉ

SIDI

ORMACH

BOSCOLÓN

IPONA

Gasota Tribe

NOR-VIO

AMMAR

ZIVNYR

SEA'LAER

SOUTHWESTERN
GANTHIC

48

HEALING BALM

The fruit bears thorns.

And is a healing balm.

A pearl none can value.

Protect it at all costs.

—BOOK OF CRYSALAS WISDOM, 10:5

The five days' travel had been easier than Katiam expected. Onelie was a quiet companion on the road, but filled the time around the fire at night with questions about life at Pariantür, and with music from the bowl-bodied lute she played for Larozh's entertainment. Astrid had been lucky to take down two fat game birds with rocks, and while Katiam would not eat the meat, she let Astrid fry dough for her in the remaining fat.

"How long were you with the Crysalas before you took your first Aspect, Astrid?" Onelie asked one night.

"Six months," Astrid said. "Although it was done in the wrong spirit."

"What do you mean?"

"I was a silly little gossip when I became a member of the Crysalas. I took the Aspect of Discretion, and wore these rose earrings to denote that I was trustworthy. I got into a lot of trouble, and after my first year my superior said that I was to take the Aspect of Compassion as well." She pointed to the winged elbow guards. "So now people come to me with their secrets, but I am also at their beck and call if they require help."

"An Aspect as a punishment sounds more like what the Paladins subject themselves to."

"It is rather rare," Katiam said. "But not unheard of."

"It was also nearly ten years ago," Astrid said. "Since then I've taken on Form and Honor."

"I know Honor. Most of the Paladame Guards are said to have taken that."

"Form is a separate martial discipline," Astrid said.

"She's very good at it," Katiam said. "She's defeated unarmed Paladins in the wrestling ring."

"Wrestling?"

"Somewhat," Astrid said. "I can show you in the light of day sometime."

The Rotha whistled just as a twig snapped in the woods.

"What was that?" Onelie hissed.

Astrid rose, and took up her mace. The Rotha pulled itself close to Katiam and she covered it in the wrap.

"Is someone there?" Astrid called out.

"By Rose and Thorn, we come in peace," a familiar voice called out.

"Esenath?"

Their friend appeared in the glow of the fire.

"Hello," she said smiling. "May I join you?"

"Of course!" Katiam rose smiling.

"I brought company."

Children appeared out of the woods in pairs, then threes. Soon it was as though the trees themselves marched as hundreds of children came out of the woods.

"What is this?" Katiam asked as Sister Derah Baker appeared, too.

Onelie ran up to the young girl and threw her arms around her friend.

"I've brought the Moon-Eyes away from Waglysaor. You'd not believe what happened since you left."

A Paladin stepped into the light last—the familiar face of Jurgon Upona

"We've not much food," Katiam said, looking around.

"We've brought grain," Sister Baker said.

Sister Baker built up the fire and began giving orders to the children to help prepare for dinner. Meanwhile, Esenath and

Jurgon pulled Katiam and the others aside.

"When you left the city, I decided to take the little pearls and heal those with Day Blind," Esenath said. "But upon speaking with Sister Baker, we determined an even better course of action. We've spirited the Day Blind out of the city to find you and Larozh and heal the children, which will produce more pearls for others."

"But then what? We cannot take them to Pariantür."

"No. Sister Baker will take the pearls to the College, where botanists can study them and perhaps learn to replicate them without the Rotha. In the meantime, I hope to go with you and gather more pearls as we heal people in Garrou and beyond."

"Shouldn't we talk about it first?"

"We are," Esenath said. "I'm asking if you'll help. While you think about it, can we heal these children?"

"Of course," Katiam said. She gave Esenath the Rotha to show the children. While the Rotha sneezed and children laughed as their sight returned, Katiam turned to Jurgon.

"Why are you here?"

"Because you have news of my wife."

"What happened in Waglÿsaor after we left?"

"Nichal and Jined confronted Zoumerik, who brought the Saor down upon himself. The Paladins are helping the injured and putting the Moteans on trial, and then I think they're going to head east behind us."

"Then we may see them again soon."

Jurgon nodded. "The strangest thing is that Nichal is giving the fortress over to the leadership of Beltran Cautese and Dane Marric as a means to undo the darkness wrought upon the city."

"Dane Marric?" Katiam said.

"I've not seen someone change so fast, from hatred to a genuine desire to seek healing. Although he still shows a begrudging hesitance, he sat at the head table of a feast in the duke's manor and jested with Sigri Smith. I think it helps that she wears the Aspect of the Gilded Rose."

"Yes. There is no worry that she'll tempt him, nor he her."

"Nichal has refused to set foot in the fortress again," Jurgon said. "He has given it up as a holding of the Hammer, but in a public statement, Dane has claimed it as a Monument to a new faith in Grissone. They're embracing the name Gospelers of Grissone."

"And the people of the city?" Astrid asked.

"They've sworn fealty. The duke even humbled himself before Dane, declaring him his confessor. Dane looked very uncomfortable."

Katiam laughed. "I don't think he's sought authority, just that others match his zeal."

"I agree," Jurgon said.

"How is Little Maeda?" Astrid asked.

"We prayed over her, and she lives."

"Thank the Pantheon," Katiam sighed.

"But she'll never be the same, as I understand it. The burns were very bad."

"That saddens me," Astrid said.

"Now. My wife," Jurgon said.

Katiam nodded. "She lives, and has asked that you seek her when your mission is done."

"I have promised to see these children to Thementhu. After that, where shall I seek her?"

"The Veld," Katiam said.

"What?" Jurgon's eyes bulged.

Katiam described how she had been to the dream pasture, and her journey with Sabine.

"How can I get there?"

"I am not sure," Katiam said. "Perhaps some at the College would know?"

"I will start there, then."

Esenath came over.

"We're almost done. One hundred children have been healed today."

"Then Jurgon and Sister Baker will continue on to the college?"

"We're a day or two from the Bortali Dunes. From there the road south can take them over the mountains to Nemen."

"What about you?"

"I've written instructions for Sister Baker to take to the scholars I've recommended, and I'll continue with you. I doubt we've scratched the surface of what the Rotha can do. I mean to record it."

"And your book?" Katiam asked.

Esenath reached into her satchel and pulled it out.

"It is damaged and needs repair, but I can still use it."

"I am glad."

"Glad," Larozh said clearly. "Mammakat glad."

Katiam laughed, taking the Rotha from Esenath's arms with a smile.

"Yes, Larohz. Mama Kat is glad."

"Laaarohzz glad."

The others laughed and the children chattered on into the night, munching on the bread Sister Baker made over the fire. When Onelie played a lullaby on her lute, they sang together. The bread brought them comfort; the Little Rose brought them healing, and the community they shared sparked a healing balm to their hearts and to the world.

49

GLOVES OF EONS

My research at the Archives spoke of the stories of the Üterk and so I journeyed to hear them, but to my frustration I learned only of the lore of the vül. My young mind had no patience. It would be years before I came to value their moral tales, which contained knowledge of the tools of ancient days, such as the black armor and blessings of brass. Dominion over the minds of greater creatures. It was overwhelming, to know that there were so many things to learn, for I would have them all. I had to temper myself with this knowledge: that avarice was my weakness. I could not allow it to be my downfall.

—JOURNAL OF OLLISTAN GŒRNSTADT

T he Chalicians had taken up torches and stood in a line over a hundred yards from the wall. Navien wore a slight smile, though chains were still around his wrists.

"It appears the city has taken too long to make its decision," he said.

"Quiet, Navien," Hanen said.

"Why should I? It appears this godless city will finally be brought to account."

"You hardly seem a practicing man of faith," Ophedia said.

"How little you know of me," Navien said. "I nearly became a priest as a young man. I studied all the old texts."

"What changed your mind?" Hanen asked.

"I realized I could better follow the path Aben had set for me by enforcing the law."

"Sounds to me," Ophedia said, "like you and the Chalicians would make good bed partners."

"A blasphemous analogy," Navien said, though he did not scowl.

"Apropos to what your king and High Priest did in Mahn Fulhar."

"He was made High Priest by Aben's will," Navien countered. "I'll not question that."

"Did you bring a rope, Ophedia?" Hanen asked.

"Yes."

"You're just going to lower me down?" Navien asked.

"There is no one around," Hanen replied.

They tied the rope to the middle of the chains between his wrists.

"Hold on to the chain, and we'll lower the rope."

"Tell my men the word 'guildcoin' and they'll leave," Navien told them.

"How do we know that won't signal them to kill us?"

"You think very poorly of our guild," Navien said. "I expected animosity, but your suspicion speaks more of yourself than of us."

"They already threatened our lives," Hanen said. "What do you expect?"

Navien shrugged and stepped up onto the crenellations. Ophedia and Hanen provided tension on the rope and lowered him down. When he was halfway down the wall, Ophedia leaned into Hanen.

"He was far too agreeable," Ophedia said.

"I noticed," Hanen said. "He wanted us to get him to the bottom as quickly as possible. I think he saw how undefended this portion of the wall is."

"We're not far from Commander Elbay's inn. I'll warn her."

"That will connect you to Navien's escape."

"It's that or compromise the city," she said.

"You really have grown up," Hanen said.

"Yeah," Ophedia said. "I'm a responsible adult now, which is why I'm jailbreaking foreign spies and acting as an accomplice to a guy with a cloak made of darkness."

Navien touched the ground and began fumbling with the rope's knots.

"We could toss the rope down," Hanen said.

"It's a good rope," Ophedia said, "and the longer it takes to untie it, the longer it takes for him to run to the Chalicians. You run off and save your sister. I'll get my rope back and go tell Elbay."

"Come find us after this. If we're not at the inn anymore, we'll be finding our way into Düran."

Hanen ran down the stairs into the streets just as Navien called for Ophedia to drop the rope. She gave Hanen a wave and laughed a rich laugh as she looked down over the wall at the man trying to untie the knots with shackled wrists.

He found a shadowed alley. After putting the boneshroud back on under his cloak, he began wending his way from street to street as panic in the city rose with rumors of the Chalicians' warlike formations. In one of the main thoroughfares a large crowd slowly advanced toward the wall, but in another square a crowd moved the other direction with carts laden with belongings. He entered the flow of the crowd and people shied away from him because of the effects of the cloak. The crowd grew tighter until they could no longer shy away from him, however, and they were all forced to slowly trudge through the street.

"Why try leaving the city now?" Hanen asked a man next to him.

"Why not?" the man asked irritably. "If the besiegers are making their move, now is the time."

"You think they'll let people leave?"

"Haven is a free city. They can't tell us no."

Hanen pursed his lips. "Somehow I doubt that," he muttered.

He glanced sideways and saw a familiar face.

"When did you arrive in town?" Hanen asked the hairy, bearded storyteller Kash.

Kash glanced around suspiciously, not seeming to see him. The temperature seemed to drop around them, then confined itself once more.

"Do I know you?" Kash said, not looking at Hanen again.

"I know you," Hanen said.

"Are you fleeing the city as well?"

"No," Hanen said. "I'm trying to get back to my inn. When did you arrive in town? Did you come with your brother?"

"Yes, we arrived a week ago on business. Why are you here?"

Kash still did not seem to recognize him, but he looked less suspicious.

"We're seeking something," Hanen told him.

"Perhaps we seek the same thing. If I knew who you were, we could seek together."

Hanen touched the edge of his cloak, pulling it further over his face.

"What is it you seek?" Kash repeated, his curiosity intensifying.

"A story, which I'd pay you for."

"Then I have told you a story before?"

"What would you ask for in trade?" Hanen asked.

"I'd ask for a tale in return."

"That is fair."

"I shall go first. We've got time, given how slow this crowd moves. This story takes place in a land far past the east yet nearer than you know. In that place the veil between the worlds is thinnest, and it is where he crafted his trade."

"Who?" Hanen asked.

One who sought only the highest of crafts. With a hammer of rarest metal, he could take the softest gold and make the hardest tools. His was a realm of impossibility, and the most unexpected person came to watch him, darkening the doorframe and awaiting an invitation.

"Have you come to learn a craft?" the crafter asked.

"I've come to watch and to learn, and if I find you worthy, I shall requisition your service."

The crafter invited his guest to sit and watch him forge tools unimaginable. The days stretched on, and with each day another wonder was made. Yet the guest sat unimpressed.

Greater still he made each thing, and thought to whom he would give those gifts. And yet to the guest, nothing intrigued him as much as it intrigued the crafter himself. After forty days of crafting, each piece more exquisite than the last, the crafter threw his hands up in frustration and turned to his guest.

"Nothing I have made has brought a glitter to your eye. There is nothing that can compare to my skill, not even one, and yet you sit unimpressed. Has anything ever brought you joy?"

"No," said his guest. "I have experienced no joy since the day I was formed. I have only been impressed long ago, when I saw something crafted that had in its form the light of creation."

"What was this thing you saw made?"

458

The guest brought out a massive glove made of both known and mysterious metals, with runes and filigrees upon its surface. The crafter examined it and observed a kind of rust that would have taken millennia to form. Yet despite the rust it was exquisite, and a tear came to his eye.

"I saw this created, and it has never been repeated. As you can see, its long years are coming to an end now. If you could not only craft its likeness once more, but in its partner, I will loan you both for a time, and they shall help you craft greater things still with your artist's eye. For true art is found only at the very edge of madness."

"I shall both reforge the original and make its partner, putting to shame its first crafter."

The guest watched intently as work commenced and continued for weeks, but when the crafter completed the piece and stood admiring his work, he found the guest had gone. He wore the new gloves and forged even greater tools with them. For it had not wear, nor rust work into its joints as the other did. Impressed as he was by gifts made by that glove, as helpful as those tools were, none brought him memory like the time he had spent making that which he was most proud of.

They walked in silence as Hanen considered the story.

"Yet what he made was only second best," Hanen finally said. "As it was the copy of the original."

"That may be. Yet in his attempt to copy would he not also seek to improve upon the original method?"

"If he knew himself to be the greatest crafter in the world, if that were indeed true, how could his guest have seen and watched something greater still be made, and have eons since that time?"

"In the end, stories are morals, even when they don't have one."

"But this one does," Hanen said.

"And what is that?"

"If the gods ask us for something, whether for good or evil, our best is the most we can offer. But they too are tied to the rules of agreement. If the receiver of the message and order refuses in the first place, the gods cannot compel them."

"The master always has command over slave."

"They can threaten. But the slave can always refuse, and accept unjust death as reward."

"How is that a reward?"

"Because it is a victory."

"You think the crafter ought to have refused his guest?"

"I think this crafter should have sought answers first. But not been so self-involved."

"Does that teach you anything?"

"Yes. Thank you," Hanen said. "It has. A gift, no matter what it is, ought to be accepted. But whether it is used or how it is used, ought always to be considered with wisdom."

"Now," Kash said, "I ask for that story in return."

"Will you accept a riddle?"

"Only if that riddle raises more questions than answers," Kash said.

"Alright," Hanen said.

"What walks unseen between the worlds?
What seeks demise of impossibility?
What takes up glove of curse and blessing?
What brings their own curse upon those that call
them friend?"

"You know more of me than you let on," Kash said.

"Then do you know the answer?"

"If I am right, you owe me a debt."

"And if you are wrong?"

"Then I shall offer you a blessing with no curse."

"I accept," Hanen said.

"The answer is the Gift-Giver," Kash said with a smug look.

"No, for no one calls him friend. They only supplicate to him as a god, or curse him as an enemy. The answer is me."

"The answer is Kos-Yran!" Kash said.

"That is not the riddle I asked and answered," Hanen said.

"No," Kash said. "That is not the answer."

"It is. You must fulfill your promise and lift your curse."

"What curse?"

"You and your brother cursed me through my father."

"Ah. Now I know who you are, even if I cannot see you. That curse was not given by me, so I cannot lift it. But I shall give you this blessing, that when your curse is most powerful, you will still have a choice to yield to it or accept death as your unjust reward."

Hanen stopped in his tracks.

"I accept," he said.

Kash could not see him, but he stopped and looked toward the sound of his voice. "Then it is done."

"Where will you go now?" Hanen asked.

"To the Gryph Crag Inn, where a man known as Slate hides. I've heard he possesses something that shall be the basis for a new story, one I hope to be the first to tell. "

"Then you seek a new tale?"

"The world is full of many tales. But a new tale is rarely found, and if I can find a story that my brother does not know, I shall make sure he never hears the end of it."

"What if he seeks the same?"

"He has other plans this night. I need not worry."

"And will you take this thing from Slate?"

"I have sworn not to meddle in this affair, and I can say no more than that. The story already unfolds before me."

Hanen slowed down and watched Kash as he walked away. Then he followed, fighting the current of the crowd until they emerged into the less populated streets. On the corners, men and women stood in groups of two or three, carrying the clubs and axes of the mercenaries. Kash moved unchallenged by them. A few people began to approach Hanen but then thought the better of it. Kash came to a broad square and sidled off to one side, finding a barrel to sit on. When Hanen entered the square, two Sentinels rose from their stations and approached him.

"Who goes there?" one of them asked.

"I'm just passing through."

The two men faltered a step back. "But to where?"

"My inn. I'm a captain."

"No one is allowed in this neighborhood unless they answer to Commander Deggar."

"I'll be going, then." Hanen turned away just as a group of Sentinels marched into the square with a group of prisoners—the Voktorra from the inn stood in shackles, along with Rallia and Dorian. Before anyone could see his face, Hanen turned and ran to the north, keeping them from seeing him in the boneshroud and ducked behind a stack of crates, close enough to hear the conversation.

"They came into our inn and tried to rough up my grandfather," Rallia told the Sentinels that had just been questioning Hanen. She pointed a finger at the Voktorra. "They swear that we were in trouble in Mahndür, but we're from Bortali and I joined the Sentinels to feed the two of us after my parents died."

"Calm down," the Sentinel guard said. "Why did you come to town, and from where?"

"We came up from Tashar a month ago."

"What commander are you under?"

"That's the thing!" Rallia exclaimed. "None of them will see me, then these thugs came in looking to hurt me and the old man."

"Sounds like you better come with us," the Sentinel said to the Voktorra.

"You don't understand!" one of the Voktorra said. "She's lying! She is under contract with the king in Mahn Fulhar."

"Sure she is," the Sentinel said. "Sounds more like you've been looking for an excuse to stay in town. If you're from Mahn Fulhar, you're probably with the Chalicians."

"We're not!"

"We can go, then?" Rallia asked.

"Yeah, but you can't stay here. No strangers allowed in this neighborhood."

"What's the best way out of here?" Rallia asked.

"Just go. I don't care what direction."

Dorian put his arm in Rallia's, hunched over in a fake hobble, and they began walking toward Hanen. He slunk deeper into the shadows and watched them pass.

"Hanen and Ophedia went to the citadel," Rallia was muttering to Dorian. "We need to find them before they get in more trouble."

"Smooth talking back there," Dorian said.

"It's gotten me out of a few tight squeezes. Unwanted advances. That sort of thing."

"Cool heads stay out of hot water," Dorian replied, and they continued up the street. Hanen followed a couple of blocks behind them until they turned left around the Slab, whereupon he went right, traversing the final blocks to the deserted lumberyard and slipped into the workshop. The giant coffin that held the armor was gone, but something sat in the open forge. The other gauntlet lay in the embers, as black as always.

"Where did they move the armor?" he whispered to himself.

"Someplace safe," a man said from the back of the room. Hanen turned to see Slate.

"I've awaited you coming here to finish what you started."

"What is it you think I started?" Hanen asked.

"You stole something from me," Slate said. "I'd like to know what you've done with it, and what it will take for you to return it to me."

"So you can kill me? Or make me a slave to your gauntlet?"

"We could make an arrangement," Slate said.

"Let him do the talking," Searn said. "He'll talk himself into a corner."

"You have the other gauntlet," Slate continued. "I have the first one. We could share the power between us."

"What if I don't want the power?" Hanen replied.

"Who doesn't want power?" Slate said.

"Those that fear to draw the ire of greater powers."

"Kings? Paladins? High Priests?"

"No," Hanen replied. "Dark gods."

Slate laughed.

"I saw Kos-Yran in this city."

Slate hesitated. "You lie."

"The temperature dropped as he spoke to me."

Slate clutched at his chest and closed his eyes for a moment. "Suppose you are telling the truth," Slate said. "What happens now?"

"One of us leaves this place with both gauntlets," Hanen said.

There came the sound of people entering the outer room. Slate stood by the furnace now, taking hold of the door and thrusting his hand into the glowing space. It came back encased in the black metal.

"Still cool," Slate said with a wink. He made a motion with his hand and several people lurched through the doorway, reaching for Hanen as he backed up and thrust his hand into the gauntlet in his satchel. The first man broke free of the others and stumbled across the room. Hanen raised the gauntlet, palm out, and the man froze in place. When Hanen closed his fist, the coin hanging from the mindless man's neck leapt free into his palm.

"So that's how you did that," Slate said.

He walked over to ten more people now standing in the room, pointing at Hanen.

"Kill him and bring us that gauntlet."

They all came at Hanen, who swung the gauntlet with one hand and an axe with the other. The axe took one man across the face and he fell into the woman behind him, both tumbling to the ground. Hanen ran around the room, one of them circling the bench and swinging at him with a pair of clubs. Hanen stepped out of the way and the man struck the door of the forge, screaming as his knuckles touched the hot metal. Another charged Hanen, who opened his palm and slammed the man in the chest. He disappeared entirely.

"What?" Hanen cried out. "How?"

Another man swung an axe too close for Hanen's comfort. He took the man's wrist with the gauntlet and squeezed. The arm disappeared at the elbow, severed cleanly. The man cried out not in pain but in surprise.

Hanen ran from the room into the lumberyard, only to discover he was surrounded by hundreds of men and women. Not all were Sentinels, but all bore the vacant look of those under the influence of Slate's Doom Gauntlet.

50

BOND OF TWO

*I suggest you return to the citadel as soon as you are able.
Brother Himel was found dead, the Gauntlet upon his hand,
thrumming with power. I expect he discovered its secret. A pity
he died with the knowledge on his tongue.*

—SLATE TO PATER GLADEN

The Black Feather was a whirlwind of activity when Ophedia
entered it. Commander Elbay sat on the bar with a charcoal
pencil in her hand and a piece of paper on her lap.

"Commander Elbay," Ophedia said, walking up to her.

"What is it?"

"Captain Navien, the spy from Mahndür."

"What about him?"

"He escaped."

"I know," she said.

"You do?"

"Apparently, two Sentinels were seen lowering him over the
wall where our defenses were weakest." Bolla looked her in the
eye. "Why?"

"Why what?"

"Why come and tell me?"

"Because I would rather face you than the council. You see,
Captain Navien's men had my friends held hostage. We had a

short time to comply, or they'd be killed in cold blood."

"You'd sacrifice an entire city for your friends."

"So would you. For that very reason, you won't kill me."

"What makes you say that?"

"You told me you knew Searn twenty years ago out west, probably in Morriego. It's where he took you under wing, and where he left you. He probably didn't know you were carrying me, but I think he figured it out, since I think he noticed how I look like you, with Macenan auburn hair."

Bolla pursed her lips.

"You've got my sharp wit, and his oratory air." She turned back to her papers. "It's going to get you in trouble some day."

"How did you know who I was?" Ophedia said.

"As soon as you said your name. I gave it to you."

"Oh?"

"Ophedia was my mother's name, and Ishé is the name of the inn I birthed you in. I changed my name to Elbay after I made the foolish choice to abandon you. Yet you've grown up stronger than I ever was, willing to sacrifice your life for your friends."

She lowered herself off the counter and took up her crossbow.

"If this ever gets out—what you did today—you'll not be spared." She held out the crossbow. "Take this."

"I can't," Ophedia said. "I've not earned my axes."

Bolla unhooked her belt from around her waist and dropped it on the counter, with axes still hanging from it.

"Now you have. Take these and get out of here, and don't come back asking for any favors."

Ophedia took the belt off the counter and hung it over her hips. Then she took up the crossbow and left the tavern with one backward glance at Bolla, who turned away with tears brimming in her eyes.

She raced through the city to the Draek Inn, but found it empty except for Whisper, whose black form shot from under a table to her feet. Chairs were upturned; the owner was nowhere to be seen.

"Where is everyone?"

She stepped out into the street and turned south. When she came within a few blocks of the wall, she could hear angry people calling to be let out of the city. Circling the corner, the size of the crowd astounded her.

"Must be half the city here." She found a runoff chain and climbed it to the roof, standing over the crowd.

"Let us out! We're a free people and the gate must be opened for us!" someone shouted.

"That would compromise the city!" a guard called back. "It shall remain locked, by order of the citadel!"

There were a few black-cloaked Sentinels, but none of them were Rallia and Dorian. There were no groups of Voktorra in gray either. Whisper sat at the foot of the building waiting for her to descend. She dropped to the street and began to leg it north, Whisper hot on her heels. A portion of the crowd began to follow her.

"What do you want?" she called back.

"You're a Sentinel. Your council has locked the gate!"

Ophedia ran ever harder. She came to a square that was empty save for two figures walking away. One was tall with a long stick in his hand, and the other short with a head full of hair. Behind her the sounds of the crowd grew. To the north, a single black-cloaked figure ran with a familiar gait.

"Hanen!" she called.

He looked up and redoubled his speed, chased by his own mob. Ophedia and Whisper ran to him as he entered the square, although Whisper ended up veering away.

"What is happening?" she asked.

"Coin carrying, dominated shunts!" Hanen shouted. The fastest one dove at him with axes in his hands, but Hanen shoved him with the palm of the gauntlet and the man disappeared.

"How?!" she called.

"I don't even know!" he replied.

Three more rushed at him and he made a gripping motion, and three coins tore away and whisked into his gauntlet. Ophedia hacked a woman down as she charged at her. Whisper nipped at the heels of another man. Then the mindless attackers paused for a moment, and refocused solely on Hanen.

A mob of people marching toward the citadel arrived in the square. They saw the mindless attackers, half-clad in Sentinel cloaks, and charged them in anger. In the chaos, Ophedia saw a man wearing a gauntlet identical to Hanen's. She raced toward him, raising the crossbow. The man wearing the gauntlet glanced at her, his eyes widening just as she fired the crossbolt into his shoulder above the gauntlet. He cried out and slammed to the ground, the gauntlet falling off and rolling away. Those under its control hesitated briefly before continuing their attack.

Ophedia dove to grab the gauntlet, but the man took hold of her boot and she hit the ground, her jaw striking the pavement and sending stars across her vision. She kicked backward into the man's face, and he cried out. She grabbed the gauntlet, jumped to her feet, and ran back to the riot in the square, which had now melted into complete confusion. Hanen was limping to the side, Whisper rattling his scales at anyone who approached.

"Hanen!" she cried out.

He turned and gave her a weak smile.

"Here!" she said, tossing the gauntlet to him.

She hoped he knew what he was doing.

Hanen caught the gauntlet and put it on; the pair of gloves buzzed as he touched them together and turned toward the crowd. He held up the first glove and made a grasping fist. Pieces of metal shot across the plaza and into his palm, stuck together like a ball of wax. He took the other gauntlet and closed it over the pile of coins. The mass of them began to vibrate and glow, his arms feeling like they would shake loose off his shoulders. He pressed harder, and the coins glowed a bright red until he couldn't contain them anymore and threw the ball into the air. It shot into the sky, brighter than the sun setting in the west, and then exploded in a black cloud of dust over the city.

Ash fell into the plaza.

"Ophedia! Cover yourself!"

Ophedia dropped to her knees and pulled her cloak over her. Others were not so lucky. One man gasped and choked as he inhaled a black flake, falling over like a puppet with cut strings. Others did the same while those standing nearby looked on in horror. Then, those fallen to the cobbles opened their eyes with a dull purple glow.

"Noccitan," Hanen said. "What have I done?"

The weak timbers of the inn's frame shook as people surged north around it, disrupting the peal of the bell in the middle of the table. Seriah reached for the small bells and heard them roll off the table and hit the ground. She dropped to the floor, feeling around for them as Noss shouted orders to his men in the common room below. She struggled to her feet and walked to the door, which opened and threw her back. Someone helped her to her feet, and a noisy crowd of people led her out into the street, where she was disoriented and followed the mob in an unknown direction. She could hear someone getting trampled to the ground, and a blue streak appeared before Seriah, rushing toward the fallen victim.

"Please do not look upon me!" Seriah cried out, wanting to hide from her goddess.

Others fell and Nifara prepared to take them away.

"Why?" Seriah cried out. "Why do you only take and never give?"

The blue streak stopped and turned to Seriah, just as an explosion made most of the mob fall to the ground. Nifara quickly gathered the souls into her arms. Seriah sobbed and fell to her knees and felt something in the air go down her throat and into her lungs.

With a snap she was elsewhere, but Nifara was still there.

"What is this?" the goddess asked. Even through her blinds Seriah could see the blue of Nifara with the white pinpoints of souls she had gathered. All around them were little purple flames, whipping this way and that like apis pollinating flowers.

"Forgive me!" Seriah cried. "And take me away from all this misery!"

Nifara approached her. "What is there to forgive?"

"For bearing that dark message that caused your flight."

"You bear no guilt as a messenger, just as I bear no shame for those souls I take before the Judge. It is my responsibility."

One of the purple flames appeared before Seriah and rushed into her mouth. She felt a heat blazing within her, and a voice in her mind spoke with words she did not know.

"Begone," Nifara said.

Seriah turned to flee.

"Not you, my child," Nifara said. "This thing."

The heat turned to pain. The purple flame erupted from Seriah's mouth and she began to cough. "What was that?"

"I do not know what it is, nor how you and I stand with one foot in the Veld and the other in Kallattai."

"We are in the Veld?"

"Those flames anchor those that have taken in a dark mote into their souls to this Veld."

"Please take me," Seriah begged.

"Why should I?"

"They continue to haunt me, the Walker and his Kin."

"Have they not done enough to you and your soul?" the goddess asked.

She reached out and touched Seriah between the eyes. For a brief moment Seriah shared the eyes of her goddess and saw that she stood not in two worlds but in four. The verdant brightness of Lomïn, the dreary blackness and glittering lights of Noccitan, the Purple Veld where all was possible, and Kallattai... then she stood only in the latter. The blackness of her blinder filled her vision once again.

Nifara was gone, but her voice lingered on the wind. *"You have nothing more to fear from them. I have marked you as my Scale Weight. Seek your purpose, without fear of guilt or dark oppression. For you have and shall always have a choice. Choose."*

51

AFTERMATH

The ghosts of past reach toward,

The man upon the path,

He kept his eyes firm forward,

Avoiding baleful wrath,

Lest they claim his death.

—*THE TRAVELER*, EPIC POEM BY

JUREN LEIFSEN OF BORTALI

The rope still hung there as he came to the bottom. He tugged to make sure it was still secure and then shimmied up the length to the platform above. He only lost his footing twice, and soon had the hang of it and made it to the top. He crouched down to make a flame in his tinder box, and looked out over the city far below.

To the west the armies of the Chalician invaders lit hundreds of torches and split in two directions, the larger force moving south while the other approached the northern part of the wall, nearest to the citadel. Behind the wall were the torches of a secret army awaiting the Chalician attempt to scale the wall, which appeared undefended. He could also see thousands of people gathering to try and escape the imminent doom by the southern gate, while two mobs carrying torches marched toward one another from opposite directions.

"This is all just going to Noccitan on a flaming wagon, isn't it?"

The tinder took and he lit his torch, turning back to the large circular room.

He found the skeleton of the griffin, missing the skull he had taken to his place at the inn before coming back to scale the tower alone. He had only been partially honest with Pater Noss, keeping secret the remains of the man he found there, wearing armor made of the skyfall metal. He freed up the breastplate and hung it over his shoulders. The metal had been beaten extremely thin, but was as heavy as any steel breastplate. It would fit him perfectly. He crouched down and examined the other pieces. It wasn't a full suit, but most pieces were there. If he painted it with boot polish, it would appear like leather armor. The skeleton's right hand bore what looked like a leather falconer's glove—metal talons affixed to it looked menacing, like a griffin's taloned claw.

"Was he assembling his own armor, piece by piece?"

He began to put the pieces of armor in his canvas satchel. To the west a purple-hued cloud burst up over a large neighborhood before settling back down. He finished storing the armor in his satchel and lowered it down, and was just giving the tower a final look when something lodged in the griffin's ribcage caught the light of Umay. When he pulled at the remains of the large creature they collapsed, revealing what appeared to be an ancient curved sword, yet almost more axe than sword, made of skyfall metal and weighing less than he expected. He gave it a few swings and nodded to himself.

"Armor and a sword?" he muttered to himself. "Made a member of the Order of the Axe? Aurín Mateau, I think this suits you."

"What happened?" Ophedia said, as they ducked into an alley and ran toward the other end.

"I don't know," Hanen replied.

"But what did you do?"

"I don't know!" he shouted.

"Well, something happened, and those two gloves are part of it."

"I pulled the coins toward me into that ball, which I tried to use to send them wherever the gloves sent those that disappeared, and instead it just...exploded. I'm worried the dust somehow infected those people touched."

"Where did those people go?"

"I don't know," Hanen said, "but I have a feeling they weren't destroyed. Just...sent somewhere."

"Where?"

"I have no idea. But I am going to find out."

"Good," Ophedia said. "I'm going to go back and see if I can't find Rallia."

"She went north," Hanen said.

"How do you know?"

"I saw her and Dorian go that way. I think they probably went to the citadel to look for us."

He stopped and looked at Ophedia. "Where did you get a crossbow?"

"Commander Elbay made me a captain."

She took off running, leaving Hanen and Whisper standing there in the dark.

"It has been many years since I've been here," Dorian said as Rallia held the door open for him. They entered the citadel, which was unguarded and unlocked. "In fact, it was not long after the Protectorate Wars. I came on a peaceful mission to align the country of Limae with Pariantür. They were part of the league that stood alongside Ikhala, and I felt it would be good to visit and show that we had no ill-will against them."

"And did it work?"

"Not particularly. It was cordial, but certainly didn't establish friendship. Nonetheless, while I was here I learned some very interesting things about this citadel, which most historians agree was built by Pariantür so that a semblance of order could be established. But the tower that stands outside was built long before that, even."

"To what purpose?"

"I do not know. But there is a passage in Ellavon Gavalin's play, Brase Turrian, which references the tower already standing when Liman Untellian came to establish the city here."

"Seems a bit far-fetched," Rallia said. "The Dürani playwright wrote his plays over two hundred years ago. And the Untellians of Alvaria, if they ever existed, lived another five hundred years before that."

"You know your history," Dorian said.

"My father got the gift of storytelling from his grandfather."

"That great-grandfather of yours was an Unteel. The Unteels draw their line back all the way to the original leaders of Redot, who were themselves of the line of Dothar Untellian. Regardless, *Brase Turrian, Prince of Woe,* says the tower is older than the city itself. Do you recall the older story of the two Untellian brothers? The quest they journeyed on before they founded their kingdom?"

"They found a tall tower and within it they met the mysterious stranger who set them on their course."

"It is never said where the tower was located. I always wondered if this might be it."

"Why are you telling me this?"

"Because you are an Unteel, and you ought to know your heritage. I had no children by my wife, and she was also an Unteel."

There was a low boom. Dorian walked over to a window and looked out over the city.

"What was that?" Rallia said, drawing close.

"I don't know," Dorian said. "But I have a deep feeling that something very bad just happened."

The clifftop afforded her a view across the Bortali Waste, where very little lived among the dunes and sandstone rocks. If the horizon had been clear she might have seen to the other side, but a sandstorm swirled in the middle of the desert, sending out tendrils of wind. The Rotha had peeked out from its place within the wrap.

"What do you smell?" Katiam asked.

"Dry," Larohz said. "Sand."

"Yes, good."

The Rotha gave a little whistle that Katiam had come to realize was a laugh. There came the sound of a sleipnir in the woods behind her. She turned and smiled at Jined Brazstein, who smiled back when he saw her and quickened his mount.

"I wondered when you'd catch up with us," she said as he approached.

"Jurgon is with you, then?"

"He left two days ago," Katiam said, "heading south with the children."

"Then it is only the three of you?"

"Four. Esenath stayed with us."

He stepped down from his saddle and came to stand next to her, letting the sleipnir graze.

"I am glad you and I have a moment to ourselves," he said. "I've long wanted your attention, to apologize."

"Apologize?"

"I fear that I am at fault for the fall of your Dweol. I was given a warning, but then kept from sharing it."

"I think nothing could have stopped it," Katiam said. "It had to fall."

"Why?"

"For the true purpose of the Crysalas to be revealed."

"It involves whatever it is you're protecting there, doesn't it?" Jined asked. "It is what healed the Day Blind, and why Esenath insisted on taking the blind orphans from the city."

Katiam nodded. "When I was taken to meet my goddess, she revealed that by delivering this thing to some as-yet-unknown destination, I would be fulfilling the purpose she set on course eons ago."

"Why keep it secret?"

"Because the dark gods of the Black Coterie will do all in their power to stop it."

Jined looked out into the desert.

"These sands weren't here two hundred years ago. It was Glyth-Dormak the Dry-Walker who brought it here, leaving his mark."

"Is he still out there?" Katiam asked.

Jined shook his head. "I don't think so. He left after the Protectorate Wars, and I guess that was when Gold-Eater took over the local vül pack."

"Kos-Yran has cursed many, hasn't he?"

"I imagine so."

"But you're uniquely blessed by Grissone."

"Not uniquely," Jined said. "I think there have been others, such as St. Rämmon. The same could be said of you."

"There are other secrets like the one I bear, and I'm not alone."

"You mean the others that travel with you."

"Yes. We're all different flowers, but together we make a garden."

"I've brought another flower for your garden with me."

"Oh?"

"Sister Salna insisted on joining us. It is partially why we have been so slow to catch up with you."

Katiam gasped. "She is well?"

"Yes, but she tires easily."

"Let's go and see her."

"She'll not show you her face," Jined said.

"She is still bandaged, then?"

"That," Jined said, "and she has taken on the Aspects of Silence and Solitude."

"Oh, that poor girl."

"She doesn't like pity. She's made that clear."

"I'll go ahead to the camp and warn the others." She pointed down the hill toward the forest. "We're just down there. And you can ride into camp with Little Maeda soon after."

"Very well," Jined said. "Please do not hesitate to let me know how I can help you complete your mission."

"Thank you, Jined."

The sisters pulled the girl into a tender and careful embrace as a bittersweet smile played on Nichal's face.

"It may be for the best," Nichal said. "I saw her as they changed the girl's bandages a few days after the fall of the Saor. Her head had to be shaved, and the nurses think it will not grow back. The veil and hood she wears now will allow them only to picture her as she was."

Jined said, "I hope one day, when she is healed, they can see her for what she is, the trials she has faced, and respect that."

"I suppose we all wear masks to hide the wounds we have borne on our souls."

"Yet others pass through the flames and come out the better."

"You mean Dane," Nichal said.

"Yes."

"I doubt his journey is over yet."

"Nor is ours," Jined said. "We're still breathing."

The twins pointed to Onelie's lute, but she only gave them a naïve smile.

"They play, too," Pater Minoris Didus Koel translated. "They promise to break their instruments out tonight after we eat."

"Why do you think," Nichal said, "that Grissone has not appeared since we left Mahn Fulhar?"

"That question has plagued me all winter," Jined said. "But he said that would happen when we spoke last—that he had other things to attend to. It has still been hard for me, though."

"Though everything went wrong in Mahn Fulhar, I knew that he was there with you, in miracle, and that time upon the road when he admonished me has remained on my mind."

"I think he trusts you to make the right decisions. I'm sorry I stayed behind in Brazh and didn't continue on until later."

"In the end, I think it all worked out toward Grissone's will."

"Perhaps," Jined replied. "But I still regret it."

"Life is full of regrets," Nichal said, "and of actions we had to take despite the cost to our souls and our bodies. But we cannot change the past. All we can do is change our course."

Rumor flooded the city of Birin over the past weeks, of trouble in Limae and of the Church of the Common Chalice in Œron on the move to the north and south, sending countless missionaries and Praetors to the kings and queens and lords of the world to spread their news. Expatriate Œronzi living in Birin spread further rumors, that those not of the church of Œron might be forbidden from marriage if their sect took hold, and young couples, already eager for the bells of spring, needed no further prompting to rush to Chapel or the Nifaran Templum for the blessings of the Pantheon over their blessed unions.

Alodda Dülar made up her sister's hair. Runah looked in the mirror with a quaint smile that her older sister could swear bore smug satisfaction at the edges. She had practiced her wiles on Marn Clouw and the other monks to convince them to bless a marriage between herself and the youngest monk, Nidian.

"Nidian thinks we might find a parsonage under the Morriegan church up in Nemen," Runah said. "They're very welcoming there, and it's up in the mountains."

Alodda muttered in acknowledgement but wasn't listening.

They had been in the city now no longer than two weeks. That Runah hadn't already run off and married the monk surprised her. He was brash but humble, quick to righteous indignation, but slow to any true anger. Runah would have him wrapped around her little finger in a day or two.

"But would you?" Runah asked.

"Would I what?" Alodda replied.

Runah scoffed. "Aren't you listening? I asked you to come and tend our home in Nemen. You can bring money into the household with your embroidery."

Alodda looked at herself in the mirror, halfway through her twenties, blonde hair straight as straw and giving her age, invited now by her younger sister and a bride-to-be, to become her spinster housekeeper.

"Is that what this is all about?" Alodda said cooly.

"Is what *what* is about?" Runah said.

"Marrying for the chance at lording over me?"

Runah scoffed, and rolled her eyes. But Alodda detected a smirk.

"I will not go with you to Nemen,"

"Then what will you do?"

Alodda thanked the pantheon for the knock at the door..

At the door stood Marn Clouw. He bore features more closely resembling Rallia than Hanen, with greying blond hair and a matching beard, now that he had let his hair grow in again. He still wore his grey monk's habit under the Birinese street clothes he had purchased. "They are ready," he said.

Alodda nodded, took a deep breath and swallowed her pride, turning to her sister with as genuine a smile as she could muster. Runah wore a blue cape on her shoulders, over her own rich blue Mahndürian over-gown. Her smile was even broader, and she held in her hands a bundle of mid-spring flowers.

"How do I look?" Runah asked.

"Like mother," Alodda said, a tear welling in her eyes. "If she could see you now..."

Runah crossed the room and placed her hands in Alodda's.

"Thank you for this," Runah said.

"This is it though," Alodda said. "You walk through that door, there is no turning back."

"I know."

"Alright then," Alodda said, and swung the door open for her.

Runah stepped out into the hall of the city chapel of Aben, and turned to the main aisle.

Marn fell in alongside Alodda.

"There isn't much more you can say," he said. "Let her be an adult. She'll learn fast enough."

"Maybe you'll get to see Rallia do the same one day," Alodda said.

"To be honest," Marn said, "I'd much rather see Hanen at the front of this chapel right now."

"Me as well," Alodda said, and shot a look at Marn with equal parts devious smile and deep blush.

Marn chuckled and then added, "I'm thinking of returning west to find him."

Alodda started. "Really?"

Marn nodded.

Runah had come to the front of the chapel. Nidian stood with a stupid grin across his face. He wore his robes openly. The priest of Aben officiating gave them both a stern look, and began to the ceremony.

Alodda leaned in to Marn and whispered. "I will go with you."

Hanen tore back the wood from the cellar entrance and slipped in. It was dark, dusty, and hadn't had a soul in it for ages. Clearing a space in the middle of the room, he crouched down and lit a candle with tinder, after which he took out the journals and the gauntlets. He pulled both gauntlets on, and it took all his strength to touch them together as they began to buzz and glow with power. Their light suddenly split into several colors before oscillating into purple in the center of the glow. He closed his left fist and the purple light stopped moving. With the other hand he touched the light, and it tore the air, becoming a window into the purple-hued world beyond.

"*You found a way through,*" the voice of Searn said.

"What do you mean?"

"*Into the Veld, the Realm of Dream, without all the trouble Ollistan went to.*"

"You've been reading over my shoulder. "

"*I have.*"

"So what should I do now?"

"*Press the gauntlets through. I have an idea.*"

Hanen put a black gauntlet through the hole between worlds and it turned a bright silver, like a mirror.

"*Interesting,*" Searn said.

Hanen put the other gauntlet through until all that remained on his side of the window was two rings of black metal around his wrists.

"*Close the window,*" Searn said.

Hanen moved his hands around, trying to command the window to close. His left hand slipped out of its gauntlet and the window lost its clarity. When he slipped his right hand out of the second gauntlet, it closed completely. Two large black rings clattered to the ground. Hanen took up one and put it on. Nothing happened. Then he slipped the other back on his wrist and immediately the window opened again. He took the gauntlets back and the window closed.

"*That's helpful,*" Searn said. "*Now do it again.*"

Hanen opened the window and put the gauntlets in then took his hands out, catching the rings as the window closed and put them over his wrists. The window to the Veld opened again, yet this time the gloves on the other side were not silver but black. As he pulled his hands out of the gate, the gauntlets turned silver.

"*Well, that's handy. What do those do?*"

"What do you mean?"

"*You don't have two gauntlets now, Hanen. You have four. This is very, very interesting. And if these gauntlets are doubled, what does that mean for the rest of the armor?*"

"Why bother?" Hanen said. "Why not be happy with this, and see if we can't use these to our advantage?"

"*You're not just a little intrigued?*"

"No."

"*You heard what that storyteller said. He has spent lifetimes*" *seeking the answers to those gloves he was given, but he was just as intrigued by the armor that his brother Rionne wears. He covets the idea of having both gauntlets and armor. These gauntlets you wear are a reflection of that relationship. The last wearer of the armor was a fool. Nothing but a mindless warrior given invincibility. You're no fool. And with our minds working together, imagine what puzzles we could unravel."*

Hanen opened the window again and pressed the gauntlets back in, and took his hands out. He placed the two black metal rings into his satchel then pulled the boneshroud from his back and put it into the satchel as well.

"Why am I the one who has to do this?" he said to Whisper, who slunk out from under the crate he had been hiding behind, curling into Hanen. "I don't want this responsibility."

Whisper licked at his hand, asking for a scratch. Hanen obliged.

"But someone has to. Maybe it's supposed to be me. What if the curse the Deceiver placed upon our family is meant to mark me, not for greatness but for that debt Nair said he'd call in? What if I'm doomed to die alone and unknown, or as a greater villain than the Apostate was, no matter what I do?"

He scratched behind the ears of the little ynfald. "But what if I can solve these riddles and cheat the cheater. And give the tools to someone more worthy than I could ever be."

With another tap the metal chest opened, revealing a book with the smell of fresh paste coming off it. He placed the book on the desk and opened it. The pages were blank, yet each page appeared to be a different age and have a different maker. He leafed through them all and turned back to the first page after finding nothing.

"The secret to unlocking them," Beltran muttered, "was blood."

Dane took up a quill made of the same strange metal as the cracked orb at the center of town.

"Blood?" he asked.

"The Moteans draw their own blood and feed it to the page, awakening what lies within."

Dane pressed his quill into his forearm, breaking the skin so blood could soak into the quill, which he then touched to the page.

"What do I write?"

"Anything," Beltran said.

"What are you?" Dane wrote in blood.

Nothing happened. Dane sighed. Then, the blood faded into the paper and disappeared.

The same should be asked of you, words bloomed. *Where is Dusk?*

"He is dead," Dane said.

How?

"The connection has been made," Beltran said.

"Between what?" Dane asked.

"Your souls."

"Who lies within this book?" Dane asked.

I am Shear. I speak for those collected here.

"Collected?"

Yes. Has Zoumerik informed you of nothing? We have much to go over if we are to complete our mission. What is your name?

"I am your Retribution," Dane said.

That is a new name. Retribution. What is your purpose among the Brotherhood?

"Exactly what it implies."

What?

Dane stood with the book in his hand and walked to the hearth. He tossed the book into the flames without another word. The haunting cries of souls screamed out as Dane watched the book burn. Countless generations of heresies dwindled and died like a candle going out.

He turned back to Beltran.

"Give me another," he said, rubbing at the sore spot where he had drawn the bead of blood. "We have a long night ahead of us."

EPILOGUE

In bitter spite Unteel was promised a cursed fate,

Descendants marked to serve, opening enemy gate.

While Turrian as enemy—foil'd servant of the liar,

was promised that from loin, a great queen should he sire.

For choice was theirs to take or deny the offer giv'n,

Both choose in the end their blood spilled for their kin.

But all would end by choice to bring 'bout curse and woe.

Unteel and Turrian, Untellians, brothered houses long other's foe.

— FINAL STANZA OF *BRASE TURRIAN, PRINCE OF WOE*, BY
ELLAVON GAVALIN, DÜRANI PLAYWRIGHT

He walked into the square, the tall staff in his hand clacking on the cobbles. He could sense trouble in every direction. But the greatest trouble was one his Wisdom told him was nothing to fear, yet the greatest threat to all. He turned and saw him sitting atop the barrel, head covered in thick, long hair, and a beard to match.

"I watched an odd thing," the nearby figure said. "I watched men fight something I could not see."

Wisdom told him he could speak plainly, so long as he give nothing away and answer no question given.

"I see someone before me that is only seen when he wishes to be, and only walks where he wishes to walk."

"You perceive well, qavyl," the other replied, jumping off the barrel as he approached. "It is not often Wisdom chooses one of your race so young, to carry him about as a father carries a child. Has he grown so weak?"

"You walk this city, and have for days," the qavyl said. "I know by what names we might call you, but not by what name you wish now to be known."

"I travel by the name of Kash, and Coldness."

Wisdom told him to offer up a name that would not reveal his true self.

"I am Chance-Thief and Wisdom-Bearer," the qavyl replied.

"With names offered, let us establish the rules of this conversation."

"You move as one watching the final moves of a long-held plan."

"The final lines of this act," Coldness offered.

"What would you ask for in return for some enlightenment on this plot?"

"I will tell you what you ask, if Wisdom will finally offer up the name of your chosen pawns. All of us have committed a Champion save Wisdom and Destruction."

"Then even Rionne will commit one?" Chance-Thief asked.

"If he can do so past the drool dribbling from his skull, he too shall be allowed to place a weight upon the scale."

"Wisdom agrees to offer up a Scale-Weight. But first, you give up your plot."

"The Dothari Curse," Coldness said. "My brother decided finally to collect upon it and marked the bearer a generation ago, to pass to their firstborn."

"And only the firstborn bears the weight?"

"Achanerüt couldn't care less about the girl. She matters not."

"You know this?"

"I pit my gauntlet upon it. The girl means nothing."

"What of the heir of Turrian?'

"So long as she does not interfere nor seek to stop the Untellian, we shall not stop the Turrian from coming into their own. But if they do, then a curse will be brought down upon them and their lives will be forfeit."

"So long as they know this. They must have a choice."

"There is always a choice. That is the cornerstone of fate. Not moments ago I gave the Untellian the 'gift' of Fate, and nothing has changed."

"Then nothing is gained nor lost this day."

"But I gain the name of the one you choose as your Scale-Weight."

"While the Dothari Curse may allow the Deceiver to call upon its weight to tip balance in his favor, Wisdom chooses to give free choice to any Scale-Weight who takes up the War Bane."

"You do not choose a side?" Coldness laughed. "But allow any side of the scale to take up that burden to bear your blessing?"

The qavyl nodded.

"So let it be done," Kash said.

"This is no victory for you, but a promise," Chance-Taker said.

"And so you are bonded to that promise. Even if one of your own family should take up the War Bane, it may not be enough after this night."

"In what way?"

"Cannot Wisdom sense it? As we have spoken, another grain is placed upon the scales of imbalance."

Chance-Thief stopped in their tracks and Coldness continued to walk away, whistling a chaotic tune to himself.

Wisdom went silent, considering those words.

"What did he mean?" the qavyl asked Wisdom. "What does any of that mean?"

Wisdom advised him to consider the final words of the Master play, Brase Turrian, Prince of Woe.

A loud crack exploded from the square several blocks behind him, and a plume of otherworldly dust expanded across a quarter of the city. Some people blown over did not rise again, but others rose with a Veldic curse in their eyes, revenants of a bygone era.

THE END

TO BE CONTINUED IN

VOLUME FOUR OF THE

KALLATTIAN SAGA: **DREAD KNIGHT**

GLOSSARY 1

DRAMATIS PERSONAE

HANEN CLOUW (*Ha-NEHN Khl-OW*) — A Black Sentinel
mercenary and organizer of the Clouw Sentinel Merchant Detail.
Hanen is a 1st Lieutenant in the Black Sentinels, and thus has
earned his second hand axe.

RALLIA CLOUW (*Rah-LEEAH Khl-OW*) — Like her older
brother Hanen, Rallia is a 1st Lieutenant in the Black Sentinels,
though she prefers to carry a staff she had built with both of her
clubs mounted on the ends. Rallia is also deft with a razor, and
often shaves the heads and faces of fellow Black Sentinels.

JINED BRAZSTEIN (*Jih-NED BRADJ-steen*) — Rank of
Brother Excelsior. Vow of Chastity. Son of Jarl Jaegür von
Brazstein of Brazh, Jined left home to avoid execution for
murdering a fellow prince of Boroni. Jined joined the Paladins of
the Hammer as a Penitent, committing his life to Grissone, the god
of Faith.

KATIAM BORREAU (*Kah-TEE-um Burr-OH*) — A Paladame
of the Rose. Personal physician to the Matriarch Superioris and
Prima Pater. Aspects of Peace, St. Klare, and Dignity.

SERIAH YALEDÍT (*Sur-EYE-uh Yah-leh-DEET*) — Monk of
Nifara. She is known for often establishing orphanages in towns
that have none.

ABENARD NAVIEN (*Abb-ih-NARD NAY-vee-EN*) — A ranking member of the Voktorra guard guild in Mahn Fulhar.

ABITHU OMRAB (*Ab-ee-THU Om-RAB*) — Benefactor Missioner of the Church of the Common Chalice.

ABGENAS DÜLAR (*Ab-GHEE-nahs Doo-LARR*) — An old tailor who served in the Protectorate Wars.

AEGUR (*A-gur*) — Cup. Deceased Paladin of the Hammer. Rank of Brother Primus. Vow of Silence. Shade bound in a pen..

ALODDA DÜLAR (*Uh-LAW-thuh Doo-LARR*) — A seamstress and daughter of Abgenas Dülar.

ANHOUIL CHÉTAIN (*An-WEE Che-TANE*) — Praeposit of the Praetors of the Chalice.

ARTHOSS BRAZSTEIN (*ARR-thoss BRADJ-steen*) — Younger brother to Jined Brazstein

ASTRID GLASS (*AH-strid Glass*) — Paladame of the Rose. Aspects of Discretion, Compassion, and Honor.

AURÍN MATEAU (*AW-reen Ma-TOE*) — A Black Sentinel from Œron.

AVARR (*AH-var*) — A rancher

AVERIN (*AV-er-in*) — Pater Minoris of the Green Bastion.

AVINE GELDIN (*AH-veen GEL-din*) — Sister Superioris of the Vault in Zebude.

BELL (*Bell*) — A mysterious Paladin, member of the Motean sect.

BELLIGAR MAND (*BELL-ig-gar MAND*) — Saint of Nifara.

BELTRAN CAUTESE (*BELL-tran CAW-tease*) — Primus

BOLLA ELBAY (*BO-lah ELL-bay*) — Black Sentinel Commander

BROTHERS HAMMER (*Bruther HAMM-err*) — A mysterious Paladin who quotes scripture. Revealed to be the god of Faith, Grissone, in physical form.

CÄVIAN (*CAVE-ee-an*) — Paladin of the Hammer. Rank of Brother Excelsior. Vow of Silence. Twin of Loïc.

CHÖS TELMAR (*CHAHSS TEL-mar*) — A Black Sentinel.

CRÄG NARN (*KRAGG NARN*) — An old monk of Nifarah, currently acting as advisor on the Archimandrite's council.True name is Koragh Neyarn.

DANE MARRIC (*DAEN MARE-ik*) — Paladin of the Hammer. Rank of Brother Excelsior. Vow of Chastity.

DEGGAR (*DAY-gar*) — A Black Sentinel Commander.

DERAH BAKER (*DARE-ah BAY-ker*) — Head of the Moon Eyes children and a member of the Crysalas.

DIDUS KOEL (*DIE-duss COAL*) — Pater Minoris of the Paladins of the Hammer. Vow of Prayer.

DORIAN MÜR (*DOOR-ee-an MEWR*) — Prima Pater of the Paladins of the Hammer. Head of the Church of Grissone. Vow of Prayer. Became the youngest Prima Pater in history, elected almost unanimously during the Protectorate Wars. He still holds the title, seventy-five years later, at the ripe age of 95.

DUSK (*DUSK*) — A mysterious Paladin, member of Motean sect.

EIMEÉ DÜLAR (*AY-MEE Doo-LARR*) — Seamstress. Wife of Abgenas Dülar.

ERALT LOTH (*Err-ALT LAW-th*) — Paladin of the Hammer. Rank of Primus. A Motean.

ESENATH CHLOÏS (*AH-sen-oth Khloh-EES*) — Paladame of the Rose. Botanist. Sidieratan. Aspects of Cleanliness and Charity.

EUNIA HALLA (*YOU-nee-ah HA-lah*) — A Black Sentinel from southern Mahndür.

FEDELMINA BARBA (*FE-dell-MEEN-ah BAR-bah*) — Paladame of the Rose. Aspects of Clarity and Peace.

GOREG VON THOMMÜS (*GOR-eg von TOE-moos*) — Jarl of Thom in Boroni.

GUARIN (*GOO-ar-in*) — A monk of Aben.

GRUZ FORENOR (*GROOS FOR-an-ur*) — A Black Sentinel Commander

JAEGÜR von BRAZSTEIN (*YAY-goor von BRADJ-steen*) — Jarl of Brahz in Boroni.

JAMIS ZOUMERIK (*JAY-miss ZOO-mare-ick*) — Paladin of the Hammer. Rank of Pater Minoris. Vow of Poverty.

JURGON UPONA (*YOOR-gahn Oo-POH-na*) — Paladin of the Hammer. Rank of Brother Primus. The Prima Pater's Seneschal. Husband of Sabine Upona. Vow of Prayer.

KASH (*CASH*) — A storyteller.

KEREI LANT (*KEE-REE LAN-t*) — Monk of Nifara. Councillor to the Archimandrite.

KETIVAH VAUR-BRAZSTEIN (*Kah-TEE-vah VOW-r BRADJ-steen*) — Wife of Arthoss Brazstein.

KLAMMEN VON DONIGAR (*KLA-men von DOE-nee-GAHR*) — Jarl of Donig in Boroni.

KLENT RIGAL (*KHLENT Ree-GALL*) — High Priest of Aben.

LAROHZ (*LAH-rose*) — The Rotha.

LOÏC (*Low-EEK*) — Paladin of the Hammer. Rank of Brother Excelsior. Vow of Silence. Twin of Cävian. From Setera.

LOR HARDIN (*LORE HAR-din*) — A Black Sentinel Commander

LUPHINI GOLLIN (*Loo-FEE-NEE GO-lin*) — Saint of Nifara.

MAEDA SALNA (*MAY-dah SAHL-nah*) — Paladame of the Rose, "Little Maeda," Aspects of Virginity and Honor.

MARN CLOUW (*MARN Khl-OW*) — Father of Hanen and Rallia Clouw. A monk of Aben.

NAIR (*NAY-er*) — A storyteller.

NICHAL GUESS (*Nih-KAHL GESS*) — Pater Segundus of the Paladins of the Hammer. Castellan of Pariantür. Vow of Poverty.

NIDIAN (*NID-ee-an*) — A monk ofAben

ODITTE FOI (*Oh-DIE-tt Foo-AH*) — Abbess Superioris of the Crysalas Convent in Mahn Fulhar.

ONELIE CLEMMBÄKKER (*OH-Neh-lee CLEM-bah-ker*) — Daughter of the Jarl of Clehm.

OPHEDIA DEL ISHÉ (*Oh-FEE-DEE-ah del EE-shay*) — A new Black Sentinel and apprentice to Searn VeTurres.

PELLIAN NOSS (*PELL-ee-an NAH-ss*) — Paladin of the Hammer. Pater Minoris of the Piedala Fortress. Vow of Prayer.

PERRAH (*PEAR-ah*) — a Rancher

RAGNUT VON STURMGUARD (*RAG-nut von Sch-TERM-gard*) — Jarl of Sturm in Boroni.

REDDO DOTTI (*RED-do DOH-tee*) — Saint of Nifara.

RUNAH DÜLAR (*ROO-nuh Doo-LARR*) — Alodda's sister.

SAEDRIK VON CLEMMBÄKKER (*SAY-drikh CLEM-bah-ker*) — Jarl of Clehm.

SÄLLA FYFE (*SAW-luh FIE-ff*) — A Black Sentinel.

SEARN VETURRES (*SURN Veh-TOOR-ez*) — Captain of the Black Sentinels.

SERK VON GERTIGAN (*SUR-kh von GAYR-tih-ghen*) — Jarl of Gerht.

SIGRI SMITH (*SIH-gree SMITH*) — Captain of the Paladames of the Rose. Aspects of Virginity, Form, Function.

SILAS MERUN (*SIGH-luss MARE-un*) — Paladin of the Hammer. Rank of Brother Paladin. gehNichal Guess' Senechal.

SLATE (*SLATE*) — Paladin of the Hammer. Rank of Primus. Vow of Silence. Motean. Real name Yngver Morrin

STEVAN FILIP (*Ste-VAN FILL-ip*) — A Paladin almoner.

TERMIA DOMIC (*TER-mee-ah DAH-mic*) — A Black Sentinel Commander

ÜTOL VON TOSCHBRECHT (*OO-tahl von TAH-sch-BREH-kt*) — Jarl of Tosch in Boroni.

VELAB ERDTHAL II (*VELL-ab URD-thall*) — King of Mahndür.

VOLDÉ (*VOL-duh*) — A woman of Zebude.

WESKAR ABRAU (*WESS-kar AB-raoo*) — Provost of the Praetors of the Chalice. Known as the Catechist.

WHISPER (*WHISPER*) — A smaller black ynfald.

YADVI SAHNE (*YAD-vee SAN*) — A member of the Crysalas

YANAS BRODIER (*YANN-ass BRO-dee-ehr*) — A Curate of the Praetors of the Chalice.

YMBRYS VERONIA (*IM-brees Ver-OH-nee-ah*) — A qavyl spice merchant.

YULAN VORE (*YOO-lan VORR*) — A Black Sentinel Commander

ZAPA yu CARADADZ (*ZAH-PASS yoo CAR-ah-DAJ*) — A hrelgren map merchant.

ZEHAN OTEM (*ZAY-han OH-tem*) — Provost of the Order of the Chalice. Known also as the Enquêteur.

ZELLINA DOSK (*Zell-EE-na DOSK*) — Saint of Nifara.

ZHAG rm TELLIS (*ZHAW-gh rem TELL-iss*) — A young hrelgren merchant.

GLOSSARY 2

PANTHEON OF KALLATTAI

The Existence — *Maker of All* and *He That Is*. The world of Kallattai came into being at his word: BEGIN. He made first the two brother gods, and then the two sisters as their wives. Power was granted to them, and through them all was created, and the Existence was worshiped.

ABEN (*A-benn*) — *High King in Lomïn, the Ever-Day*. Made from a white star. His way is the Path. His Gray Watchers hold lanterns to guide those that seek the Path. His tenets are an Arrow, pointing the way to the green fields of Lomïn. The Chalice raised symbolizes his first domain, the sea. And from those depths the Ancient Ones sing.

WYV-THÜM (*WIHV THOOM*) — *The Three-Eyed Judge in Noccitan, the Ever-Night*. Brother to Aben, and formed by the Existence from the well of a black star. When he descended to his Realm of Noccitan he donned the title Thüm, or Judge.

CRYSANIA (*Cri-SAH-nee-ah*) — *Life Mother, Purity Resplendent, and Seamstress of the Future Tapestry* is wife to Aben. Only she can untangle the knots caused by time and see what the future holds. Her people are those that seek to protect the Dweol, the World-Roses that speak directly to her and one another, providing the Crysalas Integritas a chance to glance, ever briefly, at the Future.

SAKHARN (*Sa-KAHRN*) — *Wife to Wyv, Shepherdess of the Veld*—the Dreamscape from which the impossible is dreamed and made fact. She is the goddess of the Improbable, for she impossibly birthed the Deceiver without her husband to sire him.

THE CHILDREN OF ABEN AND CRYSANIA

LAE'ZEQ (*Lay-ZEK*) — *Firstborn of Aben, god of Wisdom, Curious One.* His people, the qavylli, follow his path into the depths of knowledge, for upon his own pages he wrote the secrets of life. Long has he now sojourned, seeking an answer to the prophecy that ties his fate to the death of his closest friend.

GRISSONE-ANKA (*Gri-ZOHN AHN-kha*) — *Twin-Souled, god of Faith.* As Grissone came of age his soul was two. The Anka, who soars above all and sees all, is joined to him. He was the creator of man, who abandoned Grissone to worship many. Now his loyal followers are few: the Paladins who seek protection of the people who no longer follow their god.

NIFARA (*NEE-FA-rah*) — *The Virgin of Justice, Soul Messenger, Once-Betrothed, Future Healer.* She learned to step between worlds from her once-betrothed, Kos-Yran, before he fell. She bears now the responsibility of that now-mad god, escorting souls between worlds they were never meant to set foot upon. Justice is her only concern, as she attempts to balance the scales perfectly.

KASNE et TERRAL (*Kaz-NEH et Teh-RAHL*) — *Prince of the Forest, Toucher of Souls,* Youngest of Aben and Crysania, Kasne strode from the forests that he had created, his people, the Minotyr on his heels. And yet it was he who agreed to leave his own people to take the enslaving Gren under his command, and from them came the Hrelgrens, touched by his hand, and blessed with a command of peace.

THE CHILDREN OF WYV AND SAKHARN

RIONNE (*Rye-OWN*) — *Firstborn of Wyv and Sakharn, Creator of Civilization, the Arbiter, The Fallen Warrior*—fallen to ruin when he was deceived by Achanerüt. Driven mad, he slew his greatest creations, and turned his own people into a scourge of the sky.

KEA'RINOUL (*Kee-AH-rih-NOOL*) — *The Scarred One, He-Who-Was-Beautiful*. Kea'Rinoul abandoned his own people, the Goranc, for he had been a god of beauty, marred by his fallen brothers. It is said he is a god who bathes in the blood of his followers, the T'Akai, wracked with torment by his own visage.

KOS-YRAN (*KOSS-EE-RAHN*) — *The Mad Gift-Giver, Once-Walker-Between-Worlds, Kashir Two-Gloves, the Walker*. Yet now he is banished to wander, gifting curses to those that seek him out. His own people, the vül, though small in number, are an infestation upon the civilized, sowing mayhem and destruction wherever they call home.

ACHANERÜT (*AH-ken-er-OOT*) — *The Deceiver, The Weaver, The Thirteen-Limbed One, Fatherless*. His thirteen limbs sow lies and weave dissension. His eyes see far, and bring kings to their knees. All that is in ruin is his attribute. All that is built up fears that he shall tear it down. The machinations of his web cannot be understood, even by the gods.

GLOSSARY 3

BLACK SENTINELS

The Black Sentinels are a mercenary organization in which each individual seeks out their own bodyguard contracts, and pays dues back to the organization, thus allowing them to wear their trademark black, peak-hooded cloak. They carry various weapons to denote their rank, which equates to their pay grade, hidden under their cloaks to keep their ability concealed.

BANDED CLUB — Initiate to the Black Sentinels carry a single club.

BLACK CLOAK — Officially marks their entry in the organization.

2ND CLUB — Sergeant rank. Common rate for their service is a full silver Baro a day in the northern nations.

HAND AXE — Lieutenants can negotiate a higher pay, armed with a more lethal weapon.

2ND AXE — 1st Lieutenants have several clients willing to give them a good reference.

CROSSBOW — Only by being promoted by the upper echelons can a Black Sentinel become a Captain.

BATTLE AXE — Commanders are rarely seen away from the Black Sentinels headquarters in Limae.

GLOSSARY 4

PALADINS OF THE HAMMER

The Paladins are the followers of Grissone, god of Faith. Each Paladin takes on one of the five active Vows. (The sixth vow, Introspection, or Blindness, is no longer taken.) The Paladins were founded in the Hrelgren Imperial Year 1111, the same year the T'Akai first appeared, launching attacks into what is now the Protectorate of Pariantür, (simultaneously against the Hrelgren Empire and Qavylli Republic.) Heeding Grissone's call, the seven apostles founded the Order, and peoples from every nation came to help them build Pariantür to defend against the T'Akai incursion. Many of the men who survived the war stayed on at Pariantür, joining the Order.

VOWS OF THE PALADINS

VOW OF PRAYER — Those that adopt this Vow ground themselves in the memorization of scripture, making the conscious effort to speak their inner thoughts directly to their god.

VOW OF POVERTY — Paladins are supported via family stipend or by their own trade. Paladins who take this vow perform additional duty to pay for their room and board and they may not keep personal items.

VOW OF CHASTITY — Those that take this Vow are forbidden from marrying. Many avoid contact with members of the opposite sex entirely.

VOW OF PACIFISM — Paladins who take this Vow never raise their hammer against another, seeking peace by any other means.

VOW OF SILENCE — Brothers who take this Vow do not speak another word for the rest of their lives, instead communicating through their hands. These brothers also give up their surnames as their founder, Sternovis did.

VOW OF BLINDNESS — This Vow is no longer taken. Those that did bound their eyes away from the world.

HOLDINGS OF THE HAMMER

The Paladins live in communities of two or more brothers and their monasteries are scattered across the world, having different sizes and designations.

BASTIONS

A least two Paladins stationed at a bastion at any given time. Can be as high as twenty-five. Most major cities and towns have a bastion and many are raised at intervals along long stretches of road between cities.

FORTRESSES

Commanding local bastons, a fortress houses upward of one hundred Paladins.

CITADELS

There are four Citadels. Each commands a network of Fortresses and Bastions.

PARIANTÜR — Pariantür is the head of the entire order and acts as guardian over the eastern lands known as the Protectorate of the Hammer. Over half of the entire order is stationed there—over seven thousand Paladins. There is enough space to house over ten thousand Paladins if necessary. The Paladames have over three-thousand sisters stationed at Pariantür.

ST. HAMUL — This citadel holds sway over the Order in the eastern nations of Ganthic. Nearly five hundred brothers are stationed there.

THE AERIE — Located in the country of Limae, the Aerie has nearly four hundred brothers stationed there. Commands Northwestern Ganthic fortresses and bastions.

AMMAR — Located in Ormach, Ammar Citadel has over one thousand Paladins stationed there. While this citadel controls the fewest Fortresses and Bastions, it boasts one of the greatest human libraries outside of Pariantür.

RANKS OF THE HAMMER

Those seeking admittance to the Order of the Hammer begin as either:

ACOLYTE — Individual who seeks out Pariantür to become a Paladin.

PENITENT — Individual who has chosen servitude over imprisonment or worse.

These lower level Acolytes and Penitents are grouped together and don brown robes and shaving their heads. They act as servants to the Hammer at Pariantür while learning to live as a Paladin.

ESTUDIATE — Having learned the Rule of St. Ikhail, Estudiates lives a life of routine and constant change as they are tested in various occupations over the course of a year. During this time they will review each Vow, and come to a decision regarding which Vow they will take. This decision marks their graduation to Neophyte.

NEOPHYTE — Having taken on a vow, the Neophyte begins study under a master in their chosen or assigned trade. They are given their hammer, which is chained to their belt by the twenty-two links, and they are given the Vow-Bead which will hang from their belt until they receive cordons.

Vow of Chastity — Haloed Hammer
Vow of Poverty — Stylized Pattern
Vow of Silence — Tower
Vow of Pacifism — Shield
Vow of Prayer — Anka's Wing
Vow of Blindness — Simple Band

PALADIN — When the Neophyte is given their armor, they are officially called a Paladin, but in name only. It is only if they proceed past this level that they will be considered a true Paladin by the Brotherhood. They have a single year to test as a Journeyman in their field if they wish to proceed. If they do not master their chosen profession, they will wait anywhere from five to ten years before being allowed to test once more.

BROTHER PALADIN — If deemed worthy, a Paladin is given the red cordons, marking them both a Master in their trade, and a Brother Paladin. Full member of the Brotherhood with full rights to vote on all matters. If leadership requires they move to a new trade, they will learn from and proceed through the same lessons and trials, however, nothing can take their rank of Brother Paladin from them.

BROTHER EXCELSIOR — Brother Excelsiors are the equivalent to a lieutenant, commanding brothers of lower rank, marked by green cordons. Quite often they are true experts or specialists in their assigned trade. A Brother Excelsior in the Smithy might be an expert at metal inlays. A baker might specialize in selecting and negotiating superior ingredients.

BROTHER ADJUTANT — Marked by white cordons, there is rarely more than a single Brother Adjutant in any occupation at a single location. They often fill vacant leadership roles when a higher rank is not present. This rank is also considered the first "true" leadership rank.

BROTHER PRIMUS — Leaders and masters, the black-cordoned Primus commands respect and authority. Primuses often hold the highest rank at Fortresses.

PATER MINORIS — A Paladin will rarely rise to this rank without there being a vacancy. Each Citadel is led by one, and many fortresses have a Pater Minoris stationed there as leader. There is a Pater Minoris representing each Vow stationed at Pariantür. Besides wearing gold cordons, their armor is also often adorned with symbology reflective of the long traditions of a Citadel. The five Pater Minorii stationed at Pariantür fill very important roles in the community.

- Pater Minoris of Prayer Hiram van Höllebon, Chaplain to Pariantür
- Pater Minoris of Poverty Mason Diggle, Keeper of Fealty
- Pater Minoris of Chastity Pol Dunkirk, Hospitaler
- Pater Minoris of Silence Daveth, Grandmaster Smith
- Pater Minoris of Pacifism Klous Girard, Groundskeeper

PATER SEGUNDUS — Under the Prima Pater rules a council of four Pater Segundii, each representing a different Vow. They are marked by blue cordons and their words hold nearly as much authority as the Prima Pater himself.

- Pater Segundus of Poverty Nichal Guess, Pariantür's Castellan
- Pater Segundus of Pacifism Gallahan Pír, Master Scribe
- Pater Segundus of Silence Athmor, Master Cellarer
- Pater Segundus of Chastity Agapius Emiro, Sacrist

PRIMA PATER — There is only one Prima Pater. A Prima Pater's armor is crafted to match the motifs and symbols of the founding saint of their Vow. When a Prima Pater's rank is passed on, one of the Pater Segundii under him will take on the role, donning armor of their own figurehead saint, thus ensuring that another Vow takes the helm.

THE CRYSALAS SOCIETAS

Followers of Crysania are known collectively as the Members of the Crysalas Societas. This includes women of the secret Vaults, known as the Crysalas Integritas, Paladames of the Rose known officially as the Crysalas Honoris, the Shieldmaidens of Boroni and Bronue, and several smaller factions of female qavylli and hrelgrens who have chosen to follow Crysania. All of these Societas meet in secret Vaults across the world of Kallattai, guarding prophecies gathered from the Dweol and each other.

Centuries ago, the Church of Aben long ago and went further into hiding. The majority of the Crysalas fled to Pariantür, where they formed the Crysalas Honoris, known as Paladame. This formation tricked down over time to changing the nature of the Crysalas Vaults to guarding women from predatory men and political leveraging.

ASPECTS OF PURITY

Across the entire organization members of the Crysalas take on Aspects of purity, rather than Vows as Paladins do. Some of these have been around since the foundation while others have developed over time. Most sisters take on an average of three Aspects, though some take on more. They are noted publicly by adornments, which creates a general customized look among the sisters who otherwise wear only white robes and headdresses. These Aspects fall into four categories:

BLOSSOM — Purity of Form
THORN — Purity of Choice
LEAF — Purity of Service
ROOT — Purity of Function

ASPECTS OF THE BLOSSOM

ASPECT OF CLEANLINESS — *(Shaven Head)* This Aspect focuses on a ritualistic and meticulous cleaning regimen.

ASPECT OF SILENCE — *(Veil)* Wears a veil over their face so they cannot be seen. They are not completely silent, talking in quiet whispers. Sisters of this aspect experience an aloneness that others naturally give them.

ASPECT OF VIRGINITY — *(Gilded Rose)* Women who select this Aspect are forbidden to marry. While most Crysalas do not marry, they are not forbidden from doing so as these sisters are.

ASPECT OF PEACE — *(Wooden Mace)* Sisters who take this Aspect vow to cause no harm to another.

ASPECT OF STRICTNESS — *(Solid Plate on Shoulder)* — Sisters who take this Aspect have no choice over their diet. They must eat what they are served, and may not leave any of it untouched, nor ask for more when the meal is concluded.

ASPECTS OF THE THORN

(It is often frowned upon that any sister take more than one Thorn Aspect, as each is known to be stringent and difficult.)

ASPECT OF SANCTITY — *(Gloves)* Sisters who take on the Aspect of Sanctity do not feel the touch of another save through their gloves.

ASPECT OF SOLITUDE — *(Fetter Hat)* The fetter hat is a very recognizable adornment. It forces the wearer to look towards their feet at all times.

ASPECT OF SOLEMNITY — *(Black Circlet)* One of the harder Aspects to master, the Aspect of Solemnity allows no outward emotion.

ASPECT OF PRESERVATION — *(Leaves—no roses on uniform)* Those who take this Aspect may not eat meat of any kind.

ASPECT OF ST. KLARE — *(Thorn Necklace)* This Aspect was developed when members of the Aspect of Preservation employed a workaround for their abstinence from meat by excess drink. St. Klare developed a variant that was ascetic, allowing the eating of breads, insects, water, and certain fruits and vegetables.

ASPECTS OF THE LEAF

ASPECT OF DISCRETION — (*Rose Earrings*) This Aspect requires a sister to listen intently to others without interrupting.

ASPECT OF CHARITY — (*Brown Robe*) The Charitable Sisters are very often found matched with the Paladins who take on the Vow of Poverty.

ASPECT OF COMPASSION — (*Dwov Elbow Guards*) These sisters are required to serve those with needs that can be met.

ASPECT OF OBEDIENCE — (*Bell Earrings*) The Aspect of Obedience is not a slaving Aspect, but one that allows one to be congenial, and helpful as requested.

ASPECT OF DIGNITY — (*Bound Sleeves*) — Those sisters who practice this Aspect seek to restore the dignity of those that are ailing or are elderly.

ASPECTS OF THE ROOT

ASPECT OF HUMILITY — (*Heavy Boots*) — The menial, janitorial tasks of a sister of the Aspect of Humility keep the order continuing as they do what no one else wants.

ASPECT OF CLARITY — (*Scroll Front Cloth*) Those sisters with a knack for memory, or wish to develop such a gift take on this Aspect. They are constantly testing one another with the recitation of verse.

ASPECT OF HONOR — (*Thorn Spiked Mace*) Of all the Aspects, this is the most practiced among the Paladames at Pariantür. While they do not go out on patrol against the T'Akai, they act as guards at all the hidden Vaults across Ganthic.

ASPECT OF FORM — (*Plain Bracers*) The Aspect of Form practiced hand to hand techniques, to grapple and contain opponents.

ASPECT OF FUNCTION — (*Utility Belt*) Those that seek to master an art or craft will take on this Aspect and delve as deeply as they can into their art.

GLOSSARY 6

MONKS OF NIFARA

The Monastic Order of the Staff, or the Monks of Nifara as they are more commonly known, are perhaps the oldest religious organization on Kallattai, and make up the sole followers of Nifara. While the largest community of monks are humans, Nifarans can be found in every race on Kallattai. Their purpose is to offer judgment between two arguing parties. They rule fairly, impartially, and quickly. Some deem their judgments too harsh, but this is tempered by their consistency. When a monk of Nifara is addressed, the correct honorific in the lands of man is Nefer. This is said to be a very old title, dating back to an older name for Nifara, Nefereh. When a judgment is made, a stick is broken, and given to each side of the argument, in memoriam. Nine times a judgment has been made that was deemed world-shifting. When that occurred, the monk broke not a stick, but their staff. These nine are honored above all others, with statuary made in their likeness at the Templum of Nifara in Birin. While there are many myths surrounding the Nine Saints, the most interesting fact is that none of their tales reference how they died.

GLOSSARY 7

PRAETORS OF THE CHALICE

Until recently, the Church of the Common Chalice has remained an isolationist branch of the Abecinian Church, remaining in nearly total isolation in Œron.

The military arm of the church is known as the Praetors of the Chalice, and bear some similarities to the Order of the Hammer, in that they built their organizational ranks loosely off their Eastern rivals. The learned class is open to all members of the Church of the Common Chalice who purchase a seat at the university, however, anyone not of Œronzi heritage will rarely rise to rank of Praetor. Exceptions have been made.

Those seeking admittance to the Order of the Chalice begin as an:

ACOLYTE — When sufficient training has occurred to indoctrinate the Acolyte, they rise to the role of level of Etudiant.

ETUDIANT — The Etudiant lives a life of routine and constant change as they are tested on various subjects. This is generally a ten year training.

PRAETOR – To be a Praetor is equivalent to a Paladin Excelsior. This provides them with a graduating rank above that of most Paladins.

CHAMBERLAIN – Equivalent of the Brother Adjutant, but considered first among the Lay.

CURATE – Equivalent of a Primus. Considered the first of the Leadership ranks. Generally those of Curate rank hold lands. Assigned holdings are treated as owing allegiance to the church, and not the country in which they are located.

PREFECT – Equivalent of a Pater Minoris. It is believed that there are three to five Prefects serving each Provost.

PROVOST – Equivalent of a Pater Segundus. There are an unknown number of Provosts.A Praetor can only be made Provost by agreement between Praeposit and Benefactor. And it is from the Provosts that the Benefactor chooses replacements for Praeposit.

PRAEPOSIT – Equivalent of the Prima Pater of the Hammer.

BENEFACTOR – Head of the Church of the Common Chalice. Considered a living prophet.

AFTERWORD

That you've read Gloves of Eons tells me that you are now officially invested in the lives of our heroes (even if they themselves don't wish to be viewed as such.) They've had their trials just in this book alone, and obviously have many more to come, and each will reach destinations expected and unexpected.

Over the creation of this book in particular I've come to realize in myself a penchant for "writing in twos." I strive to offer resolution in each book I write, but it also seems that each book I write breaks down into two halves (each with a denouement) and each pair of books acts as two halves of a whole. As I am currently writing the next book in the Kallattian Saga, *Dread Knight*, I find the same happening again. *Gloves of Eons* and *Dread Knight* are two halves of a whole story just as *Deathless Beast* and *Bone Shroud* were. Just as Kallattian Saga books 1-4 will be one half of the whole completed in Kallattian Saga book 5-8. This is not so bad a thing, certainly. It helps curb any potential cliffhangers, and ensures enough answers are given that you as a reader feel satisfied enough to close the book, but intrigued enough to want the next book immediately.

Speaking of that feeling you're having right now. Hold on to that while you wait for the next book. And if you feel the urge to act on it, please share, review, like, and spread the word to get more friends reading. That's what enables me to write the next one:

You, the reader.

Until the next book, may that road continue on with new vistas and new lessons.

—Andrew D Meredith

ABOUT THE AUTHOR

Andrew D Meredith's journey has taken him to many fantastical places. From selling books in the wilds of western Washington to designing and publishing board games for *Fantasy Flight Games/Asmodee*. He's now committed to the quest he was called to so long ago: the telling of fantastical tales, and bringing to life underestimated characters willing to take on the responsibilities no one else will.

AndrewDMeredith.com

@AndrewDMth

GLOVES OF EONS

Milton Keynes UK
Ingram Content Group UK Ltd.
UKHW031955281024
450365UK00009B/524

9 798330 450251